THREE-EDGED SWORD

THREE-EDGED SWORD

JEFF LINDSAY

ORION

This edition first published in Great Britain in 2022 by Orion Fiction,
an imprint of The Orion Publishing Group Ltd.,
Carmelite House, 50 Victoria Embankment
London EC4Y 0DZ

A Hachette UK Company

A CIP catalogue record for this book
is available from the British Library.

ISBN (Hardback) 978 1398 70659 0
ISBN (Export Trade Paperback) 978 1 3987 0660 6
ISBN (eBook) 978 1 3987 0662 0

Printed in Great Britain by Clays Ltd, Elcograf S.p.A.

www.orionbooks.co.uk

For what it's worth, this book is dedicated to all the people
who keep fighting, even when it seems hopeless.
We need a lot more of them.

PROLOGUE

Babloki Letsholo was not easily intimidated. After all, he held an important position, and he had earned it. He had served a term in the BDF, the Botswana Defence Force, and that had qualified him for a job in security when his military service was over. He worked hard in this new job, and he followed his father's advice: "Keep a smile in one hand and a fist in the other." Babloki had used both hands with wisdom and restraint, and it had been noticed. His rise had been swift, and now, at the age of twenty-eight, he was a security supervisor at the Keresemose Mine, a large open-pit diamond mine that was one of Botswana's most lucrative and prestigious.

The man standing impatiently before him clearly expected the smiling hand to be extended, but Babloki was not so sure. The paperwork seemed to be correct, but . . . "You are alone," he said to the man. "Mister . . ." He glanced at his clipboard. "Kleinhesselink?"

"Kleinhesselink, *ja*, *Doctor* Kleinhesselink," the man said with unnecessary emphasis. He frowned and pushed up his glasses, battered black horn-rims, with a forefinger. "I should like to get started, if you don't mind?"

Babloki returned the frown and looked this man over. He was average height and build, with shaggy reddish-brown hair and a beard of the same color, trimmed short, and he spoke with the flat and harsh Afrikaans accent. He was dressed in sturdy but well-worn clothing, and his white skin was battered and weathered, too, as would be expected of a mine inspector. But inspectors did not generally come to the mines alone; they came in a group, half a dozen or more at a time. This Dr. Kleinhesselink had showed up by himself. And he seemed in a hurry, which was also out of place. Still . . . "The paperwork appears to be in order," Babloki said dubiously. "But where are the other inspectors?"

"They will be here shortly," Kleinhesselink said. "I wanted to get started, so I came ahead." He shifted his feet impatiently. "Is there some kind of problem?"

Once more, Babloki flipped through the man's papers. He could find no fault with them. Even the ministry seal was correct. But something bothered him, something he could not quite name. He looked up at Kleinhesselink again, blinking back at him with his pale blue eyes—and he asked himself if perhaps this was what gave him pause. Was it because this man was so very much Afrikaans, and white? Anyone who knew the history of this part of Africa might harbor resentment for such a man. But Babloki had no patience with prejudice, no matter which way it cut, and he refused to let it color his judgment.

He frowned again and looked up. Dr. Kleinhesselink looked steadily back, and Babloki saw no trace of uneasiness or deception in his glance. He made his decision.

"If you will wait for one minute, please, Doctor?" he said. "I will arrange for an escort." Kleinhesselink nodded, and Babloki turned and went back inside the small building that housed the security office.

He made one very brief phone call, hung up, and went back outside. "Dr. Kleinhesselink?" he called as he stepped, blinking, back out into the bright sunlight.

But there was no reply. Dr. Kleinhesselink was gone.

Botswana is one of the most sparsely populated countries in the world. There is a very good reason for that. Seventy percent of the country is the Kalahari Desert, a bleak, hot land consisting mostly of bare earth and a few sparse patches of greenery. The Kalahari is not a place most would want to live, or even visit, unless there was a truly outstanding reason to do so.

As it happens, there is one.

Diamonds.

Some of the richest diamond deposits in the world have been found here, and so the mining companies have come, too. The Karowe mine, where some of the largest diamonds in history have been found— including one mammoth stone of 1,758 carats—is here.

Belle Journée, a French-owned mining company, is also here, on one corner of the Kalahari Desert. Belle Journée operates the Keresemose Mine, a large open pit surrounded by a few outbuildings and covered by a shimmering haze of brutal Kalahari heat. And although Keresemose was French-owned, it paid heavy taxes to the Botswana government for the privilege of operating here, just as all the diamond mines in the country did. Because of this income, Botswana was now an upper-middle-income country with one of the fastest-growing economies in the world. In a region that had seen more than its share of troubles, it was a stable and prosperous democracy.

But this piece of Botswana, where the Keresemose was situated, was still a desert. And now, rolling across this bleak landscape and

3

mixing with the shimmer of Kalahari heat was a very loud and persistent alarm. It screamed out across the whole facility, from the front gate to the airstrip. Dr. Kleinhesselink heard it—it was impossible not to. The sound squealed at him with near violence, echoing off the processing equipment and rolling around in the deep pit in the center of the operation. But Kleinhesselink did not respond, beyond looking up briefly before continuing on his way. He moved quickly, without appearing to be in any kind of haste, working his way around the large pit where the actual mining took place, ducking past the huge metallic sprawl of the crusher.

"Hey!" The voice came from above, and Kleinhesselink looked up. A very bulky man in work-stained clothing stood above him on the scaffold that surrounded the crusher. "Don't you hear the alarm? We're in lockdown!" the man called. Kleinhesselink just nodded and kept walking. He didn't go any faster, even when he heard the bulky man clatter down the stairs and run up behind him.

"Who the hell are you?" the man said. "You just hold it there—I'm calling security!" He put a beefy hand on the doctor's shoulder. He was clearly not expecting the reply he got.

Without hesitation, Kleinhesselink grabbed the man's fingers and twisted, forcing the man to double over or risk a broken arm. And then he ran the man headfirst into the side of the crusher's metal stairway. There was a loud *BONG!* and the bulky man sprawled unconscious on the walkway.

Kleinhesselink nudged the body with a toe and then continued around the crusher to the lip of the pit. There was a sudden flurry of activity coming from the security building, and the inspector picked up his pace as he went around the pit. Halfway around he cut away and hurried in the direction of the mine's landing strip. Two small planes crouched in the shadow of the tower, a corporate jet and a DC-3. Kleinhesselink ignored the planes and went past them to a small concrete-block building next to the tower. He walked quickly up to the front door, where two guards were posted.

Dr. Kleinhesselink approached the guards with the confidence natural to his exalted position as an official inspector of mines. "You cannot enter, sir," the guard on the left doorpost said. "Not while a security lockdown is in progress."

"Yes, but I must go inside," Kleinhesselink said. "I have a special order from the minister. Here—I will show you."

Kleinhesselink opened his battered attaché case and reached inside. "Here—look at this," he said. The guard politely bent his head to look. But what he saw was not a document. It was a puff of some kind of mist with a medicinal smell. He jerked his head back—but not before he had inhaled some of the vapor. For a moment he swayed where he was, looking stunned.

"Here! What have you done to him?!" the second guard demanded.

"I did nothing! Look for yourself!" Kleinhesselink said indignantly. He held the attaché case out to the second guard, pushing it right into the man's face.

"Get that out of my face! You can't— Oh . . ." A second puff of vapor shot up, and his face assumed the same stunned expression as the first guard's. Kleinhesselink took a step back and watched as one guard, then the other, slumped to the ground beside the door.

"Sleep well, gentlemen," Kleinhesselink said softly. "My apologies for the coming headache." And then he stepped past the unconscious guards to the door they had been guarding. It was locked. He reached again into his attaché case and took out a small black leather pouch. From this he extracted a few small tools and bent over the lock. In a matter of seconds, he had the door open. He stepped through into the dim coolness of the building's interior.

He moved quickly past the unoccupied reception area and down a hall on the left. Three doors down the hall he stopped. There was only one visible difference between this door and the others. Mounted on the right side of the door's frame was an electronic keypad. Once again Kleinhesselink reached into the attaché case, this time coming out with a metallic black box, slightly larger than a deck of playing cards. He held it up beside the keypad, pushed a silver button in the center of the box, and waited. A moment passed, and then a *beep beep beep* sounded. Kleinhesselink smiled and opened the door.

He stepped through the doorway and into a space the size of a small conference room. A beautiful dark mahogany table, with six chairs pushed neatly into it, split the room. Each place at the table had an inlaid square of lighter wood, about the size of a sheet of paper. Each square framed a pad of black velvet. The room's walls were painted a muted green, and there was a Rothko painting on one wall. In the center of the wall opposite this painting was a large steel panel— a state-of-the-art safe.

This was the room in which the mine's output of high-quality diamonds was shown to potential customers, and the safe contained several million dollars' worth of stones ready to be shown. Kleinhesselink nodded. It was all exactly what he had expected to see—except for one small detail.

At the far end of the room, at the head of the beautiful table, invisible until Kleinhesselink was all the way into the room, there were four more guards. Another stepped out from behind the door. And they were pointing automatic weapons directly at him.

"We have been expecting you," the tallest guard said. "Put down the case and put up your hands, please."

Kleinhesselink raised his attaché case meekly, to show he was dropping it as instructed. For just a second he appeared to fumble with the outer pocket, but then he threw the case to the floor.

Instantly there was a flash of light, a screeching noise, and a huge cloud of thick smoke filled the room. There was a moment of stunned silence—and then guards began to shout and also to curse as they bumped forcefully into furniture as they tried to move through the room blindly.

A thick tendril of smoke poured out of the room and into the hall. And under it, on the floor, Kleinhesselink rolled out of the room, dragging a briefcase. He kicked the door shut behind him. Then with remarkable agility for a mine inspector, he rolled onto his feet and dashed down the hallway—but in the opposite direction from the front door where he had entered. He was at the end of the hall and into the last room, door closed behind him, before the five guards stumbled out of the showroom, coughing.

Inside this last room the inspector paused, took a deep breath, and looked around. He was in an office, beautifully and elegantly furnished. There was a desk, two heavy teak chairs facing it, a potted palm in the corner, and a Vermeer painting on the wall behind the desk. There was also a good-sized picture window. Kleinhesselink's gaze fell on the window, and in the time it takes to blink an eye, he had stepped forward, snatched up one of the teak chairs, and used it to shatter the window. Two seconds later he was through the window and outside again, in the shimmering heat of the desert.

He did not run out into the Kalahari, however. Instead, he faced the building he'd just escaped and, after taking a step away from it, ran forward, put a foot on the windowsill, and leapt upward. He grabbed the edge of the roof, flipped himself upward, and tumbled onto the tiles of the rooftop.

In the same smooth motion he rolled to his feet and into a stoop and duck walked forward carefully, until he was crouching over the front door.

For a moment, Kleinhesselink peered back across the grounds of the Keresemose Mine. Through the hot, hazy air he could see a cluster of guards. They were headed his way rapidly.

Below him he heard the front door open, and the guards who had surprised him in the showroom clattered out. Kleinhesselink ducked down quickly and crawled back to the rear side of the building. He paused at the edge of the roof. Heading out across the Kalahari Desert was not an option. No one could last long out there unless they'd been raised to do it, like the small and hardy Bushmen who made it their home.

But the sounds of pursuit were coming closer. If he was going to get away, it had to be now.

He turned his head right, then left—to the control tower of the small landing strip. Beyond it sat the jet and the DC-3.

Kleinhesselink nodded. That was it—the only possible escape. He looked around once more to be certain; yes, that was absolutely the only way out. Decision made, he was off the roof and sprinting for the landing strip. Ducking under the jet, he went past it to the DC-3.

These propeller-driven airplanes had been in service longer, and in more parts of the world, than any other aircraft in history. Also known as the Gooney Bird, the DC-3 could take off and land in a very small space with a surprisingly heavy cargo, and they were utterly reliable, even when shot full of holes. They were also easy to fly. If this one had even a half tank of fuel, it would get him away.

Kleinhesselink raced across the tarmac and under the DC-3 to the far side. His luck was holding; the hatch was open! Without pausing, he leaped, grabbed the lip of the airplane's doorway, and pulled himself up into the plane's interior. For a moment he paused just inside the door as his eyes adjusted to the relative gloom in the cabin area. Then he raised up on one knee—but before he could fully stand, a voice came from the far end of the cabin: "But see, amid the mimic rout, a crawling shape intrude!"

Kleinhesselink froze, then climbed slowly to his feet.

The cockpit was to his right, and he had intended to head directly there, start the engines, and be airborne before the guards figured out where he was. But that plan was now obviously off now. Kleinhesselink slowly turned in the direction from which the voice had come.

The cabin was furnished in surprising luxury for an old Gooney Bird. There was a velvet settee and a scattering of glove-leather captain's chairs. At the far end was a gleaming steel bar with three stools. Sitting on the left stool, leaning back against the bar, was a man. He appeared to be in his sixties, with silver hair, a nice and even tan, and a patrician face. He wore a suit that said the noble face was not a coincidence, and he was pointing a gun directly at Kleinhesselink.

The inspector blinked and took a half step backward before jolting to an abrupt halt when he felt a second gun poke into his back. He turned his head slightly, just enough to see a large man with a scarred face jamming the gun into his spine and smirking at him. And behind him, hovering in the doorway of the cockpit, two more men who might have been clones of the first.

Kleinhesselink sighed, lifted his hands up, and turned his head to face the bar. The man on the stool was not smirking, but he looked like he was fighting the urge only half successfully, and he stared at

Kleinhesselink for a few moments with a nearly tangible satisfaction before he finally spoke.

"Well, well, well," the silver-haired man on the stool drawled in an accent that was pure Boston Brahmin. "Riley fucking Wolfe. We've been expecting you." And now he smiled. "What a pleasure to meet you at last."

PART 1

CHAPTER

1

Amahle Khumalo hurried through the hallway of the exclusive, private, very expensive extended-care facility where she worked as a nurse. She was in a near panic because she could not find her phone, and like any modern woman, she felt lost without it. It was a small nursing home, and she was being paid very, very well to look after only one patient. The extra money was badly needed, so she was extremely diligent. She stayed close to her patient, leaving only to go to the lunchroom, the lounge, or on small errands like getting supplies from storage.

So there were only a few places Amahle might have left her phone. She had checked the nurses' lounge, a room where she spent her time between checkups, since her patient was stable and nonresponsive. The phone was not there.

She was now quite sure she must have left her phone in her patient's room. She had been working on a crossword puzzle on the phone when she went into the room on her last check. No doubt she had put it down on the little bedside table by the window in order to check vital signs and record them on the chart. And then her friend Lesedi stuck her head through the door and asked for her help with Mr. Van der Merwe, who had dementia and had wandered off again.

Amahle had rushed out to help, and Mr. Van der Merwe had been surprisingly elusive for an old man. By the time they had him back in his room and calmed down, it was time for lunch, which she and Lesedi spent talking as they ate. And so it had been nearly two hours until she noticed that her phone was missing. If she *had* left it there on the little table by the window . . .

In two hours, the sun had moved across the sky, of course—just enough so that the light would be pouring through the window of her patient's room. And it would be shining its intense heat and light on that small table by the window. If she had really left her phone there, it would be in direct sunlight. That South African sunlight was hot; hot enough that if you left a metal object in its light for too long, it would burn your fingers when you picked it up. If you left electronic devices in that kind of heat, it could be fatal to the circuits.

As she raced into the room, the sun was pouring in through the curtained window as if it had been released from a large dam. It was relentlessly bright, and it lit up the entire room like a searchlight. The window was closed, of course, and there was a soft flow of air-conditioned air blowing through, but even so, Amahle could feel the heat.

The phone was there, on the table by the window, in the full glare of the sunlight. Amahle crossed the room quickly and picked up her phone—and swore as it burned her fingers. She hurriedly wrapped it in the hem of her scrub shirt, a pale lavender today. She juggled it clumsily for a moment, found a secure grip that was not too hot to hold, and breathlessly touched the screen.

It lit up, showing the picture of her nephew, Gabriel. The phone was not broken. "Thank you, Jesus!" she said.

"... What ... ?"

The voice that came from behind her was a terrible dry croak, almost inaudible, but it froze Amahle where she stood, because it came from a place where no voice could have been.

Her comatose patient.

The patient who was nonresponsive, and had been for several months.

Amahle turned. The attractive young woman in the bed looked at her with wide-open eyes. She was awake.

Immediately, amazement faded and a nurse's calm sense of purpose took over. Amahle dropped the phone into the pocket of her scrubs and stepped to the patient's bedside.

"... What—where, what?" the woman whispered.

"Hush, dear, don't try to speak," Amahle said as she hurriedly checked the woman's vital signs. Blood pressure good; heartbeat steady—a little elevated at ninety beats per minute, but that was to be expected of someone waking up in a strange room with no idea how they'd gotten there. "You are in hospital," Amahle said. "A private hospital—a very *good* private hospital."

"But, but . . . Ha-how, how . . . *where*?" the patient repeated in an insistent croak.

"Cape Town, of course," Amahle said. She turned from the bed and reached for the call button. "Now be quiet and lay still, dear, while I call Doctor."

"But . . ."

"I said lay still," Amahle said with the stern authority all nurses develop. And then, relenting slightly, she gave the woman a tender smile. "Don't worry your head, dear," she said. "You are going to be just fine."

Amahle patted the woman's hand reassuringly. Then she left the room to tell Dr. Sipoyo the news. But she did not go directly to find the doctor. Instead, she paused at the door to a supply closet. She looked carefully around to make sure no one was looking. Then she stepped inside the closet and closed the door.

Amahle took out her phone. It was still very warm, but it was usable. She flipped to her Contacts page and called a number there. It rang three times. Then a mechanical-sounding voice said, "Yes."

Amahle was not sure why, but she was a little frightened. But the extra money was enough to make a very large difference, and she had already decided to do this. So she took a breath and did it.

"She's awake," she said.

There was a pause on the other end, then the same flat, metallic voice said, "Good," and the connection broke.

Feeling slightly dizzy, Amahle put her phone away. She tried to swallow and found that her mouth and throat were almost too dry. But it was done.

Amahle took another, deeper breath and slipped out of the closet to find Dr. Sipoyo.

CHAPTER
2

I t was not a pleasure for me, of course. Not at all.

It was a setup from the very start. How had they known I'd come here, to Keresemose? Simple. They knew I had been in South Africa for a while, just sitting around and waiting and probably getting bored. It was an easy guess that eventually I'd want to find something to do, and with me that meant just one thing: stealing something. And in South Africa, where would a bored thief go? A diamond mine, of course. So they put out the word about the upcoming showing to make sure it was *this* diamond mine. And I had walked right into their trap.

When you look at how it turned out, it seems stupid. But the thing that made me the best ever is doing impossible things, and there's a really thin line between impossible and stupid. So if I cross the line into pure stupid now and then—well, shit. I usually make it back, and with the score, too.

This time, though, it wasn't really about the score. I was just bored. And mixed in with the boredom was enough real anxiety to turn that boredom into the kind that makes you jumpy. Like, you're on edge all the time even though you know there's no good reason and nothing you can do about it, and the only smart thing you can do is to find a good book and just sit there and read it. And what you really want to do is light your hair on fire and run screaming into the night.

I had good reasons, for both the boredom and the worry. I'd been sitting in South Africa for six weeks, waiting for Monique to come out of her coma. She hadn't so far, and the doctors were not being really encouraging. And Monique—she is one of the only two people in the world I really give a crap about. I almost trust Monique, which is as near to it as I can get. I trust her enough to work with her, and that's hard, because trust makes you vulnerable. She's never betrayed me, though. And I don't want to work with anybody else, because she is hands down the best art forger in the world. She can make a copy of absolutely anything. Nobody else comes close.

And I like her. I mean, we aren't in love or anything. We had one night, celebrating a great heist we did together, when we got ripped and jumped in the sack, and it was legendary. For both of us, I'm positive about that. But she insisted that it had been a mistake, a one-timer, and so far it has stayed that way.

Last time out she got dragged into a truly bad thing, and because of me. I got her out of it, but along the way she got smacked on the head by a freakishly strong psycho. I got her to Cape Town, the closest good hospital, and waited for the doctors to bring her around.

Six weeks later, I was still in Cape Town, and still waiting. I wasn't going anywhere, because I had to be there when she came out of it. She would come out of it; I knew that for sure. Not from what the doctors said. They'd shake their heads and tell me not to be too optimistic, the odds were very long, there might have been brain damage, she'd sustained a serious blah blah blah. I didn't care. They didn't know

Monique. I did, and I knew she would wake up, and she'd be fine. And I would be there when it happened.

After a week, the hospital waiting room lost its charm, so I rented a house nearby. After three weeks, I'd read seventeen books and forty-two magazines. And after four weeks, I was chewing my teeth and looking for something to hit. I knew if this kept up I was going to do something that would inflict serious bodily harm on myself and others. That is not the best way to maintain a low profile, which is usually a good idea for someone in my line of work. I knew I had to find something to take my mind off Monique and keep me busy for a few days. And what could that possibly be? Well, I am, after all, the greatest thief in the world. I had to believe that if I looked around a little, I could find something interesting to do in my line of work. Something nearby, close to Monique.

So I did something stupid. If you don't look at it too closely, it made perfect sense. I mean, this is me, world's greatest thief, and here I am in South Africa. And South Africa is known for what, exactly? Go ahead, guess. Hint: If you're thinking "Nelson Mandela," or "vuvuzelas," or even "That amazing fake sign language translator guy when Barack Obama was there," you're on the wrong page. You must have missed the part where I said "world's greatest thief."

Because if you look at it from that angle, South Africa is also known as the home of the greatest diamond mines on earth. And do you know what great diamond mines have that no place else in the world has?

That's right.

And if I need to say that diamonds are worth a lot of money, you probably should stick with the vuvuzela thing.

So I did a quick check around, and I found the Keresemose, just across the border in Botswana. They'd been dragging up some unbelievable stones lately, huge monsters with perfect color and clarity. Even better—they had announced a showing for select bidders in three weeks. That meant they'd have their best stones all clean and pretty in one handy location. That made it a perfect setup for somebody like me.

A little more checking, and I came up with a plan that looked perfect. I would do it in plain sight, in broad daylight, as a mine inspector. I could grab the stones and be away before they knew anything was happening. Boom, perfect, why not.

Getting the paperwork was easy, and so was finding an outfit of suitably beat-up clothing. The Afrikaans accent took a little work, though. It's tricky; kind of close to an Aussie accent, which I already had in the bank, but there are enough differences to trip you up easily, and the locals would know if I screwed up. But I worked it, tried it out in a few places around Cape Town, and got away with it. I was ready.

Now here's where the stupid part comes in. Like I said, bored and anxious, and that made me impatient. That's a mortal sin in my occupation. In the past, I was always extra careful about details when I planned. Always. Except this time, I wasn't. I was just so damn antsy to *do* something, I jumped into it too soon, only half ready. I figured I could get away with it just this once.

I was wrong. And so here I was, looking down the barrel of a pistol.

CHAPTER

3

They didn't even handcuff me. No rope, no chains, not even duct tape. Nothing. Maybe I should have taken that as a major put-down, like, *Hey this guy's a lightweight. Why bother?* But of course, there was the matter of the four well-armed assholes pointing stuff at me, everything from two Tasers to a Heckler & Koch MP5. So I guess the real message was, *We are more badass than you can imagine and we would love it if you would try something.* Or maybe, *We're all profession-als here, why screw around?* And all the stuff pointed at me? That was just so I knew they were serious.

Okay, got it. You're serious. You probably figured, who the hell needs chains? Riley knows the score. And of course, there was also the fact that, only a minute or two after I put my hands up, the old Gooney Bird had lurched up into the sky and started winging away to wherever the fuck they were taking me. I have done a lot of totally impossible things—and yeah, I am always looking for more. But jumping out of an airplane without a parachute is not on the list.

And I did know the score. These guys were clearly professionals. You can always tell by the way they move, the way they keep it just business, no unnecessary sadism, little tells like that. And we were already flying at a few thousand feet, which was not ideal jump-without-a-parachute altitude. So when you are in the air and surrounded by exceedingly ugly professionals with lots of weapons, it was not the time or the place to go all Jason Statham on them and make your daring escape. That time would come. It always has before, and it always will again. Because there is always a way, and the whole reason I got to be the very best ever is that I believe that—I *know* that—and I am smart enough to wait for it and know it when I see it.

So okay, they had me. They were being civilized about it and not stapling me to a chair or wrapping me up with duct tape, so fine. I can play the polite and elegant game, too. As soon as we were up in the air and leveled off, I strolled back to the bar. Two of the large ugly guys strolled with me, but I ignored them. I found a bottle of pretty good brandy, poured some in a glass, and stuck my butt onto one of the bar chairs.

"Okay," I said. I lifted my glass in a toast to the silver-haired guy. "Cheers." I took a sip. "Now what?"

He nodded back at me. "Good," he said. "I had heard that you were not prone to pissing into the wind."

I studied him a little more carefully. Obviously I'd been looking him over and trying to figure out who the fuck he was and what he wanted with me. From the custom-tailored suit to dropping the quote from Edgar Allan Poe, that bit about "a crawling shape intrude," the picture was definitely *I'm smarter and much classier than you or anybody you know.* Like us trailer park guys never read "The Conqueror Worm," or "The Raven," or any of that stuff. On top of that, his whole attitude was *I own everything and I went to Yale so fuck you,* and I'd figured he was some kind of billionaire CEO who wanted some weird favor only I could get for him. One glance at his born-into-it face, with its perfect nose and you-are-not-real blue eyes, told me who he was. Strictly hereditary member of the .1 percent, the stupid-rich, inherited money and power assholes who make me want to get them alone some dark night on the roof of a very tall building.

But now he comes out with "pissing into the wind"? It was the kind of thing you say to make sure everybody knows yeah, you're Ivy League and you own everything, but you're a tough guy, too, and you don't mind kicking somebody in the balls. It said, *Yeah, I know which fork to use, but sometimes I use it to stab people like you in the eye.*

I study people very carefully, all types of people. Not because they're so damned interesting, but because when I'm working, I need to *become* all types. So I recognized that this guy had a very definite character trait of a certain kind of person, and "CEO" was not in the top ten. One option was a lot more likely. On the theory that my luck had been kind of shitty today and it was time for it to change, I took a guess.

"So what's with the old plane?" I said. "Agency budget cuts?"

His lips twitched briefly, telling me I was right. "Pass that bottle over here, would you?"

I did, and he poured out a nice slug of the brandy for himself. Then he leaned over to the bar, grabbed the ice bucket, and dropped two chunks of ice into the glass. And I need to emphasize: *ice cubes.* Into a glass of *brandy.* Forget about born into class, the man was a barbarian, no matter how much the suit cost.

He sipped. The ice cubes rattled, underlining what a savage he was. Fucking *ice* in *brandy*; is nothing sacred anymore?

"My name is Prescott," he said. He nodded. "As you have guessed, I am with a government entity." He swirled the glass. "One of the

'Alphabet Agencies,' you would probably say. No need to specify, is there?"

"Not for me," I said. "They're all about the same for my purposes." I sipped. "Carry on."

"Very good," he said, swirling the ice again without really thinking about it. "That will save us some time." He took another sip.

"Oh, good. So now we have more time for—what, exactly?"

He looked at me like he'd never seen something like *that* before and wasn't quite sure what it was or what to do with it. And he held the stare, long enough that it got kind of uncomfortable. Finally, he figured he'd built the suspense enough.

"Do you love your country, Riley?"

Oh, boy. That set off a very loud *ding ding ding* in my cranium, the alarm that goes off when I am about to be fed a line of crap—and, most likely, fed to the sharks, too. Those words were meant to shame me into something really stupid, something with no real hope of my pulling it off in one piece, so they had to go with emotional blackmail. And since this guy was with An Agency, it was going to be some kind of impossible heist against a foreign military installation—and probably for free, too. Which is the worst possible situation. Military bases have very tight security, with lots of guess what? Right! Lethal force! Lots of it, from guys who practice it a lot! Because they're *military*! Guys who shoot at you, no warning shots. And of course I'd just love to do it for free—yeah, naturally, because after all, I do love my country, right?

I could see what was coming, and it totally sucked. Still, you have to play out the hand, right? "Yeah, sure. Of course," I said. "I love my country."

"Oh, good, you do. You do love your country. Okay. And we're talking about the same country? The United States of America?"

"Seriously?" I said. "You want to see my birth certificate?"

"I've seen it," he said. "In fact, I've seen three or four of them. And I have no doubt you could show me a few more."

Well, shit. He truly had my number. So I just shrugged. "Why not?" I said. "They're pretty cheap."

"I'm aware," he said. He sipped again. "So if the first one is real—if you actually are, or *were*, J.R. Weiner"—he winced a little, like it hurt his mouth to say that kind of name—"then you are, in fact, a real American. And you love your country. The United States of America, *that* country."

"Weren't we saving time?" I said. I mean, what the fuck. Where was this going? "Can we cut to the chase and go to dinner?"

He nodded. "Very well," he said. "You, Riley Wolfe"—he said my name like it had quotation marks around it—"are a country-loving American. So let me ask you—" He leaned forward and looked pissed off. He was pretty good at that. "What the fuck have you ever done for this country you love so much?"

Oh. He was going there, huh. "I never stole the Constitution," I said.

"Cute. I am laughing on the inside. And because I am so wildly amused, I will abandon this embarrassing topic and move on, is that it?"

"Something like that," I said. I mean, what else could I say? He got me.

"So the real answer, of course, is that you have never done *anything* for your beloved country," he said, and I had to admire the way he packed so much sarcasm onto the words and still kept a straight face. Who says Yale doesn't teach practical skills?

"This is going somewhere, right?"

"It is," he said. "It is going to Riley Wolfe, the man who loves his country so much he has never done one motherfucking thing for it. Have you ever even *voted*, Riley?"

I mean, shit. Have I ever *voted*? Really? Technically I don't even exist; how am I going to vote? Oh, sure, I could spend a couple of bucks and get a birth certificate for Riley Wolfe. And guess what? I show up at a polling station, cast my vote—and fifty Feds and cops are waiting for me.

So I shrugged. "It's not exactly easy for me," I said.

"Right. Not easy. And you only do easy things."

That stung a little. It was getting a little close to the bone. "Yeah, sure, just the simple shit," I said. "That's why you snatched me, right?"

He sneered at me for a minute, then drained his glass. "I snatched you, as you so elegantly phrase it"—he poured another slug of brandy . . . and added another ice cube, the asshole—"to give you an opportunity to actually do a job for this country you love so much that you have never even voted."

"Very generous," I said. "I've waited my whole life for this opportunity. But shouldn't you be playing 'Battle Hymn of the Republic' in the background?"

"Go ahead, indulge your wit, such as it is. But there are a few of us who actually do more than merely *say* we love America. We devote our lives to serving it. And far too often, we sacrifice our lives. Difficult for someone like you to grasp, I know, but we make that sacrifice willingly. Because we serve a much greater cause. A noble cause, Riley. If that doesn't embarrass you."

I drained my glass and reached past him for the bottle. "What embarrasses me," I said, as I poured, "is listening to bald-faced emotional blackmail at the point of a gun."

"Four guns, in fact," he said. "And two more in the cockpit."

"I can count," I said, pouring more brandy. A lot more, because I was pretty sure I was going to need some anesthetic even to listen to this.

"And it is only emotional blackmail if you are susceptible," he said. "If you actually do, in fact, love your country."

"God bless America, land that I love," I said. "Let's hear it."

He looked at me a little longer, just to make sure I was intimidated. Then he stood up and said, "Come over here. I'll show you the file." He turned and walked over to a couple of pilot's chairs with a table between. There was a stack of paper and file folders on it.

I sighed. I was trapped, at least for now. And this was going to be a flaming-hot shit show, I could already tell that much. The only comfort I had was that, whatever it was, I would figure it out and get it done. And while I did it, at least Mom and Monique were safe.

So I sat down and heard his pitch. And guess what?

I was right. A total flaming shit show.

But the capper really grabbed my attention.

CHAPTER
4

Arthur Kondor was not actually happy. Nothing bad had happened or was happening, as far as he knew. He just didn't do happy. He had learned long ago that there was no point to it. A long stretch in Special Forces taught him that. An even longer career in less creditable civilian activities drove it home. Happiness was a dangerous distraction. It got in the way, affected your judgment, might even make you hesitate for that half second that gave somebody the opening to end you. And what the hell, happy never lasted long anyway, so why bother?

So he wasn't happy. That didn't matter. At the moment, he was satisfied, which was better. He was doing a job for a client he respected. The guy paid quickly, and he paid a lot. And he expected first-rate results. Kondor produced them, and that was another source of satisfaction. He was very damn good at what he did. This job was not hard, just keeping an anonymous eye on the guy's mother. Pretty simple—she wasn't going anywhere. She was in a coma and hooked up to a bunch of machines. So no trouble from her, and none from anybody else so far. All he had to do was hang back and watch. If anybody got too close to her, he took care of it and them. He was very damn good at that, too.

So sure, he was satisfied. That was about the best it got for him. Things were going smoothly, the way they should go. Just the way he had planned it.

Of course, even something as meager as satisfaction never lasts long. And it didn't now.

It started to unravel the moment he got out of his car, a brand-new Dodge Challenger SRT Hellcat. That was courtesy of the last job he had done for this client. Kondor loved muscle cars. This was one of the best to come along in years. So when he got out, he locked the car carefully, clicked on the aftermarket alarm, and stood up.

That was when he saw the guy leaning on the car in the next space. The guy was watching him. That was bad enough. But when he realized the guy was somebody he knew, that was worse.

"Hey, Artie. How's it going?"

Kondor stared at him. His right hand drifted toward his Glock in its waistband holster. That face was from a bad time, and he didn't like seeing it now. The name came back to him. "Blanda," he said. Then he waited. He knew this was not a happy coincidence, two old friends meeting by chance. There was no such thing as coincidence, not in Kondor's line of work. And Blanda was not a friend.

Blanda waited, too. But he couldn't outwait Kondor. Finally, he nodded and said, "Okay, sure. Just business, right? That how you figure it, Artie?"

Kondor moved. He was incredibly quick for a large man, and

he had a hand on Blanda's throat before the other man could do more than twitch. "Don't call me Artie," Kondor said. "Or I will hurt you."

"I wouldn't do that," Blanda croaked. "Take a look at your chest."

For a moment, Kondor refused to take the bait. But Blanda looked so goddamned smug. There had to be a reason for that. So he looked.

There were three red dots on Arthur Kondor's chest. The kind of red dots laser sights make.

He blinked.

"There's a couple more on your back," Blanda rasped.

Kondor looked up at Blanda.

"Could you maybe let go?" Blanda choked out. "This is really uncomfortable."

Kondor squeezed, just a little more, just enough to make Blanda's eyes bug out. Then he dropped his hand. And for just a moment, looking at Blanda coughing and gasping, he felt a final little bit of satisfaction.

Then he shook it off and took a step back. Blanda being here at all told him everything he needed to know. He was in a bad spot, about to be forced into a bad choice. He had no idea what it was, but he knew that much. And he knew that Blanda's agency thought it was important enough to track him down, which was not easy and not cheap. They had deployed a team including five snipers. That was expensive, too. A lot of time and money, all to force him to listen.

It could have been much worse. At least they were giving him a chance, instead of killing him outright. And some kind of opening would come up later. As long as he lived through right now.

So Kondor shrugged off satisfaction and all other emotions. This was not the time for anything but that hard choice.

He nodded at Blanda. "Let's hear it," he said.

Well, then," Dr. Sipoyo said, standing up and giving his patient a very good, very bright smile. It was the kind of smile doctors always give patients when they want to reassure and encourage. It was seldom a totally genuine smile. But the sheer wattage of Dr. Sipoyo's version of the smile seemed sincere. And why not? This woman had been unresponsive for quite some time. And now she was conscious. As a physician, that made him very happy.

But of course, with a traumatic brain injury, there was a great deal more to the picture than consciousness. Dr. Sipoyo was a leading expert in the field, and he was quite well aware that a full mental recovery was a very rare thing.

"Your vital signs are all quite good, considering," the doctor said. The woman looked back at him without comprehension. "But there is a very long road ahead of you, young lady." Dr. Sipoyo dropped his smile and adopted a serious expression. "You have suffered a very serious injury to your brain. You may not understand words—even when you are saying them. Or you may say things that are not appropriate." He nodded. "This is perfectly normal. And so is laughing or crying for no real reason, hm? I think you will recover, but it will take a great deal of time—and a great deal of work." He did not tell her that the odds of recovery were slim. "You must begin a very strict regimen of therapy. And there are many tests we must run. Above all, you must avoid exerting yourself too strenuously. Give your brain time to heal."

The young woman began to look alarmed, and Dr. Sipoyo relented. He sat back down on the side of her bed and took her hand. "But please do not be unhappy. You have already beaten the odds, just by waking up. And we are all very proud of you."

"What what," the woman rasped. "What what where—what where why what what—" She broke off in confusion, a look of panic spreading across her face.

"Now relax; as I said, this is very normal," Dr. Sipoyo said reassuringly, patting her hand. "It will be some time before words make sense to you. Even your own words."

She shook her head. "But but—but I but but—" She stuttered to a stop, looking even more confused.

"Don't try to talk just now," Dr. Sipoyo said. "Words will not mean what they should, they will come out in the wrong order, and they will not come to you as easily. This may frighten you, but it is normal," he repeated. "Perfectly normal," and he emphasized the word. "It all takes time, but we have time for you. And you have made a wonderful start."

Dr. Sipoyo gave her the very bright smile again and stood up. "For now, you must rest, and tomorrow we will begin to—"

There was the sound of shouting in the hall, and then a few very odd sounds—some thumps and grunts and feet scuffling on the high polish of the hall's floor. This should not be; the regulations said this area of the hospital must be kept quiet, and no visitors were allowed. Frowning, Dr. Sipoyo turned toward the door. Nurse Amahle was backing into the room with her hands raised. And beyond her, stretched out on the floor and bleeding from a head wound, was one of the janitors, a newly hired Zulu man Dr. Sipoyo did not know.

While Dr. Sipoyo was still staring in disbelief, Amahle, obviously pushed hard, stumbled all the way into the room and turned to face him. "Doctor?" she said, her voice trembling. Behind her, two strange men stepped into view.

Really, Dr. Sipoyo thought, *Nurse ought to know better than this*. "What is it, Nurse?" he said.

"These men are, ah . . ." Her eyes were wide, as if she was frightened. "Please, Doctor, you must talk to these men."

Dr. Sipoyo stood up. "I will gladly talk to them," he said. "And I will tell them that they must leave."

One of the men pushed roughly past the nurse. He was in his forties, and in spite of a good suit, he looked like a very tough customer. He was also nursing a split lip and looking displeased. "Sure, we're gonna leave, Doc," he said. His accent was American, and the bleeding lip leaked blood onto his teeth, so his smile was not pleasant. "But we're taking her with us." He nodded at the woman in the bed, who was now sitting bolt upright and looking well past pure terror.

"That is impossible, dangerous, outrageous," Dr. Sipoyo said. "This woman cannot be moved—she has just come out of a coma!"

The other man looked at his partner. The two of them shared a smirk. Then he turned back to Dr. Sipoyo. He held out some papers and nodded at them. "You best take a look at this," he said.

Dr. Sipoyo looked at the papers, then at the man holding them. "But that's—No, I must insist, this is—"

"Read it, Doc," the man said. He was no longer smiling, and suddenly Dr. Sipoyo understood the nurse's frightened look, because he was feeling afraid himself.

Without saying anything more, Dr. Sipoyo took the papers and began to read.

CHAPTER

5

'd like to tell you a story," Prescott said. "But let me ask you: As a man who loves his country—" That again. The bastard wouldn't let go of it. "—have you heard of something called the Cold War?"

"No, not me," I said, fighting to keep a snarl off my face. So typical of all these overprivileged assholes. How could I know things? I hadn't gone to Yale. "I never even heard of the Soviet Union, the Red Menace, the Cuban Missile Crisis, none of that. And I have no idea why December of 1991 means anything."

"All right," Prescott said. "Don't get snarky, I'll start to feel like you don't like me." He frowned and looked away. "The eighties and nineties were a wild time." Almost to himself, he recited, "There was much of the beautiful, much of the wanton, much of the bizarre, something of the terrible, and much that inspired disgust." Quoting Poe again, almost. He mangled the line, though. "All the players had come to know each other, and even like each other sometimes." He shrugged. "There's a lot of common ground, after all. But all of us were scrambling. We could tell it was winding down, coming to some kind of conclusion, so there was a lot of . . . Both sides formed certain . . ."

Prescott made a vague gesture with his left hand and looked away out the plane's porthole. I looked out my window, just to be sure I wasn't missing anything. Nope. Still over the Kalahari. So Prescott wasn't really seeing what was out there below us. He was seeing his vanished youth and innocence. Too bad I didn't have a violin to accompany him.

Don't you just love it when people go pensive on you? I was pretty sure it was part of the performance, but what could I do except wait for him to get on with it?

So I waited. After a couple of minutes, he looked back at me. "Fuck it," he said. "It was a wild time. I was young, eager, full of bullshit idealism." He gave a snort of not-funny amusement. "That didn't last long." He shrugged again. "Everything is very different now. But—this might sound peculiar, but those were good times," he said. "It was an utterly clear struggle, good versus evil, and I was on the side of the angels."

"I'm sure they were grateful for the help," I said. I mean, how long was I supposed to hold it in?

He made a face but plowed ahead with it. "I was in the Baltic Soviet satellite countries, working a string of operatives," he said. "My first big job in the field. And one of these agents was producing some remarkable results."

He reached for his glass, saw it was empty, and went to the bar, bringing the bottle back and pouring more into his glass. With more ice, of course.

"My prize agent was GRU, and we had flipped him," he said as he sat back down. "Russian military intelligence. He assured us he hated communism, despised the Soviets, was eager to help us." He shrugged. "They all say that crap. Like it's from some sort of traitor's manual." Snort. "But I kept setting the bar higher and higher, and he kept clearing it, bringing more and more absolutely top-shelf intel. I rode him all the way to the end—collapse of the Soviets, reordering of Europe, all that. It made my career." A thin smile. "He did well out of it, too. One thing about black ops. There's always plenty of ways to make a lot of money. It's part of the tradecraft, because it's the only way we can afford to operate. So he was selling intel, too. The agencies look the other way. The only real trick is to get *enough* money so you can—"

He looked up, like he was surprised at something he'd heard. He covered it with another sip. "When things began to collapse, it was utter chaos. Everyone trying to figure out the new teams, the new rules, where the advantages would lie. Ivo took another route. He still had money—a lot of it. He took it home to Lithuania, bought himself a small island off the coast. A special island." Prescott nodded wisely. "It looked perfectly normal, a small lighthouse and a cabin. But"—he raised a finger to show me that he was making a point—"very few people knew it, although of course Ivo knew—but there was a Soviet missile silo hidden under the lighthouse. One of their top secret advance launch sites. The Soviets had naturally done all they could to make it inaccessible. Of course the missiles left with the Soviets, but Ivo improved on their out-of-date security measures until he had a very nice little place no one could approach without fatal results."

"A Fortress of Solitude," I said. Just to show I was still here.

Prescott shook his head. "Not quite solitude. Ivo used some of his leftover operating capital to hire some of the old Spetsnaz troopers. The collapse had left them high and dry, and they were happy to have a job, particularly with an old tovarich. And there he sat." He nodded, looking as satisfied as if he'd said something special.

"Fascinating," I said. I mean, I know I had to listen, but couldn't he cut to the chase?

He ignored me. Why not? I was a peasant. "I was perfectly content simply to leave him there," he went on. "He was no threat, and we'd done well by each other. But." He raised his finger again. Annoying as hell, but he liked it. "A few years later, a new order emerged from the chaos, and with it, a new and very ugly threat." He raised an eyebrow at me. "Putin."

"I've heard of him," I said.

He nodded. "Putin wanted to restore Soviet glory." Prescott snorted. "An oxymoron if ever there was one. But he began to make rather bold moves, spreading his tentacles outward. And frankly, we began to worry." He sipped. "Then I began to hear things—just rumors, but rather persistent. Some kind of new and devastating weapons system. Something that would give Russia a huge edge if it was deployed. So I had to find out whatever it was—absolutely had to.

"I went back to Ivo. Why not? He'd always produced in the past, and I rather trusted him. Stupid of me."

Prescott closed his eyes and took in a deep breath through his nostrils. I wondered if maybe he'd taken on a little too much of that brandy. I mean, he had really been putting it away.

He opened his eyes again. "Well. We live and we learn. Once again, with my help, Ivo succeeded brilliantly. He got the specifications of the weapons system and got safely back to his fortress, with the whole thing on a flash drive. But then—he kept it. And he began, very quietly, to put out word that he had it and would listen to offers."

He really didn't need to finish. I knew what was coming. It would be the part where he got really solemn and said, "Twelve brave men have died trying to retrieve it. Now it's your turn." So I thought I'd save him the trouble.

"No," I said.

He turned his icy-blue Ivy League eyes on me. "That is not an option," he said.

"Yeah, it is, and it's the option I'm taking. No. You expect me to sneak into a heavily guarded, inaccessible missile silo and steal something so small it could be hidden anywhere?"

"No, Mr. Wolfe—I expect you to die." And the asshole cackled like a grandma with a winning bingo card. "Sorry. Couldn't help it. Yes, that's what I expect you to do."

"No," I said. "Not gonna happen. Find some other dumbfuck to die for you."

His lips twitched, like he was trying to smile but couldn't remember how. "The appeal to patriotism didn't move you?"

"Sure it did," I said. "I've decided to vote next time. But this? No. No way."

He reached back into the folder and took out a couple of eight-by-ten glossy photos. "Let me urge you to reconsider," he said, flipping the pictures at me.

I didn't touch them. I mean, I had no idea what the pictures would show, but I was pretty sure I wouldn't like it.

I was wrong.

Photo number one made my eyes pop out of my head. It was a color shot, the kind you take for a museum's exhibition catalog of a Russian Orthodox icon.

I don't know what you think of when you hear the word "icon." Maybe you think it's some little trinket that only means something to somebody who believes in whatever the trinket stands for. Like, a Star of David if you're Jewish, or a crucifix for Catholics. If that's the picture in your head, toss it out now. Russian Orthodox icons are paintings, usually on wood, sometimes on copper. They're kind of stylized—like, somewhere in between Byzantine art and medieval European. So the figures are stretched out, too long to be human, and their expressions are pure cartoon. And the paintings depict stuff that's supposed to inspire awe and reverence when you see them—or maybe I should say, when you *behold* them, just to stick with the theme.

Generally speaking, they're a little gawky and they feel foreign and kind of funny, at least to me. Of course, I'm not Orthodox. This one was different. It wasn't just a bleeding Jesus. It was still Jesus—but he was in midstride on top of the water, water that was a brilliant blue so sharp it almost hurt. He was walking toward a boat rendered in gold, with two guys in it holding up their arms for help. And all around them was one of those incredible, intricate mosaiclike backgrounds of a starry sky. And the stars—I mean, there's only so much you can tell from a photo, right? But I was ready to bet my teeth that the stars were actually gems stuck onto the picture.

Like I said, I was impressed. The lines of the figure were so perfect and sharp, the colors all so eyeball-smacking clean and bright, it probably meant just one thing.

I looked up at Prescott. "Simon Ushakov?"

He nodded. "Good eye. Yes, it's Ushakov. So are these." He threw down a couple more photos, and they were just as good. So beautiful it could almost make you want to go to church—even a Russian church. I mean, everything I said about icons in general? Throw it out the window. Simon Ushakov made icons that were *art*. The shapes that seemed clumsy in the others came alive when he painted them, and what he did with color was so amazing there ought to be other words for it, because "blue" and "red" just didn't describe it. It was tough to tear my eyes away, but I finally managed. "Okay, I'm impressed. What's the connection?"

"As I said, I think I've come to know you well," he said. "I was fairly certain you would decline to serve your country, at least without compensation."

I shrugged. Okay, he had me pegged. "All right, so?"

"So," he said, and this time with a crocodile smile, "these are from the collection of Ivo Balodis. The greatest collection of seventeenth-century icons in the world. Including seven Ushakovs." The smile got bigger. "He keeps them in the same vault, with the flash drive."

I looked at that shit-eating smile on Prescott's face and wanted nothing to do with him or his job. And then I looked again at the photo. "I'm in," I said.

He nodded. "I thought you'd say that," he said.

CHAPTER 6

The old Gooney Bird landed eventually. I mean they have to, generally speaking. After about forty minutes of flying time, we put
down on a little strip and climbed into a couple of black SUVs. I
was a little disappointed that Prescott would stick with that kind of
cliché. Black SUVs? Really? And in Africa? Why not just carry a ban-
ner reading, HERE COMES THE CIA? But I climbed in the back of one,
and two of the goons came in to sandwich me in the middle of the seat.

It was a short drive into a little town, and we all climbed out at
something that looked like an office building. Three stories, painted
lime green, big glass doors on the front. We all trooped inside, and
they led me up two flights of stairs to the top floor.

"There's a conference room down the hall," Prescott said. "We'll
set up there and work out how you're going to do this."

I just shrugged and trudged along. We got to the end of the hall and
went through a door on the right. As advertised, a conference room.
Long table in the middle, a bunch of chairs around it, a whiteboard on

the wall at the far end, under a pull-down screen. Prescott took out the file with all the intel on Balodis and tossed it onto the table. "All right," he said. "Let's get started."

I tossed down my attaché case so it landed on top of the file, real casual, like it was an accident. Then I sat down. The others filed in and took seats. When we were all settled, Prescott started talking. Just general bullshit, like how hard this was, we have to be careful, blah blah. I sat through a couple of minutes of it and then figured enough was too much.

"I got to use the can," I said. "I gotta pull off this beard, it itches." I held up my briefcase. "The solvent and stuff is in here."

"Of course," Prescott said. "Help yourself."

I left the room, went into the restroom, and locked the door. I figured I had about two minutes' head start, so I didn't waste time. I was out the window and down the side of the building thirty seconds after locking the door.

I wasn't ditching the whole thing. I was going to do the job, but without a snotty upper-class spook telling me how. I knew Prescott would want to tell me how to do it, when I would start, what equipment I should use, how to do everything every step of the way, yadda yadda. Tough shit; I wasn't about to do it his way. And I knew he'd get pissy about it. A type A shit bag like Prescott would just know he had to keep me on track—*his* track—so it didn't all go south. Which just goes to show that he didn't know as much about me as he thought, because if you know anything about Riley Wolfe, you ought to know this: He works alone. He doesn't want your stupid aristo face stuck into things, and he doesn't give a rodent's rectum what you think about his plans. Because I do it my way, in a way you can't even imagine, and I always get it done. Always.

So I didn't give him the opportunity to correct my sad mistakes or force me into something by the Agency book. And then, I disappeared. It's not that hard if you know what you're doing. And I had everything I needed from Prescott, all the pictures, and the file with all the dirt on Ivo Balodis and his happy little home in Lithuania.

It was all in my attaché case, and I had some other useful stuff in there, things I'd meant to use to get Dr. Kleinhesselink safely away. So just about everything I needed was in the case.

I got a ride to a bus stop from a friendly local guy who played the radio too loud and sang along off-key. I didn't really mind; it was Afro pop, and some of that is pretty good.

He was still singing when he dropped me at the bus stop. I waited about twenty minutes and caught a bus to the train station, where I lost Kleinhesselink's beard and glasses and darkened my hair. I bought some touristy clothes and tossed the good doctor's fatigue-style clothes in the trash. I was ready for some serious travel.

But first I had a couple of phone calls to make; just checking up, but it's something you have to do. Mom always said that even when you've got all your ducks in a row, you had to remind them to keep waddling now and then. Mom was always full of good advice, and I learned pretty young to listen to it. Good, solid, practical tips for living, and most of it was still usable today, all these years later. Things like "Hope for the best, prepare for the worst," and "If it seems too good to be true, it probably is," and "The Lord helps those who help themselves."

And yeah, they may sound like hackneyed, dumb sayings ripped from *The Big Book of Old Wives' Tales*. Mom knew that, but she liked to say, "Well, there's a reason they got to be *old* wives, J.R. And considering how women have been treated forever, if they got to be old, you should probably pay attention."

I did, and I still do. Mom was usually right. And I know you probably think there's something wrong with guys who are hung up on their moms. Doesn't matter. Mom is important to me. When my father died and our lives went off a cliff, we were broke, had nowhere to go, all alone in the world. I was ten years old, and I was ready to give up, sit down in the middle of the road, and cry until a semi hit me. Mom wouldn't let me. She worked two jobs to keep us fed and still had time to push me. She built me up, kept me going, taught me to take care of myself, physically and mentally. And just because she'd been in a coma for a few years, I wasn't going to abandon her.

I guess that all gave me some preparation for what was going on with Monique. I had Mom in long-term care while I looked for a way to wake her up. The doctors all told me that was never going to happen. I told all the doctors to shut the hell up and keep trying. They shook their heads, but they took my money. Of course.

I moved her to a new place every now and then to keep her safe. And I had a guy watching her, a real professional. And when I use that word, I mean one of the best people in the freaking world, which is the only kind I hire. Especially for security. I look for guys with years of training and experience at being lethal, hard-assed paranoids. I pay them better than anybody else could, and they stay loyal or they get dead.

Mom was the most important thing in the world to me, so the guy watching her was the best I ever met. He looked like a gorilla, but he was fast and mean and deadly, and if you let his looks fool you into thinking he was stupid, it would be your last mistake. This guy was smart, too, and could think like a chess master. I paid him a lot, and he never let me down.

So I needed to check in with him. To be honest, I was feeling guilty. I usually visit Mom often, tell her how I am and what I'm doing, and I hadn't done that for a while. I hadn't forgotten her—I never will. But

I'd been wrapped up in watching over Monique, and I'd left Mom on the back burner.

Mom was back in the States, of course. Monique was in South Africa, with the best brain-trauma care I could find. Both of them were in comas at the moment, but I couldn't just dump them with doctors and hope everything worked out. That's not who I am.

I found a quiet corner in the train station and took out a burner cell phone from the attaché case.

In a very secure location that you don't need to know, I had a very secure computer answering service set up. My watchers have the number, and I can call in for messages from anywhere in the world. And I do. It's always a good idea to stay in touch. All the phone commercials say so, and why would they lie?

No problem connecting, either. In this provincial train station in Mozambique, I connected right away. All good. It was just routine precaution, but that never hurt.

And damn, was it a good idea this time.

The computer-generated date stamp said the first call was from yesterday, when I'd been gearing up to be a mining inspector. It was from the guy I had watching Monique while I went after diamonds. He was a native South African, a Zulu man who'd kicked around the world as a mercenary and had some very impressive credentials. I'd gotten him a spot as a janitor at the care facility where Monique was stashed so he could keep an eye on her.

It took me a few seconds to understand what he was saying. Not because of the accent, which was the beautiful, musical Zulu-English accent. This sounded like he had a dish towel in his mouth. I rewound and listened again. "This is Solomon," it said. The guy's name. "Men from your government came to take her. I tried to stop them." A pause, a few ragged breaths. "I did not succeed. I am in hospital." Now I got it; his voice was muffled because his jaw was wired shut. He'd taken a beating.

There was a last short pause, then a deep breath and, "I failed you. I will not take your money."

That was it. It was more than enough.

They took her. They took Monique. "Men from your government," he had said. There were one or two hot possibilities for what that meant, but considering they beat the crap out of my guy, it wasn't hard to narrow it down to one. I was pretty sure what "they" from "my government" meant.

Prescott.

The bastard wanted a backup incentive plan in case I wouldn't play. He'd found a good one.

But was it the only one? I got a sudden sick hunch, one of those evil ideas that pop into your head and get you begging God to make it not true. I ran the phone messages all the way through, with a steady and pathetic *please please please* running through my head. But there was nothing from the guy I had watching Mom. He always reported regularly, but there was nothing. Total silence.

Prescott. The bastard had them both.

CHAPTER
7

T. C. Winston wasn't sure how he should feel. He had fucked up, no doubt about it. And he'd told Prescott, as he should have. And then shit had gone south, at least as far as he was concerned.

Winston had been tasked with staying with their guest, or whatever he was. Riley Wolfe. If that was really his name. Probably not. It didn't matter. Prescott said to keep an eye on him but not hurt him. And Winston gathered that even though he was working with the team now, Prescott didn't trust the guy. No wonder, with the rep this cat had. Master thief. Disguise artist. He moved pretty good, too; the way he'd come off that roof and up into the plane was impressive.

So Winston stayed with the guy when the DC-3 made its landing, on a small airstrip that was not marked on any map. The men on board climbed off and into a couple of large SUVs that had been waiting, motors running so the air conditioning would keep the interiors of the cars cool. Winston squeezed into the back seat of the second SUV and scrunched up next to Wolfe. They rode in silence for forty minutes until they got into Sussundenga, to the small office building they'd been using as HQ.

They all went inside and up the metal stairs to the third floor, to the suite of offices they were using. And on down the hall to the conference room. Wolfe tossed his attaché case on the table and sat. But a minute later, he stood up again. "I got to use the can," he said.

"Of course," Prescott said. He pointed down the hall. "Help yourself."

Winston watched as Wolfe headed out the door, his attaché case under his arm, like he didn't trust anybody else in the room. Winston caught Prescott's eye and gave him a questioning look. Prescott nodded. "Stay with him," he said.

Winston followed out the door, just in time to see Wolfe go into the bathroom. The door shut, and when Winston got there, it was locked. That wasn't alarming, but it wasn't optimum, either. And there was a quick fix. Winston stepped to the end of the hall. A key board was there on the wall. He took the key for the restroom, went back, and opened the door.

The restroom was empty.

Winston quickly checked the entire room. There was no sign of Wolfe. He sighed. It really wasn't his fault, but he knew that, for Prescott, it was on him. He wasn't looking forward to reporting this, but it was his job, his duty. He'd been dressed down a few times in the Corps, and it wasn't the yelling or name-calling that bothered him. It was the idea that he had failed in his duty. That hurt a lot. He served in the Corps, and then with the Agency, because he loved his country. Maybe that was corny or old-fashioned, but it was true. Winston loved the USA and had been happy to lay his life on the line for it.

So when he fucked up a job, he failed his country. He hated that. But he would never try to cover up, save his own ass. That was an even worse failure. So he went to the conference room to report his fuckup. Prescott looked up. "He's gone," he said. "He locked the door to the can. By the time I got it open, he was gone."

He waited for the blast, the yelling, the name-calling. He deserved it. But that was when shit had gotten weird. It hadn't come. No angry words, no telling him what an idiot he was. Instead, Prescott just nodded. "Good," he said.

Winston stood for a minute, blinking.

Prescott finally looked up at him. "For Christ's sake, sit down, Winston," he said. "He was *supposed* to get away." A nasty smile flickered across his face. "That's why I sent *you* to watch him."

That stung. Winston thought about saying something back. But he had too many years of following orders and eating whatever shit the brass threw at him. And he figured, what the hell, he was basically still a grunt. And he was still serving his country, which was what mattered most to him. So he shook it off and took his seat at the table.

This was serving, right?

CHAPTER

8

It doesn't matter how cold you are, how hard and tough and don't-give-a-shit. There are moments when the ice water in your veins boils over and you want to scream and kill everything that moves. I was having one of those moments. In fact, a whole string of them.

I went with it. I let the red fog roll over my vision and ground my teeth and clenched my fists and thought about putting my hands around Prescott's neck and squeezing, watching as his eyes bugged out and his tongue began to stick out, and squeezing some more, until I heard the crunch of his throat collapsing and watched his eyes fog over—

Fun while it lasted, but I couldn't let it last very long; just long enough to get it out of my system. Then I took a deep breath. There was truly nothing I could do about my situation—at least not now. At some point, you can bet your ass I would do plenty. But Mom had a saying for this, too. She gave it to me because when I was in my teens, I lost my temper. A lot. And because of that, bad things happened. "Go in on fire, and you'll burn down the house," she told me.

She taught me to sit down, take a few deep breaths, and do things cold and smart.

I would fix this, and I would fix Prescott for doing it. But I would do it when I had a plan. For now, all I could do was carry on with the job. And I'd do it my way. To do that, I had to get away and lose any possible tail. Because by now, he would be looking for me.

So I put strangling Prescott on the back burner and got back to travel. I wanted to take enough jumps to make sure my trail was wiped out. That meant a bunch of random trips, changing identity each time. Maybe it seems like a lot of work. But I knew Prescott would have somebody watching, and he would be a pro. So if I didn't want them to know where I was going—or, for that matter, who I was going to be—the extra travel and work were necessary.

I took a train across Mozambique to Namibia. It was no problem switching identities in Namibia. I had a couple stashed in my attaché case, all the ID and credit cards I needed. I always had a good selection of new identities on hand. They're cheap and easy to get if you know where to look. I just had to find a quiet restroom to change. I made a few small changes to my face, darkened my beard stubble and hair. Then I added a whole new wardrobe from the shops near the train station, and I put on a New Me that I thought was right for the job. When I got a bus for the airport, I was Umberto Ciccone, a business-man from Sicily. My Italian is good, and I liked the Sicilian business-man bit. Nobody asks questions.

At the airport, Umberto got a first-class seat from Namibia up to Nouadhibou Airport in Mauritania. A few hours later I was out of one desert and into the next. From the Kalahari to the edge of the Sahara. You could almost forget that Africa is supposed to be all green jungles and rain forest and that kind of thing. Which it isn't, really. There's a whole lot of sand, too.

In Mauritania, Umberto went into the trash and I came out of the restroom as Brad Skalgard, a freelance journalist from Vancouver. Brad bought a ticket to Delgado Airport in Lisbon, Portugal. There was a two-hour wait before the flight, which Brad spent in the first-class lounge, swilling the local coffee—it's not bad—and trying some native dishes. Of course I had to have some *thieboudienne*. It's their national dish, fish and rice in a red sauce. And honestly? Just, no. Maybe the fish was off that day. Either that, or they needed a new national dish. Anyway, I didn't like it.

I moved on to some roasted lamb, called *mechoui*, and that was better. Washed down with fruit juice—Mauritania is an Islamic republic, so no alcohol—and then some more of the coffee.

I made up for the airport's alcohol ban on the plane to Lisbon, putting away a couple of cognacs to kill the last lingering taste of the *thieboudienne*. Don't know if you've noticed this, but bad fish stays with you for a while.

It wasn't with me anymore by the time I landed in Lisbon. I got a flight from there to Toronto, no wait at all. By the time we were in the air and out over the Atlantic, I was asleep.

I switched again in Toronto, turning into William Skinner, a middle-aged professor of English literature at a community college in Missouri. Dr. Skinner got a flight to Atlanta, where he went into the restroom. A few cosmetic changes, stuff the attaché case into a backpack, and Dr. Skinner came out as Henry Swindell, who worked at a body shop in Hot Springs, Arkansas. Henry flew on down to Fayetteville, Arkansas. Swindell was the last ID I had on me, so there was no point in grabbing another flight. And Fayetteville was where I had stashed my truck anyway.

And there, finally, I got my truck from the long-term parking lot and headed south.

CHAPTER
9

Chase Prescott had of course studied Wolfe's profile and had been well prepared for Wolfe to take off at the first opportunity. In fact, he had planned for it. Even while they were trapping the thief at the diamond mine, Prescott's surveillance team had been deploying across Africa. They were covering train stations, airports, bus stations, and maritime ports. Good men, too, who knew what they were doing.

So Prescott was unconcerned when Wolfe vanished. The surveillance team would be careful. Wolfe wouldn't know he was being watched. He'd have the illusion of operating freely, when he would actually be under Prescott's eyes the whole time. All as it should be. He put the matter aside.

He was working through a stack of unrelated reports when a hesitant tap came on his office door. He looked up to see T.C. Winston standing in front of him, practically at attention. Prescott sighed. No matter how many years Winston had been out of the Marines, he still acted like the grunt he was, and Prescott found it irritating as hell. But the man was a very good pilot—choppers and prop planes—and he was good at the dirty jobs, as long as they weren't too complicated. So Prescott put up with the absurd Semper Fi spit-and-polish and parade-ground manners. For now.

"What is it," Prescott said, letting a little weariness show in his voice.

"It's Wolfe, sir," Winston said. And then—nothing.

"For Christ's sake, spit it out," Prescott snapped. "What about Wolfe?"

"He's dropped completely off the radar," Winston said. "We lost him in Portugal. At the Lisbon airport. After that, he was gone. No trace of him, sir."

Prescott frowned, drummed his fingers on the desk. It was a little worrisome, losing sight of Riley Wolfe. He'd put enough men on tailing him, ops who knew all the dodges and should have been prepared for any bullshit tricks Wolfe could pull. Still—Prescott was certain that his hook was in deep enough to guarantee that Wolfe would perform as he was supposed to. And if he balked at all, there was still the hole card. Two of them, in fact.

Prescott shrugged. "It doesn't matter," he said. "We've got him by the balls. He'll be in touch when he needs something." He waved a hand at Winston. "Dismissed," he said, using the military command with just a touch of mockery in it.

Winston stood another few seconds before he turned on his heel and left the room.

She woke slowly, and for several minutes she was not even aware of being awake. The thick gray fog that held her was so complete, and so comfortable, that she let it keep her, even fought to hang on to it as it began to roll away. But gradually, it seeped out anyway, and she opened her eyes.

The light was bright, and it hurt. She blinked against it and soon it didn't hurt. She was in a room, a different room from the one where she first woke up, the room with the nice woman and the smiling man. And then men had come—men who should not have been there. They were loud and rough, and they scared her. And then one of them had jabbed her with a needle—

Nothing. Just darkness.

And now she was here. She didn't know why. But she didn't know much from the other place, either. And she couldn't remember anything before that place. Before the other room there was just empty space where her life should have been. She could not remember where she had lived, or how, or who she was. There was nothing in her of her past, nothing at all. She was sure she had one, but what was it? Why couldn't she remember anything, not even who she was? She thought very hard, and her breathing got fast and ragged and there was still nothing. She closed her eyes and clenched her fists and screamed in her head for something, anything, just one small clue about who she had been—and for just a second there was some kind of sound memory of a word that—

Monique.

Her eyes popped open. She moved her lips to say the word, *Monique.* She heard the sound, and even though her voice was dry and harsh, the word was right somehow. *Monique.* She said it again and felt it roll across her lips and it was warm and soothing, and as she said it one more time, she knew what it meant. It wasn't just a word. It was a name—

Her name. Monique. That was who she was. She said it again,

Monique, and it sounded good; easy and comforting and familiar, like being home.

Monique said it again, and for the first time since she woke up, she smiled. She knew who she was. *Monique.* Her name was Monique.

That was enough for now. She closed her eyes and went happily back into the fog.

CHAPTER

10

A day and a half of driving took me south from Arkansas, and then west into Texas. I had recently bought an old rancho in the southwestern part of the state, and that was where I holed up to plan. It was cheap and way off the radar, and the old house was sound. I generally don't like Texas a whole lot, but it has a couple of outstanding qualities. One of them is that they tend to mind their own business there and just leave you alone. That was what I was looking for now, so this place was perfect. It was way the hell out in the middle of absolutely nowhere. That's another of the state's virtues. There's a whole lot of nothin' in big chunks of Texas.

My place was two hundred dusty acres that branched off a dusty road in a dry and dusty part of the state. That sounds like a big place—if you're not from Texas. Two hundred acres is nothing to brag about in a state where some people have ranchos bigger than a couple of US states. It was just enough land to put me into the charming Texas category of "all hat and no cattle." Fine; I don't like cows, except in steak form, and anyway the place was too dry for them.

Which is one reason it was relatively cheap, and just what I was looking for. I hadn't done a whole lot to fix it up yet. Just the standard modifications I make on all my places. I had an electrified perimeter fence put up and a few electronic security things, cameras and sensors and stuff. And I'd had it provisioned with a lot of food, the kind that keeps indefinitely, and a top-notch sound system, some basic books and clothes. Just the necessities. And, of course, a few more lethal toys, hidden in a special compartment in the back wall of the pantry. I don't want to be the dumbass who shows up at a gun party waving a kitchen knife, so I had a nice assortment—pistols, long guns, and a bunch of things that go boom. It was pretty much the same thing I do at all the hidey-holes I buy. I never know when I'll need a place, or what kind of shape I might be in when I get there, or even who might be coming after me. So I like my places to be ready when I check in, even without luggage, and be all set the minute I get there.

So even though I'd only been to this rancho once before, it was like coming home. Everything was familiar, because that's how I set it up. Same layout, same supplies, even the same furniture. When "home" is kind of a revolving concept, it's nice if things are familiar, even when you haven't been there much before. I tossed my backpack on the couch, cracked a bottle of Aberlour sixteen-year-old single malt Scotch, and then the most important part. I had to put on some thinking music.

Music is important to me—so important that I can't understand how some people claim to function without it. And I don't care a rusty sparrow fart whether it's rockabilly, classical, Balinese monkey chants—anything and everything, as long as it's *good*. There's a time and a place for all of it. People who can only tolerate one kind, like *it's got to be country,* or *I can't stand anything but chamber music*—what's wrong with these people? To me, that's like refusing to eat anything but peanut butter.

So I had music for all my moods, and the thinking stuff was an important part of working through a new puzzle. It put me into a state of mind that was kind of meditative; relaxed but mentally alive. And the tougher the nut I had to crack, the more important it was to get the soundtrack right. I took my time finding it.

I was used to complicated problems, and this one fit the bill. It wasn't just a hard grab at Ivo's missile silo. I've done stuff a lot harder, and once I got in, I was pretty sure I could pop Ivo's vault and get away. Of course, getting in was going to be a problem, and right off the bat I didn't see how the hell I was going to do that.

What made the deal truly complicated was not getting my icons and Prescott's super-secret plans. The real problem came because I had to find a way to get Mom and Monique away from Prescott without tipping him. The best way to do that was to have his attention focused on me and the job I was doing. Lots of tough angles, like I'd have to be in three places at once—that isn't as easy as it sounds, even for me.

So at this stage of planning, the music was crucial. I had to find something special. I flipped through my index, looking for just the right sound. I rejected a couple of old favorites: Philip Glass, Brian Eno, Keith Jarrett's *Köln Concert,* John McLaughlin's *My Goal's Beyond.* Not even the Paul Horn *Inside* recordings. Nope. I mean, all great, but not this time. I couldn't tell you why I chose a particular piece for thinking music. I can only say I go with what feels right.

So I took my time finding the right one. I paused for a minute at Jacek Muzyk's recording of the Bach cello suites. Muzyk was a French horn player, but he'd transcribed the cello suites for the horn, and somehow he made it work. But I rejected Jacek, too. When you play the horn, you have to breathe every now and then, even if you're Jacek Muzyk. If you haven't noticed, this is not a problem that afflicts cello players. I mean, they do have to breathe—but it doesn't make gaps in their playing. With the French horn, it does. And every time Muzyk paused to breathe, I noticed it. It was distracting. So no, not this time.

I thought about a recording of "Monks of the Dark Abbey." Gregorian chants, and kind of nice—but no. I was dealing with a Class One asshole, a guy who was born into the asshole caste. Prescott had a few generations of being devious and nasty in his blood, and he was in a job that had developed that inborn talent for forty years. I had to assume he wasn't telling me a lot, that most of what he did tell me was a lie, and that he would have booby traps all along the way. I needed a plan that was just as devious—and hopefully maybe a couple of steps nastier than what he had. To find that, I needed some music that was meditative, yeah, but also twisty and snaky, and Gregorian chants are too straightforward. Too relaxing. I moved on.

I finally settled on some Ravi Shankar, an assorted bunch of ragas. I mean, good old Ravi isn't nasty, not at all. But the ragas he played were not straight-line. They were complex enough to get me thinking in a twisty way, and they also pushed me into a meditative mood at the same time. Perfect. I cranked it up and sat on the couch with my Scotch.

Two days later, the bottle of Scotch was empty. So was most of a second bottle. And I didn't have a whole lot to show for it.

What seemed like the first and biggest problem was getting into the vault. I had figured a way to do that—but I needed an Ushakov icon to make it work. Normally, no big deal. I'd get Monique to whip up one of her perfect copies, and bingo. Ushakov icon. But Monique was out of play—not just in a coma, but stashed somewhere by Prescott. I'd have to get one somewhere else, and the "elses" were very limited. And then I had to get it into Ivo Balodis's hands, and from what I knew about him, that had to be done in person, face-to-face.

Which was the next problem. I couldn't very well let Ivo see my face. Even well disguised, it was a big risk, especially with somebody like him, who was suspicious by trade with a lifetime of experience. So how could I work that? Even the second bottle of Scotch hadn't helped me sprout any ideas—and it was really good Scotch, too.

And the next big problem was getting on and off Ivo's island with at least one icon for my trouble plus the flash drive, and preferably alive and in one piece. Obviously, the key to that was Balodis himself, and so far I couldn't find his weak spot.

I had gone over Prescott's file a dozen times. I knew everything about Ivo Balodis that was knowable, and a pretty good chunk of stuff that shouldn't have been. Medical history, educational history, sexual history, places he'd been, books he'd read—things you had to wonder about how Prescott got them. I mean, little things like I knew the name of the girl he lost his virginity with—Ugne, can you believe that's a girl's name? And I knew Ivo fell in love with a Frenchwoman, a double agent, but she died in prison. And he was a math prodigy and had memorized pi out to at least 150 digits. He loved American heavy metal music and *ptichye moloko*, a kind of Russian candy.

I truly didn't give a crap about most of that info, and I would never use 99 percent of it. But I studied it all, because you never know what might pop the cork and get you going.

And a lot of the material in the folder was going to be relevant no matter what plan I made. There were maps and a lot of notes on the approaches to Ivo's island, and some good details about the inside of the missile silo. The island started life as a lighthouse, because there were some bad shoals in the area. In 1963, it had gone through a Soviet

"People's Renovation" to ensure that it was politically correct. I have no idea what that means for a building, but the Soviets were big on it. And anyway, this renovation was actually a cover for what the Reds were *really* doing to the place. Which was to put a completely dark launch facility under the lighthouse.

"Dark" doesn't mean there were no lights on the island. Duh. It means that this launch site was top secret, hidden from everybody, tucked away as a kind of last-ditch surprise, just in case. It contained three silos, each one about ninety feet deep, and each designed to hold one Chusovaya MRBM, a medium-range ballistic missile. Medium range meant it was supposed to cover Western Europe, the NATO countries. I learned that the Chusovaya was propelled by a mixture of hydrazine and nitrogen tetroxide and was equipped with a 680-kilogram nuclear warhead that burst in the air with a one-to-two-megaton blast. Oh, and "Chusovaya" was the name of a river in Russia. I didn't see how any of that would come in handy—the missiles and warheads were long gone—but hey, you can never know too much, right?

Ivo's vault, the one where he was keeping the flash drive Prescott wanted—and more importantly, the gorgeous Ushakov icons—was at the bottom of one of the missile silos. Ivo had electrified the sides of the silo with fatal voltage and put in sensors and laser detectors and all kinds of security stuff. The only way to get down the shaft to the vault, in theory, was on a small lift he kept frozen in place halfway down, held there by an unbreakable security code and booby-trapped with a couple of very nasty, and very lethal, surprise traps. I had to wonder how many of Prescott's guys had been snuffed finding out about the killer surprises. I was pretty sure he couldn't tell me. He wasn't the kind of guy who gives enough of a shit to keep a count of dead peons, as long as it got him what he wanted.

At the bottom of the silo was the actual vault. Ivo had not skimped on that, either. It was state-of-the-art, hardened on the outside and lined with cobalt so you couldn't drill or cut into it. The door was massive and could withstand everything up to a nuclear blast. And maybe that, too. That would have been appropriate for a vault in a missile silo.

There was a series of what they call re-lockers built in. These are cute little buggers that detect any kind of attempt to crack the vault and, when they do, they just shut it down tight, game over, end of story, period, the end, sorry, go away now. And of course, the usual array of sensors, vibration detectors, all that. The only way in was if you knew the code on the vault's lock. It was a twelve-digit code, and of course only Ivo knew it.

Well, okay. Pretty good. I've gotten in to a few places that were just as tough. And I would get in to this one, too. There is *always* a way.

But just to spice it up a little, there were also the guards, and they were good. They were all ex-Spetsnaz. That's Russian Special Forces, their elite soldiers. They were real shooters, and they were tough, skilled, and nasty. Very disciplined, really well trained, every one of them a dead shot with anything from a Dragunov SVD sniper rifle to a slingshot. They patrolled the whole island, inside and out, on an arbitrary schedule that changed at random intervals.

So it was going to be a tough nut to crack, no question. But that still wasn't the part that really worried me. I knew I could get on the island, past the guards, down the shaft, and into the vault. I mean, I didn't know how yet, but I'd find a way. I always do. But at the same time I was doing that, I had to be on the outside, tracking down and then grabbing Monique and Mom—and also in one other place, because I had to neutralize Prescott at the same time. It's the secret to almost all really good magic tricks: "Hey, everybody! Look at my right hand!" and in the meantime you do the real trick with your left.

I had to find a way to do that to Prescott, and I had to be the left hand *and* the right hand at the same time. On top of that, I just knew he had something planned for me that I was not going to like. I didn't trust the snotty bastard as far as I can throw a Chusovaya MRBM, which is not far—they weigh 86.3 tons. No, from my reading of the guy, it was still easier to play caber toss with the missile than to trust Prescott. I had a hunch that when I came off Ivo's island with the flash drive and the icon, Prescott would be there to snatch it, and probably put an unfortunate bullet or two into nasty, low-class Riley Wolfe. Probably— hell, almost certainly. So I had to find a way to be at least four people at once. If not that, then a really good way to teleport myself.

But after another day and another bottle opened, I was still stuck with the same conclusion: I needed at least one more person to help me pull off all this. It had to be somebody I could depend on completely, and there wasn't anyone.

Monique is the only person I trust—*mostly*. But even if she was back in top shape, which she wasn't, I wasn't going to drop her into something in the field. Especially something like this, where one tiny mistake meant a Russian bullet between the eyes. And there was nobody else in the whole wide wicked world that I would even think about working with, ever. Once upon a time, years in the past, I'd partnered up for a while. It had been good while it lasted, even fun. I mean, there is something about having somebody in on the joke with you that makes it just that little bit more enjoyable. And this guy had fit the bill—the ideal partner, since he was every bit as twisted as I am. And in a slightly different direction, which meant that every now and then he could see things I couldn't.

I didn't have anybody like that now, of course. And I hadn't heard from my old partner for a long time. I'd thought about looking him up once or twice, just never had a reason. But in any case—

Ding-a-ling. *Yoo-hoo, Riley. This is an idea calling.*

Okay, Idea, come on in. What's up?

How about that old partner of yours, Riley?

I thought about it. I was pretty sure I could find him. But if he wasn't dead or in prison, he'd be pretty old, like fifty-something. And he probably wouldn't want to get back in the game anymore, either.

You could ask . . .

Naw. Sorry, Idea, that's just dumb.

Okay, Riley. What else you got?

I thought about that, too, and came up with nothing.

Well, then . . . ?

CHAPTER

11

The Cozy Posie Mobile Home Park was stuck in under the branches of an old pecan orchard on the Florida panhandle, not too far from the Georgia border. A battered old wooden sign loomed over the front gate, with a huge, dead-looking painted wooden flower curled around the name. The sign looked like it had been painted in the 1940s and never touched since. The paint was half peeled off, and two of the letters were gone, so the name read, CO Y PO IE. The grass was high at the chain-link fence surrounding the park, and Spanish moss hung from the trees, giving the place a tattered, neglected look.

But the residents of the park liked it there. They seemed to think it was a pretty comfortable place. And it was, after all, in Florida. That was why most of them were there. They were retirees for the most part, on fixed incomes, and Florida is expensive. The Cozy Posie was the only way they could afford to live there in the sunshine.

So mostly they lived there year-round. That made it a close-knit community, one where people got to know their neighbors, thanks to the many bridge tournaments, hobby clubs, and, yes, weekly bingo games sponsored by the VFW. And those neighbors became a second family, because people need family, even if it's made up of unrelated people. For the most part, it was all they had now, because one of the sad truths of the modern world is that children and grandchildren just don't come to visit like they used to. And if Grandma and Grandpa are in a trailer, even a double-wide, there really isn't room for kids, even if they wanted to come for a few days.

So it wasn't often an unfamiliar face appeared at the Cozy Posie. On the rare occasions when a stranger did show up, it seemed like it was usually bad news of some kind.

This stranger looked like he fit the bill for bad news. He was around thirty and dressed in polyester slacks and a white short-sleeved shirt. The clothes looked like they'd come from Walmart, and the tie was definitely a clip-on. A pair of black, horn-rimmed glasses and a clip-board completed the picture, and it added up to a near certainty that this man was some kind of tinhorn official. Probably from some stupid county agency, come to write people up for violations of one of the obscure asshole regulations that always seemed to pop up. Illegal awnings or substandard window shades or some damn thing.

So nobody said hello, and nobody offered to help him as he wandered through the park, looking at the numbers on the home sites. Of course, they watched him, because you never knew who he might be looking for. When he finally stopped at Lot C-27, the watchers felt some relief that it wasn't them. And a couple of them hid a smile, because that was Billy McCleod's trailer. Billy had a temper, and if this bureaucrat pushed one of Billy's buttons, he was going to get an unhappy surprise—a surprise that ought to be better entertainment than anything else going on at 3:15 on this hot Florida afternoon.

They were still watching as the man knocked and called, "License

Bureau Inspector!" Then, after a moment, he leaned toward the door as if listening to someone inside. Then he nodded, called, "All right," and pushed the door open and went into the trailer, closing the door firmly behind him. Most of the spectators turned away; the show was over. Even if they had kept watching, though, they couldn't have seen through the walls of the trailer to watch the little drama unfold inside.

And it was dramatic. When the inspector had closed the door, he paused, waiting for his eyes to adjust to the dimness inside after the bright sunshine outside. Then he looked carefully around. There was no one there—the inspector wasn't surprised. No one had answered when he called. He had pretended to hear an invitation to enter and gone inside anyway, because he felt the eyes of the watchers on him. And he actually didn't want to find anyone home. That was because there was no such thing as the "license bureau," and the inspector was not an inspector.

Who or what he really was remained unclear, but it was obvious that he was looking for something. He opened a couple of drawers and didn't find it, whatever *it* was. He moved back through the trailer, walking past the kitchen area and the closed bathroom door, toward the queen-sized bed at the far end. There was a dresser next to the bed. He bent over it and began to rummage through the drawers. Again he found nothing, and after a quick search he straightened up.

That was when he felt something cold and hard press into the back of his neck.

"This is a .357 Magnum, with a silencer. If you would like to live a little longer, very slowly, very carefully, put your hands on top of your head." The voice was soft, but something about it seemed to say that its owner had done this kind of thing before and was hoping to get a chance to pull the trigger again this time.

The inspector, or whatever he truly was, did as he was told. After a moment, the pistol's muzzle left his neck, and the voice said, "Very slowly, very carefully, turn around," and again, the inspector complied.

Facing him was the man holding the pistol. He was medium height, with a bit of a potbelly. He looked to be in his fifties and had a ponytail and a shaggy beard, and he wore battered khaki shorts and a faded Hawaiian shirt that looked like they had been pulled from a Goodwill barrel. The two men regarded each other for a long moment. Then the older man's eyes narrowed. "Well, shit," he said. And then he chuckled. "Hello, dumbfuck," he said.

CHAPTER

12

D umbfuck" was a pretty accurate description. Trying to sneak in like that, and especially trying it on this guy—that had been a dumbfuck move on my part. It wasn't the first time. It wasn't even the first time with him.

There's an old British saying that when you learn a tough lesson, and learn it the hard way, that's another wrinkle on your ass. I mean, they probably say "arse," but what the hell, they're Brits, and they don't really know how to talk. But if it's literally true, I've got one hell of a wrinkly ass. Or arse, if you're feeling old and British.

Whatever. I got the wrinkles. I went through some rough times when I was young and starting out. I know, everybody goes through rough times. I'm not whining about it. But I needed to learn an awful lot to be good at what I do, and a hell of a lot more to be the best. And considering what I am the very best at—and I am—it shouldn't be a big surprise that some of those rough times involved orange coveralls and tiny rooms with thick steel bars instead of doors.

Get the picture? Yeah, prison. I got caught.

It was a stupid mistake that landed me in the lockup, a mistake I would never make now. But like I said, I had a lot to learn. And one really great way to learn it is to get busted and thrown in the slammer.

Which I was. And just as soon as I got over the whole *Holy shit, this is scary as hell* part of prison, I started figuring how I was going to get out. Because I was going to get out, that was never a question. I spent a week or two scoping out the place, getting a feel for the rhythms and routines, checking out holes in the security. Then I made my plan and went to work.

I looked over everything I could get close to and checked out how it was watched, where the cameras were, when the duty shifts changed, all that. And after a week, I figured the best way out was through the prison laundry. Plenty of holes in the security, lots of dark places with no cameras. So I started working on getting a job there.

And exactly two days after that, another inmate sidled up to me in the exercise yard. He'd been joking with two of the guards over by the gate to the yard, and I'd seen them glancing at me and laughing a little. I didn't know why I was funny, but what the hell. You learn pretty quick you don't survive long inside unless you learn not to let that kind of shit bother you. Especially if two of the assholes laughing at you are guards. You let it slide, unless you're in one of the gangs and have somebody watching your back.

Which I wasn't and didn't. Like always, I was a solo act, and I wasn't going to change that just because I was in the joint. So I watched the guy stroll over to me, leaving the guards grinning behind him. I got the message. I mean, maybe it was the wrong message? But what I heard was that this guy was tight with the COs and I had better not fuck with him.

But I studied him. He was probably mid-forties, and he looked fit. Short hair and a dark brown beard starting to show some gray. The way he walked, the expression on his face—the whole impression was of a guy who was cocky as hell, which you don't show in prison unless you can back it up, because otherwise sure as shit somebody will knock it out of you.

He stopped about three feet away from me and looked me over, still smiling. He finally looked me in the eyes and said, "Hello, dumb-fuck." And then he just smirked at me.

Now, I definitely had a lot to learn about prison life—but this was something I knew. I mean, you'd figure if somebody challenged you, you'd take him out, hard and fast, or you'd get marked as a pussy, and before you knew it, they'd have you on your knees and wearing lipstick. That's how it is in the movies, right?

Nope. As much as I felt like decking this asshole, that was a very bad idea. First, I had no idea how he was connected. I mean, if he was top dog in the Aryan Brotherhood and I slugged him, I would be dead before the end of the week. And second, we were out in the open, in the yard. The guards were watching, and this guy had just showed me he was real chummy with two of them, and those two were real chummy with them.

And I also knew that he had some reason for approaching me. He was clearly not as much in the dark about me as I was about him, because you don't stick your hand into a dark hole unless you know what's in there. He had some kind of agenda that involved me, and until I knew what it was, it would be stupid to piss him off.

So I did the hard thing. I just nodded and said, "Howzit, Shots." As in, *shot caller*. An inmate boss.

He kept smiling. "I hear you're planning to bust out."

I blinked. All I could come up with. I mean, how the fuck did he know that? "Everybody plans that," I said.

He laughed. "Yeah, sure," he said. "Everybody *plans* it. Nobody pulls it off. Know why?"

I shook my head. "No."

"Because everybody rushes into it the same way. Trying to get a job in the laundry."

I blinked again. Not much else I could do. I mean, I was busted.

"And guess what, dumbfuck?" he said. He leaned in closer and said, "*It doesn't work.*" He let that sink in for a minute, then moved back to a normal distance. "Never works," he said. "Because that's what everybody has tried for the last fifty years. That's what they expect you to try. Get me, Slim? They're ready for you. They're actually *hoping* you try it. Because a couple of these COs are sadistic motherfuckers, and they like to hurt people. They don't get to do that often enough, but when some dumbfuck makes the old laundry move, the warden greenlights 'em. That's why there's no cameras down there, fish. That's where they take you, to a room right next to the laundry, and when you come out you don't look human anymore." He nodded, and then just stood there watching me with that smirk glued on.

I shrugged and waited, but he didn't say anything more. I mean, I was green, but that doesn't mean stupid, so I wasn't about to admit anything. On top of that, I knew there had to be some actual reason he was telling me that they were on to me. The normal thing to do was just watch, and maybe let the smirk turn into a snicker when the guards were done with me. But he was telling me, warning me not to do it, and that meant there had to be some angle to it for him.

I mean, *had* to be. He didn't know me, but he was saving me a serious ass-whipping. You don't give away shit like that. So I thought about it. And I couldn't see an angle. I was pretty sure he didn't want me for a girlfriend. And I was almost as sure he wasn't looking for a drug connection, cigarettes, hooch, any of that. Not from a fish like me.

So what did he want? I went around it a couple of times, and all I came up with was that I didn't know enough about this guy to figure what it was. I knew it was there, but I couldn't see it. I didn't even know where to look.

When you don't know what you might step in, you try not to move your feet too much. So I just said, "Okay," and waited.

He waited, too. His smile got bigger, until finally he nodded. "I'm Chaz," he said.

"Connor Franklin," I said. That was who I was when I got caught, so I stuck with it.

"Let's talk," he said, and he led me on a slow walk around the yard. We went all the way around one time in silence. I waited for him to say something, anything. He was the one who wanted to talk, and anyway, I noticed that a lot of the inmates gave him respect. Not all of them, but enough. Little things; they moved out of his way or gave him a small nod as he went by. Good to know. He had some face here—but not with me, not yet.

He started on a second lap around the yard. I followed. About half-way through he finally said something. "You don't trust me," he said. A statement, not a question.

I shrugged. "I don't know you," I said. "I got no reason to trust you."

He nodded, like that was the right thing for me to say. "I'm break-ing out," he said.

I looked at him, surprised. I mean, it's not the kind of thing you should say to anybody in the joint, unless they were going with you. And if I didn't know him, he didn't know me even more, so there was no fucking way he would even . . .

Unless he wanted something from me. Something nobody else could give him.

So I went back to thinking that over. The guy was plugged in, with guards and the way things worked here. So maybe he *did* know something about me. But Connor Franklin hadn't even existed until a few months earlier. The only things there were to know about this particular me were public record, like from my trial. And all that came out at the trial was that I was guilty of scamming a big chunk of cash. And I'd gotten a much stiffer sentence because I wouldn't say where it was or give it back. So—

The nickel dropped.

"How much you need?" I said.

He snorted. "Took you long enough," he said. "But the question is, how much do *we* need?" He stopped walking and looked at me. "You're coming with me."

I didn't say anything. After a minute, he went on. "Lookit, Slim, this tango takes two—I need a partner on this. And I need to trust him."

"You don't know me," I said.

"I know your name isn't Connor Franklin," he said. "That means you have certain skills, and they match mine."

"But why should you trust me?"

"Don't go back to being a dumbfuck," he said. "I told you I'm making a break, so you got something on me to keep me straight. And you want out. I got a plan, and I've been here long enough to know it'll work. Not like *some* people . . ." He waggled his eyebrows at me. Seriously. "But I need some quick cash to make it work, and I need a partner. And if you put that money in, that'll keep *you* straight with me. We trust each other because we have to."

I thought it over. He was right. "I'm in," I said.

He was right about his plan, too. It worked, which is the only real proof of any plan. And not by any stupid, obvious trick, like hiding in a laundry basket. Chaz didn't work like that. By the time we were on the out and safe, I didn't work that way anymore, either. And it taught me an important lesson, something I've kept with me ever since, and it's helped me see a way more than once. It was a whole new way to look at things. Not thinking outside the box, but thinking *without* the box.

Once you get it, it's simple. I thought the problem was getting Riley out of a really secure prison. Chaz taught me that the real problem was to make the prison easier to get out of. Get it? Much bigger picture. Don't change the water; change the bathtub. That might not sound like a big deal, but it is. Try it sometime.

After we got out, I stuck with Chaz for a year or so, partly because we worked well together. Mostly because I'm smart enough to know when somebody can school me on something worth knowing. We made some good scores together, a couple of them just plain con games, which was his thing. I went along and learned a lot more. Chaz was a natural seat-of-pants psychologist and a genius at reading people. He also taught me a lot about making a better disguise. You don't just change your face. You change *you*, all of you, build a new person from the inside out. And that changes everything—how you think, how you walk, how you dress and talk—everything. It changes who you are.

After one truly outstanding score, there was some heat. It seemed like a good idea to split and go to ground separately. And we just . . . I don't know. We both moved on, alone. Tough to explain; we just kind of drifted apart. No hard feelings, no real reason at all, just that we both had a nice chunk of cash to play with, and we did it in different ways. We didn't drift back together, and I hadn't seen Chaz for like fifteen years.

Until now.

CHAPTER
13

Lemme get this right now," Chaz said. He frowned, took a long pull on his bottle of PBR, and set the bottle down empty. "This government guy—and he's a spook, right?—he wants you to sneak into an old Soviet missile base, which just incidentally is guarded by a bunch of Russian Special Forces guys and who the fuck knows what else . . . And then just kinda casually slip down a booby-trapped missile silo, open a state-of-the-art vault, and steal a flash drive."

"That's about it," I said.

"Uh-huh. And you want to do this because you also get to snatch some old Russian church picture."

"An icon, yeah, that's it." I pushed the file from Prescott at him across the table. "It's all in here."

Chaz pushed the file back at me. He sighed. He got up, went back to the trailer's kitchen area, and pulled another PBR from the fridge. He popped it open, came back, and sat. "You really are a dumbfuck," he said.

"Maybe," I said. "But this Russian church picture—this icon—is gorgeous."

"Uh-huh. Is it to *die* for?"

"I won't die."

"Pfft," he said.

"And it's worth a couple million, too," I added.

He shook his head. "You know damn well you could make twice that a whole lot easier, and safer, too. And if you got to have some damn pretty Jesus painting, you could take it from a museum. They don't shoot at you there, either. Lower risk, same reward. What the fuck, Riley."

Of course he was right. But that wasn't the point. For me, the risk was part of the reward. "I don't mind if it's dangerous," I said.

"Aw, fuck, you're still just redneck trailer trash," he said. "One of those good ole boys with that whole dumbfuck 'Hold mah beer—now watch this.'" He shook his head. "Never did get that about you."

I decided not to point out that *he* was the one in the trailer. I just said, "I'll be fine."

"That's as bad as 'hold mah beer,'" he said. "All the shit you know, all the art and music and books—that didn't teach you anything?"

"Taught me art, music, and books," I said.

"I mean, maybe just once you oughta try being smart."

"I did," I said. "I came to you."

"Fuck that, I'm retired."

"Fifty percent of the take," I said.

He waved that away, slopping a little beer onto the table. "I don't need your money," he said.

"Uh-huh. You're living in a double-wide. In a rundown discount trailer park stuffed with fat old people from Ohio. Because you like the lifestyle."

"Aw, fuck you, Riley," he said. He took a hard pull on his beer. "I like it here. It's warm. Nobody tries to kill me."

"And you don't miss that?"

"No I don't." He glared at me. I looked back. After a minute, he looked away. "Maybe a little," he said.

I waited some more. He sipped his beer, but he wouldn't meet my eye. The silence got longer. It started to feel heavy. Finally, Chaz drained his beer and slammed down the empty bottle. "Fuck it," he said. "Show me the file."

We sat at the rickety little table in his crappy double-wide parked in the decaying trailer park, passing pages of the file back and forth and drinking beer. I showed him the photos of the icons as he finished his fifth or sixth beer. Chaz had never been much of an art lover and he wasn't impressed, not until he squinted at the pics. "What the fuck," he said. "Those are *gemstones*? Stuck right onto the painting?"

"Yup."

"And that's, like, real, actual gold, too?"

"It is."

"Huh," he said. "The pictures this guy collects—they're all by the same painter? Uskalev?"

"Ushakov. Simon Ushakov," I said. "Yeah, all by him. He was the very best ever at doing icons."

"Huh," he said again. "That oughta help."

"Okay," I said. "How?"

He shook his head. "Don't know yet," he said. "But I know there's something here that . . ." He flipped through the icon pictures again. "We just need a window," he said. "Some way in, some kinda thing to get you in the door." He pointed at me. "After that it's all on you."

"Just me?"

"Who else you got?" he said. "You're the fucking Tarzan clone. Climbing up the fucking wall and jumping off like a fucking flying squirrel." He meant my parkour, something I am very good at. If you don't know what it is, I'll just say it's the closest you can get to moving around like Spider-Man. He had never really approved of it, and certainly never tried it.

And from the look of his beer belly, he wasn't going to try now. "Sure as shit, *I* am not climbing down a fucking missile silo," he said.

"There's no missiles in it, you know."

"And there's no fucking elevator, either," he said. "Shut up and find something."

I shut up, but I didn't find anything, any more than I'd found the first thirty times I'd gone through the folder. I mean, that's why I'd come to Chaz—because I wanted his take on this. But what the hell. Maybe I'd find it on the thirty-first time.

I didn't. Neither did Chaz. But we kept trying. Chaz kept pounding the beers back, too. But it didn't slow him down. I knew it wouldn't, from when we'd worked together before. He was one of those guys who could drink all night with no visible effects. I've known plenty of guys who say they can handle it. They never can. But Chaz never said anything like that; he just kept drinking. Who knows, maybe it actually helped him think or something.

So I wasn't worried that he would pass out and fall forward onto the table, spilling beer all over the folder and no doubt smashing the crappy little table. I just kept reading and thinking.

Four hours and two six-packs later, Chaz looked up, frowning at me across the little table. "This is it," he said. He tapped the page from the file he'd been studying. "This is our window."

I took the paper and glanced at it. "This? Why? I mean, how?"

He snatched it back. "Goddamn it, this better not mean you've gotten stupid—not with my ass on the line." He slapped the folder onto the table. "Wake up and use your fucking head," he said. "Fake documents are totally fucking easy. We both speak the language—we just need a story. And this will give it to us." He waved the paper in the air. "This is perfect."

Maybe it was the beer. I mean, I had to try to keep up with him, beer for beer. So I had, and because of that, I just didn't see his window.

"Tell me," I said.

He gave me a wide smile. At least three teeth were missing, but it was a smile. "It's simple," he said. "*Écoute.*"

CHAPTER
14

T. C. Winston was pissed off.

He didn't want to be. He'd been in the game long enough to know that hurt feelings got you nothing but more hurt. Besides, it was part of his job to take shit from Top Sergeant, always had been, and that didn't change just because the Top was a pogue in a suit nowadays. He knew what he was for. He was a grunt, a foot soldier, a strong back and a weak mind.

But it wasn't right to have his nose pushed into it every fucking day. He knew his place, he did his job—and Prescott still kept riding him like he was a boot who couldn't figure out which end of his rifle to hold.

Like today. Prescott had called him in and given him that happy sneer. The one that said, *I'm really enjoying what a dumbass you are.* And he'd said, "We have a pickup at the airport. Think you can pull that off without losing the vehicle?"

"Yessir," Winston said woodenly.

Prescott raised an eyebrow. "Really. And you remember how to drive a car, Winston?"

That hurt. Winston could not only drive a car—he could drive any chopper, from a light civilian up to a military Chinook. Plus any fixed-wing aircraft short of an F-22. But he just said, "Yessir," and didn't let anything show on his face.

"Good, very good. Just had to be sure," Prescott said. "You know, considering that it's you. His flight lands in two hours. Don't be late."

"Nosir," Winston said, and headed for the door.

"Oh, Winston?" Prescott called when he had his hand on the doorknob.

"Sir?"

"Would you like to know who you're picking up?" And that smirk again, even bigger and nastier.

Well, he had walked into that. Wanted to get away from that smirk so bad, he'd let it cloud his head. Should've known better—he *did* know better, so it was on him. Even so, he was still pissed off, two hours later. Fucking Prescott. Even now, sitting there at the airport, it was all he could think about. And it threw him so far off his game that he didn't even see the guy he was picking up until the passenger door of the big SUV clicked open and the guy slid onto the seat.

"Hey. It's Winston, right?" he said as he closed the door.

"Yessir," Winston said.

"Oh, fuck that, *sir*?" He laughed. "Come on, buddy, I'm not a sir." He shook his head. "Besides, I got enough of that shit growing up. My dad was in the Corps. Uh, the Marines, you know?"

"I know," Winston said. "So was I."

"Oh, yeah? Well, Semper Fi."

"Right," Winston said. He slid the car into gear and pulled away into traffic. For a couple of minutes, he just drove in silence. But he felt the guy's eyes on him, and finally he flicked a glance over. "What?" he said.

"None of my business maybe, but—something wrong?"

Winston frowned. "What do you mean?"

"Just, you know. I know you're a pro, but you didn't see me approach the vehicle, and—I dunno. You seem kind of . . ." He shrugged. "None of my business."

Winston didn't say anything for a minute. Then he figured, what the hell, it wasn't this guy's fault. He might as well act civilized. "Just pissed off today," he said. He shrugged. "Nothing special. Goes with the job."

"Yeah, I get it," the guy said. "Can't be easy working for a dickless desk jockey like Prescott."

"It isn't. And I just—" Winston jerked his head around to stare at the guy. "I didn't say anything about—"

"Oh, hell, you didn't have to. Prescott could piss off the pope. And I know what my dad used to say, from his time in the Corps? You know, about the kind of asshole who just sits behind a desk and gives orders to people who have to do the work. And when he's a trust fund trooper like Prescott? Forget it."

"Yeah. He's hard to take. But it's part of the job, so . . ."

"Right. Soldier on, soldier."

"That's about it."

They talked a little more during the half-hour drive back to the office. For some reason, it made Winston feel a little better. Hard to say why. Just, the guy seemed to understand. And even if he hadn't actually been in the Corps himself, his father had, and this guy clearly got it.

So when he pulled the big black SUV into the lot at the office, he felt like he could face Prescott again. He was almost cheerful as he took the guy up, saw him into the room with Prescott, and left them together without waiting for the snotty comment he knew would come if he hung around. He just closed the door on them and walked away.

And he realized it was just because this guy had talked to him like he was a real human being. That and the connection with Corps, which made him practically family. After all the crap he'd been told about this guy, too. It just went to show you couldn't trust what other people told you. Especially Prescott. He said this guy couldn't be trusted, total monster, stab you in the back, all that. But he turned out to be an okay guy. At least, he seemed like one to Winston.

Anyway, this Riley Wolfe was a whole shitload better than Prescott any day, that was for sure.

Chase Prescott knew he was being an asshole. He didn't care. People like Winston would make anybody with a brain sneer and snarl. His goddamned Boy Scout worship of the flag and all the pretty lies it stood for set Prescott's teeth on edge, and he took every chance he got to poke at it, and at Winston, and take them both down a notch. He couldn't help it. When he encountered that sort of thing, that sort of person, it was automatic. He didn't even think about it anymore.

It was a good thing he didn't. If he'd probed the reasons behind his near-violent reaction to Winston and other happy patriots, he might have realized that it was because he had been like that once. But his love of country, and his own self-image reflected by it, had been tarnished and then shattered.

Chase had been born into a very fine old-money family, the only son, and he had done all he should have, all that tradition dictated for a Prescott: gone to the right schools, joined the appropriate clubs. He got a degree in literature—from Yale, of course, all Prescotts went to Yale. His thesis, "Edgar Allan Poe and the Birth of the American

Imagination," had actually been published in an obscure scholarly magazine. And, as his father commented, Poe was a fine foundation for a law degree, which Chase received at Harvard Law. All according to plan and family precedent. And then, he had gone off the track. Fresh out of law school and filled with a new and unexpected appreciation for the country that had made his family's longtime prosperity possible, Chase Prescott had taken a job with the Agency.

His father, Benson Prescott, had tried to talk him out of it. Under the influence of a little too much very good Scotch, he had explained to young Chase that the spook trade and all that sort of thing was nonsense. "The business of America is business," he intoned solemnly.

"That's very good, Dad, you should write it down," Chase said.

"You're being an idiot. With your law degree and your family connections, you can do very well very quickly. But this? Nonsense," Benson said, pouring more Scotch into his glass.

"I owe something to this country," Chase said.

"You owe it to your *family*! You owe it to *me*!" his father had said, spilling his Scotch.

Chase hadn't listened. And now, far too late, he realized his father had been right. Country didn't matter, the flag didn't care, and half a lifetime of service meant nothing. Whether you were a country, a business, or an embittered old spy, all that mattered was the money. Well, that would come. Soon.

Prescott poured himself a drink—not Scotch. He couldn't stand the stuff. Brandy with ice in it was his drink. He half-filled a cut-stone glass with Philbert Rare Cask and added some ice. He sipped, then tossed off the whole glass and poured another. Leaning back in his chair, he sipped the second drink slowly and thought through his plans. Once he had the thing back in his hands, everything would move forward properly again. He would slowly and carefully let the news filter out that the auction was still on, but it had a different ring-master. And then the bids would come in, he would play them against one another, and the high bid would take it. It didn't matter in the slightest who that would be. He was betting on China, but you never really knew. Whoever it was didn't matter. The payout would be huge, and Prescott would take it and disappear. Perhaps he'd arrange a few accidents for his soldiers, just to muddy the trail. Especially that insufferable clot Winston.

Prescott smiled and raised the glass to his lips. The ice rattled, but the brandy was gone. He stared at it, surprised, then shrugged it off and poured more. The plan would work. It would all fall the way it should, and end with Prescott on top.

But it all depended on one undependable, and very slippery, thief.

He'll get it, he thought. *He really is good. He'll get it.*

He took another sip. *Goddamn it*, he thought, *he* has *to get it . . .*

CHAPTER
15

Prescott and his gang were all done in Africa. They had only been there to snag me, and I was more or less snagged. So they'd moved the entire circus back to their former location, an isolated spot in northern Germany, not too far from Peenemünde.

When I flew in to meet with him, it was more a fishing expedition than anything else. I mean, I had a general outline of what I was going to do. But there were some very large pieces missing, and I was hoping I might see or hear something while I was with Prescott, some tiny spark that would light up the missing pieces. Since a couple of those pieces involved getting back the hostages Prescott was holding to keep me tamed—Mom and Monique, the only two people in the world I really cared about—I really needed to get this right. And to do that, I was willing to put up with King Asshole for a couple of hours.

Lucky for me, it didn't take that long. In fact, the minute I climbed into the car at the airport, I had it. I knew right away this was it. It was just a question of using a little bit of subtle persuasion. And that I can definitely do.

People see and hear what they want to see and hear. That's a basic law of human nature. It doesn't matter how extremely weird what they're expecting might be, either. If somebody thinks they'll see a dragon and a dachshund shows up, they'll swear the damn wiener dog was breathing fire.

And a kind of parallel law to that one? If you know what you're doing, you can make people look at the dachshund and see a real dragon.

When I climbed into the black SUV at the Khama International Airport back in Botswana, I had known I had a big problem. I hadn't solved it since then. I'd gone over it with Chaz, and I'd pounded at it solo in my head. Nothing. And I was still turning the wheels at the Peenemünde airport when I opened the door and climbed into the front seat. But the second I saw the guy sitting behind the wheel, something clicked into place. I just knew. This guy was the missing piece. I couldn't tell you how or why I knew; it was just something about the way he sat there, kind of at attention but slumped, like he was totally pissed off but trained not to show it. I knew without thinking about it why he was pissed off: He worked for Prescott.

And the training part only took another second. Sticking out of the cuff of his jacket I could just see half a tattoo that showed part of a globe of the earth with the bottom part of an anchor, and some rope wrapped around the anchor. US Marines, absolutely no question. I had turned myself into a Marine once on a job, and to prepare I had learned everything I could about the Corps—like, they call it "the Corps."

So those two things came together—and my brain did whatever mental magic we do when things just go *click* and we don't know why, and I had a solution. This guy, right here. He was it. I just had to work him a little. And I knew I could do that. I'm good at making people see the dragon.

Any half-decent time-share salesman can tell you the first step to making somebody like you and trust you is to call them by name, like you're already good buddies. Half a second more, and I remembered this guy's name, Winston. So I called him by name. That surprised him, and just like it's supposed to, it loosened him up a little, and I went to work showing him my dragon.

By the time I strolled into Prescott's office, I was halfway home with getting Winston where I needed him to be. And I was feeling so good about that I didn't even let King Asshole's attitude bother me. I just sat in the chair across from his and got comfortable, while he was still making me wait by pretending to be really busy with a ton of vitally important shit. That paid off right away, when Prescott said, "Have a seat, Riley," without looking up to see that I already had. When I didn't say anything, he glanced at me, frowned because I was already sitting, and then pretended to get back to his Important Work.

When he figured he'd made me wait long enough, he looked up, frowned again, and pushed a stack of papers to one side.

"So you need something, is that it?" he said.

"Sure, I need something," I said. "Why else would I come to see you?"

He frowned bigger. That was probably going to be his line, and I'd stolen it. Now he had to think of something to say that was just as sarcastic. He didn't, so he said, "You understand, I hope, that any help I offer is limited to—"

"You're broke, I get that," I said, cutting him off. "Money's not a problem for me."

He didn't like that, but since he still wanted me on his side, he swallowed it. "All right," he said. "What do you need?"

"It's simple," I said. "Just a question of resources you have and I don't."

He raised an eyebrow. "It would be very helpful if you could be specific," he said.

So I told him. Specifically, too. And it was simple, and it wouldn't cost him anything. I mean, one phone call and it was done. But because he was a blue-blood type A asshole, he had to add on a riff about how it was a lot harder than I seemed to realize. Then he frowned in a very serious way and drummed his fingers on the desktop. "Clearly you have some kind of plan," he said with a tone in his voice like he knew the plan had to be stupid, since he hadn't made it up.

"Yes, I do," I said.

"And?"

"And I have a plan."

He waited for me to tell him, and when I didn't, he went back to drumming his fingers. "And that's it? Just get this 'package' into the diplomatic pouch to Langley?"

I nodded. "And then have Langley forward it." I tossed a piece of paper to him. "To this address. Where Winston picks it up and delivers it to an address I'll give him later."

"Why Winston?"

I shrugged. "I like him," I said.

"You have shitty taste in friends," he said.

"Sure. I'm hanging out with you, aren't I?"

He scowled for a minute. When I didn't start to tremble, he said, "I don't like it."

"You don't have to like it," I said. "You just have to do it."

He really hated that. It was too much like he was taking orders, and from a peon, too—somebody who hadn't even gone to Yale. So he scowled some more and waited for me to melt under his steely patrician gaze and give in. I didn't melt. Finally, he shook his head and said, "I'm sticking my neck out here. I think I need to know a little more."

I nodded, like that was reasonable. "Okay. Sure. Here's some more: If you can't do this one simple thing, I'm all done." To make sure he knew what that meant, I gave him a little wave, the kind you'd do to a baby. "Bye-bye," I said.

"Cut the shit," Prescott snapped. "I've got no reason to trust you."

I shrugged. "Should've thought of that before you blackmailed me into doing this."

"It was not blackmail," he said. "Clearly you don't understand that word. We made a deal—the icons, remember?"

"It's blackmail when you're holding my mother and my partner until you get what you want," I said.

I could see it hit him that I'd already found out, but only for a second. "You'll get them back," he said, not very convincingly. "When this is over."

"Good to know. And I better get them back in good shape."

"You're *threatening* me?" he sneered. "You're one little guy, Wolfe. That doesn't stack up against what I can bring to the table."

"Ever hear of Patrick Boniface, the biggest, most badass arms dealer in the world?" I smiled at him. "Know what I did to him?"

He slammed a hand on the desk. "I can break you into little pieces."

"Good luck finding my replacement."

He took a big breath and looked like he was going to blow a fuse, do a little recreational shouting and name-calling. I have sensitive ears, so I cut him off before he could start. "Drop the attitude, Prescott. You do this my way, you get your prize. You don't, I can't do my part. Very simple."

He snarled for a second, and then spun his chair away and stared out the window for a minute. Then he turned back around and shrugged. "I suppose I can manage it," he said.

"If you're not sure, you could ask Winston to help you," I said. And that wasn't just sticking in a needle. I mean, it was that, too. But it definitely had a purpose. I wanted Prescott to be extra snarky to Winston, and I was pretty sure I'd done that.

"Winston," he sneered. "He could get lost in a phone booth."

"That's pretty good," I said. "Considering how hard it is to find a phone booth nowadays."

He just blew out a breath and worked the frown muscles for a minute. "All right," he said. "I'll see what I can do."

I stood up. "That would be super cool," I said. "Especially if you want that flash drive." I opened the door and then turned back. "Can I get Winston to drive me back to the airport?"

"Send him in," he said. "I'll tell him to take you."

CHAPTER
16

T. C. Winston was not really a moody guy. In fact, he mostly lived on the easygoing side of the street. He hit sour patches, just like everybody did, but they didn't last. So when he stepped back into the office, he had mostly gotten over feeling pissed off at Prescott, who was, after all, way higher in the service of his country than Winston was himself. And since service to his country was the most important thing in the world, a little bit of hurt feelings didn't amount to a goddamn thing. Besides, there was no point to hanging on to it, staying all up in his feelings: Let it go, get on with it.

Winston did. He was pretty much all the way back to his normal, sunny outlook.

That didn't last long.

In fact, it didn't last any longer than when Winston came into the office and closed the door, and Prescott greeted him with "Think you can find the airport?"

Later, Winston told himself he really shouldn't have been surprised at a random slap from Prescott. That was who he was, a total shit bag. But at the time, it caught him off guard. He blinked stupidly, and all he could think of to say was, "I was just there. Sir."

"Well, from what I know about you, that's no guarantee," Prescott said.

"I can find it," Winston said. And he deliberately left off saying "sir."

But Prescott didn't seem to notice the insult. He just snorted and said, "Take Mr. Wolfe to the airport, then. If you're really sure."

Winston stared at him for a few seconds, just to see if there was more—until Prescott made a shooing motion with his hands and said, "Go on. Get. Airport, remember?"

Winston turned and left, but he was back to being pissed off, and he stayed that way for a while this time. After all, what was the goddamn point? Why did Prescott have to insult him every fucking time? He knew damn well Winston just had to take it and not respond. So what was the goddamn point? There'd been times in the Corps when a sergeant would ride his ass, call him names, give him more than his share of shit work. But there'd always been a reason. Not like this. Prescott didn't have any reason for it. He was just being a bully, sniping at somebody who couldn't fire back. And that really chewed at Winston's ass. He was still fuming a good fifteen minutes into driving Wolfe to the airport.

"He's starting to get to you, huh?"

The voice jarred him out of his brown funk, and he snapped his head around for a quick look at Wolfe, sitting beside him in the front seat. He put his eyes back on the road. "I didn't think it showed," he said.

"You've been chewing your teeth ever since I got in the car," Wolfe said.

Winston sighed. "It's part of the job," he said. "Prescott is a four-star asshole, but so what. I can take it."

"Sure, of course you can take it. But you shouldn't have to. I mean, why do a job where you're not appreciated?"

"Because," Winston said. "This is— I mean, I love my country, okay? I did twenty years in the Corps, and—it wasn't enough. I wanted to, I don't know. To keep serving? Maybe something more—"

"More active? More aggressive?"

"That's it," Winston said, nodding. "I mean, the Corps was great, I loved it, but—it's mostly standing around at attention and shit. I wanted more. Keep serving my country, but like you said, more active." He shrugged, still gripping the wheel. "And I thought this would be it. I mean, there's a lot more action, but—I don't know. It's not what I thought."

"Yeah, well—Semper Gumby, right?"

"Sure, and I've *been* flexible. I've done shit I wasn't sure about. Because it's all . . . I mean, I don't want to sound corny and shit, but it's in service to my country."

"Oh," Wolfe said. "Then you don't—Nothing, never mind."

The silence just hung there. Winston waited for Wolfe to say more. He didn't. Finally, he couldn't take it any longer. "What?" he said.

Wolfe shook his head. "Nothing. You know, just—nothing." And he turned to look out the window.

"Come on, Wolfe," Winston said. "It was something, or you wouldn't have said it."

Still looking out the window, Wolfe shook his head and sighed. "I shouldn't have said anything," he said. "I just—I mean, it surprised me that . . . You know, you being a jarhead and all, so I thought— No, it's cool, I'm not going to, you know."

Winston jerked the car over onto the shoulder and stuck it into park. Wolfe looked at him, surprised. "Hey, I don't want to miss my flight."

"Spit it out," Winston said. "What the fuck are you not saying because it's nothing?"

Wolfe shook his head. "I shouldn't have said anything," he said again.

"But you did. What was it?"

Wolfe bit his lip and frowned. "It's not definite. Not yet."

"But?"

"I'm not sure Prescott is completely, um . . ."

"Human?" Winston suggested.

"Yeah, that," Wolfe said. "But it doesn't add up that— Look, I think the guy might not be a hundred percent right, okay?"

Winston shrugged. "It's the trade," he said. "Spooks always seem a little off. But they're usually not."

"Right, I get that, so like I said, it's probably nothing. But something he said made me wonder, so— Listen. I asked Prescott to get me a piece of equipment. Russian stuff, classified, and they don't let anybody but their own operatives have it. I just kind of pretended that I thought Langley had them, which they don't. And he sort of walked around it for a minute, and then said okay, he can get it."

"Shit," Winston said. "But that doesn't mean—you know."

"No, it doesn't," Wolfe said. "But, uh— Look, I don't pretend to be all in on the side of the angels, okay?"

"Yeah, I kind of got that," Winston said drily. "From your reputation."

"Right, so, anyway. I have a few contacts in the SVR? That's Russian Foreign Intel—"

"I know what it is," Winston said. "What're you doing over there, bro?"

Wolfe shrugged. "I'm a thief," he said. "I get something, I sell it to the highest bidder. And lately, the Russian oligarchs have been throwing money around, so—I keep a line open."

"All right," Winston said. "So?"

"So I'm going to get one of my contacts to watch for this, for somebody to ask for this piece of equipment. And to verify that it was Prescott. And if that happens—"

"It means Prescott is dirty," Winston finished.

"Yeah, pretty much," Wolfe said. "I mean, it sure does quack like a duck, doesn't it?"

"Sure as shit does."

"I asked for you to pick it up and bring it to me. You okay with that?"

"Yeah, sure, why not?"

Wolfe nodded, reached into his jacket pocket, and handed Winston a cell phone. "This is a burner. Keep it hidden. I'll call and tell you where to pick up the package and where to bring it. And the guy who gives it to you will tell you yes or no on Prescott. Okay?"

"Yeah," Winston said. "Shit. I never . . . Shit."

"I could be wrong," Wolfe said.

"Yeah, sure," Winston said. But he didn't sound convinced. He sat for another minute, looking down and frowning.

"Hey, I kind of need to get to the airport?" Wolfe said at last.

"Right. Sorry," Winston said. He put the car back in gear and steered out onto the road.

They were mostly quiet the rest of the way to the airport. But if it was true—if Prescott had gone off the reservation and was into something that wasn't exactly in the best interests of the USA, and he was dragging Winston along with him . . .

Winston thought about that for a long time.

CHAPTER 17

The sun was starting to slide down in the winter sky, but Patrick Mordelet wished it would sink a little faster. He was tired, and he was bored, and the day had been long and uninteresting. Perhaps one might say the same of every day in the working life of a provincial bureaucrat. *Eh bien*, it was true, and so? He had not taken this job for the thrills, because he knew there would be none. Patrick had become a clerk here, at the Rennes Bureau of Records, because it was a government job, which meant it was steady, paid a decent wage, and had good benefits.

So it had been, and Patrick had risen to the top position in the little bureau. But every now and then the boredom got to him. As it had today. Perhaps it was the change in weather. Winter always brought with it a certain bitterness. A darkness, if you will. How was it that Rimbaud had put it? "The evening shadows making faces." Something like that. They were not happy faces; one knew that by knowing Rimbaud. In any case, winter brought on something very close to depression. It might be that as the cold seeped in, it woke all the regrets that usually lived so quietly inside.

But this, too, was a part of life, and Patrick had a cure, waiting for him at home in the form of a rabbit. It had been slow-cooking all day in a Crockpot: *lapin à la cocotte*, slowly simmering in a red-wine sauce. And he had a half bottle of very decent wine to go with it, a lovely pinot noir he had been saving. After that, with a fire going in the old stone fireplace and a glass of Armagnac, winter could go whistle.

But not yet. There was still half an hour to go in this endless day, and Patrick had to endure it. He had sent the other clerks home already, and he was alone, finishing some minor paperwork. He had always been scrupulous in observing the posted hours of operation, so he would wait it out, however slowly the time might drag. And it was most definitely dragging. He half wished that something out of the ordinary would occur to help the time pass. Not that it ever did, not here in the Bureau of Records. Still, one could wish.

Because Patrick was French, it may be that he had never heard the expression, popular in America, "Be careful what you wish for; you might get it." And he did get it. The small silver bell above the door rang and a blast of frigid air blew in. Patrick looked up to see a figure limp in and stomp up to the counter. It was a man, somewhat elderly, wrapped in a crusty old topcoat and a scarf. He had long and greasy hair, and pinned to his filthy coat was a military medal of some kind. The man sneezed violently, then blew his nose on his scarf. *"Merde,"* he said in a gravelly voice. He coughed once, then straightened and addressed Patrick.

"I wish to get a copy of some birth records," he growled.

"Of course," Patrick said.

"Are the records here? In this building?"

"Yes, certainly," Patrick said.

"Where?" he demanded. "Where are they kept?"

"They are in the files, m'sieu," Patrick said patiently.

"And where is that?" the old man growled. He jabbed a filthy finger at the door to the file room. "In there? Is that it?"

"Yes, that's it," Patrick said. "But I am afraid I must go get them myself."

"And why is that?" the man said, cocking his head to one side as if he suspected some kind of trick.

"Only bureau employees are allowed in the files, I'm afraid."

"Uhrrr," the old man growled. He coughed again, forcing Patrick to take a step back. "All right, then," he said when he was done coughing. "Let's have it." He waved a grimy hand. "Bring it to me."

Patrick nodded and reached for a pen. "The name?"

"The name?" the old man demanded suspiciously. "What do you mean? Do you want my name, or the name on the birth records?"

"Let us start with the name on the birth certificate," Patrick said patiently. "And then—"

The door burst open again, and a man Patrick did not know stuck his head in the door. "Fire!" he yelled in a panic-filled voice. "Around the side— Your building is on fire!" Then he disappeared.

Patrick frowned. If there was a fire, he should have been made aware of it by the building's fire alarms. Even so, alarms can fail, and he could not risk damage to the vast assortment of paper records in his charge. So Patrick stepped around the counter and opened the front door. A blast of bitterly cold wind blew into his face, and he blinked and then looked to the left. And sure enough—a black plume of smoke was streaming away from the side of the building. Patrick forgot the cold, forgot the crusty old man, forgot everything except the fire. Slamming the door behind him, he sprinted for the fire.

Back inside the office, the old man watched the door for a moment. When Patrick didn't return, he slouched over to the door and stuck his head out, just in time to see Patrick disappear around the corner.

The old man nodded and went back inside. And then, moving with surprising speed for someone who had been limping a moment earlier, he hurried around the counter and into the back room where the files were kept.

And five minutes after that, Patrick came back to his place behind the counter, still shivering from the cold. The fire had been nothing but some kind of prank, a pile of oily rags set alight in the dumpster. A joke, perhaps, but Patrick did not find it amusing. He had run out into the cold without his coat, and he was frozen to the bone. Why some people thought this sort of thing was funny, he would never understand. Would they still laugh if he caught pneumonia? Probably they would. The kind of person who would do such a thing—

At least the grumpy old man was gone. That was something. Just to be absolutely certain, Patrick looked into the file room. No, it was empty. He was alone once more. And now, only eleven minutes to go before he could lock up and leave. Perhaps he would start with a small glass of the Armagnac to ease the chill in his bones. Just a little—he did not want to kill his taste buds. Not with that *lapin à la cocotte* waiting.

The State Tretyakov Gallery in Moscow holds the finest and most comprehensive collection of Russian art in the world. One hundred fifty thousand visitors stroll in through the gallery's fairy-tale facade each year, past Zurab Tsereteli's gigantic statue of Peter the Great, over ninety-four meters tall. Among the 130,000-some exhibits, the visitor will find works by Wassily Kandinsky and most of the other well-known Russian artists. Even in winter, as it was now, people come. And no wonder; you can spend all day wandering through the galleries and not see even a fraction of the marvelous works housed in the Tretyakov.

And of course, one of the most popular exhibits is the display of Russian Orthodox icons. These unique and colorful painted religious images are wonderful, and without question the most wonderful of them all are the ones painted by the great seventeenth-century artist Simon Ushakov. For the faithful, they are objects of spiritual veneration. But for the art lover, they are adored nearly as much. Ushakov's use of chiaroscuro and perspective, the brilliance of his colors, and the way he somehow filled his figures with more light and emotion than other icon painters, made his work uniquely moving to the connoisseur as well as the devout.

So even now, in the bitter Moscow winter, people came to the Tretyakov. Of course this is a good thing, and exactly as it should be. But there is a downside, too, especially if you are one of the museum's security guards. More visitors means more work, and more work means fewer chances to sit for a moment with a cup of tea. And standing or walking all day means that your feet will hurt.

Galina Zaitseva's feet did, in fact, hurt. They hurt a lot. She had been standing or walking through the galleries for five hours without a break. So when the lunch hour came around and the crowds dispersed for a few merciful minutes, Galina embraced the opportunity to rest her poor, throbbing feet. She hurried into the back room reserved for the staff's lunch breaks and practically dove into a chair.

She did not take off her shoes, as much as she truly wanted to.

She was quite sure that if she did, her feet would swell up so she could not get the shoes back on. Then she would have to massage her feet, perhaps even soak them in cold water. That would have meant a much longer break, and Galina was conscientious in her work habits. She simply closed her eyes and sat for a few minutes with her feet on the table. Far too soon, she opened her eyes again, blew out a breath, and stomped back to her post in the gallery that housed the icons.

As she entered the gallery, Galina experienced one of those odd moments when you look at something utterly familiar and suddenly it seems wrong, different, changed. Ordinarily when this occurs it is merely a matter of a different kind of light, or perhaps low blood sugar. And at first, Galina dismissed the feeling.

She was almost halfway across the gallery when she realized that, actually, something *was* different. She stopped in her tracks, and then spun to the wall on her left.

"*Blyat*," she muttered, the Russian equivalent of "No fucking way."

But it was true. There was a bare spot on the wall, where one of the icons had been.

Aside from being diligent in her duties, Galina was also fairly quick-minded. The moment she realized the piece was missing, she spun around and sprinted for the nearest exit. She rushed out the door into the bitter cold and through the courtyard. Dashing into the street, she looked in all directions. The sun was already low on the horizon, and it cast long shadows, and her eyes were tearing from the cold, making it difficult to see clearly. But something moved—there, across the street! It seemed impossible, but someone was moving straight up the side of the building. And strapped to their back was a package the size of the missing icon.

Galina took a step forward, and then stopped. There was no point; she was not a monkey. She would never catch the thief. She would have to report that someone had stolen the icon, right under her very nose. And worse: After the sprint through the museum and into the street, her feet hurt even more.

"*Gavno*," she said. *Shit.*

Galina turned and went back into the Tretyakov.

CHAPTER

18

Something was wrong.

Monique did not know how she knew that. She'd been living inside that fog, and it had rolled in to separate her from everything, past and present. She knew that she'd had some other life once, and now and then small bits of it would come back. Snapshots, quick film loops, sometimes a taste or a feeling. But none of it seemed real somehow. Not present, not connected to her. And it was just so hard to think clearly about any of it—so hard to think at all. Words and ideas thundered through her head, just out of her reach. She knew they were there, but when she reached for one, it skipped away and left her with nothing. But now, here—no. She did not know where this was, or why she was here, or what was supposed to happen to her here. She only knew one thing.

This was wrong. This was not where she should be.

She began to cry, although she wasn't sure why. She looked around her, searching for something, *anything*, that made sense, something she might remember. There was nothing. She was still in a room with a nurse, but it was a *different* nurse. And the room was different, too, and wrong. She didn't think it was a—the word would not come. The word for that place where nurses were. And and and—the other one, more than a nurse, but—

Doctor. There should be a doctor. There had been one before. He said they would work to, to . . . Maybe help her get all the fuzz out of her head? Something like that. That doctor had been nice.

But she had not seen that doctor in a while. Not since they had moved her. And now—what? It was so hard to put thoughts in a row. If she concentrated really hard, she could remember that this vague blankness that had taken over her head was new—she had been different before. Smarter. She knew more words before. But before what? There was just a blank space, a place where something must have happened. But she had no memory of it, no clue what it might have been. Just the feeling that she should be more, more, more . . .

The door opened.

The woman who came in was white, and she wore a white coat. Was she another doctor? She came to the foot of the bed and smiled, but Monique knew the smile was not real. One look at this woman made her think she was not able to make a real smile. Everything about her was harsh, severe. She was very thin, and her face looked like a painted-over skull. Her grayish hair was pulled back into a bun, pulled so tight it looked painful.

"No. No. No," Monique heard her voice say. She was afraid and felt like hiding. But she was in a small bed. There was nowhere to hide. "Well, then," the woman said, still with the awful smile in place. And her voice was as cold and sharp as a winter wind. "How are we feeling today?"

A dozen words rattled and clacked through Monique's brain. None of them made any sense, and none of them held still long enough for her to grab them and say them. She just shook her head.

The skeletal woman nodded. "Perfectly normal," she said.

"Doc. Doc-Doctor?" Monique managed. She pointed at the woman to make her meaning clear.

The woman nodded. "Yes," she said. "I am Dr. Arnsdale. I will be looking after you for a little while."

"White white—you are white . . . Why?" The last word, the *right* word, burst out of her, and she felt a little better when she heard it.

"We are going to keep you here for a little while," Dr. Arnsdale said. "While you wait for—for *treatment*." And she tacked on another death's-head smile.

Monique knew she was lying. Not just because the smile was so false. Everything about this "doctor" felt like a lie, and Monique wanted to stand up and tell this woman she knew it was a lie. But her legs were weak, and she couldn't think of what to say, or how to say it, so she said nothing. Instead she retreated into the gray fog in her mind and lay nearly motionless while Dr. Arnsdale went through all the standard tests: temperature, blood pressure, oxygen level. And then a series of physical tests, to determine how well Monique could move. All the muscles worked, but very feebly. The doctor moved Monique as needed, but not like she was caring for a patient. She manipulated Monique as though she were pushing furniture into a different position, pausing between each test to write the results on her clipboard.

When Dr. Arnsdale was finished, she got up and marched to the door without a word. She pulled the door open, and then paused. In the hall outside the room Monique saw a man in a chair. He looked up, and she could see his face. He looked mean, too, just like the doctor.

Dr. Arnsdale turned back around like she'd forgotten something.

She stared at Monique for a moment as if reminding herself of some final task. Then she twitched a last awful smile in Monique's direction and spun around and left the room.

Monique watched her go. Even if she could remember things, remember the right words and what they meant, the doctor's performance would have left her too frightened to speak. It was so strange, mechanical, unhuman, and Monique did not know what to do, or even what she could do. She just stared at the door for a long time. And the only thought she had was the same one she had started with. She started to cry again.

Something was wrong.

Arthur Kondor had been sitting in the small dim room for a long time. The walls were stone and looked old, and they sweated with condensation. There was a small drain in one corner, and some old metal fittings on one wall that looked like they'd been used for chaining prisoners to the wall. The place had all the feel of a genuine no-kidding dungeon.

Well, he'd been in much worse. At least it was not dirty or cold. There was a toilet in one corner, and a sink. Meals were brought to him on a regular schedule, and they weren't horrible. Mostly, they tasted like an Army cook had made them, using the same old recipes, but for just a few people instead of a few hundred, so sometimes they were over-spiced instead of standard GI bland. But there was enough of it, and it was fresh and wholesome. He ate it all.

He wasn't bored. Next to the barrack-style bed was a bookshelf that held some so-called classics. *Treasure Island*, *A Tale of Two Cities*, *The Complete Plays of Shakespeare*. Stuff like that. Most of it he'd read before. But Shakespeare was always worth rereading. You discovered something new every time, especially since he'd learned what some of the odd words and phrases meant. And there was even a chair he could sit in while he read.

But it was still a small room, and he was locked in. He didn't like that, but they hadn't given him much choice—stay put or we kill you. So he sat. It could have been a lot worse. In his life, it had been, many times. He had spent much longer times in worse places, almost always without Shakespeare. It didn't bother him. By nature and by training, he was patient. He wouldn't be here forever. That was certain. One way or another, he would get out. But not now. Not for a while. For now he would wait.

There were several important reasons to be patient. First, because at the moment there was no other choice. Second, he didn't have a plan yet. He would, but not yet. And not now, even if he did have a plan. It was too soon to make a move. He knew from long experience that guards were more watchful at the beginning. After a while, when the prisoner acted like he knew he was stuck there, the situation became normal, and they began to relax. By then, he would have been watching long enough to see a way out, and he would take it.

But the most important reason to stay put was that he had been given a job: Stay with the comatose woman and keep her safe. He hadn't, and that hurt. Kondor didn't like to fail. It made him feel small, messy, useless. He was not very good at a lot of things, but the things he could do he did well. There were not many people in the world near as good as he was. And when he took a job, he did it, and he did it right. He did not fail often. He had no intention of giving up and accepting failure now. But the time was not right, not yet.

So he would wait and watch. He would continue to do his daily program of exercises, simple things designed to keep him sharp and in shape when he was in confinement. It would do no good to see a chance at last and be too sluggish to take it.

He sat in the chair and opened Shakespeare, flipping to *Coriolanus*. He'd never really understood the play, so he'd give it another shot. And he would wait.

For now.

CHAPTER
19

In spite of tensions that go far beyond the current Russian regime, the United States has diplomatic relations with Russia. Or perhaps more accurately, *because of* those tensions. When the possible result of a misunderstanding might mean cataclysmic destruction on a global scale, it's always a good idea to have a way to communicate face-to-face, quickly and unambiguously, with the other side. That means there is a Russian embassy in Washington, and there is a US embassy in Moscow, their capital city. And where there is a US embassy, there is an FBI presence, too.

As presently constituted, Russia is not a dear and trusted friend of the USA. Therefore, the Special Agent in Charge at the embassy is chiefly concerned with counterintelligence and security, of course. And at the embassy representing the USA in the capital city of such an old and crafty adversary, the Bureau assigns an SAC with experience and seniority.

This assignment is generally considered something of a plum, a prestigious reward for a record of excellence. In this tense political climate, the Bureau had assigned one of its most celebrated senior agents, a man who had, until now, turned down command positions and promotions so that he could continue to do the work he loved, pursuing bad guys in the field. But the time comes, even for such very successful crime fighters, when they have to accept the mark of the Bureau's esteem—a prestigious posting like SAC, Moscow embassy. And this particular successful agent had at last yielded to the writing on the wall and accepted, if not gracefully and gratefully, then at least without open insubordination.

So it was that Special Agent in Charge Frank Delgado found himself in Moscow. He did not like it there. The weather was far too cold for someone who had grown up in Florida, and the job required a constant paranoid vigilance, staring at shadows around the clock. He had to assume that anyone and everyone with whom he came in contact was an agent of one of the Russian intelligence services, and a very high percentage of them actually were.

As the son of parents who had fled a dictatorship with a heavy Soviet thumbprint on it, Delgado had no problem maintaining the required wary alertness. He was perfectly willing to suspect everyone, all the time. But constant watching and wondering did tend to wear on the spirit after a while.

So it was a relief to sit down occasionally with someone about whom there was absolutely no doubt at all. And at least once a week he did so, in semiofficial meetings with his Russian counterpart, Vasily Drosdov. Vasily was the liaison from the Russian security bureau, the Federal'naya Sluzhba Bezopasnosti Rossiyskoi Federatsii. And he spoke very good English, which was fortunate for Delgado; his language skills had so far proved unequal to the task of learning to speak Russian. Since there could be no question of where Vasily's loyalties lay, Delgado did not have to question every statement and action, looking for hidden motives. All of Vasily's actions were overt, calculated to further his government's designs against the USA. That meant Delgado could lower his guard and spend a little time in real human interaction.

As had become their custom, Delgado and Vasily dealt with formal issues first. Today they had discussed a few of the usual security and diplomatic problems, some of them patently absurd, some of them so very innocent that they clearly hid some more sinister maneuver by someone higher up in one of their governments. And when these matters had been thoroughly discussed or deferred, Vasily opened his attaché case and removed a bottle of vodka, which had also become a ritual for the two men. The bottle was wrapped in a roll of Styrofoam to keep it cold. No proper Russian would drink warm vodka, not even in winter. Vasily carefully removed the insulation and poured two water glasses half full, handing one to Delgado.

Delgado took the glass and lifted it. "*Boodym zdarovy*," he said, somewhat clumsily.

Vasily laughed, a great booming sound. "Frank! *Moy brat!* You have been practicing! *Boodym zdarovy* indeed!" And he tossed off the entire glass of vodka effortlessly.

Delgado, with a little bit of difficulty, did the same. The first few times he had tried to sip the vodka. That proved impossible—partly because he didn't like the taste, but mostly because Vasily would not permit it. He had made a point of instructing Delgado at their first meeting. And when Delgado had taken that first sip, Vasily had reached across the table and held his wrist.

"No, Frank, no—please, do not insult me and my proud nation. This is not how you must drink vodka. Not in Russia. Like this!" he had said, and he had poured himself a second glass and tossed that off quickly. "You see? The Russian way. As ever, it is far superior to the decadent and effeminate habits you Westerners embrace. We Russians do everything with joy—we even weep that way!"

That was the first time Delgado had heard Vasily's huge laugh, and it had been so infectious that Delgado had smiled in response and lifted his glass. "*Nostrovya*," he said.

"No! Never! No! You must not say this!" Vasily had slammed the palm of his hand on the table. "No. No, no, NO! Please, Frank, I beg you, do not say *nostrovya* like some brainless tourist from Ohio." He had paused and cocked his head to one side. "You are not from Ohio?"

"Miami," Delgado said.

"Good. Much better," he said. "No, we do not say *nostrovya*. Please. We say *boodym zdarovy*. You try it. Now."

"*Bo-dim . . . Varovy.*"

"Feh," Vasily said. "Terrible. But drink anyway."

In the weeks since that time, an odd and cautious friendship had grown between the two men. Certainly not trust, but instead a watchful, mutual liking. They would have a drink or two and just chat for a while, discussing news of the day. And today, after the toast and the drink, Vasily had led the way.

"Well, Frank," he said in a bantering tone, "I do not wish to compete with your country's proud record in the field of crime, but this week we have had a notable theft—right here, in Moscow! Terrible."

"Even here," Delgado said with a small smile. "How many bottles were stolen?"

"You would think it might be bottles, yes?" Vasily said. "What else would a Russian think was worth stealing? Mmm, perhaps toilet paper? But no. This was a priceless work of art." He cocked an eyebrow at Delgado. "We do have them, you know."

"Yes, I know," Delgado said. "What was stolen—another Fabergé egg?"

"Even worse," Vasily said. "It was an icon—not merely a beautiful work of art, but an object of veneration as well." He shook his head. "Terrible. Not bottles at all—perhaps it was an American thief?"

"How was it done?" Delgado said.

"In broad daylight," Vasily said. "Someone simply came into the State Tretyakov Gallery and took it—in the afternoon, while the guards were distracted."

"Meaning they were in the back room on a vodka break?" Delgado asked with a hint of a smile.

"And who could blame them if so?" Vasily asked. "Imagine having to stand in an art gallery all day! Crowds of loud and stupid tourists—and so many of them *French*!" He made a face, then shrugged. "I do not envy these guards. But yes—one of them came out in time to see the back of the thief as he fled."

"He is sure he saw the thief?"

"It was *she*, Frank. Unlike your country, we understand that women deserve equal opportunity," Vasily said with massive pomposity. "And yes, she is sure. The thief had something the proper size and shape—like this," he said, moving his hands apart to show the size. "Like perhaps a flat-screen TV, hm? But narrower. The thief had it strapped to his back. It was wrapped in a green case of some kind."

"She didn't pursue the thief?" Delgado asked.

Vasily shrugged. "Difficult, or impossible," he said. "By the time she saw him, the thief was running up the face of the building across the street." He reached for the bottle. "That's what she said, running straight up the wall, like some kind of chimpanzee."

Delgado's stomach did a quick flip-flop. He was intensely aware of one particular thief who stole precious artworks and ran up buildings.

Was it even possible . . . ? But no, it couldn't be. Not in Moscow, not in the dead of winter. He was letting his obsession show. So all he said was, "Interesting."

But later that day, he made a routine stop in the embassy's mail room. And laying on top of a stack of dispatches destined for the diplomatic pouch home to Washington, he saw something that brought that suspicion back to the front burner.

A large green package. About the size and shape of the stolen icon Vasily had described.

"Where did this come from?" he asked the mail clerk.

"Oh, hey, isn't that something?" the clerk said. "A guy brought it in this morning."

"What guy?" Delgado asked.

"I didn't get a good look at his face," the clerk said. "I mean, I was kind of busy—the big bag from Stateside had just come in? And anyway, he had a cap pulled down, sort of over his face."

Delgado nodded and reached for the package. "Um, sir—no, sir," the clerk said quickly. Delgado looked at him.

"I'm really sorry," the clerk said. "But that thing is sealed? Nobody's supposed to touch it?"

Delgado said nothing, just raised an eyebrow.

"Yeah, I know, but— It's for *Langley,* sir, and . . ." He shrugged.

Delgado looked down at the package, wanting very badly to open it. But the message was clear. There was only one destination to speak of in Langley, and no one was permitted to look into their sealed packages—not even the ambassador, unless she had clearance from the Director of National Intelligence. He looked for a moment longer, frowned, and left without another word.

Ten minutes later he was seated in front of a monitor and scrolling through the morning's security videos. He watched a steady stream of routine traffic coming in and out of the embassy until, after about fifteen minutes of searching, he found it.

A figure approached, probably a man. He carried the package Delgado had seen in the mail room. But his face was hidden by a cap pulled low, just as the clerk had said. Delgado used the time code and found the same figure from several angles, but nothing more was visible from any of them. Nothing but an indistinct profile that could have been anyone.

Delgado sat back and thought. He knew he was wasting his time. Theft from a Moscow art museum was very far outside of his duties. In any case, he had no idea what the thief he had in mind really looked like. And the few clues he had did not really add up. To begin with, the theft had apparently been very easy to accomplish, and that was not consistent with the pattern Delgado knew so well. There was no mistaking the rest of the MO, but there were other thieves who were proficient in parkour and could have done the same things. And this was headed for Langley—the CIA, of course. That did not fit, not at all.

And yet . . .

Delgado thought about it a long time. But he didn't have enough to form any conclusion beyond his original, and admittedly irrational, suspicion. He was finally called back to work, and he tried to put the whole thing out of his mind. Mostly, he succeeded.

But for the next few days, every now and then it snuck back in.

CHAPTER

20

T. C. Winston was feeling kind of relieved to be away from the team. Normally, he wanted to be right there at the center of things. It was partly because he was a team player, always had been, and the Corps had just made that preference stronger. But it was also because he didn't want to miss anything. He liked the feeling of being right there where things happened, a part of important events and actions that helped to shape the world, even though most of the world would never know it. And to be honest, he had to admit that was another part of the attraction, that feeling of being on the inside of important secrets.

But with what he now suspected about Prescott, it was getting kind of hard to feel like he was playing on the right team. So he was glad to get away for a while. And sure, Winston understood that this Riley Wolfe character had a reputation, and he was somebody you maybe shouldn't really trust. But this trip ought to provide some evidence, one way or the other, and he could either get over it and get back to work, or else . . . Well, if there was going to be an "or else," he'd have to give the whole thing some serious thought.

He took a regular commercial flight back to the States, to Dulles International. He rented a big Chevy SUV and took I-395 southwest to the intersection where it connected to I-495. He rode this to I-66 and headed west until he lost most of the Beltway traffic, and then he went down an off-ramp and pulled into a service station. He parked at the far end of the lot, took out the burner phone Wolfe had given him, and called. A mechanical-sounding voice answered, "Yes?"

"Is Rudy there?" he asked, as he'd been instructed.

"No, but he left a message," the voice responded. "Shelter One at Bull Run Park, three thirty. Rudy will be wearing a dark blue beret." The connection broke.

Winston put the burner away and took out his own smartphone. Bull Run was not far. He could make it with time to spare.

He drove back up onto the freeway and headed west.

In about forty-five minutes he got to the right exit and slid off the freeway. The park itself was well maintained, with good roads, mani-cured trails, and several play areas for children. He drove on through until he found Shelter One and pulled into the parking area. The shel-ter was what you'd expect, a concrete slab protected by a roof, open on all four sides. There were picnic tables under the roof.

Winston got out and strolled over, sitting on the bench at one of the tables, facing out, with a view of the parking lot and the road. He checked his watch: ten minutes to go. He leaned back and waited.

A couple of cars drove past. A few birds chittered in the near dis-tance. After five minutes, a man walked off a nearby trail and went past, limping slightly. He had a full beard and a nasty scar down one side of his face. Winston watched him go, wondering idly what caused the scar. Knife? It would have to have been a hell of a big one. Maybe a burn? Didn't matter, just idle curiosity. Nothing else happened for a few more minutes. Winston checked his watch again. It was 3:38. The guy, Rudy, whatever, was late. Sometimes that meant trouble—the meeting compromised, the contact taken by Federal agents; a lot of things could go wrong. He'd give it just five minutes more, and then—

"Hello," a voice called from behind him. He turned to look. It was the man who had walked by a few minutes earlier, the guy with the scar. But now he was wearing a blue beret and carrying a large package, wrapped in green cloth. "May I share your picnic table?"

"Help yourself," Winston said.

"Rudy" nodded and came under the roof. He sat on the opposite side of the table. He placed the package on the table and pushed it across to Winston. "This is for you," he said. And Winston thought he had a very slight accent—an accent that was probably Russian.

"Okay," Winston said. He waited.

"Rudy" nodded. "Also, I was told to tell you, 'Yes, it is true,'" he said. "And you would know what that means. You understand?"

Winston nodded. "I get it," he said.

"Yes. Well," the man said. "I won't keep you." He stood up and limped away the way he'd come.

Winston didn't move for a few minutes. His mind was stuck in a kind of angry loop, and it just repeated, "Shit. Shit. Shit." Over and over. He'd been fooled into doing the worst thing he could think of—betraying his country. He wanted to get back on a plane, right to Prescott, and beat him to death with his bare hands.

But after a couple of minutes he got control of himself, just enough to stand up, put the package under one arm, and walk back to his rental car. He put the package in back, climbed in behind the wheel, and got back up onto the freeway, heading west.

The directions Wolfe had given him were good, and Winston made good time. After the first hundred miles he began to relax. *Fuck Prescott*, he thought. *One way or another, he has bought himself a farm. The kind that's eight by three by six feet deep.* And that was coming, he was certain. Prescott had screwed the pooch, and the bill was coming due.

The thought cheered him up a lot. And as the miles unrolled and he got into the rhythm of long-distance driving in America, he started to feel almost happy. It was great to be Stateside again, and behind the wheel of an American vehicle like this one. And listening to American tunes on the radio again was especially cool.

Two days later, when Winston got to Texas, he felt like he'd managed to shake off all the crappy feelings Prescott had been painting him with. He began to feel like he was himself again, the old model, free and in charge and good at what he did. It was a good feeling.

And that good feeling just increased when Wolfe opened the door. "Hey, T.C.! Come on in!" Wolfe said with a big smile that made him feel like he really was welcome. There was music playing inside; he was pretty sure it was Bruno Mars, what was the name of the song? "24K Magic," that was it. He liked that song, and it made him feel even more welcome.

Winston went in, looking around with more than a little curiosity. Wolfe was supposed to have money, since he was, like, probably the most successful thief in the world. Winston had wondered how a guy like that would live, what kind of stuff he'd have, what the house would look like, all that.

He had some money, no doubt. Winston had seen all the telltales for the security system as he came in the gate and down the long driveway to the house, and he could tell Wolfe had spared no expense. But the house itself was definitely not a mansion like he'd half expected. It was just an old one-story ranch house. And the interior—well, shit, it was just kind of normal, like any regular guy might have. The furniture looked beat-up, and the wooden floor had worn patches. The only things that stuck out were the first-class sound system and the huge bookshelf that took up one whole wall of the living room and was lined with books—real ones, not the kind with fancy leather bindings some people bought from a decorator.

"That's it there?" Wolfe said, pointing to the large package Winston had leaned against the doorjamb so he could knock. "Bring it in—here, I'll take it." He took the package from Winston. "Grab a seat, I'll be right back." And he was off down the hall, package under his arm.

Winston looked around and spotted a chair—not the big overstuffed one, that was clearly meant for the king of the castle. But there was another facing it that looked comfortable, and Winston settled into it.

He had been sitting for only a moment when Wolfe breezed back into the room. "Damn, it's good to get that done. I've been kind of— Oh! Shit, I'm sorry, you had a long-ass drive, right? You must be whupped. Let me get you a cold one." And he was gone into the hall again, this time the other way. "Heya, here ya go," Wolfe said, sailing back into the room with two long-neck bottles of Lone Star beer, already beading up with condensation.

"Thanks," Winston said, taking a bottle. "Cheers," he said, and took a sip. It was ice-cold, and it cut right through all the dirt and dust and tension of a two-day drive across the country. "That's good," he said.

"Yep," Wolfe said, slipping into a pretty damn good Texas drawl. "It cuts the dust, don't it?"

Winston sipped, looked down. Now that he was here, he couldn't quite think how to ask the questions that were on his mind. He took another sip. Wolfe was right, he was just about "whupped," and now that he was here and sitting in a comfortable chair with a cold beer in his hand, the miles started to catch up with him. He closed his eyes for just a second, deliberately letting go of it all. Then he took a deep breath and opened his eyes. "All right," he said. "Let's talk."

Wolfe nodded. "I didn't want to rush you," he said. "Like I said, I know it was a long-ass drive. But I would like to know what happened in—where exactly did you make this pickup?"

Winston snorted. "Picnic table in a park," he said. "This guy—Rudy?"

Wolfe shrugged. "He uses a lot of names. If the GRU tracks him down—hell, you know how that goes."

"Yeah, I do. Well, he shows up just a few minutes late, hands me the package, and says, 'I was told to tell you yes, it's true.'" He took a long pull on his beer and looked down. "I really didn't want it to be true. About Prescott. Because that means—" Even now, he couldn't make himself say it.

He didn't have to. Wolfe said it instead. "It means he's a Russian asset. Which means you are, too."

Winston nodded and looked up at Wolfe. "How reliable is this Rudy character?"

Wolfe raised his eyebrows. "He's always been on target with me," he said. "But it's always, you know, which oligarch might want something I've got." He flashed a brief smile. "Or something I can get. Which honestly? Is just about anything." He got serious again. "But something like this, to do with spy stuff? I don't know. I just don't know, because, you know. It's not my game. But Rudy makes really good money off the commissions I give him. I think it's his retirement package? And I don't think he'd risk that by lying." He shook his head. "And it might not count for much, but my gut has been telling me all along not to trust Prescott. Something about him is just, you know. *Wrong*."

"Yeah," Winston said. "You got that right."

"But I don't want to sell you on this. You have to be convinced on your own, and if not—screw it. Handshake, so long, and back to plan A, Prescott's way, okay?"

"Suppose I say I believe it," Winston said. "What happens then?"

Wolfe smiled, a kind of *who, me?* grin. "Purely by coincidence, I have had a few thoughts about that."

Winston stared at Wolfe, eyes narrowed. It suddenly occurred to him that this whole thing could be some kind of scam Wolfe was working on him, for some twisted reason of his own. But Wolfe just looked back, apparently as honest and open as you could be, and Winston thought, *But why? To do what?* And he couldn't think of any way that Prescott being wrong would work for the thief.

So at last, Winston relaxed, nodded, and said, "Okay. What do I do?"

CHAPTER
21

W hy couldn't you pick a homburg or something?" Chaz said. "I felt like a total dick in that beret."

I smiled, because I knew that. "That was the point," I said.

"Well, fuck you," he said. "Keep it up and I'll get you in high heels someday, asshole."

"Fine," I said. "I got the legs for it."

Chaz popped open a Lone Star. "What about the guy, what's his name? Did he buy into it?"

"He did."

"He did? Just like that? You're sure?"

"He's a man of honor. Don't laugh," I said. "He feels, what—violated." I shrugged. "That's easy to work with."

"Well, shit," Chaz said. He drained about half the Lone Star and belched. "I didn't think you'd pull that off. Not so easy anyway."

I gave him my very best crocodile smile. "O ye of little faith," I said.

"Oh, shit, don't start that crap," Chaz said. "That Jesus picture got to you already?"

"It has," I admitted. "But not that way. It's beautiful, Chaz. Knocks your socks off."

"Not my socks," he said sourly. "I don't care a rusty raccoon fart about that stuff. But if it'll do what you say—"

"It will," I said. "That's the only thing I'm a hundred percent sure about."

"I hope so," he said. "It's my ass on the line if you're wrong."

"I'm not wrong," I told him. Which was not really necessary. Chaz didn't need reassurance. He was just grumbling, like he always did when we started out. And I really was sure, too. The painting was the real deal, an Ushakov icon, and it had been in the news that this particular one had been stolen. Balodis would know that; he would have a Google news alert or a clipping service, whatever. Just something to let him know what was happening in the Ushakov universe. Aside from collecting secrets and hiding them on his island, the icons were what he cared about. I was sure he'd heard; he might even be looking into it. And when he saw it, he wouldn't be able to resist it.

"But you're really sure about this guy?" he asked again. "I mean, you trust him?"

"I think so," I said. "He's always faithful."

Chaz snorted. "Sure, funny, why not funny," he said. "You know damn well this spook, Ascott—"

"Prescott," I said.

"Whatever. Same fucking thing. The point is, the second you hand over the flash drive, he'll kill you. You know that, right?"

"Naw, he gave me his word," I said. Chaz gave me such a look I had to laugh. "Just kidding," I said. "I won't give him the chance."

"Sure—*if* this other guy comes through for you."

"He will."

"And Ascott could find out and kill *both* of you."

"I'll take that chance."

Chaz opened his mouth, then snapped it shut hard enough that I heard his teeth click. He frowned and cocked his head to one side and studied me for a few seconds before he finally said, "Are you being stupid because he's got your mom? And you figure if I get her out while he's putting a slug in your empty fucking head it's worth it?"

And now I got quiet for a few seconds. I mean, what could I say? He was right. I'd trade my life for Mom's any day. You can say it's not much of a life, hooked up to machines and brain dead, and maybe you're right. But I owed her. When you throw Monique into the bargain, then hell yes, it was worth it.

I wasn't going to say all that out loud, not to Chaz. So I just said, "It'll work, Chaz."

"*What* will work, Riley?" he demanded. "I mean, you don't even know that yet, and you're betting your fuckin' life on coming up with something!"

"I will come up with something."

"Well, fuck, you better! Because otherwise you're toast—and I don't get my cut!"

"Chaz—"

He held up a hand to cut me off. "All right, fine, I don't give a shit—it's *your* ass if you're wrong."

"When have I ever been wrong?"

He scowled at me. "You want a list? Just don't be wrong this time."

"I'm not wrong," I said.

"Because you are going to be so alone it's like you were on the moon. And what happens if you *are* wrong? You're on the moon with no oxygen. I mean, it gets truly ugly, Riley."

"I'm not wrong," I said again.

"And if that happens—well, fuck. I don't get paid, and that sucks," he said.

"You do love me," I said.

"I'll love you a lot more when this shit is done and we're counting the take," he said.

"It's going to work, Chaz."

"Sure, of course," he said. He put on a prissy face and a whiny voice. "'There's always a way, Chaz.' Fuck that." He finished the beer and threw the bottle in the general direction of the trash can.

He missed the can by two feet. "I still don't like it," he said. "For shit's sake, Riley, you don't even know how you're going to get out of there. I mean, that ought to worry you a little. How the fuck are you getting out—with a bunch of big, heavy pictures, huh?" He opened another beer.

"I haven't seen the place, Chaz," I said. "When I've been inside it, I'll see a way out."

"You're so goddamn sure?" he said. "What if there isn't a way out this time?"

I shook my head. "There's always a way."

"Aw, fuck you and always a way," he said. "You always say that when you don't have a fucking clue."

"I'm always right."

"So far," he said. "You only got to be wrong once."

"I'm not wrong."

"So you say," he said. He took a pull on his beer. "Shit, you're going to do this no matter what I say."

"That's right."

"Dumbfuck," he said.

I just smiled. It's nice to have people who care.

"Well, shit," he said. He finished his beer and threw it. It missed the trash can by an even wider margin than the first one. "I guess we might as well do this thing."

"Might as well," I said.

CHAPTER 22

Prescott was waiting in the conference room, and he didn't waste any time on amenities. Neither did I.

"All right," I said. I unrolled my map and spread it out on the conference table. Prescott stood and came to stand beside me. I pointed out Balodis's place, on the coast. "It's pretty much isolated, nothing nearby."

"Well, he's not going to put his operation in a big city just for your convenience."

I looked at him. Some people could say something like that with a merry twinkle in their eye, and it would be okay, just friendly joking. Prescott said it with his upper-crust sneer curled up at the edges so you would know it was definitely not friendly. "Gosh," I said. "I never even thought of that. Thanks. Now pay attention, this part is a little complicated for some people." I smiled at him. I can play, too.

"All right," I said. "So your part starts here, at the end of the causeway to the lighthouse. You'll have to have your guys meet me there."

"You seem pretty goddamn sure you can get that far by yourself," he said.

I just nodded and said, "I am," like it was no big deal.

"Really? And what makes you think so?"

"Because I really am that good," I said.

"Are you, though?" he said.

"If I'm not, why am I here? Are you saying you made a mistake in judgment? That's not going to look good."

He frowned. "Screw it," he said. "If you don't make it that far, you're dead. No sweat for us."

"That's incredibly sweet," I said. "Can we get on with this?" I tapped the map. "Okay. Big problem. The road at the beach end of the causeway," I said, pointing. "They'll be watching that, and it's the only way to approach with a vehicle."

"Is it, though?" he said. He pointed at a spot east of the causeway. "Just about fifteen clicks away, we've got a dirt road, ending here."

"You know this area pretty well," I said.

He snorted. "I should. We've been watching it long enough."

"How?" I said. I mean, I was curious, but there was a whole lot behind my curiosity.

"Every damn way you can think of," he said. "Electronically, satellite, we keep live operators on the ground. And we do flyovers. Nice and low so we can scan it all with cameras, infrared, everything."

"They don't notice the plane?"

"Hell yes they notice. But they can't very well do anything about it except hide. And we come at irregular intervals so they're not expecting it. And I want them to know we're watching." He jabbed at the map again with his finger. "So I know this dirt road will work."

"But this dirt road of yours," I said. "It ends, what, fifteen clicks away—that's like nine miles? Too far."

"It would be," he said. "But it connects with a trail you can get a bicycle on." He glanced at me. "Or a motorcycle."

I didn't say anything. I thought I knew where he was going, because it's where I hoped he would go. And if he hadn't, I would have steered him there. Much better if he thought of it all by himself. But I gave it a push anyway. "Even if I ride double on somebody's motorcycle, it's not going to work," I said. "I'm going to have around two hundred pounds of icons. Or did you forget why I'm doing this?"

It was just what he wanted. It let him get in two jabs at once. "I never forget what kind of true patriot you are," he sneered. "But did you forget that motorcycles can pull trailers?"

"Oh," I said.

"I thought so," he said, and he looked very happy he'd stung me.

"I guess that would work," I said.

"It'll work. We'll move the crew in, what—say two weeks after you're inside? That should be plenty of time to get cozy with Balodis and get into the vault."

I thought about it. "Make it three," I said. "Just to be safe."

"Fine, three weeks," he said. "We'll have two full crews, in shifts. You signal us, we'll have them there in five minutes. Five men to lay down covering fire if it's needed, a utility trailer for your precious icons."

"And me?" I said, trying to sound offended. "Am I supposed to run alongside the bikes?"

"We'll bring an extra motorcycle for you," he said. "On the trailer. Offload the bike, load on the icons, we're gone in under two minutes."

I frowned, like I was thinking about it. Which I was, but what I was thinking was, *Damn—he thinks I'm that stupid!* I mean, would I really believe him? I really thought he'd let me leave Lithuania alive and holding my icons? Sure, human nature is a beautiful thing—especially in the goddamn .1 percent, people like him who were born into money, power, and privilege. Prescott had proved he was overflowing with the milk of human kindness. So why not trust him?

I thought it was kind of nice that he thought I'd buy into that. And what I said was, "Okay. That works."

"It works," he said. "But it doesn't work for you unless you hand us the flash drive first."

"I'll have the flash drive," I said.

He stared at me, like he thought he would break me down and I'd admit I couldn't get the flash drive. I stared back because, come on. It's me. I'd get it.

Prescott finally nodded. "All right, then," he said. "We'll be watching. Now, how will you signal us?"

"The lighthouse," I said. "I'll get up to the top."

"What if they're blocking the stairs?"

I sighed and shook my head. I mean first, did he have to question everything? And second, he must have read my file, so—can I climb up the outside of an old lighthouse? Really? "I'll go around them," I said. "And the signal is easy. I'm taking along a Day-Glo orange T-shirt, and I just wave it out the east window, right? I mean, your guys will be watching, won't they?"

"We'll be watching," he said again, and it was the first thing he'd said that I believed. "You want to tell me how you're going to get into the vault?"

"No."

Prescott narrowed his eyes and glared at me, like he was trying to use his magical power to make me tell him. It didn't work. After a minute, he gave up. "All right. Anything else?" He raised an eyebrow at me, and I shook my head. "All right, then," he said. "We have a plan."

"Yup," I said. He was right. We did have a plan. But the part I didn't tell him?

Actually, we had two of them.

Winston drove me back to the airport. I didn't ask, but I got the idea that he'd volunteered so we could talk. And I was ready. I'd gotten my missing piece from my meeting with Prescott. I thought it would work, but not without Winston's help. So I needed a couple of minutes alone with him to sound him out. This was the most important part of my plan, since it was about getting me out alive. And knowing the spook mind in general, and Prescott in particular, I was feeling cautious. There was no way he would let me live once I handed him the flash drive. That meant there was also no way in the world I would get out doing it his way. The whole motorcycle thing? I'd gone along with that so he'd get smug and careless and think he had me wrapped up.

He didn't. I would go my own way and use his plan to distract him while I did—and that meant I needed Winston's help. So I wrote out a quick note on a piece of paper as Winston was starting the engine. I tapped him on the shoulder, put a finger to my lips meaning, "Shh," and handed him the note.

He looked at the note, crumpled it, nodded to me. "Nobody listening," he said. "I sweep the car myself every morning." I didn't get it, and I must have looked like it, because he added, "Sweep it electronically. For bugs, trackers, all that."

"Gotcha," I said.

"So what is it you don't want anybody to hear?"

"Let's get on the road first," I said.

He nodded. "Right. Because—lip-readers."

"You never know," I said. But I hoped he was kidding.

135

He put the car in gear, and I waited while he steered us out onto the road. "You thought about what I said?" I asked him.

Winston nodded. "Shit, yeah. Haven't thought about anything else practically."

"And you still want to do this?"

He frowned and got quiet for a minute. Any nudging I did would probably push him the wrong way, so I waited him out. "Okay," he said at last. "I guess I believe that Prescott has gone off the reservation."

"I think he *lives* off it," I said.

"Right. So if that's true . . . Well, shit. Like I said, I thought about it a lot. And the more I thought, the more it made sense. Something happened, I don't know, like five years ago? Whatever it was, it turned him. Prescott got mean, bitter, nasty all the time."

"He wasn't always like that?" I said.

Winston snorted. "I wouldn't have stayed on if he was. I mean, he always made sure you knew you were an insect and he was the boot-heel, but—I don't know. In a nice way, if that makes sense?"

"Okay," I said. "Any idea what turned him?"

"Nope," he said. "He never said a word about it. Just like I said, he got permanently nasty." He shook his head. I could see his hands tightening on the steering wheel. "Whatever it was that happened, it changed him. And yeah, it makes sense that—I mean, knowing Prescott, whatever happened, he'd have to do something about it. Get even or whatever. So it makes sense that he'd, you know. Cross over to the dark side."

"And take you with him," I said. "Without filling you in that you'd just switched sides."

He sighed and looked miserable. "Yeah, I guess so."

He was quiet for a while. "How's it make you feel?" I said at last.

He glared at me. "Like shit and you know it," he said. "I told you,

I've given my whole life to my country. I mean, Semper Fi and all that—I take it real serious."

"I know," I said. "I believe you. So?"

He slammed both hands on the wheel. "Well, fuck it," he said. "So—I'm in." He glanced at me again. "Whatever you got in mind, if it helps Uncle Sugar and screws Prescott?"

"It does," I said.

"Then I'm on board."

"You won't regret it," I said. And if I was lying, who knew for sure?

"What do you need me to do?" he said.

"Prescott says you do flyovers?" I said. "You know, of my target area at the lighthouse?"

"Yeah, sure," he said. "Every day or so, random intervals."

"And you fly 'em? I mean, you're the pilot on the team, right?"

He shrugged. "Mostly, yeah. There's two other guys can fly a Gooney Bird," he said. "But mostly I do it."

"Okay, good," I said. "Just out of curiosity, if you really wanted to—could you drop a small package, like out the window or something?"

"Yeah, sure, no problem."

"Great," I said. "That's excellent."

"That's it? That's all I got to do, drop a package?" he said.

"Actually, there's more. But to do it, I need to know what else you can do with that plane."

He gave a half laugh. "Hell, the Gooney Bird can do just about anything except go fast." He glanced at me again, then back at the road. "What've you got in mind?"

"Something I heard about once," I said. "Military thing."

"I've done 'em all," he said. "What is it?"

I told him what I had in mind, and he gave a low whistle. "Wow. You don't screw around, do you?"

"I try not to," I said.

He frowned, then nodded. "So yeah, okay. It'll take some weird-ass prep, a quick refit, but—I make a refuel stop on this little unmarked field? I can do it there." He frowned suddenly. "Oh, hey— Listen, the second I modify the bird, everybody knows something is up. So I got to do it right before. Like on my way to get you."

"Yeah, that makes sense."

"Right, okay. So how do we coordinate this?"

"It has to be on a schedule we set now," I said.

He whistled. "Wow. You don't think it's hard enough—you got to do it on a schedule?" He laughed. "Well, shit, I guess we're about to find out if you're as good as they say."

"Better," I said.

"You better be," he said. "Or else." He pointed at me and dropped his thumb, *ka-pow*. "And when we do it? I mean with all that extra weight? It's going to hurt like hell."

I sighed. I should have expected it, because there's always a price tag. But what the hell? If it worked, I was home free. "I'm used to it," I said.

CHAPTER
23

I t's always the same. That's important. Doing the prep the same way every time guarantees that it will work, because I did it this way last time and last time it worked.

So every time, it's as close to identical as I can make it. I sit in front of a full-length mirror and I start my music. Same songs in the same order. And for the first few minutes I just concentrate on my reflection. Not just because I'm putting this face away for a while, saying good-bye to what I really look like. I'm also visualizing the changes I've planned to make.

I start with the face. It's important because the changes will turn that face into who I am going to be for a while, and if it looks too much like Riley Wolfe, I might as well save time and shoot myself. I make changes. It has to be subtle; there's only so much you can do with makeup, dyes, small prosthetic touches. Plastic surgery would be a lot easier, of course. But finding somebody who can do it the way you want is hard enough. When you add on that you are literally trusting them with your life, it turns hard into impossible. Because there is nobody in this wide wicked world you can trust that much. Don't believe me? You can try it—once. And as you're lying there dying, remember one thing: I told you so.

So plastic surgery is out. And anyway, it's too permanent for me. I like my face. It's also kind of nice to have one thing I always go back to. I don't really have a home, a place that feels like I've always belonged and always will. I come back to my face, and that works for me.

When I'm done staring, I start to change myself, and I do it the old-fashioned way. Slowly, carefully, one small touch at a time. It takes longer, but at this stage of the game I've got time. And I have a huge incentive to make it right.

One small addition to the routine this time. There's a photograph taped to the mirror. Not my new face or my old one. It's a picture of the woman who was the key to the whole thing. I've studied that picture for hours, looking for something about that face that I might echo in mine—my new one, that is. I found a couple of things I can do. I can go with contact lenses to make my eyes brown, and I will. But I need a few other strokes, more subtle touches, too. A very small prosthetic to make my new nose just a little different. Dye the eyebrows to make them a few shades darker. Like that. When I'm done, Riley will be gone and New Me will take his place.

My playlist is more than halfway through when I finish with my face. I move on to clothes. There's an old saying: "The clothes make the man." It's true. Maybe not the way the saying means, but true anyway. What you wear, and how you wear it, tells as much about you as your face—maybe more. And people who have to deal with disguises every day know that and study it. You know, people like intelligence agents? They learn to suss out somebody by their clothes pretty quickly. And this time, I am dealing with an old and savvy pro, so what I wear is just as important. One mistake and the game is over.

When I'm dressed, I spend some time getting the feel of my new wardrobe. You might not have noticed it, but your clothes affect the way you move. And it's not always just the way your pants make you walk different. When you wear a tuxedo, for instance, you feel different. So you *move* different, too. More graceful, even elegant, if you can pull that off. You may not even know you're doing it, but you are. Subconsciously or not, you don't want to let down the tuxedo.

Same with any clothes. Sweatpants make you slouch a little more. Wearing a tie makes you stand up a little straighter. Cowboy boots make you lean back a little and take things slower.

Every outfit moves you in a different way. And to somebody who knows what to look for, the way you move tells every bit as much as your face. People who face conflict their whole life walk on the balls of their feet, their eyes moving everywhere. I mean real conflict, life-or-death stuff, where sudden violence can come and kill you at any second. That's different from a boxer or MMA fighter. They know they've got nothing coming at them when they're not in the ring, so they move with a kind of swagger.

When I had my new costume on, I moved around in it for a while. Walk across the room, jump, run a few steps, even try a couple of dance moves. When I had the feel of it, I went back in front of the mirror. And right on cue, my playlist started over from the top: Tupac, "All Eyez on Me." When that song ended, I was finished.

I turned off the music. Everything was in place. All the wheels were turning. And now, the last thing was done. I wasn't Riley anymore.

I was ready.

CHAPTER
24

Monique thought in pictures. She did not wonder if that was normal for her. Those concepts of normal and herself as opposed to others had not really seeped back into her brain so far. Since she returned to consciousness, she had been a kind of natural solipsist. She only knew that her thoughts were real and that she existed. Nothing else could really attain enough reality for her to consider it tangible.

That had begun to change, as things began to come back to her. But when names and places and items did return, they mostly came in pictures. Sometimes it would be a place, or a painting, or even a dish of food. These pictures came and went, and they did not leave any meaning or identity behind when they were gone. But one of the recurring pictures was a face—a man's face, and it meant something. She could not say what that was, but she knew it was important, that this man was himself important to her. He had meant something in her forgotten life, and that was important. More than that, she knew that somehow he would come for her. Why she thought that or who he might be eluded her, but she was sure it was true.

The other repeating picture was of a skyline of tall buildings. It was called New York. Again, she knew it was an important piece of who she was, but she did not know why. So it remained for a long time. Both of those pictures, the face and the buildings, meant a lot. They were keys to who she was. Monique worked at this puzzle as if it were a stubborn knot in a shoelace, but nothing came. She thought about it as she paced her cell in what was now several daily periods of exercise. Several times as she walked back and forth it felt like something was right on the other side of a thin mental wall, quivering and pulsing and trying to hammer its way through to her. And one evening she walked much longer than usual, trying to break that thin wall.

She walked longer and faster, until sweat began to drip from her nose, as much from the effort of trying to make understanding burst into her as from walking. Nothing happened, no new insight or revelation came. She went to bed frustrated, angry, and unable to say why—which made her feel much worse. But the next morning when she woke, the picture was there in her mind, and it had two labels on it. The first was the one she already knew, "New York." But the other one was new and went with the first word. It was "Home."

That was it. New York was her home. That was why she felt like she was part of it—she was! And if it was her home, then she knew where she was supposed to be! It flooded her with excitement.

But that led to another, even more important question: Was she there now? Was this room, with the scary doctor, in New York? Was this *home*? She didn't think so—she really hoped it was not—but how could she know for sure?

She was still thinking about it when her breakfast came in, carried by an older woman whose skin was dark, like Monique's. This woman gave Monique the tray, with scrambled eggs and toast today. Monique ate it while the older woman scurried around the room, straightening things that were already straight, dusting clean surfaces with a rag, and talking softly to herself the whole time.

This morning she also went over to the window, which was high up on the wall, and said, "Well, let's let in a little light this morning, all right, honey?" Monique laughed, without knowing why, and said, "You are brown." The woman just nodded and smiled as if that had made sense. She pulled the curtains apart, and a powerful beam of sunlight came in, flooding the whole room with brightness. "There now, isn't that better? You all done yet, darlin'?"

Monique was. "He did not cut his own ear off. I think a friend. A friend. A friend." She had no idea what that meant, and she could tell the other woman didn't either. But the woman just smiled again and collected the tray and left with a kindly "You have a nice day now."

When she was gone, Monique's thoughts returned to the revelation that had woken with her. *New York. Home.* And as she bent her mind toward the picture of the tall buildings and their labels, a terrible thought forced its way back in. What if this really was New York? This little room that she was not allowed to leave—what if this was her home? It was an appalling thought, and it frightened her. She'd been thinking for no real reason that the man whose face she remembered would come for her, take her home—but what if she was already there?

Monique began to cry. It was almost unbearable, and the awfulness of the idea drove her up out of the bed and onto her feet. This couldn't be Home! No one could live like this, not forever! She would rather not live at all than know that she belonged here and she was here forever. It couldn't be true!

She began to pace, and she tried to think. If this was really Home, then what were the tall buildings she thought of as New York and

Home? And even more, if this was where she lived, how did she even have the picture of New York in her mind? That made absolutely no sense—she *had* to have seen it, been in it. She absolutely *knew* that was true. She had done things there, some of them with the man who was coming for her, and she had been happy. She was not happy here—she could never be happy here. This place, whatever it was, this was not New York, and it was not Home.

But how to be sure?

She completed one short circuit of the room in her pacing and turned so she was facing the window, and she blinked as the bright light hit her eyes. A new thought swam into her mind, a thought about windows. They didn't just let in light; they also let you look out! And if she could do that, she could see where she was! She would do it—she would look out! If the tall buildings were there, she was Home, and as crushing as that was, at least she would know. But if not . . . If no tall buildings were outside, then she was not Home, and she had to get out of here.

Right: That made sense. Look out the window and know for sure! But the window was high up on the wall. The bottom edge was a good eight feet above the floor. Even without trying, Monique knew she was not tall enough to reach that high. So how could she get up there?

She glanced around the room. There—that one metal chair, the only other piece of furniture she had aside from the bed and its small accompanying nightstand. If she stood on that . . .

Moving quickly and as quietly as possible, so nobody would hear and stop her, she lifted the chair to a place under the window. She shook it once to be sure it was steady and then climbed up onto its seat.

Standing there, rising up on her tiptoes, Monique could just barely see over the window's bottom lip, and all she could see was blue sky. A bird flew past. And that was all. She was still not up high enough.

She got down off the chair and looked around. How could she get higher, high enough to see? There was nothing else in the room except the bed and—the nightstand!

Quickly, Monique cleared away the tidy cluster of objects on the nightstand: a plastic water bottle, a plastic flower in a plastic vase. She placed them on the bed, bent, and grabbed the sides of the nightstand, lifting it carefully and placing it on the seat of the chair. It was small enough that it did not quite cover the entire seat of the chair. That left a small lip on the seat of the chair, just wide enough that she could get her toes onto it.

Bracing herself on the wall, Monique hop-climbed up onto the chair. She touched the nightstand, and it wobbled. It might fall, and she would fall with it onto the hard floor. But she had to try. She had to know.

Reaching up above her, she grabbed the bottom edge of the window with both hands. Half-lifting herself, she gingerly pulled herself up onto the top of the nightstand. Still clutching the stone edges of the window's aperture, she looked out.

A wide swath of water reflected the bright sunlight back up at her, and she blinked and then squinted to see better. On the far side of the water was the shore, and there she saw a number of buildings—but they were not tall! She turned and looked both ways—there were no tall buildings anywhere! Just low and grubby-looking things. In fact, the building she was in seemed to be the tallest one around. She leaned forward a bit and looked farther to the right. She could see the sides of her building. They were stone, and down at the far end there was a— what was it called? Something you found on old castles—tower? Turret? That might be it. But why—

With one great lurching wobble, the nightstand slipped from under her and crashed to the floor, and for a moment Monique clung to the window's lip. And then her fingers slid away and she tumbled down to the floor. Luckily she landed mostly on her feet and she sprawled onto her butt without hurting herself.

As Monique staggered to her feet, the guard was already rushing into the room, yelling something or other, but she didn't listen. She was laughing too hard. She just climbed back into bed. And she smiled. Because now she knew.

This was not New York and it was not Home and she did not belong here. That meant that she would get out of here because the man whose face she knew would come for her.

And that was the best thought she'd had in a long time.

PART 2

CHAPTER
25

In a barren, isolated spot on the Lithuanian shore of the Baltic there is a large tract of empty land. One small, roughly paved road runs through it, leading from the village of Delnuva on one end, some eighty kilometers inland, to the Baltic shore on the other. The road does not end at the shore. It continues just a little farther, past the beach on a narrow causeway across the water and over a drawbridge that is almost always raised. At the far end is a small island. For two hundred years, this island has held a lighthouse, warning mariners away from the treacherous shifting shoals just off the shore.

The lighthouse remained in operation until just after World War II, when the area was occupied by the Soviet Union and Lithuania became a Soviet satellite. The occupiers kept the lighthouse—but they made a few minor changes to the island, in great secrecy. They dug carefully and clandestinely under the little lighthouse, carving out a deep and cavernous area. This they lined with hardened concrete, installing special shielding to block everything from radio waves to infrared—and even including radiation—and then they turned this artificial cavern into a top secret clandestine forward launch site for a Chusovaya medium-range ballistic missile with a 680-megaton nuclear warhead, carefully and invisibly tucked away under the lighthouse. Around the silo they built commodious living quarters, since the soldiers and technicians occupying the base must remain hidden underground for weeks at a time.

The Soviets were gone now, and they'd taken their Chusovaya MRBM with them. But the missile silo remained, and so did the accommodations that were built underground around the silo.

When the Soviets left and Lithuania became an independent republic, very few people knew the secret of the lighthouse. But one man did; he had been highly placed in the Soviet intelligence system, and when properties formerly owned by the Soviet state and now deemed useless by the new Lithuanian government were put up for sale, this man bought the lighthouse and the small island that held it, and he turned it into a minor Baltic version of a Fortress of Solitude—except for the "solitude" part. He staffed it with a group of very tough-looking men. Their appearance was not deceiving; they were all exceedingly tough and well practiced in all the violent arts. Every one of them was a veteran of the Spetsnaz, the elite Soviet Special Forces unit.

The ex-soldiers were not the only form of security guarding the island. All the angles of approach were monitored by every electronic measure known to man—and some that were known only to very few people. And anything the monitors detected was then liable to instant destruction—not merely from the soldiers, but from the massive array of booby traps, auto-focused weapons, and other lethal roadblocks with which the causeway and the island were equipped.

It would take an exceptionally wealthy person to go to all the trouble and expense of guarding the island so thoroughly. It would also take an extremely paranoid person—for instance, someone with things they needed to hide and guard, something that determined and dangerous people might want to take from them.

Ivo Balodis was both wealthy and paranoid. He also had something to hide. Balodis collected and sold secrets. The kind that can shift world power, change the map, or even lead to war. It was not merely dangerous people who wanted what he had. It was nations.

And so he bought the island. And he stayed underground most of the time, surrounded by the truly impressive security. Every day, weather permitting, he would go up onto the island and walk the perimeter a few times, just enough to stretch his legs and get the blood moving through his veins. Through the long and bitter winter, weather had not often permitted. But now, spring seemed to be arriving at last.

This year, however, spring came to the Baltic shore in fits and starts. One day the sun would shine and the temperatures would flutter up into a warmth that melted the ice and made small green shoots poke cautiously out of the ground. And then the next day, that terrible Baltic winter wind would blow, viciously cold and wet at the same time, and the tiny green shoots would cringe away under the soil, the ground would freeze over, and it would be winter again.

Ivo Balodis needed some fresh air. He was not feeling well, and the schizophrenic weather did not help. His stomach hurt almost all the time, and when that frigid wind came up off the Baltic, it made the pain seem even worse. But they'd had three warm days in a row now. Perhaps it would stay spring this time. And perhaps if it did, the pain would go away.

Not likely, Ivo thought. More likely to get worse. It felt like something was trapped in his stomach and chewing its way out. The feeling had been with him for several months now, and he suspected it was here to stay. *It's the stress*, he told himself. *So many years of stress.* And now even this small thing, waiting for something that was very far from a life-and-death matter, and he felt stress merely because the man was late. *Why can't anyone be punctual?*

"Ivo."

The voice came from the doorway, behind him, but he knew who it was without looking. Only one person on the island used his first name. "Yes, Grisha," he answered without looking. "What is it?"

"He is here."

Now Ivo turned and looked. Grisha stood in the doorway, a dark-haired man of less than two meters in height, with a slight build. His physique was misleading. Grisha had been a Spetsnaz instructor in unarmed combat, and Ivo had seen him in action. The man was terrifying. He fought with a combination of ferocity, inhuman speed, and moves that would challenge a circus acrobat. Ivo had hired him to run the security force for his island.

"Does he have it?" Ivo asked, fighting to keep the anxiety out of his voice.

Apparently it didn't work. Grisha knew him too well. His lips twitched in what passed for a broad grin. "He has a package. It's the right size and shape, but he won't show it to anyone but you."

Ivo stood. "Where is he?"

"He will not come onto the island." Grisha shook his head slightly. "I could force him, but—"

"No, you did right," Ivo said. "He is on the shore, then?"

"He is," Grisha said. "And he would like to see the money before he lets go of the package."

"Is he an idiot?" Ivo said. "He must know we could simply kill him and take it."

And now Grisha actually smiled, which for him was the equivalent of a belly-shaking laugh. "He says the package is booby-trapped," Grisha said. "Only he can disarm it."

"*Kozel*," Ivo swore. "Only half an idiot, perhaps." He sighed. "All right, we will do as he says. Humility is good for the soul." He leaned under his desk and pulled out an attaché case. It held the agreed amount of money, half a million euros—cheap for an Ushakov, but this man, Herr Krupp, would want to unload it quickly. He would know the Russians were looking for him. That was never a good thing.

Ivo straightened and handed the case to Grisha. "Let's go," he said.

The sun was actually shining when they emerged from the lighthouse, although there were dark clouds gathering to the northwest, across the Baltic. Still, Ivo hoped the sunshine was a good sign, a small and superstitious indication that the Ushakov would be genuine. He was very nearly an expert at identifying Ushakov forgeries, but he had been burned once. He'd been too keen to believe the icon was real, and he'd let that eagerness lead him into a mistake.

Not this time; not any time since.

As they started across the causeway the breeze picked up. But it was from the west and would help to keep the clouds away. He could see the man, Krupp, waiting on the far end, and as they approached him Ivo examined him. His hair was long and greasy, but he had a neatly shaped stubble-length beard. He wore a cheap and shabby blue blazer and a pair of faded blue jeans, and he clutched the package tightly, shifting his grip as he watched them approach.

Ivo stopped about six feet away. "Herr Krupp," he said in German. "I am Ivo Balodis."

Krupp squinted at Ivo, then nodded. "*Ja*, it is you, I recognize the face. From the photographs."

Ivo noted that he spoke with a Tyrolian accent, softer and not as clipped as German was spoken farther north. "May I see it?" Ivo said.

"I told your man I do not show it until I see the money," Krupp said rather petulantly.

Ivo nodded. "Grisha?" he said, without looking away from Krupp.

Grisha stepped forward and opened the attaché case. Krupp took a step forward, and Grisha immediately snapped the case shut. "Show me," Ivo said.

Krupp hissed once, then nodded. "So," he said. He placed the bottom edge of the package on the ground and unwrapped it, turning it to face Ivo. "And there it is," he said. "You are satisfied?"

Ivo stepped closer and went to one knee to see better, and for a moment he forgot to breathe. Ushakov always had this effect on him, and this was no exception. It was wonderful, better than he had hoped. The blues were radiant, and the central figure was clearly St. Paul, raising his eyes to the heavens, where two angels fluttered. He moved closer to see better—and Krupp jerked the icon away.

"The money!" he said.

Ivo stood up. "I must be certain it's genuine," he said. "Surely you can appreciate that, Herr Krupp."

"I have told you it is," Krupp said.

"I don't know you," Ivo said, still very reasonably. "I simply need to look closer. That is my standard policy."

"No, absolutely not," Krupp said. "First I must have the money—and that is *my* standard policy."

Ivo sighed. "Very well. Grisha? Please kill Herr Krupp. Do not get blood on the icon."

"*Ja wohl,*" Grisha said, pulling a pistol from its holster at his belt.

"What? No—wait!" Krupp stammered. "The booby trap! We will all die!"

"Regrettable if true," Ivo said. "But I think you are bluffing. So—Grisha?"

Grisha stepped forward, raising his GSh-18 pistol.

Krupp took a step backward, raising the icon in front of him. "Wait! This is— I think perhaps I can make an exception—just this once."

"That is very kind," Ivo said. He stepped close and again went to one knee. He examined the painted surface carefully, first with the naked eye, then with a magnifying glass, and finally by shining a small ultraviolet flashlight.

Ivo stood up abruptly and looked into Krupp's face. The German was sweating heavily, and he did not look happy. "Grisha," Ivo said, watching Krupp flinch. He let the moment last, enjoying Krupp's discomfort. But finally he relented and nodded. "Give him the money," he said.

Krupp lurched forward to grab the attaché case. He did not count what was inside; he simply held the case tightly to his chest and hurried away, limping rapidly toward his car, a small Mercedes, clearly rented.

Ivo watched him with amusement until he got into the car and drove away. Then he picked up his wonderful new Ushakov. "Perhaps we should have shot him anyway," he said.

"Perhaps," Grisha said. "But here on the shore? They always find out. And it was difficult to appease the local authorities last time."

"Yes. And expensive. Well," Ivo said, "I have a wonderful new Ushakov, hm?" No response from Grisha, of course. He was completely insensitive to the beauties of Ushakov's work. "All right, then," Ivo said. "Let's put it safely in the vault, Grisha."

"Of course," Grisha said.

CHAPTER
26

The routine had not changed. The same people came in every day and did the same things and they added up to the same thing. Nothing. None of it made sense or added to the nothing Monique knew. And it was still just *wrong*.

At least her head was clearing; slowly, a little bit at a time, but improving. Not because of anything the weird and scary Dr. Arnsdale did, of course. She just came in every day and took Monique's temperature and pulse and hit her with one of her scary fake smiles. But Monique's brain was definitely starting to work better, form words and memories more clearly. She thought it might be because of what she was doing herself, walking back and forth, as far as she could go in the cramped space.

The first few days had been scary—she could do no more than walk to the door, lean against it and rest for a minute, and then walk back to the bed. How could that be? She remembered being able to walk. And she hadn't forgotten how; it was just that her legs wouldn't do it anymore. They were too weak. They shook and wobbled when she tried to use them for the first week. She had cried a lot. She had also laughed a lot, and sometimes when she realized it was for no reason, she would cry some more.

But she was so weak. Monique tried to understand how that could happen, that she couldn't walk anymore. Because the bad *something* had happened? Or because she had been in bed so long? Why? It didn't make sense to her at first. Nothing did.

But the exercise helped, and she kept at it. Slowly, day after day, the little walks got bigger; back and forth, and then back and forth twice, adding laps as she was able. Finally she was walking back and forth for ten or fifteen minutes every day.

Monique felt a sense of growing triumph. She also felt more and more things coming back to her in bits and chunks, as if their return was somehow tied to her walking. Whatever the cause, she was remembering—words, names, places, and faces. New York, of course. And the man's face, the man who would come for her. And there were flashes, lots of them, of a big room, with tables that were covered with colored stuff, tubes with color in them. And—

Paintings. That was the right word. The tubes were filled with paint, and they were used to make paintings—did she do that? Make paintings? It felt right. And she could almost feel it in her hand, the— the *brush*. That was what you used to put the paint on and make paintings!

It filled Monique with a funny kind of pride and happiness to re- member. She was doing it herself, with no help. She was remembering. She still could not remember why she had stopped painting or being in New York. Something bad had happened, and it had made her like this. But soon the other things would come back, too, and by then she would be strong enough to . . .

To what? She didn't know. But she knew she would have to do something. This wasn't right, being in a little room all the time. And she didn't want to stay here—but the door was locked. And there was someone outside the door, she could hear them moving, sometimes coughing or talking. Without knowing why, Monique was sure they were there to keep her from leaving. So at some point, she would have to do something to get out.

Monique didn't think she could get out by herself, even if she got strong again. That made her sad at first, and then angry. But she felt better every time she remembered: *The man is going to come to help me.* No more details came to her, but she knew it would happen. He would come for her. She just knew it. He would come. She would have to be ready when he did.

So she kept walking, more laps every day. The more she walked the more she remembered. When she remembered enough, she would re-member who was coming and why. And then she would know what to do. And she would be strong enough to do it.

Arthur Kondor had no idea how the small scrap of paper got into his sandwich.

The sandwich was thin-sliced chicken on soft white bread. Not what he would have chosen. And mayonnaise, which he thought was disgusting.

He liked dark rye, some ham slices, and brown mustard. But no complaints; he'd had to eat some awful things in his life, and he'd had to go without any food at all, too. At least these people were feeding him. They brought him three decent meals every day, no fooling around with crappy food or thin soup, none of that. There was never anything in it that shouldn't be there.

Until today. Today there was a piece of paper. And Kondor was pretty sure it wasn't a piece of wrapper or something that had accidentally fallen in while they made the sandwich. This little piece of paper felt too thick—construction paper, the heavy stuff grade school kids played with. That was how he had known what it was. He had almost missed it, had come very close to chewing it up and swallowing it. But he hadn't. He had bitten down and felt something different, just a hint of a different texture. Too thick to be the deli-cut chicken, and when he felt it with his tongue, it was much rougher than anything that should have been on a sandwich.

Kondor was an old hand. He knew better than to spit it out or yell, "What the fuck?!" Two guards were standing there, watching him eat, as they did every day. Standard practice, just to make sure he didn't try anything he shouldn't. And it was a better-than-even chance that somebody had put the paper in there on purpose. Not to fuck with him—that would have been something worse than heavy paper. Who-ever put the paper in his sandwich wanted it to be secret, or they would've just handed it to him or told a guard to.

So Kondor pushed the paper up with his tongue and wedged it in between his upper teeth and his cheek. He finished his lunch, waited patiently for the guards to clear it away—one of them picking up the tray while the other stood well back and watched. Very good practice, these people were pros.

So was Kondor. He waited for them both to leave. Then he waited some more. Finally, when he thought it was safe, he removed the paper from his mouth. But he didn't just pull it out. He didn't know if there were any hidden cameras, but he assumed there were. So he put a fist to his mouth and coughed, tonguing the paper into his fist as he did. Then he picked up the big Shakespeare book again, opened it. He smoothed the page with his hand, dropping the paper and letting it unfold on the page.

The message had smeared some from being soaked by his saliva, and it was not easy to read. But it was short, simple, just five words, and after a moment, its meaning was clear.

Soon. Be ready. Password SWORDFISH.

He read it again to be sure. "Swordfish"—that was funny. Whoever sent this was a Marx Brothers fan. Kondor didn't laugh, though. His face didn't change at all. He palmed the note, coughed again, this time putting the paper back in his mouth. He swallowed it, took a sip of water, and went back to his book.

CHAPTER
27

think you should see this," Grisha said.

Ivo looked up. Grisha stood in the doorway of the office, one hand on the door's frame. It was not possible to read his face—he never showed real emotion, and Ivo had often wondered if he ever felt anything. So it was not possible to guess why he thought Ivo should see whatever it was. From what Ivo knew about Grisha and his deadpan face, it could be anything from a pretty sunset to a nuclear attack.

Probably not a sunset; not Grisha.

"You should see this," Grisha said again.

Grisha was empty-handed—there was nothing to see. Ivo raised an eyebrow in inquiry.

"In the guard room," Grisha said, jerking his head to his right, toward the room where the cameras and electronic sensors were monitored.

Ivo frowned. He had a great deal to do. But he trusted Grisha and trusted his judgment. So he nodded and stood. "Show me," he said.

Grisha led him down the hall, around a corner, and into the guard room. It was the size of a moderate conference room, with walls painted a soothing institutional gray-green. One entire wall was lined with control consoles. Three men sat watching them, all of them also former Spetsnaz and selected by Grisha for their toughness and intelligence.

Ivo followed down to the far end, where Yevgeny, one of the guards, sat in front of a video monitor. He looked up as they approached. "No change," he said. He shrugged. "He just sits there."

Grisha looked at Ivo and nodded toward the screen. "There," he said. "Look."

Ivo leaned forward, placing a hand on the back of Yevgeny's chair, and looked at the screen. It showed the view from one of their high-resolution cameras, the one that covered the shore side of the cause-way that led out to the island. Sitting there on the ground, perhaps three meters back from the causeway, was a man. He appeared to be young, perhaps twenty-five or thirty, and he was holding a large poster-board sign. There was a photograph on the sign, apparently a woman's face. And the woman—

"Zoom in," Ivo said. "On the sign."

Yevgeny obeyed and the picture grew closer and more clear.

"*Moy Bog,*" Ivo whispered. He felt a crushing pain in his chest, and for a moment he couldn't breathe. He could only stare at the face on the poster that the camera had revealed, and he could not move at all until he felt Grisha's hand on his shoulder, gently shaking him.

"Ivo," Grisha said. "Ivo, what is it? Are you all right?"

Ivo straightened and took a deep, ragged breath. "Go," he said. "Get him and bring him to me. Safely and unhurt, Grisha."

Grisha looked at him blankly. "For now," Ivo said. "Unhurt for now."

The young man did not appear to be nervous. He sat in the chair where Grisha had placed him, hands folded in his lap, and simply waited. This struck Ivo as very odd. After all, he had been brought across the causeway at gunpoint and then led through all the security protocols—scanning, hand search, even body cavity search—and then brought into the lighthouse. They did not take him through the hidden entrance and down into the silo, which might have been too much. Even to Ivo it seemed rather like the secret lair of a James Bond villain. It was enough to shake the composure of any normal person. And although this young man could not know it, he really should be nervous. Ivo had a rule that anybody who saw the inside of his keep was either part of the team or disposed of quickly. He had too many enemies, and he had no desire for any of them to discover details about his lair.

So now they sat facing each other in the kitchen of the little cottage at the foot of the lighthouse. And so far, this young man seemed completely unfazed. To someone with Ivo's background, that could mean several things, and none of them were particularly pleasant to contemplate. But which one? He realized that he wanted it to be something that would give him a reason to kill this intruder, because he had made Ivo angry. To show up and display that picture—*her* picture—felt like a slap on the face.

But Ivo was well schooled in controlling his emotions, setting them aside so they would never affect his judgment. He set the anger aside now and studied his "guest" very carefully. The face did not show much, other than determination. It was not a bad-looking face, but not extraordinary, either. But Ivo took his time and examined everything about him, the whole picture. Little details told big stories if you knew what to look for. After so many years as a field operative, Ivo had a considerable amount of tradecraft, and he knew.

The shoes and the jeans were French, and the thin belt around his waist was, too. The contents of his pockets revealed nothing: two hundred thirty-four euros, half a roll of Mentos, a small pocketknife. No identification, no credit cards. Ivo looked at his hands. The nails were cut in the square manner favored by most Europeans, and the hands were marked with a few faded scars, souvenirs of some past form of manual labor.

Altogether, this told Ivo a grand total of nothing. He went back to the face. There was something vaguely familiar about it, but—

Never mind. Find out who he was, why he was there, and then Grisha could dispose of him.

"What is your name?" Ivo asked, in French, since that seemed indicated.

"Stefan," the stranger replied, also in French. "Stefan Laurent."

Ivo nodded. The accent indicated Brittany, in the north of France. That made a small flicker of feeling flare up again, but he pushed it down and concentrated on the young man in front of him. "Why did you come to my island, Stefan?"

"To meet you," Stefan said.

"Really. Why not just walk across the causeway and knock?"

Stefan's mouth twitched as he suppressed a smile. "I was told you could be very unwelcoming."

"And so I am," Ivo said. "I do not encourage visitors." He frowned and flicked the poster with a fingertip. "And why did you choose that particular photograph?"

Stefan made a face to show he thought that a stupid question. "Because obviously, I thought it would get your attention. Perhaps even get me past all the traps and obstacles." He shrugged. "It did, yes?"

"But why *that* face?" Ivo insisted. "Do you know who she is?"

"*Was*," Stefan corrected. "She is dead."

"Very well, *was*. And do you know who she was?"

"Her name was Simone Beauclair," Stefan said. "As you know very well."

A much larger flare of feeling at that name, but Ivo just nodded and showed nothing. "Yes," he said. "Did you know her?"

Again, Stefan's mouth twitched with a suppressed smile. "I knew her very well," he said.

"Really? And how is that?"

"Because," Stefan said. "She was my mother." And before Ivo could recover from the enormous jolt of shock, Stefan leaned forward and said, "And I believe that *you* are my father."

CHAPTER
28

It can be very hard to let go of a longtime obsession. Even if it's a hobby that most people would regard as frivolous, or even when the obsession is harming your health or your job, leaving behind something you've been fixated on passionately is difficult, as tough as breaking any other kind of addiction. When the obsession is focused on fixing something that tarnishes your self-image, it is even harder to let it go.

And so for years, in spite of repeated urging, and increasingly insistent warnings, Special Agent in Charge Frank Delgado had found it very hard to move on from his obsessive determination to put Riley Wolfe behind bars. It was not just Wolfe's success as a grand-scale thief, and not even the ruthless methods, often including murder, he used to achieve success so many times. More to the point, it was because Delgado had tracked Riley Wolfe multiple times and cornered him.

Or so he thought. Because each time, somehow, Wolfe had wriggled away.

Frank Delgado was committed to winning, and in his career at the FBI he had won almost every time—so often, in fact, that he had acquired a reputation among his fellow agents as the Bureau's own version of a Canadian Mountie: the guy who always got his man. And Delgado almost always did, with one glaring exception.

Riley Wolfe.

Worse, he had missed on Wolfe four times now. That made it an epic failure.

Delgado felt that failure keenly, took it personally, and it stung. For the last ten years he had spent all his spare time and energy trying to track and capture Wolfe. So far, he didn't even know what the master thief really looked like.

When the assignment in Moscow had been handed to him, he had intended to refuse. After all, the chances that Wolfe would be in Moscow were exceedingly slim. When he had been told, quietly and off the record, that, in fact, he *would* take the assignment, he accepted with something approaching good grace. And Delgado had started out well in his new post in Moscow. For the first six months he had concentrated on the job at hand, overseeing security and counterintelligence in the capital city of a hostile foreign power. He'd thought about Riley Wolfe now and then, of course; it was unavoidable. But he had not focused any real time or energy on tracking the elusive thief. There were simply too many demands on his time as he accustomed himself to his new position, and Delgado had been sure Wolfe was nowhere near Russia. And if things had continued on this path for six more months, who could say what might have happened? It was possible Delgado might have been cured of his long addiction.

But then, as if to remind Delgado that he was neglecting something vitally important, Riley Wolfe had appeared in Moscow. Delgado was sure that it had been Wolfe. The more he thought about it—and he couldn't avoid thinking about it—the more convinced he became. Stealing the icon in broad daylight, while the museum was open, would have been a foolish risk for any other thief. For Riley Wolfe, it was a necessary flourish, an added element of hazard to what might have been too simple otherwise. Wolfe needed risk as much as he needed to breathe. And then to make his escape up the facade of a building and away across the rooftops—that was pure Wolfe. Added together, it was as clear as a signature.

The only thing that was uncharacteristic was the connection to Langley. Not because Delgado had a naïve notion that the Agency would never work with someone like Wolfe. Of course they would. They did, all the time. And while it was true that Wolfe worked alone, and he certainly avoided any entanglement with government agencies, he had been coerced into cooperation with others in the past, and the intelligence agencies didn't have any scruples about using the talents of criminals even worse than Wolfe. Even his own agency, the FBI, had done so when the greater good was served by doing it. If Wolfe had some connection to the Agency, it was a curious touch, but it didn't change the big picture. Delgado was certain it had been Riley Wolfe who had stolen the picture and then dropped it at the embassy to be sent to Langley in a top secret diplomatic pouch.

To almost anyone else who was smart and in the know—and Delgado was both—finding that Langley was involved, probably controlling Wolfe, would have served as a very clear and ominous warning to stay away. They played hardball at Langley, and they got away with it. All the many layers of government power routinely rolled over when one of the Ivy League suits from the Agency whispered, "National security." That was well known, and anyone who wanted to avoid a confrontation that could easily go far beyond unpleasant would be wise to back off.

Not Frank Delgado. To him it was a lead, a useful tool for tracking Riley Wolfe.

Furthermore, he had not gone digging for it. It had come to him, had actually been shoved under his nose and begged for his attention. That removed any small and cautious impulse to stay away and stick to his assigned duties. Instead, it reignited his obsession, until it flared up into something he could not possibly ignore.

But how to start? How to use this connection in a way that was both helpful and somewhat low-key? Delgado was willing to risk a confrontation, either with the Agency or with his own superiors, but he would rather avoid it if he could. Going into this recklessly might provoke both. So he spent the next two days considering and rejecting different approaches. In the end, he decided to explore the connection itself and hope it would lead him to a more substantial link. So: Why was Riley Wolfe working with—or for—the Agency? He would not do it willingly, not from patriotism or the promise of monetary reward or any other inducement that might be offered. He would have to be coerced.

Delgado went back over all he knew about Wolfe. His only real point of vulnerability was his mother. She had been in a coma for years, but Wolfe poured a fortune into keeping her alive, at least in the technical sense of keeping her heart beating. In the past, Wolfe had been forced into servitude by threats to his mother. If the Agency wanted his services, they would know that much, if only by looking at the FBI case file created by Delgado himself. And they would certainly not have any scruples about using the mother to get to Wolfe.

Maybe he was wrong about that, but Delgado decided it was a good starting point. It was also something he could track. He knew the kind of care Wolfe's mother required, and he knew the list of medications that went with it. He had tracked her down by this method once before, only to have Wolfe pull a switch on him at the last second, substituting a different comatose woman for his mother. Still, it had led Delgado to her, and he thought it might work again. Wherever they might have stashed her, she would need those meds, some of them quite rare, and that could be tracked. It was at least worth a try.

The downside to this method was that it involved a very long search, matching the whole laundry list of drugs the mother required against the patients in every extended-care facility in the country. Realistically, it was a full-time job, and Delgado could not spend that kind of time on anything outside his Moscow duties right now. Despite his obsession, Delgado believed the work here was important, and he intended to do it well.

It took him only half a day to see a solution. Because so much international hostility and aggression had moved into cyberspace, the embassy had a very good IT section. Delgado had had a few dealings with them already, and he had been impressed in particular with the most junior member of the team, a young graduate of MIT named Miranda Shaleki. She was incredibly bright and quick, which naturally made her impatient with others who were less so. And since this included most of the rest of the world, Miranda was not popular with the others in her department.

But she was inarguably very, very good. And Delgado felt something of a sympathetic bond with her. Like her, he had swum against the current in his career, and he instinctively felt that anyone else who did that was on the same team. And he was confident that Miranda would not dive into the regulations and object to a project that was outside the mission statement of the embassy.

He found Miranda in her cubicle in the IT section. No surprise; she generally even ate her lunch at her computer. As she was apparently doing today—there was a half-eaten sandwich beside her, and a can of Diet Coke with a metal straw in it. She was wearing earbuds and typing away furiously, jerking to the rhythm of something only she could hear, and her short, dark hair flipped with the beat as she moved. Delgado stood behind her for a moment, watching the rapid and nearly violent movement of her hands on the keyboard. Then he cleared his throat to get her attention; she didn't hear him. Of course not; the earbuds. He leaned forward and tapped her shoulder.

"Fuck off," she snarled, lurching away from his hand. "I finished it two hours ago, okay?"

Delgado leaned around her, put a hand in front of her screen, and waved.

"I said fuck *off*!" Miranda snapped, spinning her chair around. Her face was set in a mask of righteous indignation. Delgado could not help noticing that it was a very nice face. When she saw *his* face, she blinked and looked mildly alarmed as she popped out her earbuds. "Oh. I thought, uh—should I have said, 'Fuck off, *sir*?'"

Delgado couldn't help it. He smiled. "Just plain fuck off is fine," he said.

"Super, thanks," she said. "You going to fuck off?"

He shook his head. "I have a problem," he said. "I thought you might be able to help me."

She cocked her head. "You're the FBI guy, right? Delmonico?"

"Delgado," he said. "Cuban, not Italian."

"Right, and that's soooo important," she said.

"It kind of is," he said.

"Oh, okay, *lo siento mucho*," she said with an exaggerated Anglicized accent. "Why me?"

"Well, this problem is very challenging," he said. "It might offer some unique opportunities to explore—" He stopped because she made a rude noise.

"Bro, come on," Miranda said. "Like, seriously. Why me? Nobody told you I was the bad apple?"

"Actually, I was counting on that," Delgado said. "This is something that's not totally . . . official?"

"Okay, epic," Miranda said. "You want something done and you don't want anybody to know because it's not totally cool, and you figured nobody talks to me, so . . ."

"Sure, that's part of it," he said. "But also, I think you're the best brain in the department."

"Oh, my," she said, fake-fanning her face with a hand. "You could turn a girl's head." She dropped her hands into her lap and gave him a world-weary look. "Come on, boomer, just give it to me straight."

"All right," he said. "I'm trying to find somebody. They're in a coma, extended care. I have a list of the medications she needs to take, and they're distinctive enough that not too many patients take all of them. But there are hundreds of facilities where she might be, and to check all of them—"

"Right, I get it," Miranda said. "So you want me to write a program that can track it quickly."

"That's it," he said. "Can you do it?"

Miranda snorted. "Of course I can fucking do it," she said. "Question is, why would I?"

"Um," Delgado said, a little startled at the question. "I don't know. Because you're not supposed to?"

Now Miranda looked surprised. "Shit," she said. "I think you got me figured. Oh—you're a detective, right."

Delgado smiled. "Right," he said. "So how about it?"

She chewed her lower lip for a few seconds. "Yeah, what the fuck," she said. She held out a hand. "Gimme the list of meds."

CHAPTER

29

He is not your son," Grisha said.

Ivo shrugged. "Perhaps not," he said. He tipped his head at the dark blue duffel bag in Grisha's hand. "That is his bag?"

"Yes. It was on the shore, under a bush." Grisha unzipped the bag. "I have scanned it and searched it carefully."

"Yes? What did you find?"

Grisha shrugged. "Socks, underwear, two shirts, one pair of jeans. A bright orange T-shirt." He frowned. "All cheap French brands." He reached into the bag and held something up. "His wallet," he said, tossing a battered canvas wallet into Ivo's lap. "A European Union French passport." He dropped the burgundy-colored passport next to the wallet. It was dog-eared and worn, like the wallet. "And this." He held up a creased and distressed sheet of often-folded paper. "A birth certificate, from Rennes, France."

"Rennes, yes," Ivo said, carefully taking the document. "That was her home. Most likely, he brought it as proof. So I don't kill him out of hand, hm?" He examined the birth certificate. "Is it authentic?"

Grisha shrugged. "It appears to be," he said. "I sent Ivan down to Rennes to check. On his motorcycle."

"A Bugatti, yes?" Ivo said absently. They all knew that Ivan loved to ride his motorcycle and looked for any excuse to take it out.

"Yes," Grisha said. "A Bugatti Veyron."

"Hmp, all right," Ivo said. He put the birth certificate down and looked up. "What else?"

"An old iPod," Grisha said, holding it up. The earbuds dangled down. "Apparently he likes metal music." He shook his head.

"Does he?" Ivo smiled. He, too, was fond of the old metal bands—Black Sabbath, Def Leppard . . . Was it possible that such a taste could be transmitted through DNA? He had read of experiments in which the music was played to laboratory animals, and—

"It is too perfect," Grisha said, interrupting his musing. "He is not your son."

"We'll see. Perhaps you are right," Ivo said. He was in no mood for an argument, or anything at all that might cause anxiety, tension, worry. His stomach was hurting, worse than ever lately, and any kind of stress made the pain worse.

"Shall I kill him, then?" Grisha said.

The pain flared in Ivo's stomach. "No," he said. "I forbid it."

Grisha said nothing. But he did not go away, either, as Ivo devoutly wished he would. "Grisha," he said. "There is a possibility that Stefan is who he says he is."

"You are a fool if you believe that," Grisha said.

"Then I am a fool. But I need to be absolutely certain."

"All right," Grisha said. "I will interrogate him."

"You will *not*!" Ivo snarled. Grisha's interrogation methods tended to be extreme. It was possible to survive his questioning, but those who did were never quite the same afterward. For just a moment, at the thought of permanent damage done to the boy, Ivo's anger shined brighter than the pain in his stomach. But only for a moment, and then the pain came back even worse, and Ivo clutched at his middle and folded halfway over. He straightened slowly and, when the pain had subsided, he looked at Grisha. "Grisha," he said. "I appreciate that you want to be cautious. I agree, we will be cautious. But Stefan . . ." He paused, looked away, sighed.

"You loved her," Grisha said. He made it sound half question and half accusation.

"I did," Ivo said. "And the boy looks like her somehow. He has her eyes, nose, or—I don't know," he said. "Something about him is just—" He shrugged. "I don't know," he said again.

"You see what you want to see," Grisha said.

"And if I do?" Ivo demanded. "That is my privilege! I do not want him harmed—not at all, not in any way, is that clear?" The pain was worse than ever, and for a moment he could not go on. He closed his eyes.

Grisha studied him without answering. Finally he said, "Ivo. You need to see a doctor."

"And to see a doctor I have to leave the island, and if I leave the island, I am vulnerable," Ivo said wearily. "You know they're watching, hoping I do just that, and this—" He made a face and waved one hand. "It is nothing, at worst an ulcer. It will pass."

"I can bring a doctor here," Grisha said.

"He will have no equipment, no X-rays or—and then he has seen inside the lighthouse, and we will have to— No, Grisha," he said. "I will be fine."

"You do not look fine."

"Thank you for the compliment," Ivo said. He closed his eyes again briefly. "Where is the boy now?" he said.

"You keep calling him a boy," Grisha said. "He is thirty-one years old."

"To me, to both of us, Grisha," Ivo said, opening his eyes and smiling slightly, "that is very young."

Grisha shrugged. "I suppose," he said.

"And where is he?"

"Nikko is showing him the lighthouse," Grisha said. "I did not want him poking about down here."

"He can come below," Ivo said. Grisha said nothing, but his frown was eloquent. "You can watch him. But subtly, all right?"

"Very well," Grisha said.

"Grisha! Without hurting him!"

Grisha looked at him without blinking. Then he turned and left.

Ivo watched him go. He could not decide what to do about the boy—the man, Stefan, whatever. He knew Grisha was correct; the story Stefan told was preposterous, and it was foolish to trust him. But he looked so much like her, like Simone. He had loved her deeply, the only real love of his life. Her death still hurt. Ivo desperately wanted to believe that some small piece of her still lived. And more—he had never married. Between the demands of his work and his feelings for Simone, he had felt no need. But now—to have a son would be a very good thing. To have some small piece of himself, too, that went on after his death. Which could come at any time.

A sudden spasm of pain in his stomach underlined that thought. He bent with the pain for a moment, then straightened again. A great weariness enveloped him and mingled with the pain in his stomach, and for a moment he gave in to it and let the feelings run through him and turn him old and weak, and once more he closed his eyes.

Perhaps I should see a doctor, he thought.

A nd here, as you perhaps now are possible to looking, big view," Nikko said in his clumsy French. Stefan nodded and looked where the other was pointing.

"Very big," he said, peering politely out the windows at the top of the lighthouse.

"Very," Nikko said. "Is Baltic Lake—lake? No. Is correctful?"

"*La mer,*" Stefan said. "The sea."

"Ah. Good. Baltic *Sea*. So."

The radio clipped to Nikko's tunic fired a burst of static and a few muffled words. Nikko pressed the TALK button. "*Da*, Nikko." He was answered with a quick torrent of words that Stefan assumed was Russian. He did not speak the language, but he was aware that everyone else on the island did. Nikko had been assigned to guide him on this tour of the upper island because he claimed to speak French. He was very nearly right about that, but Stefan had to struggle to understand him at times.

Perhaps I will learn Russian, he thought. He watched as Nikko nodded, said "*Da*" a few more times. Then he dropped his hand from the radio and looked up at Stefan.

"He say, come down now," Nikko said.

"Lead on," Stefan said.

Nikko led him down the narrow winding staircase and into the house at the base of the light. They walked to the back of the house, farthest away from the shore, and stopped in front of what appeared to be the pantry. But Nikko pushed aside a large jar of olives to reveal a keypad. He punched in five numbers, too quickly for Stefan to see what they were, and the entire wall swung inward. "Come," Nikko said, gesturing at the dark space he had revealed. "Down."

Stefan followed. They went down another spiral staircase, only about three or four meters, and came into a small room with an ordinary elevator door on one side. Nikko pushed a button, the door slid open, and they stepped into a large metallic elevator car. The car bumped and began its descent. It was impossible to tell how far down they went. The car moved very smoothly, and in less than a minute it bumped to a stop and the doors slid open.

"*Mon Dieu,*" Stefan breathed. For spread out in front of him was a deep concrete cavern. Directly in front of him was a steel pipe railing, but beyond that a great pit opened up. It was only about five or six meters across, but it shot straight down, and Stefan could not see the bottom.

"Is in past for rocket," Nikko said. "Soviet bomb rocket, yes?"

"Missile," Stefan corrected absently, still staring.

"Missile, yes," Nikko said cheerfully. "Paris, London, Berlin— boom!" He chuckled, which Stefan found so odd he broke away from staring to look at Nikko. "Is gone now, rocket," he reassured Stefan. "Rocket—MOO-sill?"

"Missile," Stefan said. He looked around him. To the left and the right, narrow hallways led away. Other than that, there was not a great deal to see. He stepped to the steel railing and looked down. The depths were dimly lit, and he could not make out any details, but the silo appeared to be about thirty meters deeper than the corridor where he stood. He bent over the railing, squinted, trying to see a little better.

Nikko touched his arm, and Stefan looked up, startled.

"This way," Nikko said, nodding toward the hall on the left. It was narrow, just wide enough for two people to walk side by side. There were fluorescent light strips on the ceiling, and a cluster of pipes, wrapped in insulation, along the right-hand wall.

A short way down the hall Nikko turned to the left into another hall, virtually identical to the first one. He stopped in front of a dark red door and knocked. "*Voydite*," said a muffled voice on the other side of the door.

Nikko put a hand on the doorknob and nodded to Stefan. "He say, go in."

Stefan took a deep breath. *Here we go*, he thought. But aloud he said only, "All right," and Nikko opened the door.

CHAPTER
30

I t started awkwardly. Naturally it would. Ivo did not quite know what to say. Beyond that, he could not even fathom what his role should be. He was long accustomed to interviewing people. He was also quite at his ease interrogating them, which was very different. And if it went beyond that to more extreme and painful measures, it was simple for him to adjust to that, too, and he certainly was not going to feel queasy when blood and body parts hit the floor. In his career he had killed many people, too many to count, and doing so had long ceased to bother him. If it came to killing Stefan, he would do it without a qualm, and before that, he'd cheerfully watch Grisha extract from Stefan the truth behind his arrival here at the lighthouse.

All these things, and far worse, Ivo could do easily. But to simply *talk* to someone? That was not as easy. And when that someone was a newly discovered son—*might be*, he corrected himself—Ivo had absolutely no experience to guide him. How did a father act when meeting his adult son for the first time? How did one act if it was only possibly his son? Should he be cold and questioning? Warm and welcoming? Somewhere in between? If there was a guidebook for such situations, Ivo had never seen it, and he had no experience to rely on.

And so, after fumbling with a few ill-chosen sentences and quickly abandoning them, Ivo switched to automatic pilot while he tried to think of how to proceed. He gave Stefan an explanation of his home and its history, without in any way indicating how he had known of its existence. And then, when that topic was exhausted and no new inspiration had come to him, he lapsed into silence.

Stefan seemed to have nothing at all to add. So for several minutes, he simply looked at Stefan, looked away, and looked back again. And for his part, Stefan did the same. He did not offer any hint on how to proceed—and why should he? He would naturally expect Ivo to take the lead.

But what *was* the lead? Ivo hadn't a clue, and so he sat and looked. Finally, when the silence was nearly unbearable, he had a brilliant inspiration. "Oh!" he said abruptly. "Would you like, ah—tea? Or perhaps some coffee? Mm, something stronger, such as beer or wine? Or—"

Stefan smiled. Was he enjoying Ivo's clearly visible awkwardness? But all he said was, "Some coffee, please?"

"Yes, of course," Ivo said. "Forgive me, I should have— Yes, let me take care of that." He swiveled his chair and spoke into the phone for a moment, then turned back to face Stefan. "Well, then. Stefan," he said. And there he was stuck.

Stefan was helpful at last. "Yes," he said. "Stefan. Stefan Laurent."

"Uh-huh. Yes, so you said," Ivo said. "But tell me—why Laurent? Not your mother's name, nor mine, and I— Oh! Did Simone marry? I mean, your mother?"

"I know who you mean," Stefan said. And now he was clearly

enjoying Ivo's discomfiture. "No, she did not marry. She died in prison." Some of the amusement left his face as he had said this. Was he angry? Resentful? Ivo couldn't tell.

"I knew that," he said. "But I never . . ." He could not find the words for a long moment. "Was it bad?" he said at last.

"Bad," Stefan said, almost spitting the word. "For her? Yes, of course. It was cancer. I don't think that's ever good." He clenched his fists and looked down at them. "For me? What do you think? I was an orphan. A bastard orphan. It was bad, and it stayed that way."

"Yes, of course," Ivo said, eager to change the subject. "But the name, ah—Laurent?"

Stefan shrugged. "I was raised by an aunt. A widow. It made things much simpler if she adopted me—bureaucratic things that occur for a child, such as parental consent, hm?"

"I see."

"And on weekends she would take me to the prison, Centre Pénitentiaire de Rennes, to see Mother." He made a small and bitter smile. "Until she died, of course."

"Of course," Ivo said. He felt heat in his cheeks—was it possible he was blushing? "But then," he said awkwardly, wanting to change the subject quickly. "After—did you attend university?"

Stefan shrugged. "Just for a year. At Lyon."

"Really? The technical school?"

"Yes," he said, and shrugged again. "I had some interest in mathematics. I thought perhaps . . . Eh. It didn't work out for me."

"Mathematics! Really? That was always my passion," Ivo said. He felt a pulse of excitement. Could such things be passed through the genes? Why not?

"It was not for me," Stefan said.

"Why not?"

"Eh," Stefan said. "It was all so—they try to make it all so—so much about formulas and equations? And they did not like questions."

"I see," Ivo said. "And then, after Lyon?"

He shrugged yet again. "A couple of years in the Army," he said. He gave a short and derisive laugh. "That was even worse than university."

"It can be difficult," Ivo said with sympathy. "So much, what. Regimentation?"

"Yes, that's it," Stefan said. "And ultimately not terribly practical. So, not for me."

"No, I can see that," Ivo said. "I think that— Come!"

The door opened; it was Sasha, who served as their cook. He came into the room with a tray holding a coffeepot, creamer and sugar bowl, and two cups.

"Would you like me to pour it?" Sasha asked.

"No, we can manage, thank you, Sash," Ivo said, and he nodded and left.

For a few moments, they were occupied with the coffee: pouring, adding cream and sugar, stirring, and taking a first sip. But when that ritual was finished and they were back to looking at each other, the awkwardness fell back over them like a thick, wet blanket. Ivo sipped again and tried to recall what they had said before Sasha had come in, so he could pick up that thread of conversation again. After struggling for a few seconds, he remembered.

"Ah, yes," Ivo said. "That's right. So, after the Army, then. What next? A job, a girlfriend, travel—what have you done with yourself?"

Stefan stared at him for a moment and then broke into laughter.

"Is that funny?" Ivo said. "I don't see the joke."

"No. I'm sorry," Stefan said, regaining control of himself. "It's just— I'm sorry, but . . . You sounded exactly like a father."

For a moment Ivo was filled with so much odd emotion that he could only blink. "Well, that's . . . That is to say, ah," he stammered at last. "I hope you don't think I'm, you know. Prying into personal matters? But, ah . . ."

"Yes," Stefan said, still smiling. "I know."

"It's just that, that I—" Ivo blew out a long breath. "Well, after all . . ."

Ivo found himself looking at his fingernails. They were fine. He looked up at Stefan, who was still smiling. He felt that he should smile back. But instead, he found himself growing irritated. This boy—man, person, whatever—seemed to be completely relaxed. Instead of feeling discomfort as Ivo did, he appeared to be mocking Ivo for feeling it. How could he be so cocksure? He fought the negative feelings, seeking to push them away. He failed, and so at last he let them burst out. "What exactly is it that you expect from me?" he said, and he was surprised to hear petulance in his voice.

It didn't affect Stefan, who gave him a light and mocking smile. "I? Nothing. Nothing at all." He shrugged. "I just wanted to see you, to know who you are. It seems natural to me, wanting to know who your father was, hm?"

"I suppose so," Ivo said. "But why did you wait, hm? Why now and not years ago?"

"I only found out recently," Stefan said. "When my aunt died. I went through her papers and things, you know." He shrugged again. "As one does when someone dies. And I found some old letters my mother had written." He cocked an eyebrow. "She did not want me to know about you," he said. "She was afraid that somehow it would compromise you. I don't understand how, but . . ." Another shrug. "She told everything to my aunt. Who you were, this place here, you know. Apparently she actually loved you."

"Yes, that's— I, uh . . . I see," Ivo finished lamely. He had wanted to say that yes, he had loved her, too, that their time together was the only time in his life he had felt anything—but it seemed impossible to get the words out to someone who was, after all, a stranger. And so instead, he let the silence grow and turn once more into a stifling pall. He broke it at last with a rather clumsy, "Well . . . Ah, you must have a great many questions? For me, I mean?"

"No," said Stefan. "Not really."

"I see," Ivo said. And there he was stumped. He very much wanted to keep the conversation going, learn more about Stefan, perhaps get him to open up a bit. But he could think of no more, beyond something utterly moronic like, "Are you really my son?" So once again, silence fell on the room.

After a few painful moments of this, Ivo's stomach began to hurt, and that made him irritable. *Enough of this*, he thought. "I must get back to work," he said. And then, fearing that this had sounded petulant, he added, "You are free to wander around, but certain areas must remain off-limits, you understand?"

"Of course," Stefan said.

"I will have someone find you a room. And if you think of any questions, come and ask them. To me."

Stefan stood up. "Yes," he said. "I will."

"All right, then," Ivo said, waving a hand dismissively.

Stefan left, and only a moment later, Grisha came back in. He stood silently until Ivo said, "Yes? What is it, Grisha?"

"Ivan has just left," he said. "For Rennes."

"Oh? Is that a problem?"

"No," Grisha said. And then, most annoyingly, he was silent.

"Grisha, please," Ivo said. "Is there a reason you mention this?"

"He could check on this story of the aunt," Grisha said. "Laurent."

"Grisha—"

"This is an elementary precaution, Ivo," Grisha said.

For a moment Ivo thought he would lose his temper—Grisha had been listening? But a vast jolt of pain shot into his stomach, and instead he doubled over and closed his eyes. When he could breathe again, he waved one hand at Grisha. "All right," he said wearily. "Tell him to check."

He heard Grisha leave and close the door behind him, but he did not open his eyes for several more minutes.

CHAPTER
31

Frank Delgado was a busy man, now more so than usual. As SAC at the Moscow embassy, he had more to do every day than could be done in twenty hours, let alone the ten or twelve he routinely spent on the job. So it was several days before he went back to the IT section to see if Miranda Shaleki had made any progress on designing a search program he could use to track Riley Wolfe's mother. He knew she would be busy, too, and didn't want to pressure her. She was, after all, doing him a big favor.

When he dropped in on Miranda, he expected it to be just a quick visit for a progress report. That was not what he got.

He found Miranda Shaleki, as expected, at her computer, earbuds in, pounding the keyboard rapidly in time to some music only she could hear. This time, he didn't bother clearing his throat to get her attention. He simply leaned in and tapped her on the shoulder.

Miranda instantly spun around with a hostile glare on her face. A second later, when she recognized Delgado, it softened. "Oh," she said.

"I wondered when you were going to come for this." She held up a small black thumb drive.

"I'm impressed," Delgado said. "You finished writing the program."

"What? Oh. Hell, yes, I did that in about three hours. Then I wanted to see how well it worked, so I went ahead and ran it. And—" She wiggled the thumb drive at him. "Here you go."

Somewhat stunned, Delgado took the thumb drive. "So wait—what, you ran the program? And so this is . . ." He trailed off, shaking his head.

Miranda snorted. "That's the results, dude. Shit, it wasn't hard. Get that weird look off your face."

"I just— I'm having trouble believing it's done so quickly," Delgado said.

"Yeah, well, believe it," she said, looking just a little smug.

"I don't, uh— I mean, this is it? The whole thing? The program, the search, the results, and—" He broke off, shaking his head again.

"Bro, what did I say? Is there a better language I can use? I'm not real strong on Spanish," she said, clearly only a little exasperated, but mostly very pleased at his reaction.

Delgado took a breath, then nodded. "Well, okay," he said. "Now I'm *really* impressed." He pulled over a chair from the adjoining cubicle and sat beside Miranda. "Tell me about it."

"Sure, so . . ." Miranda frowned and chewed on her bottom lip. "Okay, so like I said, the program was easy. And how I set it up, all I had to do was enter the variables—which was the list of meds?—and then turn it loose." She shrugged. "Okay, so I did one dumbass thing."

"Hard to believe," Delgado said.

Miranda ignored him. "I forgot age and gender. Stupid. And I got like, four thousand hits? Way too many."

"Yes, it is."

"So I fixed that, and tweaked a couple of minor bugs, and yeah." She shrugged. "I got three hits that matched what you said. Uh . . ." She chewed on her lower lip again. "I mean—there was one more? But it was at a private house . . . ?"

Delgado frowned. "A private house? Like somebody's home?"

"Well, yeah, sure," she said. "But, so, the question was, *whose* house, right? And I hacked into the property records, and it kind of made sense because it's just some lady doctor living there? I mean, at first."

"At first?" he said, puzzled. "What does that mean?"

"Well, so, I was just wondering, you know," Miranda said. "And I was already into the property records, so—I checked some more. Check this out." Miranda spun around, hit a few quick, percussive strokes on her keyboard, and an image came up on her monitor.

Delgado leaned closer to look and blinked at what he saw. It was a castle, right out of a fairy tale. There was water on all sides of it—a castle on an island? And why was Miranda showing it to him?

"What am I looking at?" he said, genuinely puzzled.

Miranda snorted. "It's a *castle*, dude. What, you never saw any of the Disney princess flicks?"

"Not many," he said. "And why are you showing me a castle?"

"Because *this*," she said, running the cursor over the picture, "*this* is the 'private house' the lady doctor lives in."

Delgado grunted. "Nice house."

"Right? And, like, who owns something like this? Which is a real question, I mean—so I followed the paperwork, and it turns out she doesn't really own it—it's some weird holding corporation." She punched the keyboard rapidly. "Civil Property Management—which sounds all straight and everything, okay, but maybe *too* straight? And I go deeper, and Civil is owned by *another* corporation, and another one owns them, and then another—it's like the babushka dolls, you know. One inside another—and they're all registered in Delaware to the same PO box." She looked up at him. "In case you missed class that day at the FBI Academy, you're supposed to be, like, automatically suspicious of corporations registered in Delaware?"

"No, I was there for that class," Delgado said. "And if a bunch of them are registered to the same PO box, even more."

"Right? And when you add the castle, which is totally isolated on the Canadian border, north of Syracuse and out in the middle of the St. Lawrence Seaway—I start to get this picture? Like, my techie radar says back the fuck off, cuz . . . It's got to be some kind of spy guys."

Delgado had been listening with pleasure that bordered on awe. And now, he actually smiled. "You are exactly right," he said. "So you should forget this ever happened. Thank you."

"Uh-huh. Why do I get the feeling you are not going to follow your own advice?"

Delgado just kept smiling. "I owe you a big favor," he said. "Collect anytime. Thanks, Miranda."

"No worries," she said. Delgado stood up, and she was already turned back around to her computer.

He took the flash drive back to his office and plugged it in. The drive's directory listed what was clearly the program, a Word file labeled, "KEEP OUT," and something called, "RSLTS." Assuming that meant "Results," he opened that file first. There were three entries, all extended-care facilities. One of them was in Oak Park, Illinois. The second was located in Lakeland, Florida, and the third in Boone, North Carolina. There was a patient's name and room number with each one.

Delgado frowned, considering carefully. Any of the three was possible, but the fourth Miranda had mentioned, the castle, seemed most likely. He went back to the directory. Either Miranda hadn't included it, or it would be in "KEEP OUT." An odd title, but considering the source, it made sense.

He called it up on his screen and looked it over. A nineteenth-century robber baron had brought the castle over from Germany, stone by stone, and had it reassembled on an island in the St. Lawrence, just barely on the US side of the border with Canada. His family had used it as a vacation house for two generations until, as so often happened, the baron's descendants had squandered the last of his fortune and sold the castle.

And now it was owned by Civil Property Management, a holding corporation that had made some effort to hide. Delgado thought about it. It was exactly the sort of move an intelligence agency would make—especially if they were operating within the borders of the USA. Strictly speaking, that was illegal for the CIA. Of course, that simply meant they did it covertly—exactly like this, in fact. And a castle was, by design, easy to defend. When it was approachable only by water, even more so. Better still, no one seeing it from the shore would think of it in terms of a well-defended stronghold. It was quaint scenery. And being so close to the Canadian border would be a big plus, too.

This was it. He was nearly certain. This had to be the place. The other three choices might have made sense if Riley Wolfe had picked them for his mother, but not this. The castle absolutely reeked of the Agency.

All right. The Agency had taken Wolfe's mother to leverage Wolfe into doing something for them—something that involved a Russian Orthodox icon. And knowing what he did about the way Wolfe worked, Delgado was reasonably sure the job would take some time—which gave Delgado time to prepare to do something. That left one major question:

Do *what*?

CHAPTER

32

W ell now, how are we doing this morning?"

The doctor spoke from the doorway, wearing her scary pretend smile. Monique stared, and not only because finding the right words was still difficult. Dr. Arnsdale always asked that same question—but Monique was certain she did not care at all how "we" were doing. Aside from taking the routine vital signs every day, she had never said or done anything to Monique that would show concern or a desire to help or treat or comfort. This morning, like usual, it was too confusing, too much to process, so Monique laughed and said nothing.

"Well, that's all right," Dr. Arnsdale said. "We can't expect you to be talking yet. Or maybe ever. We'll see." She approached the bed, where Monique sat, propped against the wall, and perched on the edge. "We're going to try some therapy, okay? Just nod if you understand."

Monique shook her head. She knew that word, "therapy." But what did it mean? Something about, about . . . It slid into her mind, and then right back out again. "Colonostomy. Colonoscopy. Colon colon . . ." She stopped herself abruptly, suddenly afraid.

The doctor stretched her mouth into that smile again. It didn't show in her eyes, but it hollowed out her cheeks so it was like a skull talking. "Therapy is an *activity*," she said. "Do you know that word? Ack-TIV-ity. Hm?" She didn't wait for Monique to respond. "For therapy, the activity is something we do to make you a little better," she said. "Of course in your case? Who knows." The doctor held up a notebook, the kind with blank, unlined pages. "We thought it might help your memory if you try to write things down. Perhaps better than trying to speak them." She paused and tilted her head, looking suddenly like some awful flesh-eating bird. "Do you understand?"

Monique laughed.

"Of course not," the doctor said. She put the notebook down on the bed in front of Monique, and then placed a jumbo pencil beside it, the kind that little kids use when learning their letters. "Why don't you go ahead and write down some things? Anything at all you might remember. All right? Good." And without waiting for Monique to respond, she rose and quickly left the room.

Monique watched her go and then sat unmoving for several minutes. The doctor had said to write down some things she remembered. But what Monique remembered was not words. It was images, pictures, scenes that she knew were important even though she couldn't remember why. She remembered some of the words that went with the pictures, like "New York" and "Home." But she could not remember any words for so many other things, pictures in her head that might be even more important. Like the man who was going to come and save her. She could only remember that he was important and that he would come for her. That and his face. How could she put that in words?

She thought about that, trying to frame it in her mind. "He is important, and he will come to save me." But that didn't make any new memories flow. Still, doctors were supposed to know about these things, and this doctor had said it would help. Maybe she should write it anyway.

Monique reached for the pencil, and then stopped. A new thought had come to her. Would the doctor read what she wrote? What would she do if she read, "He will come to save me"? The doctor was keeping her here. She didn't want Monique to go. So she would try to stop someone who came to take her away!

That was bad. She couldn't write about the man.

But he was important! And the more she thought about him, the more important he seemed. She couldn't write about him—but could she somehow make a picture of that face? And even if she did, would it be therapy? Would it help her? The doctor had said to write words, not pictures.

And then Monique had a wonderful thought. If she could draw something and look at it, she might remember the word that went with it. She nodded. That made sense.

But could she make a picture like that? Something that really looked like what it was? That seemed like something that would be very hard to do.

She bit her lip and thought. After a minute she nodded again. She had to try. If nothing else, just putting things on paper might help her remember words. She reached for the pencil and picked it up.

Magic happened.

Monique felt something like a jolt of electricity run from the hand holding the pencil all the way up her arm and into her brain. She stared at her hand, at the way it held the pencil.

I know this.

Holding a pencil, making lines with it, was familiar and important. She had done this before. She thought she might be able to make a picture.

Monique laughed, and just as abruptly began to cry. Hand trembling, Monique flipped open the notebook to its first blank page. She took a deep breath, and then she put the point of the pencil onto the paper. And she began to draw.

CHAPTER 33

There was really no way to tell what time it was. All hours seemed the same down here underground, except that the lights were dimmed from ten o'clock each night until six the next morning. Still, Stefan guessed that it was close to midnight. Aside from the dimmed lights, the sounds of the place were muffled. There was also that feeling that came only at night, of all things turning down a few notches, of the world listening carefully for something that might be in the shadows.

Stefan knew he should have been in the small, cell-like room he'd been given. But he did not feel like sleeping. So he had wandered out here, to the edge of the great shaft that had once held a Soviet missile. He'd seen no one in the halls, although he knew that there would be several men in the security room, and a few more patrolling the entire facility. But here at the shaft there was no one but Stefan himself, and that suited him perfectly.

He leaned on the steel pipe railing at the lip of the shaft, apparently lost in thought, for several minutes. His gaze wandered on downward, toward the floor below, which was not visible, lost in a great pool of darkness at the bottom. But to Stefan, it seemed that the darkness spread out down there, as if the shaft opened out at the bottom. Was it possible? He had no idea how these things were built, nor what the demands of a missile launch silo might be. Perhaps there was more down there than just the bottom of the shaft.

And come to that, if there was something down there, how did one get down to it? The Soviets must have built in some way to get down, if only for maintenance. Stefan leaned over and looked at the sides of the shaft. There should be some kind of ladder, or perhaps rungs mounted into the sides of the tube. But he saw nothing. Perhaps some kind of elevator or cable car?

Stefan leaned farther over. Nothing; no sign of anything at all. Maybe there was some kind of—

"What are you doing here?"

The voice came from behind him so suddenly that Stefan nearly fell into the pit. He caught himself on the railing and turned.

Grisha stood there, very close. Stefan had heard nothing of his approach. "Well?" Grisha said. "What are you doing?"

Stefan regarded him. His French was rough, but it was better than Nikko's. "I am looking down, into this pit," Stefan said.

"Why," Grisha said. A demand, not a question.

Stefan shrugged. "I wondered, that is all," he said. "Wondered what is down there."

Grisha's eyes narrowed. "Why should anything be down there?"

"Why waste space?" Stefan said. "Why not put something interesting down there?"

"Interesting," Grisha said. "Like what."

"But how should I know? A music room, a gymnasium, a cinema

theater—I don't know, I just thought there might be something there. Is that wrong?"

Grisha looked at him for a long moment without blinking. Then he took a half step forward toward Stefan, so he was only inches away. For a very long and very uncomfortable moment he simply stared, and to Stefan it seemed that the temperature around him was dropping rapidly to freezing. But he held Grisha's gaze, staring back until, finally, Grisha spoke. "Who are you," he said.

"I am Stefan Laurent," he said. "As I have said."

"I don't believe you," Grisha said.

"I'm sorry to hear it."

Grisha went back to silent staring. "Listen to me," Grisha said at last. And if reptiles could speak, their voices would sound like Grisha's did. "Stay away from the silo. It is not for you. Stay. Away. Understand?"

"Yes, of course," Stefan said. "But what is—" And he stopped speaking, because Grisha was already gone. Stefan blinked. "*Quel connard*," he muttered.

Ivo Balodis was very far from being a fool. It was impossible for fools to survive as long as he had in the world of intelligence, black ops, and international intrigue. So he was very well aware that Grisha was correct to be suspicious of Stefan. He, too, was suspicious; Stefan's story seemed too good to be true. And yet—

And yet, he was compelled to learn more. He absolutely had to be sure about Stefan. To kill him without certainty would destroy what might be the only link to the one and only love of his life. He told himself that he was being cautious and that he merely wanted to be sure one way or the other. But there was more to it than that. He wanted it to be true. He knew very well that this was exactly what Stefan would count on if he was not who he claimed. It was a basic tool of black ops: Find an emotional opening and use it against the target. He had done exactly this many times in his career. That was certainly the most reasonable explanation. The evidence that Stefan was telling the truth was almost nothing. And still Ivo wanted it to be true.

If it was true, he had a son, and a link to Simone. And Stefan could tell him more about Simone's last years. He knew almost nothing about her after she had been sent to prison. Even to look into it would have alerted people that he cared, and that would be used against him, either as a way to control him or as an excuse to officially sanction killing him. He had tried to push her out of his mind. He had failed, of course. He still felt a tremendous void where Simone had been. Stefan could fill that void. If he was real.

Since Stefan's arrival, Ivo had done little more than watch from a distance. Now it was time to get closer. He invited Stefan to dinner, just the two of them.

The meal had started just as awkwardly as their first meeting. But Ivo was determined to get Stefan talking. He refilled Stefan's wineglass frequently, hoping the alcohol might loosen his tongue. And in order to encourage Stefan to drink, Ivo drained and filled his own glass, far more often than he would normally. Ivo told himself he was a seasoned professional and it would take more than a few glasses of wine to lure him into an indiscretion.

But as the meal went on and the silence grew, his desperation grew with it. Finally, he simply blurted out, "Tell me about your mother." Stefan fixed him with what Ivo thought was a rather cold gaze, so he added, "Please?"

Stefan sipped, then nodded. "All right," he said. "What would you like to know?"

"I just— Everything, I suppose. Anything," Ivo said. "Starting with . . . after she went to prison."

"Yes," Stefan said sourly. "Prison." He drained his wineglass. "That is all I knew of her. But you . . ." Stefan cocked his head to one side and frowned. "Did you love her?"

Ivo opened his mouth, closed it. He was not accustomed to discussing or revealing any emotion at all. To admit that he did love her was to reveal great weakness. On the other hand, perhaps Stefan, of all people, had the right to know. He sighed. "Yes," he said at last. "I loved her."

Stefan shook his head. "She always said so," he said. "I thought she was a fool to believe it. If you loved her, you would not have left her. You would not have allowed her to die in prison. You would not have left *me*."

His voice had been rising into anger as he spoke. Ivo held up a hand to calm him. "Stefan, please," he said. "You have to understand that—" He broke off, aware that the only way for Stefan to understand was for Ivo to tell him a number of closely guarded secrets, and he was not prepared to do so. "It's—it's very complicated," he finished lamely.

"Yes, it always is, isn't it?" Stefan said bitterly.

Ivo looked away—far away, and back into the past. He could see her so clearly, the way she had looked the last time he had seen her. For a long moment, he stayed back there with her, in the grubby little room in Marseilles, so many years ago, just before the heavy knocks on the door came.

But as always, he came back to the lonely and painful present. He looked at Stefan, who was looking back, still clearly upset. "I loved her, Stefan," he said. "But this was at a time—this was the Cold War, yes? Neither of us was free. And in theory, we were enemies, so . . ." He shrugged. "For me to admit that I cared for her would have meant death. For both of us." He attempted a small smile. "For all three of us, apparently."

"You were some kind of—what, a spy?"

"Yes," Ivo said. "I ran an espionage circuit for the Soviet Union. I had tried to turn your mother. You know, make her come over to my side?" He smiled again. "She, of course, was trying to turn *me*, too. Neither of us turned. But we—instead, we, ah . . . It was unexpected," he said. "But it—you know. We fell in love."

"Hmp," Stefan said.

"It's true, Stefan," he said. "And for me . . ." He found no way to say it, so he drained his glass and then refilled it. "Until I met your mother, I had never considered that I could ever . . . I was, as you say, 'some kind of spy.' And love? This is not for spies. I was . . ." He waved a hand, realizing too late that the hand still held his wineglass. Half a glass of wine splattered out onto the table. Ivo stared at it, appalled.

Stefan burst out laughing. Ivo looked at him in surprise. What was funny? But apparently, his expression was funny, too, and Stefan laughed harder, nearly choking, and after a few seconds, Ivo felt the corners of his mouth twitch, then spread into a smile—and a few seconds more and he, too, was laughing.

The laughter went on for a good minute, until finally they both gasped and wheezed to a stop.

"Well, then," Ivo said.

"I think you're not accustomed to drinking so much," Stefan said. "When is the last time you were drunk?"

"Drunk? My God—forty years ago at least."

"It takes constant practice," Stefan said, still smiling. And then he stood up and came around the table. "Look at you," he said. He began to blot up the spilled wine with his napkin. "A mess."

"I'm sorry," Ivo said.

"Don't be," Stefan said. "For the first time, I can believe my mother loved you."

Ivo blinked. He could not think of anything at all to say. And if he had, he would have been unable to say it. His throat had tightened, nearly closed, and he was astonished to feel tears forming in his eyes. He quickly blotted them away, pretending he was mopping up wine, but the feelings remained. Stefan went back to his chair and the meal resumed, but later, Ivo could not recall much of what happened. Partly because yes, he was a little drunk. But mostly because of the shock of feeling so many unaccustomed emotions whipping through him.

And still later, it occurred to him that he had told Stefan a great deal more than Stefan had told him.

CHAPTER

34

Frank Delgado met with Eleanor Garvey quite often. She was the chargé d'affaires of America's Moscow embassy. Outranked only by the ambassador, she was in many ways more powerful. The ambassador was a political employee, with a limited term of office. The chargé, however, usually served a longer term, and her duties were more practical, hands-on, much like a chief operating officer of a corporation.

It was a routine part of Delgado's FBI SAC duties to meet with Garvey over routine matters of security. This time, as he stepped into her office, Delgado was aware that this was not routine. Garvey looked more tense than usual: Large dark circles had formed under her eyes, and her face looked puffy. And she was visibly grinding her teeth as she flipped through a file folder on her desk.

"Sit down, Frank," she said, waving at a chair. Delgado sat and waited while the chargé flipped to the last page and, still frowning, closed the folder. She closed her eyes, blew out a long and tense breath through her teeth, and said, "Shit." She opened her eyes and turned bloodshot eyes on him. "We have—a *problem*, Frank," she said.

Delgado nodded and waited.

Garvey held up the folder and waved it. "If this is true," she said. Another violent exhale through her teeth. "Goddamn it, it *is* true. I'm sure of it, and Washington is sure of it, and . . . To cut to the chase, Frank, we're screwed."

"In what way?" Delgado asked mildly.

"Most ways, damn it," she said. "We've been hacked. Our entire system has been breached—computers, security, cameras—we're wide open in every fucking way possible."

"How would you like to respond, ma'am?" Delgado said.

Garvey rolled her eyes and shrugged. "I'd like to shoot somebody, of course," she said. "But short of that—you know the political situation between us and Russia right now?"

"Tense," he said.

"And then some," she said. "So any response becomes political, and I just plain don't have the authority to act without approval from a high level. *Very* high level," she said, raising an eyebrow.

Delgado nodded. "What does Washington suggest?"

Garvey snorted. "What do you think? They want to hold a high-level meeting, which means find somebody to blame it on. And since they want you there, and you will be the only one present who has enough rank to be responsible but not enough to push back . . ." She closed her eyes for a moment, appearing to compose herself a little. "I'm being a bit dramatic," she said, opening her eyes.

Delgado smiled sympathetically. "I got that," he said.

"In fact, you do have to go. It makes sense for you to be there. I just wanted you to be aware that the knives will be out, because this whole thing makes them look like shit, not just us here in Moscow."

"I understand," he said. "I can take care of myself."

"I'm sure you can. In a gunfight," she said. "This is political, and that's a hell of lot messier."

"I'll be fine," he said. "Can you brief me on what happened?"

Garvey waved the folder again. "This will bring you up to speed," she said. "It's everything we've got, which isn't much. But you won't be going alone. The IT tech who discovered the breach is going with you. Washington insisted on that, too. And that makes another problem for you, because you have to keep her muzzled. And from all accounts, this woman is a loose cannon."

"Miranda Shaleki," Delgado said with a smile.

Garvey raised an eyebrow. "Really. You know her?"

"I've worked with her," Delgado said. "She's very smart, dedicated, skilled. And, as you said, kind of a loose cannon. But I like her."

"That makes it a bit easier," Garvey said. "All right, then." She pushed the folder across the desk. "You leave tomorrow morning."

As always, Delgado found Miranda at her computer. Her screen was filled with what looked like complete gibberish—Delgado assumed it was code. He tapped her on the shoulder, and this time she spun around instantly, so quickly that she ran into Delgado's legs.

"Sorry," she said. "When are we leaving?"

He opened his mouth, closed it again. He was surprised but realized he shouldn't be. Of course she would have guessed that the two of them would be traveling back to the States. It was the obvious course of action, and they were the obvious choice to carry it out. So he simply said, "Tomorrow morning."

"Fabulous. DC is beautiful when it's winter slush season. Slogging through the half-frozen crap, all the cars splashing you with lovely brown snow," she said. "I can't wait."

"I've been unofficially warned about a couple of things," he said.

"Right. 'Keep an eye on Shaleki, she can't control her mouth,'" she said with a small sardonic smile.

"Yes," he said with a matching smile. "But also, the politics is going to be very dicey."

Miranda snorted. "Politics. You mean the blame game, right?" she said. "Yeah, I figured that already."

"Good," he said. "The chargé says they'll want a scapegoat."

"You would fit pretty well, wouldn't you?" she said. "You worried?"

"A little," Delgado admitted. "But you're in the bull's-eye, too."

For the first time she looked surprised. "Me? But I found the fucking hack!"

"Right," he said. He put on an officious scowl. "And why didn't you find it sooner, Miss Shaleki? Your résumé says you're supposed to be world-class—why didn't you *stop* it, Miss Shaleki?" Delgado shrugged. "Get the idea? It doesn't have to make sense. It just has to give them cover."

"Well, shit," she said. "I guess I should update my CV."

"I've got your back," he said. "But don't give them any levers. Don't talk except to answer their questions, and keep your answers very short."

"Yes, sir, Your Honor," she said. "I promise I'll be good."

"Good. If you want, you can go home and pack now."

"I packed yesterday," she said. "Right after I reported the hack."

CHAPTER

35

The lighthouse workout room was crowded at this hour. The day shift had eaten breakfast and would take over from the night shift soon. There was just enough time for a good workout and a shower before the changing of the guard. All the former Spetsnaz troopers worked out every day. They were expected to stay in top shape, and that took a daily commitment.

The room was very well equipped, of course. There were several stationary bicycles and ellipticals for cardio, a good range of free weights, and a cluster of heavy bags and speed bags. But the largest portion of the room was taken up by training mats, the kind you would see in any dojo or other martial arts school. All the men had been well trained in hand-to-hand combat, and they knew through their long service the necessity of keeping those skills sharp with daily practice.

Several pairs were sparring, practicing holds and falls and jiujitsu ground techniques. But the largest area of the mats was taken up by Grisha. And instead of working with one partner, he sparred with three men at the same time. They would attack singly, in twos, and all three at once. It apparently made no difference to Grisha. Although he was considerably smaller than the others, he dominated. He moved through them like a dervish, whirling from one mock attacker to another, dealing quick strikes and kicks that would be either fatal or permanently crippling if delivered at full force. Each time he landed a strike he would call out, "Your left is open! Again!" or "Watch me, not my movement!" or "Like that!"

A small circle of watchers stood at the edge of the mats. It was always instructive to watch Grisha—and quite often it was fun, too. Watching your messmates get their asses handed to them was nearly always enjoyable. Additionally, it was a lot more entertaining to see somebody else take their lumps from Grisha than to take them yourself. Just watching him work was a lesson in itself. He was terrifying to see in action.

Among the watchers was Nikko. He had sparred with Grisha the day before, and he was not yet recovered enough to think about a return match. Today it was a real pleasure to see somebody else take the punishment he'd taken so recently.

"*Mon Dieu*, he is formidable." The voice came from behind Nikko, and he turned.

Of course it was Stefan. No one else would speak to him in French. Nikko smiled. He was starting to like Stefan—a good thing, since Nikko usually had the task of communicating with him. "Stefan!" he said cheerfully. "*Dobroye utro!*"

Stefan smiled back. He had been helping Nikko improve his French, and Nikko had been teaching him some Russian phrases and important words. *Good morning* was one phrase they had already practiced. "*Dobroye utro*," Stefan responded. He nodded at where Grisha now had two men pinned at the same time and was delivering a sweep to the third. "Grisha is very frightening to watch," he said.

"Ah. You are perhaps more happier to join in?" Nikko said with mock seriousness. "Shall I ask him?"

"*Merde*, no! I think he would kill me!" Stefan said.

"Oh, no, never this," Nikko said, still teasing. "No more than broken wrist, broken head maybe? Almost never does he kill you."

"Perhaps," Stefan said. "But he does not like me."

"Eh," Nikko said. "He changes his mind soon. For the *komandir*, I think."

"Perhaps," Stefan said again. "But I would rather not take the chance."

They watched for a minute in silence, until one of Grisha's victims cried out and fell to the mat. Grisha watched him for a moment, then spoke to the other two. They nodded, helped their comrade to his feet, and led him away.

Grisha picked up a towel from the edge of the mat and wiped his face. He turned and saw Stefan. For a very long moment he just looked without blinking. Then he threw the towel over a shoulder and stalked toward the door and past them—very close, closer than necessary. And as he passed, the hostility that came off him was something you could almost touch.

Stefan watched him go. When Grisha was finally gone, he realized he had been holding his breath, and he let it out. "As I said," Stefan said. "He does not like me."

Nikko shook his head slowly. "*Moy Bog*," Nikko said. "I think you are right."

——————

Ivo Balodis said a very bad word and dropped the sheaf of papers he was holding onto his desk. He leaned on his elbows and rubbed his temples to ease the throbbing in his head. He simply could not concentrate today and decided there was no point in trying.

He checked the weather on the monitor that stood at the back of his desk. Balmy temperatures, low chance of rain—very well. Perhaps a walk around the island would clear his head. He pushed back from the desk and headed out the door.

There were two guards on the door, and he nodded at them as he passed. "I'm going outside," he said, and the two fell in behind him.

Down the hall, a right turn, and he was headed for the elevator, the one that led up the lighthouse and thus outside. Going out for a walk when he could was a risk—but it was worth it. The walks made him feel better all over. Just breathing fresh air, getting the blood flowing—it was common knowledge that this improved one's health, physical and mental. So he walked whenever possible, and two of his men, armed with automatic weapons, always accompanied him, and more could be there in under a minute.

Today he truly needed his walk. He had been sitting for several hours, flipping through the same report, and he could not recall a word of it. It didn't seem to be important, not compared to other issues that assailed him. In any case, those other matters had him distracted, anxious, torn in different directions. It wasn't just the pain in his stomach, although that still seemed to be getting worse. And it wasn't the threat hanging over him, nor the secret auction for the flash drive in his vault, which had been inching along for several months.

No, he finally had to admit that the real problem was Stefan. Even with so many critical and potentially lethal possibilities surrounding him, Ivo was consumed with the problem of Stefan. There was no obvious answer. Ivo wanted to believe Stefan was his son by Simone—wanted it desperately. But he was quite aware that this powerful desire made him particularly vulnerable, too, exposed to any kind of scam or operation that Stefan might be working on him. As a career intelligence operative, he knew very well that it was exactly the kind of operation a bold and cunning adversary might attempt in order to worm their way into his confidence. The wish to believe could very easily be blinding him.

And yet . . . there was something about Stefan, some ineffable *something* that reminded him quite forcibly of Simone, his only real love.

The result was that he was torn between the extremes of ingrained paranoia from a long career in black ops and what could only be described as a desperate yearning. Grisha was totally convinced that Stefan was an imposter infiltrating for some dark purpose, although he could not provide a convincing explanation of what that purpose might be; only Ivo could possibly open the vault, and there was no way he would ever do so, son or not. Grisha wanted to kill Stefan immediately, and Grisha was usually right. Ivo generally took his advice. But in this, in a matter where his heart was so heavily invested, he simply could not. Not while there was a chance, however slim, that Stefan really was who he claimed to be.

And so he was faced with an impossible decision: what to do about Stefan. The choice was between two completely ludicrous extremes. Bluntly stated, it came down to this: Should he kill Stefan, or adopt him? Killing him was definitely the smart move, but . . . but—

Lost in thought, he turned the corner for the final approach to the elevator and very nearly collided with Stefan himself, who was staring dumbly at the keypad on the wall beside the elevator. "Oh—Stefan," he said somewhat guiltily. "I was just thinking about you."

Stefan responded with a very thin smile. "That is not necessarily a good thing, is it?"

It was a sharp observation, the kind Simone herself might have made. Ivo studied Stefan. Yes, the resemblance was definitely there, but even so . . . "What are you doing?" Ivo asked.

Stefan nodded at the elevator. "I wanted to— That is, I thought perhaps . . ." He hissed a breath between his teeth. "I am going mad being cooped up down here," he said. "I thought, if I could just go outside and breathe fresh air, see the sun, just for a little while . . ." He shrugged and slapped at the keypad. "Stupid of me, but I thought there would just be a simple UP button. And I could go outside."

Ivo regarded him intently. It was possible that Stefan was trying to flee or signal an accomplice. But it was equally possible that he simply wanted to go outside, exactly as he said. Perhaps it was even more likely; Stefan was not accustomed to living belowground.

Abruptly, he made up his mind. "That is exactly where I was going," Ivo said. "Come. Walk with me."

Stefan studied him in turn before nodding. "All right," he said.

The two of them, trailed by the two guards, stepped into the elevator and rode up. He could not help noticing that both of the men gave a friendly nod and smile to Stefan, and that pleased him.

The elevator thumped to a stop, and they trooped out onto the island. The sky was a brilliant blue, decorated with puffy clouds and a scattering of birds, and the sun was warm on their faces. It was a picture postcard day, and they stood for a moment, blinking against the light and savoring the fresh air, with its faintly salty tang.

Ivo put a hand on Stefan's elbow. "Come," he said, even attempting a smile, which did not come naturally to his face. "Let's enjoy this

215

weather while it lasts. Which," he added as they began to walk around the lighthouse, "will almost certainly not be long. The only thing predictable about Baltic weather is that it is unpredictable."

Stefan laughed, a one-syllable amusement. "A day like this, though, is worth many bad ones."

"Yes," Ivo said. "Yes it is."

They walked for a minute in companionable silence. "You seem to be adjusting—seem to be fitting in well," Ivo said.

Stefan shrugged. "I am here," he said. "Wherever I may find myself, there is no point in being miserable, and so I try to enjoy it."

"That is a very good philosophy," Ivo said. "I wish I could do it. I would have saved myself a great deal of unhappiness."

"Well," Stefan said, "I don't know exactly what you do—Mother would never say. Of course, I was very young. But I know it is something that is . . . clandestine? And very, very serious, yes?"

Ivo nodded briefly. "You could say that."

"Yes. But my point is just this: If you live in a cave, eventually you become a caveman."

Ivo blinked. "I . . . I take your meaning," he said. "I suppose that is true."

"When is the last time you have done something for no reason except that you wanted to, just to have fun?"

Ivo snorted, a short and bitter sound. "Nineteen eighty-two," he said. "I rode a bicycle down to Amsterdam, just to see the tulips bloom."

Stefan snickered. "And perhaps to sample a little cannabis?"

"What? No!" Ivo said. But Stefan continued to look at him with a raised eyebrow and a half smirk, until finally he laughed. "Well," he said. "Perhaps a little."

"Of course," Stefan said. "But this was so long ago—how can you live without some kind of— I mean, it's like trying to live without breathing. Sooner or later, you just . . . burst."

Ivo sighed. "Yes," he said. "Actually, I may be bursting now."

Stefan took him by the arm and turned him so they were face-to-face. "Is there something wrong?" he asked; quite anxiously, Ivo noted. "Your health, or—"

"No, no, nothing like that. I'm sure it's nothing."

"But it is *something*, or you wouldn't say it isn't," Stefan said.

"Well," Ivo said. He smiled and gently lifted Stefan's hand from his arm. "I guess it is something. But it's not serious. Just stomach pains." And he resumed walking.

Stefan caught up quickly. "How long have you been having these pains?" he asked.

"Stefan, don't trouble yourself with this."

"But that is— I mean, I have just located you, after wondering my whole life. And if I were to lose you now, I don't—" He broke off. "I'm sorry," he said. "I shouldn't even talk like this, 'losing you,' when it's not even . . ."

"I know what you mean," Ivo said. "There are many unanswered questions. For both of us."

"I know you have men checking my story," Stefan said. He held up a hand. "No, it's all right, I understand. The whole thing sounds impossible. But . . ."

The silence was heavier this time, and it lasted for several minutes. They were halfway around the lighthouse now, on the side that faced the open water, and Stefan paused and stared out to sea. "*Merde*," he said. "It is a beautiful day. And I get so very serious, when I have just been lecturing you on the hazards of being serious." He laughed. "Fuck it!" he cried. "This is what matters!" He waved his arms to take in the water, the sky.

217

Ivo stood beside Stefan, and he had to smile. "Perhaps so," he said. The heaviness lifted, and they stood there for a few minutes, doing nothing more than enjoying the sunshine, the wind, and the waves.

Stefan broke the silence. "Are there fish?" he asked. "Here, in the water?"

"Well," Ivo said, "I am led to believe that the water is where they are often found. Unless on a platter."

"Yes," Stefan said, smiling at him. "And I am interested in relocating them, from water to platter. Could I try to catch them sometimes? Here, on the shore?"

"I don't see why not," Ivo said. "I believe Gregor has some equipment you could use."

"And I should call you every time? So you can open the elevator?"

Perhaps he was feeling a bond with Stefan. Perhaps it was just the beauty of the day. Whatever the case, Ivo gave in to impulse and said, "Nonsense. I will give you the code. Come fishing whenever you like."

Stefan looked up at the sky, then down to the water. "I would like that," he said.

CHAPTER
36

Grisha was becoming obsessed.

It was not normally in his nature to fixate on a problem to the exclusion of other matters. But in this case, no one else seemed to see it as a problem. That meant no one else would see the danger until it was too late—danger that Grisha was certain was coming. And so he felt compelled to see it ahead of time and stop it dead.

He had been watching Stefan for two weeks now, sometimes openly, more often covertly, as the *komandir* had asked. He had not yet seen Stefan do anything that was clearly suspicious—at least not clearly enough for Grisha to use it as proof that Stefan was up to something. But he knew that sooner or later, Stefan would reveal his true colors, and when he did, Grisha would be there to see it and pounce.

So it was no coincidence that he saw Stefan heading for the elevator to the surface, and when he did, Grisha went to meet him. He arrived as Stefan was punching in the code to summon the elevator.

"What are you doing?" he demanded.

JEFF LINDSAY

Surprised by the sudden voice behind him, Stefan jerked around to face Grisha. "*Merde*, you startled me," he said.

"I said, what are you doing?" Grisha repeated.

Stefan shook his head in mock wonder. "I am going up to catch a fish," he said, holding up the fishing tackle in his hand. "See?"

"And that?" said Grisha, nodding at a shovel in Stefan's other hand. "Are you looking for fish in the dirt?"

Stefan shook his head. "I see you don't know anything about fishing," he said. "Let me explain. To catch a fish, you must persuade them to bite the hook." He held up the rod again and nodded at the hook. "See? With me so far?" He raised his eyebrows. Grisha said nothing. "Well, a fish will not bite a hook if he knows it is a hook. So we fishermen like to put something on the hook, something that will disguise it and at the same time seduce the fish." He lowered his voice, as if imparting a great secret. "Food works best," he said confidingly. "But fish do not eat the same things we do. Many of them like to eat worms, which we do not. Or, at least, I do not. Perhaps you . . . ? No? Well. I can see you are impatient. So I will skip ahead and tell you that the shovel is so I can dig in the dirt and find worms, which I will then put on the hook and hope the fish will bite. All right?"

Grisha's face had not changed during Stefan's mocking speech. But his voice was noticeably colder. "What kind of fish do you think you'll catch with worms?"

"Mostly sea trout and perch," he said. "Would you like me to catch one for you? They're delicious—and very good brain food."

Grisha said nothing. For a long moment Stefan looked back silently. Finally, though, he shook his head and sighed. "What is it, Grisha? Why are you always jumping out at me, everywhere I go? What have I done?"

"Nothing yet," Grisha said.

220

"Then what is it you imagine I will do? And with a shovel and a fishing rod, at that? Did you think I would catch explosive fish? What?"

Grisha took a step forward so that he was much too close to Stefan. "I don't know what you will do," he said. "But I know you will do something. And when you do . . . I will be there." He held Stefan's gaze for a long moment. Then he turned abruptly and walked away.

Stefan watched him go. Then he shook his head and turned back to the elevator's keypad and punched in the code. The elevator arrived, and he stepped in and rode it to the surface.

He stepped outside into a day with bright sun and a parade of thick clouds that pushed in front of it and then scudded away. A blustery wind blew in frequent gusts, kicking up whitecaps on the water. Stefan paused for a moment to take it all in and then proceeded to the spot he'd chosen for fishing, at a point on the shore where the bottom dropped abruptly, creating the kind of deep pool that fish like.

He put his gear down beside a large rock and began to dig in the soft earth beside it, on the side closest to the water. He lifted up a shovel full of dirt, then another and another. He dumped it, and sifted through it, looking for worms. Soon he had several, and he tossed them into a cup. He shoveled the dirt back into the hole he'd made and put down the shovel. He sorted through the worms in the cup, selected one, and began to fish.

What is he doing now?"

The voice was only two inches from Andrei's ear, and he jumped. He hadn't known that anybody was behind him as he sat at the security console. But somebody was, and it was Grisha, which was a little frightening, even though they had known each other for many years. Those years did not make a difference; you treated Grisha with respect. No other option ever occurred to Andrei, nor to any other member of the Balodis team.

"There, number four," Grisha said, jabbing a finger at the #4 monitor.

"He is just sitting," Andrei said, in answer to Grisha's demand. "He is fishing."

Grisha grunted, a single syllable that somehow conveyed doubt and menace at the same time. "Has anything else happened? Anything at all?"

"Uh, that plane went over again. You know, the American spy plane?"

Grisha was instantly more intense. "When was this?"

"That was, ah—twenty-six minutes ago," Andrei said, very glad he'd written it down.

"What did he do when the plane came?"

"Nothing, nothing at all. He just sat. That is, he looked up, but nothing more," Andrei said.

"And that's it? He didn't wave or signal? Nothing at all?"

Andrei almost said, *Nothing that I noticed.* But this was Grisha. Andrei knew that such a response would make Grisha angry, and he would demand to know how he could be sure nothing happened that he did not notice. Andrei was acquainted with Grisha's anger, and he never again wanted to renew that acquaintance. So instead, Andrei said, "Nothing else. He cast the line out when he got there, and since then he just sits and waits."

"Waits," Grisha said.

"For a fish to bite, Grisha," Andrei said. "As I said, he is *fishing.*"

Grisha made no response at all, and for a moment, Andrei was afraid he'd said too much. But Grisha only narrowed his eyes, stood up straight, and said, "Tell me if anything happens. Anything at all, understand?"

"Yes, of course," Andrei said. Grisha stalked off, and Andrei took a deep breath of relief. It was impossible to tell what might set off Grisha's temper, which could have sudden and painful consequences. But Andrei was in the clear, and he returned to his task, watching the several monitors that switched from camera to camera around the perimeter, staying ten seconds with each before clicking to the next. But because Grisha had shown an interest in the feed from one particular camera, Andrei punched in a new command, rerouting the other cameras on Screen #4 to Screen #3 and leaving #4 fixed on this one target.

Briefly, Andrei wondered why the scene was so important. But it didn't matter. If Grisha wanted him to watch it, he would watch it, no matter how dull.

But he did hope that at least Stefan would catch a fish, if only to break the monotony.

CHAPTER
37

Running an espionage network, whether for a government or for yourself, is not as romantic and interesting as it might sound. It requires a great deal of routine paperwork, usually having to do with money. An informant wants more of it, a source wants to be reimbursed for questionable expenses, a client thinks they paid too much. All routine, and all irritating.

So Ivo Balodis was busy. He was in the middle of a dispute involving payment with an informant, highly placed in the Second Department, the Chinese military intelligence agency. This informant had asked to be paid in cryptocurrency, and Ivo had complied. But between the time of the request and the payment, the cryptocurrency had lost value. The informant wanted a further payment to bring his total up to the original price.

This informant was a valued and reliable source—but Ivo thought the request was ridiculous. Anyone who wanted payment in cryptocurrency should understand the risk. He didn't want to pay what he thought was a spurious claim, but he also did not want to offend the source. The Chinese were most likely to be the high bidders in the auction for the prize item in his vault right now.

And so he was not in the best of moods when he looked up and saw Grisha in the office doorway. "What is it?" he said.

"Ivan has reported," Grisha said.

Ivo frowned. "Ivan—oh, he was off on a motorcycle trip, yes?"

"He was in France," Grisha said. "Checking Stefan's story."

"Yes, that's right, the official paper trail. And he has done so?"

"Yes," Grisha said.

"Excellent. And what did he find?"

Grisha frowned. "The birth certificate appears to be genuine. Certificate of adoption matches what he told us. The aunt, Gabrielle Laurent, was real. She died four years ago." He looked up at Ivo, who motioned for him to go on. He did. "A driver's license exists, for Stefan Laurent. It seems authentic. Two years ago he received a warning for impaired driving."

"That's all of it?"

"Yes."

"Well, good. Then that's settled," Ivo said. He felt a small glow of happiness. Stefan was not lying. He had a son.

Grisha shrugged. "Perhaps."

"If the official record matches his story, he is telling the truth," Ivo said. "It's time to put all this behind us and get on with business."

Grisha didn't move.

Ivo sighed. "What is it now, Grisha?"

"I want Ivan to check the logbook at the prison. To see if any such person visited Simone."

Ivo gritted his teeth. "Why?" he said.

"Records can be forged," he said.

225

Ivo felt his patience eroding. He caught it just in time and dragged it back. "Yes, Grisha, I suppose they can. Are you suggesting that these records were forged?"

"Yes."

"Because?"

He shook his head, once. "It doesn't make sense otherwise."

"Which part doesn't make sense? That Stefan would have authentic documentation? Or that I might be capable of fathering a son?"

"He is not your son."

"The records say he is. I believe them, and I believe him."

"You believe him because you want to believe him," Grisha said. "He counted on you doing just that."

"So Stefan is a brilliant forger, a master of disguise, and who knows what else—and he has dedicated himself to making a fool of me? That makes more sense to you?"

"Yes."

"For the love of God, Grisha! He would have to be some kind of superman to do all those things! Such people do not exist!"

"There are a few of them," Grisha said.

Ivo stood up abruptly, knocking his chair over backward. "No more!" he shouted. "Enough! You will stop this bullshit now! That's an order!"

"Ivo—"

"No! No more! Get out!" he shouted, jabbing his finger at the office door.

Grisha said nothing, merely looked at Ivo for a moment. Then he turned and left the office.

Ivo remained standing, looking after Grisha. The man was obsessed with proving that Stefan was up to something—but what? There was no possible motive for anyone to go to all the trouble it would take. And for what possible reward? Everything of value was either in his head or in his vault, and getting into either without him was simply impossible. Was Grisha really suspicious? Or was he jealous, afraid that Stefan would get more of Ivo's attention? It didn't matter—his attitude was infuriating, and—

A very sharp spasm of pain shot through his stomach, and Ivo bent over for a moment, eyes closed. The pain was worse than ever, but it passed; it always passed eventually. But this time, it seemed to dig deeper and last longer. Was it getting worse? Or was it just his anger?

Never mind. It passed. Ivo straightened and took a deep breath. He realized he was shaking, either from pain or anger, and he sank back into his chair.

He is my son, he said to himself. *Stefan is my son—and Simone's.* And then he said it out loud. "He is my son."

He said it with conviction and authority. It still sounded hollow, as though he was trying to convince himself, and he closed his eyes. *My son*, he thought. *Stefan is my son.*

But he couldn't help thinking, *But is he really?*

CHAPTER
38

Monique was concentrating fiercely on her drawing. It was nearly finished, but it wasn't quite right, not yet. None of them were quite right. She was also endlessly repeating, "Appropriate. Inappropriate. Appropriate. Inappropriate," in a low voice as she worked. But she didn't really hear herself. She just kept drawing, but something was missing, and she didn't know what. It had been frustrating, and that was now about to boil over into rage. What was it? What part of the face was she failing to remember? If she could only remember what—

A hand reached down and plucked at the notebook. Monique scrabbled frantically to hang on to it, but the hand was too quick. Monique looked up angrily to the face that hand belonged to, and froze.

Of course it was Dr. Arnsdale. Who else could it be? No one other than the doctor came into her room. Usually Monique heard footsteps approaching, and then the lock turning, and she was prepared when Dr. Arnsdale entered. But this time, she had been lost in trying to get the drawing right. She'd been concentrating furiously, and that had taken her far away from her room, to a place where she hadn't heard the door open, and so she hadn't noticed Dr. Arnsdale until too late.

"Well," the doctor said. "You've been busy, haven't you?" She flipped open the notebook. "Just drawings? Can't remember all the letters? Mm-hmm." Dr. Arnsdale held the drawing up to the light and examined it. Then she flipped to the next page, and the next. "You keep drawing that face," Dr. Arnsdale said. "The same face, over and over again." She frowned, like she was offended at something, and added, "Why?"

"Inappropriate," Monique said.

"Who is it?"

Monique shrugged. "Appropriate," she said.

"Really. A boyfriend?"

Monique concentrated very hard for a moment. "Friend," she said. She felt herself begin to shake.

"Does he have a name?"

Monique frowned. "Yes. But, but—"

"But you can't remember it?"

Feeling oddly ashamed, Monique hung her head and then began to laugh. She stopped immediately and said, "Appropriate. Inappropriate."

"Well, that's what I expected," the doctor said. "I told them you'd had too much brain damage, but they said try anyway. I said this isn't really my area, but they didn't care, and since I lost my license to practice, I needed a job. And when the wolf is at the door, you take what there is. So fine." She tossed the notebook down on the bed beside Monique. "Do what you can," she said. "Try to remember a couple of words, all right?"

Again without waiting for an answer, Dr. Arnsdale whirled around and left the room. Monique heard the lock click and she was alone again. But she didn't move for a couple of minutes. She just sat with her head down and her fists clenched, letting the anger run through her veins. Why did the doctor treat her like that? Saying all those awful things right in front of her. Like she was just some kind of *thing*, a piece of furniture that couldn't hear or understand? "Too much brain damage," which she kept saying. And then other things that made no sense at all, like losing her license and the wolf at the door and—

For a minute, Monique couldn't breathe. Because she had remembered something. Something very important.

"Wolf." That word was connected to home, like "New York." It was part of—of the face!

Excited now, Monique picked up the notebook. She studied the drawing she'd just been working on. It was a face, and even though it was starting to look right, it was still a man's face. And "Wolf" was an animal, a big wild dog. Why did it feel like that word went with the face? Her lips moved, forming the word "wolf" over and over. And it fit. The word went with the face. But how? She thought about it as hard as she could, and although she became even more certain that she was right, she could not come at the meaning.

But it didn't matter. She had a place to start. It would help, and she would remember. Sooner or later, she would remember. Because now she had the key to everything.

She bent back over and began a new drawing: the long face, the pointed ears, sharp teeth . . .

CHAPTER
39

vo Balodis was restless. There was a great deal happening right now, most of it vital, but he couldn't focus on any of it. For his entire career, both during the Cold War and then after, when he went into business for himself, he had been hugely successful, largely because he was unaffected by emotions and able to avoid distractions. Now, though, when the stakes were higher than ever, he could not. His attention was being pulled away from all that was important, and he felt the tug of strange and powerful new emotions.

He pushed aside the pile of reports on the desk in front of him and rubbed his eyes. *It's too much*, he thought. *It's all just too much.* And although he did not name the "it," he didn't have to.

Stefan.

The records are real, he thought. *I have a son.*

And yet . . .

He had spent his life in a world where no one was what they seemed, every fact was suspect, nothing was ever what it claimed to be. For something like this to be true—something that he devoutly wished *was* true—his logical brain cried out that it had to be a lie. He needed more proof, something incontrovertible.

But he doubted he would ever find it. Either he could accept the "facts"—the paper records from France, the resemblance Stefan bore to Simone—and acknowledge that Stefan was his son, or else . . .

He pushed back from the desk and abruptly stood up. "Enough," he said aloud. He strode out of the office and down the hall with no clear destination in mind. He simply had to move around for a few minutes, and hopefully get the blood flowing back into his brain. Because this was stupid, counterproductive, self-destructive.

He turned the corner and jerked to a halt. Ten feet in front of him, Stefan was standing, his body jerking spasmodically. For a moment, Ivo thought the boy was having some kind of fit. Then he saw the white wires hanging from Stefan's ears: earbuds. He was listening to music, dancing in a way that Ivo recognized—but that kind of dancing went with music from a long time ago. Ivo watched him, wondering if it was possible.

As if he felt himself watched, Stefan suddenly snapped his head up. He saw Ivo and jerked the earbuds from his ears, letting them dangle onto his chest.

"What are you listening to?" Ivo said.

Stefan swallowed uneasily and shifted his weight from one foot to the other, like a little boy caught stealing cookies. "Some music," he said.

Ivo nodded. "That was my first guess," he said. "What is it?"

"The music? Oh, it's just, I don't— You wouldn't like it."

"You can't know what I like," Ivo said.

"Oh, but this— No, it's heavy metal. Very old metal. Most people hate it. It's, you know. Loud and annoying."

Ivo grabbed the right earbud and put it in his ear. He frowned, and then his face lit up with delighted surprise.

"It's Ratt!" he exclaimed. "'Lay It Down'! I haven't heard this in years!"

He nodded at Stefan, who was gaping at him, astonished.

"That's not— You couldn't possibly—"

"Stefan," Ivo said. "That first album—*Out of the Cellar*, of course—it came out in—I think it was 1984? I'm the one who should be amazed that *you've* heard of Ratt." Stefan continued to gape, and Ivo smiled. "I also really liked Helstar and Saigon Kick. But you've probably never heard of them, have you?"

Stefan just shook his head dumbly.

"Well, then," Ivo said with a slight edge of mocking satisfaction. He dropped the earbud back on Stefan's chest. "There is much I can teach you. Stop shaking your head like that, you'll hurt your neck."

Stefan's head jerked to a stop. "I really can't believe it," he said. "Nobody I know listens to this music."

"You don't know enough old people," Ivo said. "Like me."

"But of all the things to have in common," Stefan said.

"It's quite odd, isn't it?"

"It's absurd!" Stefan said. "But wait—what about Holocaust, and Blitzkrieg—"

"And Korpse, Raven, Diamond Head," Ivo added.

"I've never heard of Diamond Head," Stefan said. "But Raven is great!"

When a person has an obscure passion, finding someone who shares it can feel like discovering a best friend you didn't know you had, and for a long moment they beamed at each other, ludicrously pleased to share this bond. It was nearly twenty seconds before the look turned awkward and Stefan dropped his eyes to the floor.

Ivo kept looking at Stefan, but the tone of his gaze changed. *Could this be the further evidence I wanted?* he thought. *Is it possible that a taste for a specific kind of music can be genetic? That this is really my son?* He stared at Stefan, his head churning, ready to believe, *wanting* to believe. But caution returned and his gaze turned hard and harsh. So many thoughts came at him that he couldn't grasp one singly, and finally he shook his head.

"What do you want, Stefan?" Ivo blurted abruptly. Stefan jerked his head back up and met Ivo's eyes.

"Want?" he said.

"Yes," Ivo said, and he was very cold now. "What do you want? From me? Why did you come here?"

Stefan flushed, whether from embarrassment or guilt, it was impossible to say. "I wanted to find my father," he said. "And I thought..." He looked away, and then went on in a rush: "You go your whole life knowing that somewhere is a man who gave you life, gave you half your DNA, and not knowing who that is, who the stranger is that made your hair brown, or your hands the size they are, and then— then to have a chance to meet him? Meet the man who— I know," he said, raising a hand to cut off an objection that Ivo was not making. "There is a very good chance that you are not that man, and if that turns out to be the case, you will kill me. But"—he shrugged—"at a certain point, you decide the gamble is worth it." And he gave Ivo a look of pained uncertainty. "Can you understand that? At all?"

"Yes," Ivo said. His voice sounded odd, and he cleared his throat. "Yes, I understand," he said.

"Well, then," Stefan said. "And so, here I am."

"Here you are," Ivo murmured.

Stefan shrugged. "And now what?" he said.

Ivo shook his head. "That is the question," he said. He had no answer to that question. But even though it made no sense at all, the love for heavy metal he shared with Stefan seemed nearly conclusive. And deep inside, pushing its way upward like a flower shoving up through rocky soil, was the growing conviction that Stefan really was his son.

It's the same thing, every time, for a week now, Grisha," Andrei said. He nodded at the monitor screen. "He digs, sorts through the dirt and gets a few worms. And then he fills in the hole and sits down to fish." Andrei shrugged. "Nothing else, nothing changes."

Grisha frowned at the screen, as if looking for some new and telling detail. There were none to see. "That's it," he said accusingly. "He does nothing else, and nothing else happens."

"He catches fish sometimes," Andrei said. Grisha glared at him. "And the American plane went over again, twice, but Stefan didn't even look up."

Grisha looked at the screen a minute longer while Andrei worked very hard not to squirm from the great discomfort he was feeling. Finally, Grisha straightened. "Keep watching," he said, and he turned and left.

Andrei kept watching, and it went the same way, exactly the same, every day. Stefan would go to the same spot by the big rock, dig a hole, remove worms, fill in the hole again. Then he sat and fished.

Sometimes he caught a fish, even two. But what could this possibly matter? Watch a young man go fishing every day? It was ludicrous.

But Grisha had told him to keep watching. He did, but he watched with a little less focus every time. After all, what did Grisha expect to happen? Because very clearly, whatever it was, it was not going to happen.

And so at the end of the second week, he did not notice when something did, in fact, happen.

Two somethings, in fact.

First, the American plane went over again. That was not really significant. It had been going over at irregular intervals for months. The Americans wanted the *komandir*'s flash drive, too. Anyone who knew about the auction would kill to get it. But the Americans were most persistent and obvious. Their surveillance had been very tight, very thorough, but no real bother. Andrei glanced at the screen to be certain that Stefan was not signaling the plane. He wasn't. Of course he wasn't. He didn't even look up. Andrei shook his head. Seriously, Grisha had become a little crazy on the subject of Stefan. Why would he signal the American plane? What did Grisha think the plane would do in response?

Andrei looked away, and so he missed the first significant something.

Just before it passed over the lighthouse, the plane dropped a package that hit the water fifty meters from the shore, where Stefan sat fishing.

Andrei missed the second something, too.

When Stefan's image on the screen began to move, Andrei glanced again. He looked long enough to register that the movement was Stefan reeling in his fishing line. "Huh, good for him," Andrei said. "He caught one." And then he went back to checking the other screens.

CHAPTER

40

Chase Prescott was in a very bad mood. That was not unusual for him, but this time it was worse and lasting longer. He told himself he had plenty of reasons to justify the black cloud he had surrounded himself with, but he knew that most of them were excuses, not reasons. In reality, he knew it all came down to one cause.

Riley Wolfe.

In the first place, he had no idea what the thief was really up to, and that was unacceptable. Additionally, he knew he did not, could not, control Wolfe, and he hated that. He always needed to be in control of his operations, and now more than ever. This was far and away the most important operation of his life, and if it failed . . . But no, it couldn't fail, that was unthinkable. Because if it did—death and dishonor. At best, prison for the rest of his life. And it would not be one of the so-called country club prisons, either. Treasonous spies didn't get that option.

And that was what he was. Treasonous. A traitor to his country, his family, the Agency—he knew that well. Had known it when he made the decision to recover the flash drive, make himself the auction's seller, and offload it to the highest bidder.

Since that moment five and a half years ago, he had known that when the time was right, he would sell out his country in a heartbeat and disappear. For five years now he had taken every opportunity that arose to grab any money that came his way, and for five years his well-hidden offshore savings had grown. He grabbed with both hands and got away with it. The Agency always looked the other way at extracurricular fund-raising. It was the only way agents could fund the more important black ops.

And as they continued to look away, Prescott grew increasingly reckless. He took more and more—but it was never enough to vanish into the life he wanted, the life he *deserved*, goddamn it! He had grown up deserving that opulent retirement, expecting it as a matter of course.

And then his father had died and everything changed.

He had not spoken to the old man for years beyond an occasional quick phone call to say happy birthday or merry Christmas. Old Benson Prescott had made it clear that he detested what Chase had done with his life. But so what? He didn't need his father's approval. As the only son, he would inherit a great deal of money when Benson died, and that was as certain as the sun rising in the east. His father hung on for an indecent number of years, up into his nineties, but Chase waited. Sooner or later, the biological inevitability would occur, and when it did, Chase would be very wealthy. He could retire in luxury after a long and dirty career.

Then came the news that Benson Prescott had finally had the good grace to die. Chase put on proper mourning attire for the funeral and kept it on for the reading of the will. There was no doubt at all about what the will would decree; Chase would inherit. But appearances are important, and Chase kept on his somber clothing and sober face as the lawyer went through all the boring preliminaries and legal necessities. He waited patiently through a long series of pointless bequests to cousins, charities, and museums.

The lawyer finally came to the important part. "'And to my only son, Chase Melchior Prescott, I leave the summer house on Saco Bay—and nothing else.'"

At first Chase had been certain he'd misheard. Or perhaps it was one of the old man's stupid non-funny jokes. It had to be some kind of mistake.

It wasn't. The rest of the will made that quite clear. Chase was disinherited. The lawyer made it even more clear. "Your father was bitterly disappointed in the way you threw away your life." He raised a hand to head off objections. "His words, not mine. He never forgave you for your failure to follow in his footsteps, and as he grew older, the resentment grew. I assure you he was of sound mind, though. We have certificates from three eminent psychologists attesting to the fact, because he thought you would initiate a legal battle. You see, he wasn't going to leave you anything," the lawyer said with a shrug. "But I advised him that doing so might provide grounds for a suit to overturn the provision of the will. This way, it becomes much more difficult." He gave Chase a thin-lipped smile. "I will not tell you this is airtight, Mr. Prescott. You are free to contest the will. But I promise you it will take years and a great deal of money, and in the end, this will stand exactly as your father wished."

Chase actually had consulted a lawyer, and he had been told exactly the same thing. The will would stand, and he was out of luck. And Chase Prescott, born of wealth and privilege, had nothing but a meager government salary and an even skimpier pension.

It burned at him. He had never thought about wealth before; it was a basic assumption, like not wondering if the atmosphere was breathable. Of course it was, and of course Chase would always have money.

And now he didn't, all because he had chosen to serve his country. The country did not shower him with gratitude, either. It expected him to give a lifetime of dangerous, exhausting, difficult, often fatal work, and at the end get no more than a clap on the back and a polite thank-you.

The devotion to his country that had started him on this path soured very quickly. He began to resent the nation that would ask such a total sacrifice for so paltry a recompense. And if that was their attitude, he would bloody well take compensation everywhere he found it.

He did, but it went too slowly. He was a professional, and he knew how to vanish into disguised luxury, but he also knew it took a great deal of money, and that remained elusive.

Until the flash drive came along.

Chase knew how important it was to recover it by the amount of sheer terror its loss generated in the upper ranks of the Agency. After a little digging, he found out what it was—no specifics, but enough generalities to make him salivate. This was it, his ticket to a safe and secure disappearance.

He made his plan carefully, meticulously, and he was certain it would work if he could find the right man and the means to control him. He had found Wolfe, known immediately that he was the one, and easy enough to control with the two hostages. But with no idea what Wolfe was doing, Prescott had lost control. All his suspicion and mistrust came to the surface. This *had* to work, and it all depended on one totally undependable element.

Riley Wolfe . . .

CHAPTER
41

S tefan awoke to the sound of gunfire. Before he was even conscious
or aware of what he was doing, he rolled onto the floor and crawled
to the desk for shelter. But before he could hunker down under it,
the door opened. For a moment, Ivo stood there, framed in the doorway and backlit, holding a wicked-looking pistol in one hand. "Stefan!" he called in an urgent whisper.

"Here," Stefan said from the floor beside the desk. "What is
happening?"

Without answering, Ivo hurried across the room and grabbed his
arm. "Quickly," Ivo said. "Come with me."

Stefan stared and blinked, looking up at Ivo, who pulled at his arm.

"Quickly!" Ivo said. "We are in danger."

Stefan stood and fumbled on a shirt and said, "What danger—
what is happening?"

"We are under attack," Ivo said. "Come!"

Ivo strode out of the room and Stefan hurried after him. "Where are we going?" he asked.

"A safe place," Ivo said. "This way, quickly!"

Stefan hurried along after Ivo, following him to the main corridor, and then down the hallway toward the silo. At the lip of the silo, Ivo paused, and Stefan finally caught up. "Why is this safe?" he said. "This is in the open, by the main entrance—"

"Hush," Ivo said. He fumbled in his pocket and pulled out a small black box. It looked like a remote control for something, Stefan thought. But for what?

The question was answered before he could even ask it. Ivo pointed the box down and held it there for a moment. Almost immediately, Stefan heard a new sound—the well-greased whispering of some kind of machine. A few seconds later, a metallic platform appeared in the shaft, moving upward. It went past them, and a moment after that, it became apparent that the platform was the top of an elevator cage. It clicked to a halt even with the walkway where they stood. Ivo reached for a latch on the railing and swung it upward. "Get in," he said. "Hurry."

Stefan scrambled into the car and Ivo followed, pushing the button on the black box as he did, and the car went quickly and smoothly down the side of the silo. Stefan watched the sides of the launch tube go by. It seemed to be covered by some kind of metal mesh, and he reached a hand toward it.

Ivo slapped his hand away. "Do not touch anything!" he said. "The walls here are electrified with a lethal voltage." He shook his head. "And many other things that will kill you."

"Oh," Stefan said. "But—why?"

The car bumped gently to a stop at the bottom. "I will show you," Ivo said. "Come."

Stefan followed as Ivo hurried away from the car and toward an area of darkness on the left side, apparently a tunnel or hallway. As Stefan followed Ivo, he saw that there was, in fact, a short hallway, hidden by the shadows. Ivo flipped a switch on the wall, and a muted light came on, revealing that about five meters ahead, the hall ended at a massive steel door.

"There. You see?" Ivo said as he arrived at the door.

"What is it? A safe? Why do you need a safe?"

"My paintings," Ivo said, waving his pistol vaguely. He turned the light off again so the two of them were in semidarkness. "Here, you are in my field of fire. Stand out of the way."

"Field of— Oh! Yes," Stefan said. He glanced back toward the lift. From here, they could see the lift and most of the bottom of the shaft, which was still lighted. Ivo would have a clear field of fire, and he'd be invisible to anyone who managed to get past his guards and down the shaft. Stefan moved to the side, looking curiously at the vault's door. "It looks very solid."

"It is state-of-the-art. Perhaps better," Ivo said.

"Better," Stefan said. He ran a hand over the metal of the door, then turned back around to watch with Ivo. "Who is attacking us?"

Ivo waved vaguely. "I have many enemies," he said.

"Oh . . . So you don't know which . . . ?"

"They are probably Russian," Ivo said.

"Russian?!" Stefan exclaimed. "But I thought you—and this place . . ."

"I am Lithuanian," he said. "I worked for the Soviet Union. But I have no love for the thugs and criminals who rule Russia now."

"And so that's why—but an attack, with guns and—Why would they do that?"

Ivo shrugged without taking his eyes away from his field of fire.

"As I said, I have secrets. Things other people want. Other governments. Especially Russia." He glanced quickly at Stefan, then away. "Perhaps I can tell you about them, if—that is . . ." He broke off, frowning, as a flurry of shots broke out quite near. The shots died away, and all was still. "There, you see?" He turned quickly and flashed a small smile. "No one ever gets this far."

"So far," Stefan said.

"Yes, of course."

The two lapsed into silence. Above them, very faintly, they still heard an occasional gunshot, but little else. Stefan watched Ivo, who was watching the lift area with fierce concentration. Several shots echoed down the missile shaft. Ivo tensed, then bent at the waist slightly and grimaced as if in pain. But he quickly straightened up. There was another cluster of shots, and then, just visible to them in the dimness, a body sailed down the shaft to land with a wet thud.

But the man was not dead. He gave a soft moan, and Ivo walked to the man and knelt. He tilted his head over as the man said something Stefan couldn't hear. Then Ivo stood, fired a single shot into the man's head, and strolled back to Stefan. "Russian," he said. "I thought so."

Wide-eyed, Stefan gaped at Ivo, who shrugged. "Sometimes they make it this far, but only like that." He pointed at the dead body and gave Stefan an odd half smile that was meant to be reassuring. There was another cluster of shots, and Ivo jerked his head back around to focus on the area now occupied by the corpse. A half-audible yell, a burst of automatic fire, and then a pause.

"Why did you bring me down here?" Stefan asked abruptly.

Ivo frowned. "What's that?"

"Why bring me? I am grateful to be safe, but—why?"

For a moment, Ivo focused entirely on Stefan. "Why—Stefan, it is because you . . . If you are—" There were shouts and shots above, very

244

near, and Ivo looked away from Stefan, without finishing his sentence. But then they heard three single shots, spaced evenly, and he relaxed visibly.

There was a pause of several minutes in the firing. Stefan broke the silence at last. "What kind of paintings?" he asked.

"What?"

"You said paintings. In the safe," Stefan said.

"It's a vault, not a safe," Ivo said.

"Yes, of course. What kind of paintings?"

"Icons," Ivo said absently. "Russian Orthodox icons."

"Huh," Stefan said. "You mean the kind of thing with those odd stick figures and lots of gold paint? Why would you put them in a safe—in a *vault*," he corrected himself.

"These are very different, special," Ivo said. "They are remarkably beautiful. Very valuable, too," he added, as if that was not really important.

"Is that why these people are attacking?" Stefan said. "To get your paintings, your icons?"

Ivo shook his head. "I have other things, perhaps more valuable," he said. He glanced at Stefan. "Those things must remain secret. For now."

"But someone is willing to kill us all to get these secrets?"

"Yes, of course," Ivo said, as if this was patently obvious.

Stefan was silent. He heard a burst of automatic weapon fire, then silence. "What happens if we lose?"

Ivo smiled. "We will not," he said.

More silence followed, broken by a few isolated single shots, and Ivo again relaxed visibly. "Yes," he said. "So you see, it is over. And we did not lose."

"How can you tell?" Stefan said.

"The single shots," Ivo said. "My men are cleaning up."

"Cleaning up? What does—oh . . ." Stefan trailed off as he realized what Ivo meant. Cleaning up meant killing any survivors. "Will they, um, 'clean up' everyone?" he asked.

Ivo shrugged. "They will keep one alive. For now." He glanced at Stefan to see how he was taking this. "Grisha will question him." He shook his head with mock disapproval. "I think he actually enjoys that," he said. "But it is not pretty to see."

As Stefan was digesting this, he heard a crackle of static. Ivo reached into a pocket and pulled out a small radio. He pushed the button on the side. "*Da*," he said. Stefan heard a few words in Russian, and Ivo answered in the same language. Then he put the radio back in his pocket. "It is over," he said. He turned toward the shaft and said nothing for several moments. "Well," he said at last, "and here we are, just the two of us."

"Yes, I can see that," Stefan said.

Ivo opened his mouth, closed it, and then took a deep breath. "Stefan," he said, and his voice was very much more human and hesitant than it had been. "I have wanted a chance to . . ." He looked at Stefan, then away again. "You took a very great risk coming here with such an extraordinary claim," he said.

"I knew it was a gamble," Stefan said. "But I had to know. And I thought that, you know. If it was true, we would both know it."

"And the truth always wins out?" Ivo shook his head. "It never works that way. Not in the real world."

"Perhaps not," Stefan said.

"But in this case," Ivo said. He turned toward Stefan, who raised his hands, frightened. Ivo frowned, then looked down at his hands. He still held his pistol, and it was now pointed at Stefan. "Oh, I'm sorry," he said. Ivo tucked his pistol into a pocket. "That is quite the opposite of what I meant to say."

"Good," Stefan said. "I do not really want you to shoot me."

"No, of course not. And I do not want to shoot you. In fact, what I wanted to say . . . I have come to believe that you . . . That is—" He turned away again. "This is incredibly difficult," he said. He seemed to be shaking, and Stefan was amazed to see what looked like a tear roll down his cheek. "My God," he said softly. "I have not had this kind of feeling since . . ." He took a ragged breath and faced Stefan. "I will just say it." He took a step forward. "Stefan, I believe that you really are—"

Ivo froze suddenly and turned visibly pale. And then he lurched over and clutched his stomach with both hands. He looked at Stefan, gasping.

"What is it?" Stefan said. "What—Ivo, are you all right?"

Ivo gasped. "I . . . just . . ." Then he made an almost inaudible sound of strangled pain, gasped again, and fell over.

Stefan knelt quickly at Ivo's side. "Ivo? Ivo, answer me!"

But Ivo did not answer. Stefan felt for a pulse, found one. It was very rapid. Stefan nodded and looked behind him, toward the lift. Then he felt in Ivo's pocket and took out the little black box that controlled the lift. He stood, stuck the box into his own pocket, and then stooped again, grabbing Ivo's wrists and pulling him toward the lighted area at the bottom of the shaft where the lift waited.

Andrei Sidorov stepped into the hall and glanced toward the missile silo. Grisha had sent him to make a report on the action to the *komandir*. It had not lasted long, but the attack had been very well planned and executed, and there had been a point when it was not certain which way it would go. That had been some very hot action, but only for a minute or two. And now, it was over, and Grisha had sent Andrei on his way and gone to work on the lone survivor of the attacking force.

Secretly, Andrei was very glad to have this task—any task at all, in fact, that took him away from where Grisha was interrogating the survivor. "Interrogating" was perhaps a little mild for what was happening. Andrei shivered. He respected Grisha a great deal—who would not? The man had been a legend in the Spetsnaz. And Andrei had seen for himself that the stories about him were true. Like most of the others here at the silo, Andrei worked hard to be like him, as much as possible. But the things Grisha did to encourage a captive to talk—No. This was something Andrei could not imagine he would ever do. It turned his stomach just to watch.

So it was pleasant to have a legitimate excuse to get away from Grisha at work. He began walking toward the lift. Three bodies littered the hall in his path. They wore black paramilitary clothing with no identifying marks or patches, but they were Russian, there was really no doubt. One of them was still alive; he groaned and reached a bloody, imploring hand up at Andrei. "Please," he croaked. Andrei just stepped over him and continued toward the lift. The *komandir* should be coming up from the vault at any moment.

Sure enough, the car rose into sight, and Andrei hurried to meet it. But as it rose to the level of the walkway, he stumbled to a stop. Balodis was there, yes—but he lay on the floor of the lift, motionless, with Stefan standing anxiously over him.

"Help! Quickly!" Stefan called—in French. Andrei did not speak the language, but the meaning was clear, and he sprinted the last few meters, arriving as the lift came to a halt.

"What is it? What happened—is he shot?"

Stefan shook his head. "*Nyet Russki*," he said pointing to himself. Clumsy—but Andrei understood that it meant Stefan didn't speak Russian. Of course not—he had known that, but seeing Balodis lying there, apparently lifeless, had shocked him. Stefan gestured, clearly signing "Help me."

"What is it? What happened?" Andrei asked again as they pulled Balodis off the lift.

Stefan patted his stomach, then clutched it and mimed Balodis falling over.

"Ah, the stomach, yes," Andrei said. "Stop here," he added as they came even with the elevator that led up to the lighthouse. He grabbed his radio and spoke urgently for a moment. He nodded, signed off, and turned to Stefan. "They are coming," he said.

Stefan nodded. "*Hôpital*," he said, and as Andrei looked confused, he added, "Ospedale. Ah—*Krankenhaus!*"

"Ah," Andrei said. "Yes, I see. They will come, and Grisha will say what happens. You understand? Grisha?"

But Stefan shook his head urgently. "No! *Krankenhaus!*" And he unleashed a torrent of French that Andrei took to mean that this was an emergency, Balodis was very ill, only a hospital could help him—

"Please," Andrei said, holding up a hand. "It is not for us to decide. It must be Grisha's decision. Grisha—yes? Understand?"

Stefan took a ragged breath and ran a hand over his forehead. He seemed to be very upset. Perhaps there was something to it after all— perhaps he really was Balodis's son. That would explain his concern. But he simply nodded. "*Oui*," he said. "*Je comprends.*"

They stood in silence for a moment. Stefan put his hands in his pockets, frowned, pulled out the remote control for the lift. "Ah," he said. He pushed one of the buttons, and the lift descended to the bottom of the shaft. Then he shoved it back into his pocket. "Where are they? Why haven't they come?" he said.

Andrei made a patting gesture in the air. *Be patient.*

Only a minute later Grisha arrived, two other men trailing him. He hurried toward them until he came to the three fallen invaders. The one who had reached for Andrei reached for Grisha, too. He glanced down, drove a heel into the man's throat, and stepped over as the man made faint choking sounds and then stopped moving.

Grisha glanced at Balodis, then fixed his stare on Stefan. But Stefan shook his head. "Please," he said, and there was real pain in his voice. "He needs the hospital." He pointed at Balodis. "He is very ill—please help him."

Grisha knelt and felt for a pulse. Then he nodded and stood. "What happened?" he asked.

Andrei shook his head. "They were down below, at the vault?" he said. "And—in truth, I am not sure what happened. I don't speak French, and Stefan—" He nodded toward Stefan.

"Yes, I know, he doesn't speak Russian," Grisha said impatiently.

Andrei shrugged. "Well, in any case, Stefan brought him up. I think he is saying we must get Balodis to a hospital. He said '*kranken-haus.*' That's German for 'hospital'?"

"I know that, you idiot," Grisha said. "But why? Why would he want the hospital?"

"Ask him," Andrei said. "You speak French."

Grisha spun abruptly and took a step closer to Stefan. "What did you do?" he said.

"I—I brought him up," Stefan stammered. "He just—he clutched his stomach and fell over and I . . . I couldn't revive him, so I just, I brought him to get help." Grisha narrowed his eyes and said nothing.

"Grisha, please," Stefan said. "Whatever your feelings about me, Ivo needs help. You have to get him to a hospital, at once."

It was Andrei who broke the long silence. "Grisha, the *komandir* does seem very sick," Andrei said.

Grisha glanced at him, then at Balodis. At last he nodded. "Call Michail," he said. Then he knelt by Balodis again.

Andrei took a shaky breath, as if he was going to say something. But he changed his mind and reached for his radio. Grisha's order did, after all, make sense as a first step. Michail was their medic. He was very good with bullet or knife wounds, and even venereal disease, but he was a military medic, not a real doctor. There would be little he could do for something like this. But one did not question Grisha, not when he was clearly in a mood.

It did not take Michail long. He came down the elevator from above with his medical kit and hurried over. "What happened?" he said.

"Stefan says he grabbed at his stomach and fell over," Andrei said.

"Stomach. That again," Michail said. He went to his knees beside Balodis and checked him over quickly. When he was done, he shook his head and stood.

"Well?" Grisha demanded.

"This is far beyond me," Michail said. "Normally, I would say he should go to the hospital. But under our circumstance?" He shrugged. "I can't say, Grisha. I'm sorry, but I think it is for you to decide."

"How bad is he?" Grisha said.

"I can't say," Michail said. "He is unconscious and—that isn't good. There could be internal bleeding—I have no way to tell. But that would be very bad."

"Life-threatening?" Grisha said.

"Probably."

Grisha nodded. "Get a stretcher. We will carry him," he said to

Michail. Michail nodded and hurried away. Grisha turned again to Andrei. "Call Leonid. Tell him to take a squad and move two vehicles onto the causeway. We will take the *komandir* to the hospital. I will meet him there."

"You are going, too, Grisha?" Andrei asked, a little surprised.

"I think I must," Grisha said. "The *komandir* will be too vulnerable, an easy target in the hospital. He needs me there."

A moment later Michail returned, accompanied by two men carrying a stretcher. They quickly and carefully loaded Balodis onto it and began to carry him away. Stefan, still looking terribly worried, began to follow them.

Grisha put a hand on Stefan's chest and stopped him. "You are staying here," he said.

"But no—I should be with my—with Ivo!" Stefan protested.

Grisha gave his head a single small shake. It was somehow more definitely negative than a long speech. "You do not leave the island," he said. "You stay here."

"But that's— I need to—"

"No." He spoke that single syllable in a way that was impossible to argue with.

Mouth still moving, as if he was looking for an argument that didn't exist, Stefan took a step backward. Grisha looked at him a moment longer before turning his back and starting after the stretcher. "Andrei," he said. "You will be in charge while I am gone," he said.

"Yes, of course, certainly," Andrei said. "You will stay there, at the hospital? If they want to keep him overnight?"

Grisha turned and glanced briefly at Stefan. "Of course," Grisha said. "I will stay there with the *komandir* as long as it takes."

CHAPTER
42

Sometimes you have to work your ass off to make things happen. You have to get all the ten thousand details all lined up just right, and then get all the plates spinning in the same direction. It takes time, brains, and five gallons of sweat, and it's never enough. Because sure as shit, one of the plates falls anyway and you have to be ready to sweep it up and get a new plate spinning. More sweat, and this time there's a taste of flop sweat to it. But you keep going, you get all the plates spinning again, and hope they stay up there this time. Like I said, sometimes it's all work.

And sometimes, things just fall into your lap. That can be just as upsetting as a falling plate, because you're thinking, no way, it can't be that easy. But it is; I mean, sometimes. Not often. But when it does happen, you have to be just as quick to see it and go with it. Because every now and then, it happens. The grand prize just floats down and lands in your lap.

You can call that luck if you want, and maybe you're right—if luck means sweating like a fountain to get everything going the way you planned, and then getting yourself into the right place so when "luck" does fall, your lap is right under it. Because every time I've had real good luck, it's because I made it happen, one way or another, and I was ready to grab it when it did.

And this time? I was ready. In fact, I was actually waiting for it—because I needed it. I really needed some serious luck. The kind I call Sweat Luck.

I had planned and sweated and worked to do something everybody else thought was impossible. Of course it was; why else would I do it? And I did it. I got myself into place in Ivo's special hidey-hole. And I'd been suffering through hanging on there and not giving myself away. Even more important, so far I'd kept that psycho Grisha from deciding he really had to kill me, no matter what Ivo said. I had done it. I was alive, in place, and ready. All I needed was one small chunk of luck, because without it, I was going to end up one-on-one with Grisha, and I had a pretty good idea that wouldn't end well for me.

So I was there, and I was ready. But there was one big hole in my master plan, the one Chaz had been totally pissed about, and that was that I had no goddamn idea in the world how I was going to be able to get down to the vault without somebody—and most especially Grisha—catching me at it and doing something unfortunate and permanent to me. Chaz was right to worry. And hell, I worried, too. What I knew about Ivo's security measures was truly scary. And I'd run into a few Spetsnaz guys in the past, and they were nothing but solid trouble, the real deal. Any one of Ivo's guys could kill me quicker and easier than you could cut a toenail. Somehow I had to get around a whole flock of them, all at once, and at the same time find a way to keep the electronic stuff from killing me. And I went in without a clue how I'd do it, with nothing at all except my wits and stupid confidence.

Because damn it, there is always a way. I just didn't know what it was this time.

Of course Chaz caught that, and he pushed me to come up with something. But shit, I didn't even know how many of them there were, or the floor plan of the place, or anything at all, really. So how could I figure a way to dodge them when I didn't even know where there was a linen closet to duck into? I shrugged it off and told Chaz I knew something would occur to me, and mostly I was sure it would. It usually did, because of my Sweat Luck.

And now, with Ivo's collapse, it had. The plate had fallen, and I was there to catch it.

Half of Ivo's troops were out of the way in one fell swoop, off to the hospital, without me lifting a finger. Even better, Grisha the Psycho was going with them. That meant the remaining men would be too busy to watch me. And the icing on the cake? In all the excitement of getting Ivo to the hospital, nobody thought to ask about the remote control for the lift that went down to the vault. It was still in my pocket. Without it, my plan had been to turn off the security somehow and climb down the side of the shaft, hoping like hell I could be down before it all got turned back on. Now I didn't have to. I could disable the camera in the shaft, making it look like the attackers had done it, and ride down in comfort, like a gentleman. And all because of Sweat Luck.

So I followed the stretcher up and outside, and I waited around on the surface while the guys got ready to take Ivo away, and when I say I waited, I hovered like I was watching my dear wife give birth to triplets. It didn't take long. The Spetsnaz guys are good, very efficient, and they had the whole parade loaded and on the road in under ten minutes. I watched from the island end of the causeway until they disappeared, with Nikko beside me the whole time. They'd left him behind so there was someone to talk to me—I mean, "Stefan"—while they were away. Which was nice, because I was sort of getting to like his fractured French. He stood with me, clumsily patting my shoulder and telling me no worry, good doctor, hospital expert, *komandir* is to be fine, yes, none of worry, okay?

I nodded, and then, when the parade was gone, I trudged back down, looking like a kid at the circus who just heard the clown had died. Nikko rode down with me, and when the doors opened down below, I told him I needed to be alone and I was going to my room to wait for news. He gave my shoulder one more awkward pat and promised to tell me when there was any news. I mean, I think that was what he said. As usual, understanding his French required some imagination. It didn't really matter. Ivo was gone, and he'd taken half his guards with him. Even better, he took Grisha.

I was pretty sure they'd be at the hospital for a nice long time, too. Maybe Ivo would even die. More likely he'd wake up in pain to find out his precious flash drive was gone, and his "son" was a fake who had played him like cheap maracas, and that would hurt even more. Did that bother me? That I snuck in on Ivo and dropped him into a world of hurt? Hell, no. Ivo had been playing all sides against one another for years, torturing and killing people left and right along the way. The way he'd shot that Russian soldier, like he was brushing dirt off the floor, showed what he really was. And anybody who kept an animal like Grisha around? The bastard had it coming.

I stayed in my room for about fifteen minutes. Then I slipped out the door and down the hall to the missile shaft. All the troops were either outside on guard duty or in the control center, so it was quiet and empty all the way. I carefully disabled the camera, used the little black controller and got the lift up, climbed aboard, and rode it on down.

That was the easy part. From here on things got a little delicate.

First, there was the door to the vault. You know, the super-duper, beyond-state-of-the-art, impossible-to-open-unless-you're-Ivo-Balodis vault door? The one with the super encrypted space-age electronic lock and the forget-it-you'll-never-guess-it combination?

Yeah, that door. I had to open it. And like you've probably guessed, that was going to be tricky. The designers of the vault had thought of just about everything. No matter what you might try, you were not getting it open without the combination.

So let's go through the conventional safe-cracker stuff. First, you can't get through the vault's skin. It's built with cobalt plates behind the steel facade, and sure, the very best drill bits in the world can get through that. But it would take all day and you'd use up maybe a dozen drill bits. And generally speaking, time is a factor when you're trying to bust open a vault—in my case, even more so.

Okay, you say. Drilling is out. So I'll *burn* my way through, blast a hole in the door so I can release the lock. That'll work, right?

Wrong. There's a layer of aluminum in there, which may not sound like a big deal. It is. Aluminum dissipates heat, meaning you have to use a lot more of it, and it takes four times as long. And now you're up to *two days*. But let's say just for giggles you have all that extra time and maybe a little more heat. How about that?

Again, nope. Sorry. Because there's a layer of copper in there, too. You start to burn with enough heat to penetrate the skin and beat the aluminum, the copper inside melts, and the minute you turn off the heat, the copper flows to the hole you just made, resolidifies, and seals the hole.

Okay, fine, let's just attack the lock, okay?

Sure. And good luck—you are going to need so much luck it's basically an act of God.

First, the electronic lock would not fail, ever. Anything you do to it that it doesn't like triggers a whole series of what they call re-lockers. They come in a bunch of different flavors, too. There's seismic, electronic, mechanical—forget it, they've got this covered. If the lock loses power, the mechanical re-lockers kick in and shut the door down solid. If you hammer or drill, the seismic ones do the same. Try a fancy electronic hack, the electronic ones not only lock it down, they set off a high-pitched siren at 150 decibels, which will have you rolling around on the floor trying to stuff things into your ears.

Get the idea? Unless you have the right combination, that vault was impossible to open.

So how could I do it if it was impossible? Simple: I could do it *because* it was impossible. Because remember me? Riley Wolfe? The guy who starts where everybody else gives up?

It really wasn't all that impossible. I mean, in theory, I'd figured out a way to do it—I just didn't know yet if it had worked. But it really *should* work, because I would have the right combination, straight from Ivo's own personal hand.

Now, you may be thinking, hold on here. Ivo would never, ever, no matter what, give me, or anybody, the combination, would he? And he wouldn't even let anybody near enough to see or film the numbers when he was opening the vault. In fact, he never let anybody within ten meters when he was opening it. You would basically have to get the combination from him without being there, which sounds just a little *Alice in Wonderland*–ish.

But it's true. And it's exactly what I had done.

Of course I had a little help. I happened to have a friend who spoke fluent German, and I'd seen him use it and fool people into thinking he was a German health official, an astrophysicist, an engineer—so I was pretty sure he could do a convincing nervous German with a hot work of art.

And I also had in my possession a really nice icon, painted by the great Simon Ushakov and freshly lifted from a Moscow museum, and I knew it would make Ivo drool. I mean, it made me drool, too, so I was pretty sure. And at a truly ridiculous cheap price, Ivo was guaranteed to bite.

If you're not up to speed yet and you're wondering why I'd go to all the bother of stealing that icon and selling it at a steep discount . . .

Retail stores have a thing called a "loss leader." That's some item they mark down to a really low price so the suckers flock in to buy it. And experience has proved that mostly they buy a lot more stuff, at full price, while they're at that store and feeling good about how much money they saved. And the store makes out like a bandit.

The Ushakov we sold back to Ivo dirt cheap was my loss leader. Naturally, Ivo grabbed it and, because it was so gorgeous, stuffed it into his vault with his other Ushakovs. But why does that matter? How does it help me get the vault open?

Simple. That beautiful Ushakov icon didn't go into the vault alone. Buried in the frame of the icon was a tiny little chip. And that chip had been made for only one purpose: to monitor and record nearby electronic activity. You know, activity like radio waves, or cell phones, or, um . . . somebody punching in the combination on an electronic lock? Even if it was one of the super-duper space-age ones, it still gives off an electronic signal.

The last time Ivo opened the vault, he'd been holding that icon right next to the lock, and that little chip had captured his secret combination. All I had to do was recover the recording. My cell phone was set up to do that, and they hadn't taken it away because it was impossible to make or receive calls in or on their island. But it was not impossible to collect the combination from my genius little chip.

It was tough, though. The vault's door provided shielding, and it was airtight. In the end, I had to get right up onto the door, and it took twice as long as it should have because the signal was so faint, and twelve digits took a while. But I got the combination at last, and I was good to go. I took a deep breath and punched it in.

For what seemed like an incredibly long time, nothing happened. I was getting a little antsy. I had to do this fast, or somebody was going to notice. But at last, the lock spat out three *beeps* and a big click. The door was open.

I grabbed and turned the handle and pulled the vault open. There it was stretched out in front of me: metal strongboxes, stacks of file folders sealed with red Top Secret tape, and a whole flock of drop-dead gorgeous Ushakovs in a neat rack. All the treasures of the world. All mine. I took a few seconds to enjoy it, and then I stepped inside.

First job was to find the flash drive. Not that it was more important than the icons; just that I could see the paintings and they weren't going anywhere. The flash drive would be tucked away somewhere, and that required some search time.

I figured it would be in one of the strongboxes, so I started on them. Funny thing about a strongbox—most of the time it does live up to its name. The box is really and truly strong, and it is very difficult to break one. I didn't even try. Didn't need to—because yeah, the box is strong. But the locks are almost always pathetic, and this time it was no different. It took me about thirty seconds to pick it and pry up the lid.

The first box was just the kind of boring crap you'd expect. Stacks of big-denomination cash—euros and American dollars—and a dozen passports from different countries. The second box was a little more interesting. It had a bunch of small leather bags inside. More from curiosity than anything else, I opened one up, and it was chock-full of cut diamonds, probably a couple of million dollars' worth, and easy to sell anywhere in the world.

Not what I was after, but what the hell. This whole shit show had started with diamonds, and after all, I'm a thief. I stuffed the bag into my pocket.

The third box was the jackpot. There was a stack of grainy photographs on top. I flipped through them: a few weird jets, some kind of naval vessel, and a couple of shots of people having sex. It was a funny place to keep your porn stash, but I looked at the third sex pic, and I got it. The guy in the shot was somebody who just about anybody in the world would recognize, and the things he was doing—and having done to him—were not what most people would even call "sex." And he was naked, and nowhere near to looking like a pinup. I thought about keeping that one, just in case I needed some political pressure, but I decided not to. Blackmail is not something I can do and still like myself. It just isn't clean, like theft and murder. I put the photo back and dug my way down to the bottom of the box.

There was a small cardboard box at the bottom, holding some tape cassettes and CDs. And even better, sitting next to them, was a flash drive. I picked it up and looked it over. Stamped into the plastic in block letters, it read, "TOP SECRET," in English. Next to it there was an eagle stamped in, the kind you see on the USA's Great Seal. That was surprising and weird; Prescott had said the thing was Russian. But what the hell, I was in a hurry, and there weren't any others; this had to be it. I could worry about what it meant later. I tucked it into a different pocket and turned to go.

I didn't go. I stopped. Because the door to the vault was partly blocked, and even though it wasn't all that big, I did not think I could get around this particular obstacle.

Grisha. He didn't look pleased to see me.

"I thought so," he said.

CHAPTER
43

I knew Grisha was going to kick my ass. There was no way around it. I mean, if somebody sort of normal takes a swing at me, I'm not helpless. I know some tricks, and I don't mind fighting dirty. I've fought when I had to, and there are two things I've learned from it. Rule One of Unarmed Combat is that you avoid it any way you can, because anybody can get lucky. If that doesn't work and you absolutely have to fight, Rule Two is fight to win. No Queensberry, no Bro Code, no sense of "honor." All that crap is for boxing. Fighting is different. So you do whatever it takes and do it first and fast.

Normally, that's how I play it. But with Grisha, I knew Rule Two wouldn't work, because I'd watched him practice and that's exactly how he always fought. His fast was a lot faster, everything he did hurt a whole lot more, and he had a hell of a lot more experience. I was pretty sure Rule One was out, too, because I was cornered in a vault and he was standing in the only exit. I needed a Rule Three, and I didn't have one. And without it, I was about to get my ass handed to me. The very best I could hope for was that he wouldn't actually kill me. No, he would want to do that later, slowly and carefully, after he got Ivo's okay.

I had to do something, but what? No way out, no way around, no way to stop him—what was left?

Grisha took a step forward. I was out of time.

"It was open," I blurted out. Even as I heard the words come out of my mouth, I couldn't believe I was saying them. It was beyond stupid, something only a seven-year-old kid would say. But I'd said it—and amazingly, Grisha paused.

"Really," he said. He was almost smiling, and who could blame him?

Well, if it got him to stop for a few seconds, I figured I might as well go with it. "Yes, of course," I said. "How else could I get in? Everyone knows that only Ivo can open it."

"So Ivo left it open?" he said.

"I'm sure he meant to close it—but he fainted and so—as you see."

He nodded. Not because he believed me. He was having fun, and he wanted it to last a little longer. "And so you enter the vault. To make sure nothing was missing."

"Listen, I know how it looks," I said. "But I was curious. I hear so much about 'Protect the vault,' 'The vault is important,' this and that—naturally I wanted to see inside. But that's all—just to have a look. Which I have done!" I said cheerfully. "So I'll go back to my room now."

I took a step forward. So did Grisha.

"I don't think so," he said. He was close enough to hit me, grab me, whatever he wanted, and I knew if he did that it was game over. I also knew there was no way to stop him from doing it. Except possibly one little thing that probably wouldn't work—but I didn't have anything else, so—

"Grisha, listen," I said. "Nothing is missing—nothing has been touched. See for yourself!" And I half turned away and pointed, stepping back with my right foot at the same time. If he would only look where I pointed, just for a second.

He did. Out of the corner of my eye I saw him turn his head to look. That was all I needed.

Driving off my right foot and putting all my weight behind it, I spun back around and threw a fist at Grisha. Not at his head, that's for amateurs. Anybody is twice as likely to see and react if something comes at their face. If your ass is on the line, and mine truly was, you go for the gut. Right in the center, where the ribs end and the diaphragm sits. One good slam there and no matter how many sit-ups you do every day, you're going to double over and spend some time trying to remember how to breathe. And while you're bent over and you can't breathe, you are helpless, and I can finish it off any way I want.

So I threw my fastest, hardest, very best Sunday punch right at Grisha's diaphragm.

You've heard the old expression "Eyes in the back of his head," right? Here's a new one for you: "Eyes in his diaphragm." I'd never heard of it, never seen it—until now. The second I started my punch, Grisha spun back around, so fast I swear I heard a sonic boom. He knocked my fist to one side, grabbed my wrist, and pulled. My own momentum drove me forward, and he stuck out his foot. I tripped over it and went down on my face, with Grisha still holding my arm.

It hurt. Really, a whole lot. I thought my arm would come out of the socket. But that was not enough to satisfy Grisha. He put a foot on my back and twisted my arm, pulling up until I thought he would just pull my arm off and beat me with it. Then he gave it one extra twist, let go, and stepped back.

I didn't move at first. I mean, first of all, I hurt too much. But more than that, I knew he hadn't changed his mind. He was still going to beat me half to death—or maybe a little further. So what was up now? Why did he let go of my arm? I waited and did nothing. So did Grisha.

Finally, the suspense was too much for me. I pushed up on the arm that still worked and turned my head. He stood there with his arms crossed, watching me the way a little boy watches a bug when he's thinking about pulling off all its legs, one at a time.

"Too easy," he said. "Try again."

Sure. I should have known. Grisha liked a challenge. He couldn't just pound me into something that looked like three-day-old roadkill on the interstate. He had to have fun, too, stretch himself a little so he wouldn't get stale. He wanted me to think I had a chance, and to stand up.

I didn't really feel like falling for that, but what choice did I have? He obviously wanted to make a game of it, make sure I suffered longer. You know, death by a thousand cuts instead of a quick beheading. It wouldn't be a lot of fun for me. But if I stayed on the floor, I was pretty sure he'd just kick me to death when he got bored. On my feet, at least I had a chance. It was close to the same chance a three-legged mouse has at a cat convention, but it was a chance.

I took it. Moving slowly and never taking my eyes off Grisha, I climbed to my feet. "All right," I said. "But—"

He kicked me. The sole of his boot thumped into my kneecap. I never saw it coming. It hurt like hell, and it knocked me back a step. "No talking," he said.

I decided to go along with that. What I couldn't decide was what to do instead. I put some weight on the leg he'd kicked. It still held me. Just barely. I put my fists up and, very cautiously, I stepped toward him, trying to watch his feet and hands at the same time.

It didn't matter. He hit me anyway, right in the solar plexus. I bent over. Like I said, you can't help it. If you get hit there, you bend over. And when I did, Grisha slapped me twice, once on each cheek. The slaps were hard enough to make me see stars, but I knew he could have hit harder. He was toying with me, trying to shame me with face slaps.

"Not even a boy," he said. "A baby."

I straightened up. It was hard work. I still couldn't breathe right, but I could get in just enough air. I put my fists back up. And once again, he hit me, this time on the left shoulder. That arm went numb and dropped to my side. I rubbed it with my right, trying to get some feeling back into it. And feeling started to come back, but it was all bad, and I couldn't use the arm at all yet.

That didn't really matter. I could have had more arms than an octopus family as far as Grisha was concerned. He stepped in and grabbed the numb arm. I didn't pull away; I would've lost the arm. Instead I stepped in and snapped a right at his ear.

That is, I tried to. He just moved his head to one side and watched my punch go by, and then twisted my left arm behind my back, turned me, and ran me face-first into the wall. He dropped my arm. But before I could move, he threw a shot at my kidney. And while I was wishing I could get enough air into my lungs to scream, he stepped back and waited.

I used the time to find my left arm. It felt kind of far away, but when I looked it was still there. I took a few more seconds to start breathing again. Then I turned around.

"You have not hit me," he said. "Not even once." He beckoned me forward. "Come, try harder. Look, I put one hand behind my back so it's fair, hm?"

And he did, of course. It was even his right hand, to show me how pathetic I was. It wasn't necessary. I felt plenty pathetic already. But I had to try something, anything, and this was probably as good as it would get. I started to shuffle forward, trying to get my left arm working again. I tried to circle to my left, to keep the injured arm away from him. Grisha let me. He turned to keep facing me as I circled. I moved back, circled left, moved in again. I tried to shake some feeling into my left arm, and it came halfway back to life. I couldn't do anything with it, but I could raise it. So I did. I shuffled one more step forward.

Grisha waited patiently until I was close enough. Then he raised his fist up like he was going to crush me with it, and when I moved my arm up to block, he stomped on my instep.

I managed to stumble back before he could pull my ears off with his teeth, but it was hard. Everything hurt, and moving made it all hurt worse. This couldn't last a whole lot longer. If nothing else, I was going to run out of moving parts that I could actually move. But I had no bright ideas about what to try.

He didn't give me any time to get one, either. He slid forward and threw a shot at my head. I jerked to one side so it missed. That was what he wanted me to do. He gave me a shove in the direction I'd ducked and while I was off-balance, he kicked my feet out from under me. I fell and slid over next to the shelves. I was down again. At least it wasn't on my face this time.

Unfortunately, it was flat on my back. That knocked the wind out of me. Again. Grisha waited patiently. It took me a few seconds longer to get to my feet again. Halfway up I saw the stack of folders on the shelf and thought, why not? I grabbed one and threw it at his head. He blocked it, easily, but it burst open and papers scattered through the air. For just a second he couldn't see and I jumped toward him and launched a kick at his crotch.

And of course, he didn't need to see. He caught my foot, yanked it up, and turned me halfway upside down before dropping me. I had my arms out, but the left one was still not much help, and my head hit the floor. I saw stars, which was kind of nice, because they were pretty, and when they went away a few seconds later my head felt like a jack-o'-lantern three weeks after Halloween. Except a lot more painful.

I heard Grisha scuffle forward. He stooped and picked something up. "Well," he said. "And nothing is missing? This is yours?"

Slowly, and very painfully, I rolled myself over. He looked at me and shook his head. "Shame on you," he said, and he held up something.

The bag of diamonds. Of course they had to fall out of my pocket, right at his feet.

"This is how you repay our hospitality? Shame."

There wasn't a lot I could say, so I didn't. I just staggered back up to my feet and stood there for a second, swaying. I wondered how I could be so completely exhausted when I hadn't done anything except get hit and fall down. But I was; I was completely spent. I knew I had to do something, but my brain seemed to be off duty, too.

I looked around for something I could throw or hit him with. Nothing—but I saw that I was now much closer to the door of the vault. Maybe—

"Yes, please try to run," Grisha said. "I would like that very much."

I looked back at him. His smile was bigger. And I knew that, in the shape I was in right now, I might get one step outside the vault before he pulled me down and ripped out my liver.

Forget it. I put my hands up.

Grisha looked at me and shook his head again. "Come, you are not trying," he said. He smiled a small and nasty grin. "Here—I will make it easy for you. I will turn my back." And he did. The evil, rotten son of a bitch turned away from me so he was facing the wall. "Your turn, baby," he said. "Come get me."

I thought about that. I knew damn well that I would never land a punch. Or a kick, or a spitball, or even a few harsh words. My first move and he would whip around and break off a piece of me. And I couldn't spare any. So I just stood for a minute. That was not a good choice. Grisha got impatient. He didn't even turn around. He just launched a back kick and landed it on my other kneecap, the one that he hadn't walloped before.

I staggered back again and smacked into the metal shelf along the vault's wall. "Come on, baby," Grisha said. "You will not get another chance."

Well, all right. That was probably true. But it was just as true that nothing I could try would do more than give Grisha a fit of giggles. I leaned back against the shelf and, for just a second I thought, oh, hell, why not get it over with? Let him clock me, fall down, the end. But there was a small something inside me that wouldn't buy quitting. I'm not saying it was my proud and unbroken spirit—more like my loud and dangerous stupidity. Whatever, I had to give it a shot.

I pushed off the shelf to stand straight, and as I did, the shelf wobbled. *Huh*, I thought, *it isn't bolted to the wall.* Just one of those empty random thoughts, and I shoved it away to think about more important stuff, like staying alive.

It shoved back. It told me *it* was more important and to pay attention. So I did. *Okay, Shelf Not Bolted to Wall. So?*

So, stupid, it said, *you are right beside the door. Grisha is farther inside.*

Again, so? It doesn't matter how close to the door I am. We did this already. If I take a single baby step toward the door, he'll be on me like the wrath of God.

Not if you slow him down, my random thought said.

I can't even touch him—how can I slow him?

I could almost hear it sigh. *The shelf is not bolted to the wall*, it said again.

Slowly, very slowly, the nickel dropped. Maybe a little too slowly—Grisha was getting grumpy. "Come on, baby," he called. "You are boring me. Shall I turn around and finish this?"

I stepped sideways, toward the door, reached behind me with my right hand, and grabbed the shelf. "Here I come," I said. And I pulled hard and jumped back at the same time.

The bookshelf toppled with a crash, scattering piles of papers and folders and thumping into the far wall.

It didn't hit Grisha, of course. He heard it falling, or felt it, or used his spider sense—whatever, he dodged it, sliding sideways to the back of the vault. He caught my eye and nodded, and I could tell he was about to let fly with another real zinger to help me realize my true lack of worth. I almost wanted to hear it—almost. But I wanted to live a little more.

So I took the last step out of the vault, leaned against the door, and pushed as hard as I could.

The door was very heavy, especially in my half-shattered state, but it moved; slowly at first, far too slowly. I heard Grisha scrambling over the fallen shelf and coming for me. I pushed harder. The door moved a little faster—but Grisha was close, almost to the door.

"Now," he said, and he was so near his voice was almost in my ear. "Now we end this and—"

BOOM. The door was closed. I heard the lock click shut, but some small shrill voice in my head was still screaming with terror and I kept pushing, and pushing, with everything I had left, and I pushed until I saw stars again and slid to the floor. I closed my eyes and leaned my face against the vault's door. It was cool and soothing. It felt good. I didn't have room for any other thoughts, but that was enough for now.

CHAPTER
44

Chase Prescott had no idea whether Wolfe was alive or dead. He didn't like not knowing, not when it was this important. The three weeks he and Wolfe had agreed on had passed, and it was time for action, and there was no signal from Wolfe. The last thing Prescott knew for sure was that the team had seen Wolfe taken inside the lighthouse at gunpoint. Since then, nothing except that the son of a bitch was fishing. Just sitting and fishing. Prescott hated the silence and not knowing, and he hated more that there was nothing he could do about it. It was out of his control, and that violated all his lifelong protocols. And now, the most important mission of his life, he might as well be on a beach in Tahiti for all the oversight he had. *Goddamn it, this has to work*, he said to himself. He became aware that his jaw ached and realized he was gritting his teeth. He loosened the jaw muscles, but he didn't feel any better. *HAS to work . . .*

The door to his office opened, and Prescott looked up. It was Brett Birchette, a tall and lean Delta Force veteran, a skilled sniper and specialist in infiltration. Prescott disliked him less than most of the others, mostly because he didn't talk much and used as few words as possible when he did speak.

"What," Prescott said.

"Report from away team," he said. He frowned. "Commotion at the site. An attack team made it across the causeway and inside the lighthouse."

"Whose team?"

"Darby says they were trying to look like mercenaries. But he's sure they were Russian."

"Of course they were, nobody else would pull that shit," Prescott snapped. "What happened?"

Birchette shrugged. "Same old shit. Fourteen minutes, start to finish. Then a bunch of Balodis's guys came out with a guy on a stretcher. Loaded him into a vehicle, left, one vehicle with more troops following."

"Shit," Prescott said. The obvious conclusion was that Wolfe had been found out and either killed or nearly so. But wait, if that was the case—would they take him away on a stretcher? And with a full team in support? That didn't scan at all. "Could they tell who was on the stretcher?"

Birchette shook his head. "Darby says no way to know. But they were anxious? Treated him like he was important."

Birchette leaned patiently against the doorframe and waited while Prescott scowled and tried to make sense of it. It might still be Wolfe. But again, two vehicles and a full team? That didn't seem likely. He put all the known factors in a line and looked at them: stretcher, anxiety, two teams. Wolfe, target date here. He drummed his fingers on the desk and stopped suddenly. *Yes*, he thought. It added up. *Diversion*, he thought. *Wolfe created a diversion so he could strike.*

He looked up at Birchette. "Call the away team," he said. "Tell them to move in to ready position and stand by. This might be it."

Birchette nodded and left, closing the door behind him, and Prescott poured a tumbler half full of brandy and reached for the ice. *This damn well better be it.*

CHAPTER

45

I don't know how long I stayed there like that, half asleep, or maybe half dead, with my face pressed against the beautiful coolness of the vault's door. It must have been a while, because it was warm where my face lay against it. Once or twice I got a nightmare jolt of adrenaline and I had to open my eyes and look to make sure Grisha hadn't gotten out of the vault somehow. He hadn't.

But eventually a couple of brain cells woke up and got together to make a thought. They had to shout and repeat it a few times, but finally I got it. It was time to get up and go. I didn't want to. I did anyway.

I knew it was going to hurt. I was right. I climbed way, way up onto my feet, and every second was a brand-new shot of pain. One knee wouldn't move right even though it hurt like hell. My left arm didn't hurt, but only because it was still half dead and I couldn't feel most of it. My entire midsection felt like it had been hammered into mush, and my nose throbbed, probably broken from being slammed into the wall.

I tried a step to see what would happen, and that worked. I could move—just barely. And oh, yeah, it hurt.

I turned and stared at the vault. Grisha was locked in for the rest of his life, which wasn't going to be all that long. The vault was airtight, and at a guess he had about twelve hours of air. That was it, and he would spend those hours in complete darkness before he ran out of it. Then he could spend a few more minutes gasping like a fish on the beach before the CO_2 brought a blinding headache, unconsciousness, and death. Good. I hoped he got a double serving. Served the little shit right.

But that wasn't my concern. I mean, I was glad he would be dead soon, so glad I would have done a few dance moves if I still had a real working body. No, what I was thinking was several dozen variations of *Aw, shit*. Why? After all, I was alive, and Grisha was on his way to hell.

Because. I just spent four weeks with a bunch of Russian soldiers, and then got the crap beat out of me. That's all part of the way I work, and normally I don't mind. But that's because normally I can limp off into the sunset with something shiny and expensive I've grabbed from some rich and overprivileged asshat. This time I took the lumps and I didn't have anything to show for it. I didn't have any of the Ushakov icons, and I didn't even have my consolation prize of the diamonds, and that truly sucked. So much that I thought about going back up to my quarters and waiting a day or so and then trying again when I was sure Grisha was dead.

I didn't think that for very long. It was just plain stupid. Somebody was bound to ask where Grisha had gone and why at the same time I turned up covered with bruises and limping. None of the others were as lethal as Grisha, but they were enough to take me out, especially with me in shit shape. It was a whole lot better to split with what I had—my life. I don't crap out often, almost never. But I knew enough to admit it when I had and be glad I wasn't dead. And anyway, I had everything in place to get out now, and I wanted to. I had that sad sick feeling you get when your luck runs out and it's time to go home. Even if you have to go empty-handed.

But I wasn't, not quite. I still had the flash drive. Just to be sure, I reached into my pocket. Yeah, I had it, and it hadn't been damaged while I was getting totally crushed.

Okay, that was something; I knew the thing was worth a lot. I mean, Prescott had spent who knows how much time and money and how many lives trying to get it. And while I'd been here I had seen people literally dying to get their paws on something in the vault, and my guess was this was it. I didn't have to give the thing to Prescott. I was pretty sure somebody would pay me big bucks for it. If I could figure out exactly what it was, I'd get an idea of what it was worth. Probably more than a couple of Ushakovs.

I had an idea how to figure out what the thing was. After that, I'd know who my market was. Good; settled.

Now all I had to do was get out of here.

CHAPTER

46

Where is Grisha?"

The question came from Andrei, who stood in the doorway of the security control room. And to Nikko, it was confusing. He shook his head.

"He went to the hospital," Nikko said. "He told you he was going."

Andrei frowned. "He changed his mind," he said. "He sent Yakov in his place."

"But that's— Oh," Nikko finished lamely. "I mean, are you sure? Because I have not seen him."

Andrei sighed. "Nikko, I am sure. How can you be unsure about Grisha?"

"Well, that's—of course, you're right," Nikko said. "But I have not seen him." He gestured at the console. "Not on any of the monitors, and he has not been in here, either."

Andrei frowned at him for a moment, as if willing him to change his mind. Nikko shrugged and said, "I'm sorry."

But Andrei's expression had changed to alarm, which Nikko thought was very odd, until he realized that Andrei was looking past him, at one of the monitors. Nikko spun back around to look, and Andrei leaned in over his shoulder.

"Camera five—who is that?"

Nikko shook his head. "That is not Grisha. Whoever it is, he is limping."

"Stay with that camera and move in," Andrei said.

Nikko's fingers moved over the controls, freezing the monitor on the view it was showing and then zooming in. The screen showed a figure climbing the spiral stairs of the lighthouse, limping and leaning on the handrail. A man—the stairs twisted and he was facing the camera.

"Stefan . . . ?" Nikko said.

Another halting step, closer to the camera, and they could both see the face. There was no room for doubt: It was Stefan.

"What the fuck is he doing?" Andrei said.

Nikko shook his head. "He appears to be climbing to the top," he said.

Stefan disappeared around a turn and left the field of the camera. "Follow him," Andrei said. Nikko switched to the camera at the top of the stairs, and a moment later Stefan came into view. This time they could see he carried something in one hand, something bright orange.

"*Gavno*—what the hell . . . ?" Andrei muttered. "What is that in his hand?"

"I can't—it's something orange," Nikko said.

Andrei glared at him. "Really. And you're quite sure?"

Nikko said nothing. They both watched as Stefan slid open a

window and then shook out the orange thing. "Shirt! It's a T-shirt!" Nikko said.

"Yes," Andrei said. "But why is he hanging a T-shirt out the window?"

They both watched, puzzled, as Stefan draped the shirt so it hung outside and then secured it in place with duct tape.

"Why would anyone . . ." Andrei said.

Suddenly Nikko jerked upright. "Signal!" he said. "Andrei, it's a signal! It must be!"

"*Trakhni menya*, you're right," Andrei said. "But why—no, *who* is he signaling?"

"The American plane?" Nikko suggested. "It has been coming every day—since last week, always at the same time." He glanced at the wall clock. "That would be ten minutes from now."

"Hmm," Andrei said, wrinkling his brow. "It is possible, but—an airplane could not see the signal from that angle."

"Oh," Nikko said. "I guess not."

"Then who—"

An alarm began to beep, an annoying high-pitched sound. Reflexively, Nikko quickly slapped at the controls and switched to another camera. "There, on the shore!" he said, raising his voice to be heard over the persistent alarm.

"For the love of God, turn off that alarm!" Andrei said.

Nikko did, and then pointed at the monitor. "There—do you see?"

Andrei leaned in and saw a group of people moving toward the causeway. "Zoom in."

The camera moved closer, clearly showing a group of men on motorcycles swarming into view. And they were all heavily armed.

"Sound battle stations!" Andrei said. Nikko punched a button, and a loud klaxon began to wail. Seconds later the entire facility was filled with the clatter of troops rushing to their posts.

"They have taken a defensive position," Nikko said, nodding at the screen.

Andrei looked and saw that the body of armed men had paused, well back from the causeway. "They are waiting—but for what?"

"To attack us?" Nikko suggested.

"Absurd. In broad daylight? And then they wait around on the shore, giving us time to prepare?" Andrei said. "No, they must have some other purpose."

"They could be waiting for more men," Nikko said.

"Again, not in plain sight," Andrei said. "But I agree they are waiting for something."

"Yes, but what?"

There was a flicker of movement on the screen monitoring the top of the lighthouse. Both men glanced at it; Stefan had turned and started down the stairs.

"Of course," Andrei said. "Nikko, the men on the shore—they're waiting—"

"For Stefan!" they said in unison.

Then Nikko frowned. "But why would—Stefan wouldn't—"

"He would. He obviously has," Andrei said. "Grisha was right about him."

"It just doesn't . . ." Nikko said, shaking his head. "What should we do?"

"I think—I mean, it's clear that we must stop him," Andrei said. "Before he crosses the causeway. But—" Andrei hesitated. "We are at half strength right now. And we must also be ready in case that force on the shore moves closer."

"Send a squad to block the causeway?" Nikko suggested. "They can do both tasks at once."

"Yes, you are right, but—" Andrei paused, looked around. "Grisha should give that order," he said. "Damn it, where is he?"

It was several more minutes before Andrei could overcome his reluctance to give an order that should have been Grisha's. But he was a lifelong soldier and knew very well that when there was a hole in the chain of command, the next man in line was required to step up and take the job. Andrei was next in line. He left Nikko in the control room and led a squad up to the surface of the island. They double-timed out of the elevator and out into daylight.

"Deploy," Andrei said, and the men moved to defensive positions they had taken many times before. Andrei turned two men around with orders to watch for Stefan and stop him if he attempted to cross the causeway. Then Andrei, too, took cover, watching the group on the shore through binoculars. They stood beside their motorcycles and did nothing but watch him back.

Andrei looked them over carefully for clues to their identity. They all looked to be in their thirties and very fit. They wore nondescript fatigues that might have been issued by almost any military force in the world, the kind that were readily available at civilian stores, too. Their automatic weapons were a mix; he could see a couple of M4A1s, favored by Americans. But there was also one Canadian C8, a German MK 556, and an Israeli TAR-21. The variety suggested that either they were a force of mixed mercenaries—or they wanted to look like one.

His radio crackled to life. "Andrei—" It was Nikko's voice.

"Yes, what is it?" Andrei answered distractedly.

"I thought you should know—the American plane is about to come over."

"All right," Andrei said.

"Is there something we should do?" Nikko asked.

"About the plane? Of course not, it comes every day," Andrei said, irritated. "The real threat is here."

"All right," Nikko said. "Any sign of Stefan?"

"Not yet," Andrei said.

"He is not visible on any of the monitors."

"Keep watching," Andrei said. "We have it covered here."

"Will do," Nikko said, and signed off.

Andrei went back to studying the group on the shore. They were still doing nothing more threatening than waiting. But as he watched, the one who seemed to be the leader called an order, and they spread out into something like a skirmish line.

The American plane went over, no more than thirty or forty meters up—and the men on the shore all gaped and pointed as if they had never seen an airplane before. Perhaps it wasn't theirs, they weren't Americans, or—

His radio crackled again. "Andrei!" Nikko called urgently.

"Mother of God, what is it now?" Andrei snapped.

"The American plane—it just— Look at it, Andrei!"

"Why the fuck should I—"

"Please, Andrei—quickly!"

Reluctantly, Andrei turned. Just in time to see the American plane heading out over the Baltic. And dangling below it on a cable, rapidly rising up toward the plane, was a figure.

"What the fuck . . ." Andrei said. "They are dangling someone?"

"No—they picked him up, with a Skyhook!" Nikko said.

"But who . . ." And then Andrei stopped speaking, because it was obvious who.

Nikko told him anyway. "It's Stefan, Andrei," Nikko said. "They took Stefan."

The office door opened, and Prescott looked up. Symanski, one of his operatives, stuck his head in. "Mr. Prescott?"

"What is it?"

"Radio message from Darby," he said. "The strike force leader at the lighthouse?"

"I know who fucking Darby is," Prescott snapped. "What's the message? And give it to me quick and clear."

"Yes, sir," Symanski said. "Uh, Darby says that our recon flight went over, and uh—" He looked perplexed. "Apparently, sir, it picked up a passenger?"

"That's idiotic," Prescott snarled. "How in hell could it do that?"

"Um, Darby said—a Skyhook, sir?"

"A *what*?!"

"Skyhook, sir," Symanski said. "We use it for field extractions and—"

"I know what the fuck a Skyhook is!" Prescott said.

"Yes, sir."

"But what the hell would . . ." It hit him suddenly, and hard. "Riley Wolfe," he said. "Goddamn it, Riley fucking Wolfe . . ."

CHAPTER
47

Maybe you have never gotten to the point where you are just tired of everything hurting. Okay, sure, when you're in pain you want it to stop. This is different. This is like, you've been in constant pain for so long you can't remember not hurting. It's all been hurting so much and for so long that you're kind of used to it, and the pain has turned into something really, totally annoying. I mean, it still hurts, but you're no longer thinking, *Ow, ow, ow!* Instead, it's more like, *All right, I get it, ow. Enough, okay?*

So maybe that's never happened to you. If so, you have been luckier than me when it comes to encounters with superpowered psychos who beat the crap out of you. Because I hurt everywhere, and I was truly tired of it. I had escaped, but I didn't feel like it. I wasn't getting the big rush I normally get, the high from pulling off an impossible job and an even more impossible getaway. I just plain hurt too much.

Grisha had done a job on me. I was pretty sure I had a broken rib, maybe two. The worst of it was my left arm. It felt like it was broken.

Other than that, one knee wouldn't bend, the other barely straightened out, and they both shot lightning bolts of pain at me with every step. It was about all I could do to get up the lighthouse stairs, and getting down again was even more painful. And I had to hurry, which made it worse.

It wasn't as bad once I got out the back door of the cottage and onto the surface of the island. I kept to cover and snuck a peek toward the causeway. Two guys were facing the front door, but the cottage would cut off their view of what I was about to do. That was good; if they had tried to stop me, there wasn't much I could do about it in my pitiful condition. And the clock was running. By the time I retrieved the package I'd buried at my fishing spot, it had just about run out, and there was still plenty left to do.

A Skyhook works like this: The guy on the ground sends up a balloon with a long and strong cable attached. On the other end of the cable there's a harness that the rescue-ee straps into. The rescue plane sees the balloon and heads straight for it. The plane has been fitted with a special thing on front, kind of a cross between a scoop and a clamp. This thing snaps onto the cable, grabs it tight, and starts reeling in the guy in the harness. In this case, me—*if* I could get it together in time.

I had all the pieces, but I had to get them operational, and like I said, time was running out. It took longer than it should have; my left arm was still not working properly, and any movement I made was too slow and hurt too much. But somehow, I got the balloon up and my harness fastened about twenty seconds before the old DC-3 came over. And then did I get to breathe a sigh of relief and relax? Hell, no. Because when the plane grabs you, it's a whole new festival of ouch. It's going eighty miles an hour, you're standing still, and then bang! suddenly *you're* going eighty miles an hour, too, and it feels like all the pieces of your whole damn body changed places with one another, which hurts a lot in a whole new way.

Winston had told me it would hurt, and that turned out to be a real understatement. When the plane hooked onto the balloon, it yanked me up so hard everything went all black, and when my sight cleared, the last three places on my body that weren't already in pain had started to howl. And all the places that hurt before got jolted hard enough to double down and hurt even more.

But I did it. I made it out. And I was kind of glad that I didn't have the icons, because with my ribs and my left arm broken and almost useless, I probably would have dropped them into the water when the Skyhook grabbed me. And if you didn't know already, salt water is not good for icons. These Ushakovs were so beautiful they made my teeth hurt, and to see them dumped into the Baltic and ruined would have been a true tragedy.

So I didn't have my Ushakovs. I didn't even have the diamonds. But every now and then, you just have to be glad you're still here, and this was one of those times. Besides, the flash drive was going to be worth something, and I thought it would be a lot. I had the flash drive, and I knew just the person to tell me why it was so important.

In the meantime, I had some important business with Winston.

I staggered up to the cockpit. He was sitting at the controls, gaining altitude as he took us out over the Baltic toward Sweden. There was an island there off the coast with a small private field. A stack of euros had changed hands, and we were cleared to land there.

Winston looked up as I stumbled in. He said something. I saw his lips move, but I couldn't really hear the words over the sound of the engines. Winston pointed at the headset hanging beside me, and I put it on. "Hey, buddy!" he said. "All good?"

"Depends," I said. "Got any ibuprofen?"

He laughed. "Your scat bag is there, under the seat," he said, nodding at the copilot's chair. I'd given him a small duffel bag to bring me with a few essentials in it. A change of clothes, some cash and some credit cards, a couple of passports, a few small essentials for changing my appearance. And, because I have had a ride on this kind of roller coaster a few times before, a big bottle of ibuprofen.

I reached under the seat and pulled out my bag, unzipped it and found the bottle, and buckled into the seat and swallowed eight tablets.

"Thanks," I said. "I mean, for everything."

"No sweat, I was ready for a change of career anyway," he said.

I closed my eyes for a minute. The ibuprofen would take some time to kick in. I kind of wished I could have had it in an IV. But hell, as long as I was wishing, I might as well wish that Grisha hadn't beat the crap out of me and that I got to keep the diamonds and a couple of the icons. Instead of just the flash drive that Prescott wanted.

Prescott—damn it. My eyes jerked open. "T.C.?"

"Yeah, buddy?"

"How soon will Prescott know I didn't walk into his trap?"

Winston shook his head. "I'm pretty sure he knows now," he said. "He's probably monitoring in real time."

"Well, shit," I said. I should have known. If he thought I'd crossed him, he'd do something nasty to Mom, or Monique, or both. So the first order of business was to get them out of his clutches. Which was exactly what he'd expect me to do, so right away, the minute we landed and I could get a phone signal, I had to call him and set up a "safe" place to meet. Kind of like the old magician's trick: Show them the right hand so they don't see what the left is doing. Which was a really nice image, but it didn't tell me how.

Or more important, *where*. "Hey, T.C.?" I said into the microphone.

"Yeah?"

"You know Prescott is holding some hostages to make sure I'm a good boy, right?"

He glanced at me, quickly looked away. "Yeah, I know," he said. "I helped take one of 'em, your, uh—partner?" He looked over and looked away again. "I'm real sorry, Riley. I didn't know—I mean, *anything*. I'm sorry, but I did it."

I reached over and patted his shoulder. "Actually, I'm glad you did," I told him. "Because that means you know where they are."

"Yeah, absolutely," he said, all cheerful and eager again. "And I know the place cold, I flew in there enough times."

"Well, then," I said. "How'd you like to start your new career right away?"

CHAPTER

48

vo Balodis came awake slowly. He lay in a fog that kept him even from forming the thought that he should wonder where he was. He just floated, wrapped in layers of cloud, his mind as dim and dark as the haze that enveloped him.

But he was awake. And gradually, waking turned to awareness. There was a steady, rhythmic blipping sound and the sharp smell of something medicinal. All right. That was not threatening. He floated a little longer.

Ever so slowly, he began to think. The blipping sound, the sharp smell—these did not belong in his memory of his home. So he was somewhere else . . . ? Where? And why?

He opened his eyes at last, blinking against the light. The ceiling was the wrong color, unfamiliar. He turned his head to the right. He saw a metal stand with several machines on it, machines with small screens that showed jagged lines making small movements—that was where the sound came from. And beyond them, a door that led out of the room to—

Hospital. He was in a hospital.

Slowly, painfully he remembered: the Russian attack, the vault, the terrible pain in his stomach, and—

"Stefan." His voice came out as a dreadful distant croak. It was answered immediately by a rustle of movement on his other side and a voice he knew. "*Komandir*, lie easy. Please, the doctor said you must lie easy."

Turning his head was harder than it should have been, but Ivo did it. In a chair at his bedside, leaning anxiously forward, was Andrei Sidorov, one of his men. "Please, *Komandir*?" Andrei repeated.

"What—what happened?" It was still a croak, but a little louder and understandable.

"Your stomach," Andrei said. "It has—we brought you to the hospital, and—I don't remember exactly what the doctor said, but there was bleeding inside—you nearly died." And then, looking alarmed at his own words, Andrei added, "But you will be fine now, *Komandir*! You must rest and not exert yourself."

"Where is Stefan?" Ivo croaked.

Andrei looked uneasy. "*Komandir*, don't worry about that now, just rest, all right?"

"Tell me," Ivo demanded.

"*Komandir* . . ." Andrei hesitated, looked away, looked back. "Sir, Stefan is gone."

"Gone?"

"Yes, sir. Gone."

For a moment Ivo felt a black wave of anguish mixed with nausea sweep over him, and he closed his eyes. Stefan gone. But how? What did that mean? "Did Grisha . . . ?"

"Kill him? No, sir."

The black wave receded, and Ivo opened his eyes. "Then what . . . ?"

Andrei looked even more uneasy. "Sir, Stefan was . . . Apparently he . . . The American spy plane took him away." Ivo looked confused, and Andrei added, "A Skyhook, sir. They took him in a Skyhook."

"Sky . . . Grisha didn't—"

And now Andrei looked absolutely ready to cry. "*Komandir*, I am very sorry, but—Grisha is missing. No one has seen him; no one knows where he went. He is just gone. The same time Stefan left."

For a long time Ivo just stared, because none of it made any sense. And then, it slowly did make sense. He had been betrayed. By one of them? Or both, working together? Had all of Grisha's hostility toward Stefan been a clever cloak, a way to disguise that they were accomplices? And if accomplices, in what?

It didn't matter. By one or by both, he had been betrayed. And of course, the one thing valuable enough for a betrayal of that scale was the flash drive. He didn't need to look. He was sure. Somehow, they had opened his impregnable vault. The flash drive was gone.

He turned away from Andrei and looked at the ceiling. He thought of all he had planned, all he had tried to do. And he thought of his trust in Grisha—misplaced. Grisha was gone. And he thought, too, of Stefan, who was apparently not really his son, and how that meant that he had been an utter fool, and that he had nothing left of Simone. Nothing at all.

Ivo closed his eyes again, and he was not sure he would ever again want to open them.

PART 3

CHAPTER
49

We landed on the Swedish island with no problem and just walked away from the Gooney Bird. Nobody stopped us, nobody questioned us. We took a ferry to the mainland and cut across to Arlanda International Airport at Stockholm. I bought Winston a ticket to New York on a flight that was already boarding, and he ran off to catch it.

Then I found a quiet spot and made a phone call. He answered on the first ring.

"What the fuck are you up to, Wolfe?" Prescott snarled at me. "If you're fucking with me, you will live just barely long enough to regret it."

"Yeah, I know, I'm scared," I said.

"You fucking well better be," he said.

"I have the flash drive," I said.

"You fucking well better," he said.

I shook my head. So repetitive. But I decided I shouldn't point out that he was overusing the word "fuck," which was really a sign of a weak mind and a bad character. "I have it," I repeated. "But I didn't get the icons."

"I thought you were the world's greatest and you never failed," he said, and I could feel the sneer through the phone.

"If you want to call it failure, fine," I said. "I just didn't get my payoff."

"Well, tough shit," he said. "That doesn't change our deal."

"No, it doesn't," I said. "What it does is, it *improves* our deal."

"What the fuck does that mean?"

There it was again, "fuck." Have you noticed that people who say it a lot never actually do it? "It means I need money," I said.

"No."

"Yes. I had expenses, and I'm not running a charity," I told him.

"That's not my problem."

"It is if you want the flash drive."

He was quiet for a minute, but I could hear the wheels turning. He was thinking that he wasn't going to give me a nickel, but on the other hand he was going to kill me anyway, so why not agree to pay me? Sure enough, when he'd thought that over, he finally said, "All right. How much?"

"Two million. In cash," I said.

"All right," he said—and if I needed any final confirmation that he was planning to kill me, that was it. I knew damn well the bastard would never part with that much cash without a fight. "But listen to me, Wolfe, if I get a single fucking hint that you're trying to sell it to anybody but me—"

"I won't," I said. And his answer told me something else. If he was worried I might try to sell it elsewhere, it was worth a lot more than he was offering. Or should I say, pretending to offer? "You can laugh at me all you want, but I do love the USA, and if this thing is that important, I want it to go to the right people. USA people."

"Then why didn't you evacuate with my team, goddamn it?"

"I don't trust you," I said. "Any more than you trust me."

"I never said I didn't trust you," he said.

"Oh, so you never kidnapped my mother and my partner? So you could blackmail me if I didn't cooperate?"

He was silent for about two seconds. "Standard procedure," he said. "So what's next?"

"We meet at a neutral location. Someplace safe," I said. "You come alone, so do I. You hand me the cash, I give you the flash drive, you take it and go save the world with it. And then you and I are *done*. Finished, *finito*, all over forever."

"Where's the meet?" he said.

"Grand Central Terminal. Track side of the clock. High noon in two days."

He was silent. I knew what he was thinking: *Wolfe thinks he'll be safe because Grand Central is public and very crowded. Amateurs think that a busy public place like that is safe, because with so many people around, nobody would dare try anything.*

Wrong. Professionals know that actually, it's *easier* in a busy public place. Because everybody's moving, in a hurry, trying not to notice anybody else. So go ahead and strangle somebody. Stick a knife in their head. Hell, cut their damn head off if you want. And if anybody sees you do it, so what? Everybody always figures somebody else will do something, and anyway they've got a train to catch. So you can just drop the body and go catch your own train. Sure, there are cameras. So what? They can't do anything about it. And by the time the cops get there and look at the pictures, you're long gone, and all the witnesses are on their way to Poughkeepsie, or in a cab for uptown.

I knew Prescott knew all that. And I knew he was so eager and greedy that he'd figure I didn't.

I was right.

"All right," he said. "High noon in two days, and you better bring the flash drive with you or you are done right then and there."

"And you bring my money, or you won't get the drive."

"Fine," he said, and hung up.

One more call, to Chaz, giving him Winston's flight information and laying out to him what had to happen. Then I went into the restroom and got rid of Stefan. I pulled a New Me out of my bag, Henry Davis, a high school history teacher from Indiana. Henry went back out and bought a ticket to Manchester.

CHAPTER

50

Manchester, England, is not normally a destination of choice for the discriminating tourist, but it's where I had to go. There was a ninety-minute wait for my flight, longer than it took to hop across the channel. But I boarded with no problems and landed a few minutes ahead of schedule.

As soon as I cleared customs, I rented a car and drove out of town. No matter how many times I do it, I can't really get comfortable driving on the wrong side of the road.

But I made it to my destination with only a couple of near-death experiences. I parked my wrong-side rental inside the battered gate and headed in. The building didn't look like much, except what it was, which was an old and abandoned factory. What mattered was what was inside. In the first place, it wasn't totally abandoned. Because nestled down snug inside was somebody very special.

Things being what they are nowadays, everybody needs a hacker.

I mean, if you sell hand sanitizer at the flea market, maybe not. But just about anything more complicated than that, then yeah, you better know somebody who can unscramble computer codes. Somebody who can look at a string of garbage numbers and letters and symbols and go, *Yeah, sure. I got this.*

So everybody needs a hacker. And if you are the world's greatest thief, it doesn't hurt to have the world's greatest hacker on a string. I thought I did. If not absolutely the greatest, then anyway in the top ten, no question. And she was pretty sure she was number one and didn't mind saying so. That kind of vibes with me, because, you know—it's me? World's greatest thief?

I had run into Tamiqua Coates on the dark web a few years back. All the buzz was about somebody with the handle "St. Alia of the Knife." Apparently "Alia" had hacked into a top secret super-encrypted Department of Defense site, just to show them where their unsuspected back door was. Nobody knew who St. Alia was, but a ton of people made jokes about the *Dune* reference, and everybody assumed it was "she" from the name. And nobody could find out who she really was, in spite of a couple of pretty good hackers trying to follow her trail. They couldn't because there wasn't one.

Purely by coincidence, I was looking for a good hacker at the time, somebody who could do exactly that kind of thing and not leave footprints. I made a very careful approach, all on the dark web, leaving notes and hints and teases that somebody might have some challenging and lucrative work for her. As I said, all on the dark web, and very subtle. No response.

Until a few weeks later, when I got a letter at my drop box. It was addressed to J.R. Weiner. My birth name that nobody knows. I mean, until then, I guess. It read, "Dear Riley, I'm listening. I'm expensive, but I am the best there is, and you can afford it." And it closed with an email address where I could reach her.

It was pretty impressive for eighteen words. She let me know she knew exactly who I was—both of me—and what I did. And the "expensive but I am the best" read like it was designed to reel me in.

It did. It turned out she was right on both counts—expensive but the best, as far as I could tell. In any case, she did the job I gave her, quick and clean. And then the next one, and the next. We developed a kind of mutual trust, enough so that I met her in person now. That's what I did this time. I let her know I was coming to her crumbling old factory, and she was waiting for me. She buzzed me in through a series of security devices, and I went in and down a long hall to the room where she had her workstation. It was in a large room with an old IBM mainframe at one end, a complex patch bay, half a dozen monitors of different sizes, and a bunch of electronic stuff I couldn't identify if my life depended on it. There was a poster of Bob Marley on one wall, and another of Public Enemy facing it.

Tamiqua sat at a keyboard, pounding it with blinding speed. She was in her mid-twenties and thin. She had her hair up on top of her head in a bright orange topknot, and she wore a loose shirt with what looked like a very intricate African pattern on it.

"Cheers, J.R.," she said. She called me J.R. just because, you know. She could. "Pop a squat, mate." She thundered away on the keyboard while I found a chair, lifted a pile of tangled circuit boards off it, and sat. Half a minute later she finished, spun around, and said, "Right. Wagwan?"

I pulled the flash drive from my jacket pocket. "I have this for you," I said.

"What is it?" she said.

"I'm not sure," I said. "But I need to know. Double the usual rate if you can get it fast."

She rolled her eyes at me. "Come on, mate," she said. "Have I ever been slow?"

"Not yet," I said.

"Give it," she said, holding out her hand. I stood and handed it to her. "Right," she said. "Give us five." She popped the drive into a slot, spun back around, and went to work. I sat back down and waited.

She was quiet for almost thirty seconds, and then the talk started. Not to me, not to anybody, really, except maybe the thing she was working on. Just scattered words to punctuate what she was doing. Things like, "Whaaaat?" and "Up yours, too!" and "Gotcher!"

Three minutes in she stopped dead, said, "Bloody hell, Harry," and spun around and stared at me. "J. fucking R. What the fuck are you about?"

"I don't know," I said. "But I really need to."

"Too right you do. Fucking *hell*!" She shook her head.

"Does that mean you know what's in the file?"

"Not yet," she said. "But I bloody well know where it's from."

"Okay," I said. "Where?"

She told me. And then I started swearing, too.

CHAPTER

51

The meeting took place in a conference room on the third floor of the Harry S. Truman Building. Present were several representatives of the State Department, of course. But also present were several rather high-ranking people from the various intelligence agencies, including one from his own, a woman Frank Delgado knew slightly. He smiled and nodded at her, and she returned both smile and nod.

Delgado and Miranda took side-by-side seats in the middle of the long, highly polished oak table. There was a small plastic bottle of water at each place, and Miranda opened hers at once and took a sip as she looked around the table. "My God," she whispered. "Suddenly I feel important."

"You are," he said. "You found a major leak."

She shook her head. "Don't think I like this," she muttered.

"Let's get started, shall we?" said the woman at the head of the table, a full Assistant Secretary of State named Naomi Pritkin, and the meeting began.

It went pretty much the way Frank Delgado expected. The representatives of the different agencies and departments in attendance batted blame and veiled accusations back and forth like an unending tennis match. They didn't even try to stick anything on Delgado—they were too busy tearing at one another.

In the end, no real conclusion was reached, except that it was a complete disaster and they should all study the report, write a memo of recommendations, and submit a budget proposal to bring computer security up to a much higher standard. All according to the schematic that Frank Delgado had seen played out so many times before.

The only surprise was Miranda Shaleki. She answered all their questions with a blank face, and succinctly, without too much confusing techno-talk. The only time any trace of her personality emerged was when she was questioned by Robert Hendry, a career drudge from the Russia desk at State. He suggested that perhaps she should have found the hack much sooner, and that laxity on her part had probably caused a great deal of harm to national security.

Miranda smiled at him politely and said, "I understand your concern, Mr. Hendry. Nearly a hundred of the Top Secret memos that were exposed to the Russians had your name on them. And if I hadn't found the hack, you would still be pumping Top Secret material to the Russians."

Delgado had to summon all his iron control to keep a smile off his face. And Hendry turned red, stammered something, and remained quiet for the rest of the meeting.

When the meeting broke up, Delgado had to answer a few general questions, say a few words to some old acquaintances, and play a little bit of politics, which he hated. But he'd been in the game long enough to know it was necessary, and he did it with good grace.

When he shook his last hand and headed out of the conference room, he found Miranda waiting for him in the hall beside the door. "You were magnificent," he said. "Mr. Hendry may never recover."

"I hope he doesn't," she said. "What a dick, coming at me to cover his own ass like that."

"Well, you zapped him pretty thoroughly."

"And what about you, just now?" she said. "Jesus, that was ugly. I didn't know you had it in you."

"What?" Delgado said.

She shook her head in disgust. "Just now. All that fucking I-love-you-man shit," she said. "Shaking hands and smiling and—you know, playing that game." She shuddered. "I could never, you know?"

Delgado smiled. "You'd pick it up," he said. "You just need to grow the right calluses."

"Yeah, well, I don't want 'em. Give me a simple, straightforward viral worm any day."

"I'll see what I can find," he said. "Want to grab some lunch?" She gave him an odd look he couldn't interpret. "On the Agency's dime," he added.

She cocked her head to one side, and then shrugged. "Okay, sure, what the hell," she said. "Girl's gotta eat. Where we going? I don't know this town."

"What do you like?" he asked her. "And what do you hate?"

Miranda shuddered again. "Seafood," she said with loathing. "I can't even go into a place that's got that awful fishy smell." She added another shrug. "Other than that, I'll eat just about anything."

"Okay," he said. "I know a place that has that."

They went down in the elevator without speaking and then out to the parking lot. Delgado had a car from the FBI motor pool, a one-year-old Chevrolet sedan. He drove them to a small bistro he knew and actually found a parking spot that was no more than a three-minute walk away.

They settled at a table in the back corner, and the waiter handed them menus, first to Miranda and then, with a very odd look, to Delgado. The waiter disappeared into the back of the restaurant, and because of the strange look, Delgado watched him go. Middle-aged man, or a little older, red hair and a neat goatee the same color, obviously both dyed. He disappeared quickly, but Delgado detected a slight limp.

Delgado turned back to the table to see Miranda staring at him. "What was that?" she asked. "Was the waiter hitting on you?"

He smiled and shook his head. "I don't think so," he said. "I really hope not."

"Well, he had something going on," she said.

"Maybe he recognized me," he said. "I used to come here a lot." Wondering if his favorites were still on offer, he opened his menu. And as he did, a CD in a plain paper envelope dropped out and into his lap. Delgado picked it up.

"Ha! A playlist of love songs! I told you that waiter was hitting on you," Miranda said.

Delgado didn't hear her. Because he was reading a short note, neatly printed in green ink on the back of the paper envelope.

Have one of yr IT people check this. I'll be in touch.

In the same green ink it was signed *RW*.

To Delgado those initials could only mean one thing.

Riley Wolfe.

But if it really was Wolfe, it made no sense at all. Why would Wolfe send him a CD? And why ask him to have his IT people look at it? Presumably that meant an FBI computer tech. There was some kind of code or program on the disk? Maybe—but Wolfe stayed as far from the Bureau as he could, except to occasionally taunt Delgado. And Wolfe was aware that Delgado was hunting him, had been hunting him for years. Was this some kind of a trap, to get Delgado off his back in a permanent way? Or was this a new affront, a boast about some heinous recent crime the Bureau had failed to prevent? Perhaps it was a teasing threat of something Wolfe was about to do. That made a little more sense, though he had never done anything like that in the past.

But the waiter—could that have been Wolfe in person? The thought jarred him, and he looked up to see Miranda staring at him with an odd, amused expression. "And now for the *third* time I will say, Earth to Delgado."

He held up the disc. "This might be important."

Miranda rolled her eyes. "Which means that either you kinda like the waiter's playlist, or I'm about to miss lunch, right?"

In spite of himself, Delgado smiled. "It's not a playlist," he said. "But I think we can have lunch." He stood up abruptly. "Please order me an iced tea and a chef's salad."

"What? Where are you— Damn it, Delgado!"

But he was already gone.

The kitchen door was at the end of a narrow hall that led back, past the restrooms. Delgado opened it and went in. There was the usual cluster of frantic activities from the cooks and the equally panicked parade of waiters coming in and out and yelling. There was no sign of the red-haired waiter. But Delgado spotted the headwaiter who had seated him, talking to one of the cooks, and approached him.

"Excuse me," he said.

The headwaiter glanced at him. "Sir, you can't be back here."

Delgado was ready for this. He held up his FBI shield. "FBI," he said. Out of the corner of his eye he noticed that the dishwasher and a busboy had looked up nervously and were now edging toward the back door. He turned in their direction and raised his voice. "*No tengan miedo, no soy La Migra*," he said. "*Es un asunto criminal.*" The two still looked worried, but they stopped moving toward the door.

"How can I help you, Special Agent?" the headwaiter said.

"The red-haired waiter," he said. "How long has he been working here?"

The headwaiter looked bewildered. "Uh, who exactly do you mean, sir?"

"The waiter with bright red hair, beard the same color," Delgado said. "He was here five minutes ago."

The headwaiter shook his head. "As far as I know, there's no one on our staff with bright red hair," he said.

Delgado nodded. "Thank you," he said. It was what he'd expected, but he had to check. And the question remained: Who had it been? Riley Wolfe himself, or somebody he'd hired to deliver the CD? Once again, he thought how frustrating it was that he'd been pursuing the man for so long and didn't even know what he looked like. And he had a hunch that he wouldn't find out this time, even in a face-to-face meeting.

He headed back to the table and slid back into his chair.

"So do I get to know what just happened?" Miranda said. "I mean, I'm totally thrilled I get to eat lunch, but—what the hell, Delgado? What's the mystery?"

Delgado held up the CD. "This," he said.

She shrugged. "Okay. What is it?"

"I'm hoping you can tell me," he said. "The note says to give it to a Bureau IT tech."

"Technically, I'm State Department," Miranda said.

He nodded. "But I trust you. And I know you're good."

"Good?" she demanded. "After all I've done, I'm still only *good*?"

"How about awesome?" he said.

She shuddered. "Jesus, nobody's used that word for like ten years. But I'll take it. Oh—who's the note from?"

"Have you ever heard of Riley Wolfe?"

She shook her head. "Nope. Should I have heard of him?"

"He's a thief," Delgado said. "One of the best. But a killer, too. And . . ." He hesitated. How could he explain the relationship? He decided he couldn't. "I don't trust him," was all he said. "But I need to know why he would give me this." He held up the CD.

"Well, I can't check it with my phone," Miranda said. "And I work better on a full stomach so—how's the gnocchi here?"

The gnocchi was very good, and Miranda ate it all with real gusto, followed by a piece of cheesecake and a double espresso. She didn't eat with any fake daintiness, either. She dug in and ate like she'd never seen food before. Delgado watched her with pleasure. He disliked women who ate as though they weren't really interested in food.

When they finished their coffee, Delgado paid and they walked back to their car. "I'll call ahead and get a secure computer set up for you," he said as he started the engine.

"Call ahead where—oh, the FBI headquarters? It's called the Hoover Building?"

"That's right," he said, taking out his phone.

"Yeah, no, hold on there, Slim," she said, and he paused his dialing. "They don't have the stuff I need," she said.

"It's one of the best-equipped computer sections in the country," he said.

"Yeah, sure, which means almost nothing," she said. "But what I need—if there's any code-busting or hacking involved, I've got my own toolbox."

"Of course you do," Delgado said. He put his phone away. "So where to?"

"My laptop is back at the hotel," she said.

"All right," he said. He put the car in gear.

Twenty minutes later he was sitting on the edge of the bed in Miranda's room while she sat at the small desk and hammered at her laptop. Delgado was not normally a man who fidgeted, but he did now. He had been turning it over in his mind, and he could not think of any plausible reason for Wolfe to give him a CD, no matter what was on it. But he was on fire to know, and he had to fight to stay seated and not stand right behind Miranda and peer over her shoulder as she worked. He knew her well enough by now to know she would be angry at him if he did. Aside from interrupting her work, he also had come to like her, and he didn't want to make her mad at him. So he sat ten feet away and fidgeted.

He didn't have to fidget too long. After less than ten minutes, Miranda sat bolt upright and said, "Holy shit!" in a tone that sounded almost like religious awe.

Delgado stood up. "What? You have something?"

"I know this line of code," she said. "It's St. Alia of the Knife!"

Baffled, Delgado shook his head. "Who?"

"Legendary hacker," she said. "One of the best—maybe *the* best. At least until I came along."

"Okay, so you found something?"

"Nothing yet, keep your shirt on," she said. She glanced at him quickly and added, "A least for now." She turned rapidly back to her laptop.

310

"But St. Alia of the Knife is—I know *her*, and this is . . ." She made a vague gesture and bent back over her keyboard.

Delgado sat back down, clasped and unclasped his hands, and realized he was tapping one foot rapidly. He stopped.

It seemed much longer to him, but it was only four minutes later when Miranda jerked backward, sending the little desk chair rolling away from the desk. "Oh *fuck*," she said. "Fuck fuck *FUCK*."

Delgado was across the room in a second. "What?!" he said.

Miranda shook her head. "This is— I'm not sure I should be seeing this." She ran a hand through her hair. "This is— Jesus, Delgado, I'm cleared for everything up to Secret, but . . ."

"I have Top Secret clearance," he said. "I'll take the heat. What have you got?"

"Delgado, I don't even know what it is, but I know it's above your pay grade, too. Right at the top it says, 'President's Eyes Only.'"

Delgado hesitated only a second. "Let me see it," he said. If Riley Wolfe really had something that hot, Delgado needed to know. And more than that—he needed to know *why*.

CHAPTER

52

It was a relatively small room on the top floor of a building in Mc-Lean, Virginia, over the bridge from D.C., and oddly enough, stuck in the center of the complex maze of a freeway interchange. The room was small because it was one of the most secure rooms in the world, and top secret meetings generally have a very limited guest list. This one was no exception. There were only three people present. Frank Delgado was there, of course, as the bearer of grim news. He sat in a seat at the middle of the highly polished table. The DNI, Director of National Intelligence, sat at the end of the table, and directly across from Delgado was FBI Deputy Director Holly Steele.

Deputy Director Steele was there because the director was testifying before a congressional committee today. She was more than able to fill his shoes.

"Special Agent Delgado," she said in a voice that matched her name. "I hope you understand we have a remarkably urgent threat to national security here."

"Yes, ma'am," Delgado said, with a glance at the DNI. "I believe I do."

"Who else has seen what's on that disk?" she asked.

"Other than myself and Ms. Shaleki, no one on this end," Delgado said. "On the other end—Riley Wolfe and a hacker."

"Riley Wolfe," she said.

"Yes, ma'am," Delgado said.

"You're sure it was him?"

"As sure as I can be," he said. "His initials were on the envelope. In green ink, which is what he used in the past."

The DNI spoke for the first time. "Who was the hacker?"

"Ms. Shaleki recognized some of the code," he said. "We think it was a woman known in the hacker community as St. Alia of the Knife."

The DNI frowned. "What's the significance of that name?"

"It's a female character in a well-known science fiction book, sir," Delgado said. "A book called *Dune*."

The DNI shook his head. "The president is waiting to hear this. He's cleared his schedule for the rest of the day. And I'm going to go back to the White House and tell him about a sci-fi novel. He'll love it." He sighed and sat back in his chair.

"Special Agent Delgado," Steele said. "You've chased Wolfe for years. And he's aware that you've been hunting him."

"Yes, ma'am."

"Would you say some kind of relationship has developed between you?"

Delgado hesitated, then nodded. "In a certain sense, yes, ma'am," he said. "He knows me well enough to get at me in some very specific ways."

"And you think you know him better than our profilers?" she asked.

"I think so, yes, ma'am," he said.

"But you've never even seen him," she said. "You have no idea what he looks like."

"No, ma'am."

Steele drummed her fingers on her desk. Her expression did not change. "I don't get it," she said at last. "Why would he send this to you?"

"I can only guess, ma'am."

"Then guess," she snapped.

Delgado hesitated slightly. "I think," he said slowly, "that it's part of some other plan he's got going. Something that's to his benefit."

The DNI held up the CD in its envelope. "What's on this disk is only a tiny piece of the whole. I believe it was meant to be a teaser. A sales tool, if you will. The Russians would pay a couple of billion dollars for this," he said. "With a B. The Chinese would probably pay more. Does this Wolfe character think we'll outbid them?"

"It's . . . possible?" he said.

"But you don't think so."

"No, sir," Delgado said confidently.

"Why not? He's a thief, motivated by money."

"But he's not," Delgado said. "That is, not entirely. He's made enough money to retire any time he wants to. What he's after is a challenge, a way to show the world that he can do things no one else would even try."

"Things like stealing a weapons system so secret it has Presidential Only clearance?"

"He might," Delgado admitted. "But I think it's more likely that he came across this while he was stealing something else."

"So again—why give it to you, Delgado?" Steele demanded.

"Again, ma'am—this is guesswork," he said. "But it's based on my experience with Wolfe."

"Spit it out."

"Wolfe is very good at juggling three or four things at once, in a way that makes them all come together in a payoff for him," Delgado said. "I think this is part of that kind of plan, and he needs the Bureau."

"Why the Bureau?" the DNI asked. "Why not Delta Force, or even Academi?"

"Sir, I think . . ." Delgado realized he was nervous and took a calming breath. "I think it's because of me. Because we do have a connection of sorts. He thinks—he thinks he knows what I'll do."

"Hmmp," the DNI said.

"What does he want from us?" Steele demanded.

"To use us. Either to threaten someone else, or to protect him. Possibly both," he said.

"And we don't know what until he gets in touch," she said. "And what does *that* mean? In touch how?"

Delgado almost smiled. "Some way that will surprise me and protect him," he said. "Other than that? Impossible to say."

"But you think we can trust him when he does?" the DNI asked.

"Trust him? No, sir," Delgado said. "But I do think he'll do what he says he'll do in this very limited context."

The DNI looked at Steele and raised an eyebrow. Steele simply nodded, and the DNI leaned back, apparently satisfied.

Deputy Director Steele sat for a long moment without showing any expression. Finally she said, "This Shaleki. Can we trust her?"

"Yes, ma'am, I believe we can," Delgado said firmly.

Steele nodded. "All right. Sir?"

The DNI nodded and held up the CD. "This is literally the gravest crisis in national security in the last twenty years. We have to get it back, whatever it takes." He stood up. "Whatever that turns out to be, try to keep the body count down," he said, and he left the room.

CHAPTER

53

Frank Delgado realized he was nervous. He wondered why; this was far from being the first time he'd gone to a potentially dangerous meet with a criminal. But this was, he realized, the first time he'd gone to meet Riley Wolfe. His anxiety was only partly because his life might be on the line. Oddly enough, he recognized that it also felt like the angst you might feel going on a first date with a true crush, and he almost smiled at that. But it was understandable. He had spent so many years pursuing Wolfe without so much as a glimpse of his face, and now he would meet him at last. Assuming, of course, that Wolfe actually showed up.

He checked his watch: five minutes past the agreed time. That was understandable. Wolfe was smart, cautious, and experienced. He would check out the entire area, looking for any possible backup team, before he exposed himself. That was fine. He wouldn't find anything. Delgado had won that argument, and he had come alone.

An enormously fat man came wheezing up and sat on the bench next to him. He was a little over six feet tall, and well over three hundred pounds. His face was bright red, and he wore an old-fashioned seersucker suit and a Panama hat, and the sweat was pouring off him, soaking the suit. "Oh, my," he said in a thick Southern accent. "Oh, my lord." He sat, leaning forward and gasping for a minute before he settled back against the back of the bench.

Delgado tried to think of a polite way to ask the man to move on. He couldn't expect Riley Wolfe to sit here with a stranger on the bench. And he would rightfully be suspicious that the man was an agent of some kind. Before he could frame his words, the fat man turned toward Delgado and spoke.

"Well," he said. "It certainly is a *warm* day now, isn't it?" He took a cell phone out of his jacket pocket and placed it on the bench between them. "All right, then," he said, in the same jolly drawl. "That's not really a phone. It's just a little toy to block out electronic signals. You know," he said with a wink and a smile, "just in case you're wearing a wire. Oh! How rude of me—congratulations on your promotion! How do you find those Moscow winters?"

Delgado blinked. Was it possible? He knew, of course, that Wolfe was remarkably good at the art of disguise, but this? "Riley Wolfe?" he said hesitantly.

The man nodded and smiled. "I just couldn't resist finally meeting you face-to-face. Even if it isn't really my face," he said, and then he chuckled, a fat gurgle appropriate to his character.

For a moment, Delgado just stared. Even with Wolfe two feet away, the disguise was flawless. He shook his head. "The stories were not exaggerated," he said, and he couldn't keep a tiny note of admiration out of his voice.

"Of course not, how could they be?" Wolfe said. "If anything, they're understated." And he chuckled again.

"I believe you," Delgado said. "So believe me when I tell you, you have the DNI's attention."

"Which might not be a good thing, I know," he said. "I thought it was worth the risk."

"Of course you would," Delgado said. "You have the entire document?"

"Not on me, of course," Wolfe said. "But yes."

"How much of it have you seen?"

"Yes, I can see why you'd like to know that." He shrugged. "Only enough to be scared shitless. I don't really want to know more."

Delgado nodded. Of course he would say that, but whether it was true was another thing. "What are your conditions for returning it?"

"Complete immunity, of course. Nobody touches me, tails me, tries to arrest me or shoot me. Nothing," he said. "Including some stoked-up asshole deciding later that now I'm a security risk and authorizing extreme prejudice is in the country's best interest."

"Naturally," Delgado said. "I've been authorized to offer that. What else?"

Wolfe studied him for a moment. Then he smiled. "I don't think you're asking that as a matter of form, are you? You knew there'd be more. Because you've studied me—I'd bet you even profiled me yourself, didn't you, Special Agent in Charge?"

"The Bureau's profile was—inadequate," Delgado said.

"They often are, aren't they?" He chuckled again. "Well. As it happens, I don't need any special favors. Fact is, I want to do *you* a favor."

"Why do I find that hard to believe?"

"God's truth. I want to do you a favor—a very *big* favor at that."

"All right. What do you want to do for us?"

Wolfe smiled, a big smile that grew until it spread across his fat and sweaty face. "I want to give you the US agent who stole it in the first place," he said.

CHAPTER
54

The meeting is at noon tomorrow," I said. I looked around. Chaz and Winston were watching me, Chaz looking a little bored. I didn't care. This had to go right. "Just guessing, but I think he gets here early, with as many guns as he can get. So there won't be too many of Prescott's guys at the site when you get there. Most of them will be on me. But remember, noon."

"And tomorrow, right?" Chaz said brightly. I knew that what he really wanted to say was "Yeah, we got it, shut the fuck up and get the beer." But sarcasm was Chaz's version of being polite. And yeah, okay, what I said was obvious. But there have been too many times when something was obvious to me and somebody else totally missed it. So I just nodded like I took him seriously and said, "Yes, Chaz, that's a good point. But the thing is, the timing is most important," I told them. "It has to happen just a few minutes before my meeting."

"Which is at noon," Chaz said. "Tomorrow."

I ignored him this time. "T.C.," I said. "You're dead sure this is the place?"

He nodded. "Has to be. Like I said, it's close, but totally isolated because it's on an island, in the middle of the St. Lawrence Seaway. It's a fucking castle, man, and it's off the grid. Prescott has a doctor stashed there, one who doesn't mind doing stuff that they'd lift her license for. And the Agency doesn't even know about it."

"How do you know all that?" I asked.

"Prescott bragged about it," Winston said. "Said he had a dark place to keep anybody he wanted, right in the States, and the Agency would never know."

"All right," I said. I thought about it, because there's always something you've overlooked. "The chopper," I said.

Winston nodded. "Yeah, sure, there's a field right next to the castle. Big enough to play football. I can put the chopper down there easy, done it a few times already. But it's got to be a small crew going in, four people max, including me in the pilot seat."

"We won't need four. Three is plenty. Most of his crew will be busy with me."

"Then sure, no problem," he said. "And they know me at the castle, so no worries."

"Take a pill, Riley," Chaz said. "We know what to do, we know we can do it. You just do your thing and relax. We got this."

I ran a hand through my hair. I hadn't cut it back yet, and it was still kind of shaggy, the way Stefan liked it. "Yeah, sure, okay," I said. "Well—"

"Well nothing. Let's do this," Chaz said. "Get the beer."

CHAPTER

55

In the street in front of Grand Central Terminal a work crew was clustered around a manhole. They wore orange safety vests and helmets, and like city work crews since time began, most of them leaned on shovels while one of them worked. They'd set up a temporary barricade around the site, and their van was parked just beyond the barricade, DEPARTMENT OF PUBLIC WORKS on the side above the City Seal. All perfectly normal, something that happens all over the city every day.

Inside the van, though, was a scene not quite as ordinary.

Along one side, a wall of electronic equipment blinked. A couple of them were recognizable as radios and digital recorders, and of course, several monitor screens in the center. Watching the monitors was a group of fit-looking people wearing dark jackets with FBI written on the back. Two more agents, a man and a woman, sat in front of the equipment with headphones on.

One of them was Frank Delgado. He stared at the central monitor with fierce concentration. It showed a view of the street right outside the van, the area leading up to a door into the station. His eyes flicked left and right, looking intently at each pedestrian as they passed in front of the camera, until his stare locked onto one.

Delgado lifted a microphone. "This is team leader," he said. "He's headed in. Stand by."

Arthur Kondor was halfway through *Coriolanus* for the fourth time when he heard sounds outside his door, sounds he hadn't heard here before. Far off there was a shot, then a short burst of automatic fire. In the hall outside his cell he heard his guard swear. Then there was an odd metal *clank*, as if some metal object had hit the floor. Kondor could not tell what was going on, but it was clear that something was. He put the book down and stood up.

The noise outside really told him nothing, but it was new, a break in routine. Something unusual was taking place. That could mean many things, or nothing. If it was nothing, he would go back to reading *Coriolanus*. But if it was something, he would be ready.

Kondor took one step to the side of the door, to where he would have a good line of sight if the door swung open. He listened. There was always the one guard outside his room, and he expected to hear something more from him. It might be just a greeting. Or it could be a shout of alarm, and even a shot fired.

None of that happened. No sounds came at all. Instead, there was a sudden hush, and nothing else came to fill it. There was silence for half a minute. Then, the door to his room opened. The guard stood there in the doorway for a few seconds, staring stupidly. Then he fell forward onto his face, hitting the floor with a loud and hollow *thump*. Right behind him was another man wearing gray overalls, holding an

H&K MP7. He held an olive-green shoulder bag in his other hand. Kondor had never seen this man. He quickly dropped his right leg back and got ready for anything, anything except what happened.

The man made no overt threat toward Kondor. Instead, he ripped something from his shoulder bag and thrust it at Kondor. "Put this on, quick!" he said.

Kondor glanced at it. It was a military-issue M40 gas mask. "Why?" Kondor said.

The man was already pulling a second M40 over his own head. "Goddamn it, I said *quick*!" he said. "Shit, right. Swordfish! Riley sent me!"

Kondor nodded. Now it made sense. He put the mask on and watched as the other man took a couple of gas canisters out of his bag. He opened the valve on one, rolled it out into the hall, and slammed the door.

"This'll only take a minute," the other man said, his voice muffled by the gas mask. "This stuff dissipates really fast." He nodded at the unconscious guard. "Grab that guy's weapon; we got more to do."

"All right," Kondor said. He stooped and searched the fallen guard. He found a Sig Sauer P320 in a holster on one hip and took it. There were two extra clips in one pocket and a wad of cash in the other. Kondor took that, too, and stood up. There were more shouts outside the room. Kondor checked over his new pistol; there was a round in the chamber already. He flipped the safety switch to the firing position and waited.

The shouting died down after a minute, and it got unnaturally quiet. He glanced at his rescuer. "Just another minute, to be safe," the man said.

A minute passed, and the man cautiously opened the door and looked out. "Good to go," he said. "Come on."

Kondor followed into the hall and toward the stairs at the far end. His rescuer paused, then turned to Kondor. "Gotta find Riley's mother," he said.

Kondor nodded. "They brought us in at the same time," he said. "I know where she is."

"Get her," he said. "We have to get his girlfriend, too."

"I'm on it," Kondor said, and the other man took off up the stairs. Kondor watched him go, glad to be free, and gladder to have a chance at some small redemption. And he hoped there would still be a guard watching the old lady. He was pissed at these people, and he was really hoping he could put away a couple. He smiled as he realized he'd just read the perfect line in *Coriolanus.*

"Let me have war, say I: it exceeds peace as far as day does night; it's spritely, waking, audible, and full of vent."

Shakespeare always got it right.

Kondor hurried off to find Riley's mother, and war.

Monique studied her most recent drawing. They were getting closer and closer to looking right, and this one was the best so far, but . . . No. Almost—but still not the face. Something wasn't quite right, not yet. She frowned, running a finger over the lines of the face on the page. The shape was right, but—was it the chin? Maybe not quite as strong as she'd drawn it. She smudged the chin with a thumb and re-drew it, just a little more like—that. Yes, that was it. Now it was almost perfect. But there was one last—

Badda-dadda-dat!

Monique dropped her pencil in shock. The sound was loud, and it came from somewhere nearby, a series of sharp bangs. Almost imme-diately there were three or four single sharp pops. Somebody screamed, somebody else yelled. And then more of the *badda-dadda-dat*s, several of them this time and much closer. Without thinking about why, Monique jumped up and her notebook dropped to the floor. Another *badda-dadda-dat* and this time she knew what it was.

Gunfire. Somebody was shooting, somebody was shooting back at them, and it was getting closer.

Monique realized she was standing on her bed, back against the wall and heart pounding. Gunfire meant danger. People were getting hurt, even killed, and her breath panted in and out as she looked wildly around for a way to hide, to get away, be safe. Because what if she was next? She had to run—

No. Because suddenly she knew exactly what the gunshots meant.

It was *him*. The face she'd been drawing.

He was coming to save her.

Monique had known he would come, even without knowing who he was or why he would come for her. But it had been an absolute certainty. He would come. He would save her.

And now gunfire. She was sure it was him. Who else could it be? He had come for her at last. But what should she do? Just wait here? What if he couldn't find her here in this room? Maybe she should go to meet him, somehow break down her door and rush toward the noise.

Before she could do any more than think of doing that, the door burst open by itself. Monique saw a rail-thin figure in a white lab coat: Dr. Arnsdale. She was backing into the room, in odd, jerky steps. And then she stopped moving, swayed for a moment, and fell into the room on her back. She hit the floor with a hard, wet noise, her head bounced once, and then she was still. And it was very clear why she didn't move. There were three large red circles on her chest.

Dr. Arnsdale was dead. Monique gasped, but then she realized she was glad. The doctor had been an awful person, always mean, treating her like she was some kind of *thing*. But with her dead body right here, right in front of her like that . . . It had never occurred to her that rescue would mean dead people, and suddenly Monique wasn't so sure it was really him, coming to take her out of this place. What if it was bad people, and they were killing everyone? What if—

A shout in the hallway, more footsteps, and two large men appeared in the doorway. They had guns, and they looked very frightening. "Monique," the bigger, scarier one said. "Are you Monique?"

Monique was too scared to answer. She pushed back against the wall as if she could force it to open up and hide her. "Colon. Colonostomy. Colon," she said.

The man shook his head, puzzled. "Monique," he said again.

The other man pushed past him and picked up her notebook, with the face showing. He studied it for just a second. "Check it out," he said, and showed it to the other man. "Has to be her." He gave Monique a reassuring smile and said, "My name is Chaz." He held the drawing up in front of her. "This man is our friend. He sent us to get you." He moved the drawing closer to Monique's face. "This man you drew, he sent us. Riley Wolfe."

Riley Wolfe. That was the name. The face was Riley Wolfe. Memories flooded into her brain, the two of them talking, laughing—

Monique stepped down off her bed. Things felt suddenly clear. "T-take me there," she said. "T-take me to, to, to Riley Wolfe."

The man smiled. He held out his hand. "Let's go," he said.

The two men led her out and down the hall. They came to a huge winding staircase with marble steps and handrails. Monique started down the steps, coming to a landing where the stairs turned left. She put one foot out—and jerked to a halt. There were dead bodies, one on the stairs ahead of her, two more at the foot of the stairs.

She jerked again as a hand came down on her shoulder. But it was the man called Chaz again. "It's okay," he said reassuringly. "Those are the bad guys." He nodded, gave her a half smile, and Monique continued down the stairs into a huge open hall with a great crystal chandelier hanging in the center. A suit of armor stood against one wall, holding a monstrous three-edged sword, and an enormous tapestry hung beside it. The entire hall was furnished with beautiful old things. It was all tattered and dusty but still worth a long look.

She was still gaping when she realized they'd stopped at the foot of the stairs. A third man was approaching them. He was bigger and more frightening than the others, and he carried a gun. "Appropriate. Inappropriate," Monique said. Chaz patted her again. "It's all right. He's with us," he said. And he turned his attention back to the newcomer, who looked very serious. He stopped a few feet away, closed his eyes, and shook his head.

"Oh, shit," Chaz said. "I better call and tell him."

CHAPTER
56

The Main Concourse at Grand Central is famous for several reasons. As the name implies, it's central, and most of the trains in and out of the city run to and from it. It's also got some beautiful features, like the zodiac ceiling, which was painted on backward. It may be that Cornelius Vanderbilt knew why, but if so he didn't tell anyone. There's also the Guastavino tile in the Whispering Gallery, always worth a visit. It can carry your whisper across an arch directly into just one other person's ear. And of course, putting all that aside, it's New York at its busiest, so the people watching is unparalleled.

But perhaps most famous of all is the Information Booth Clock. It's worth a look; designed and built for the new terminal in the early twentieth century, its estimated worth is twenty million dollars. And beyond that, the famous tag line, "Meet me at the clock," has been in dozens of books and movies.

The Main Concourse is always busy, and today was no exception.

People flowed through it in all directions in a nonstop flood, all of them in a hurry.

Derek Symanski sat on a bench with a nice view of the clock and watched them all come and go with real interest. But he was no casual people watcher. He was looking for one very specific person, and for a very specific reason. It was his job to make sure that this man died here today.

A stocky, dark-haired man, mid-forties, came in through the west-side door, and Symanski very casually watched him over the *Sports Illustrated* he was pretending to read. The man wore a decent gray suit, large black-framed glasses, and carried a bulky briefcase. He was clearly a businessman, hurrying to catch his train, but Symanski studied him carefully anyway. The target had seen most of the other guys on the team, but not Symanski, so it was his job to stay out front and alert everybody when the target entered. And he had to do it carefully, so the target didn't make him. Prescott was supposed to be here alone, and if any of his team was recognized, it would be over before it started.

The businessman stopped at the newsstand, just ten feet away from where Symanski was sitting with *Sports Illustrated*. He watched as the guy picked up a paper, the *Wall Street Journal*, and took it to the cashier, obviously not in any big rush.

And just as obviously, not the target. Symanski had studied dozens of pictures and was sure he'd know Wolfe on sight. And he'd been briefed all about Wolfe, how he was so good at disguise. But this guy was just too different from Wolfe. He was taller, his build was slightly pudgy, and the shape of his face was wrong. And he was taking his time, buying a paper, so now he would have the paper in one hand and the briefcase in the other, which would've been pretty stupid if it was Wolfe. He was a pro, and he knew you didn't go to a meet with your hands full. You needed to be ready to grab your weapon if it went south.

The businessman paid for the paper and started for the exit leading to the trains. He stopped as his phone rang—Symanski could hear the ringtone clearly. "Yes," the guy said into the phone. And after a pause, "I'm on my way." He pocketed the phone and moved on, and Symanski went back to pretending to read his magazine and waited.

He's not coming."

"God*damn* it!" Prescott threw an ashtray, and Darby just barely dodged it. "You fucked up a simple hit!"

"We didn't screw up," he said.

"He didn't fucking show! How do you explain that if you didn't fuck up!"

"We did it all right," Darby insisted. "He just didn't show."

Prescott scowled and looked for something else to throw. There was nothing near at hand. "Goddamn it," he said again. He drummed his fingers on the desktop. "We'll have to remind him we have his mother and his girlfriend. That'll jerk his leash."

Darby cleared his throat and looked incredibly uncomfortable. "About that, sir," he said.

In the street in front of the station, the workers in their orange vests and helmets looked like they hadn't moved more than an inch or two. They were talking and laughing, and one of them puffed lazily on a cigarette.

Inside the van, things were very different. The tension was appreciably thicker. Delgado was glaring at the monitor as if it were guilty of a felony. "Damn it, where is he going?" he said, apparently to himself.

He got an answer anyway. "He got on the crosstown train," a voice said in his headphones.

Delgado frowned even more fiercely. For a moment his gaze went unfocused. Then he nodded and spoke into the microphone. "Bring it in. It's not going to happen," he said.

He put the microphone down, and to himself he whispered, "But why?"

CHAPTER
57

I made the guy right away. I mean, it was really hard not to. He might as well have worn a sign around his neck that said, "BLACK OPS 'R' US." Because he was trying to look like a successful business guy, right? Except—no. Never. First off, he was lounging there in a nice suit, tailored, but with it he was wearing a tie that had to come from the Walmart cut-out bin, and nobody who could afford the suit would touch that thing. Also, he had on scuffed-up rubber-soled shoes, which are great for pursuing somebody, or sneaking, but not at all the thing for somebody like he was trying to impersonate. Those guys wore Italian leather shoes to show how successful they were, and those shoes *gleamed*. And on top of that, what business guy sits there reading *Sports Illustrated* in the middle of the day, like he's got all the time in the world?

So okay, some kind of spook, and he had to be one of Prescott's guys. I knew he wouldn't come alone. Not just because he meant to kill me. I had known dozens of born-rich overprivileged asshats, and they were all cowards who hid how scared they were by saying, "Oh, I would never dirty my hands by touching a grubby peon like you." He'd sent a team, and the chucklehead on the bench was one of them. Odds were he'd been put there to watch for me and alert the hit team. Oh, did they think I didn't know it was a hit? Well duh. I'd known they'd try since day one. But guess what? It wasn't going to happen. Instead, I was just going to go through the station and point out Prescott to my new best friends at the FBI. I was pretty sure the hitters wouldn't recognize me, but just to be safe, I stopped and bought a paper so the clueless goon on the bench could get a good look and be sure it wasn't me.

Then my phone rang and everything changed.

"Yes," I said.

"It's Chaz," he said, which I knew already. But then he didn't say anything for a long moment. When he finally said it, I wished he'd stuck to silence. I just stood there and watched the world turn dark and swim away. When I could think again, the hurting started. But I knew what I was going to do next.

"I'm on my way," I said.

"Riley, what about—"

I cut him off and put the phone in my pocket.

The moment I got that phone call the world turned into a dim, bad place. It was hard to see through the curtain of darkness. I got out of the station and across town, and then over to Brooklyn, but I still don't know how. I moved automatically, inside a cloud of black pain that wouldn't go away. Every now and then I saw something, like through a rift in the murky fog. The face of a scared old lady staring at me. A guy playing the violin on the subway platform. Three girls in Catholic school uniforms. I'd see these things, but none of it registered. I was moving through a world where I didn't belong, a version of life that didn't make any sense.

But I kept moving through it. I moved mechanically, taking the right steps without knowing it, without understanding how or why I did it. And somehow, it worked. Somehow I found my way to a place I had in Brooklyn. I went in and up the stairs to the spacious old loft and opened the door. And then I just sat. I didn't do anything, say anything, think anything. I just sat and watched the darkness roll in, wrap itself around me, and make itself at home.

I don't know how long I sat like that. At some point some people came in and I just blinked because I wasn't sure for a minute what it meant or who they were. The fog rolled back a little, and I knew them. Chaz, Winston, and Kondor, standing there with bleak, I'm-so-sorry expressions. They must have read how that made me feel, because they didn't say anything, just stood there watching me.

Chaz was the one who finally found the balls to speak. "I'm sorry, Riley," he said. "We were just too late. But—"

But. That set me off again. There couldn't be any "but" here. Mom was dead and there was nothing that could *but* that. I took a step toward Chaz and he moved aside—

And there was Monique.

I stood and stared at her. Tears were pouring down her face and her mouth was moving, but all that came out was, "Ruh. Ruh. Ruh. Ruh." Over and over, until finally she closed her eyes tight, clamped down her jaw, and made her hands into taut fists. "Colonostomy. Colonectomy. Colon—" She shook her head, hard. "Rriley," she said, very deliberate and careful. She opened her eyes. "Rriley." A very small and tentative smile crept onto her face, the kind of smile you might see on a little girl who hopes you've forgotten about something bad she did. "Riley," she said. The smile went away. "Riley W-wolfe . . . ?"

And then she sobbed and ran at me, and we were hugging and both of us were crying and squeezing each other like we would never let go. Monique ducked her head down onto my chest and pressed her face against me like she was trying to burrow through to my back, and I heard myself saying, "All right. All right," over and over again, and that was all there was for a while.

Monique didn't want to let go of me, which kind of limited where I could sit. I cleared off a low coffee table, and we slid onto that. The others gathered around and sat, still looking solemn. I had to sit shiva once, when I was an Orthodox gem merchant. The scene looked like that, everybody sitting together and thinking gloomy thoughts about how short life was.

Well, okay. Life is short, and it was about to end for a certain arrogant, born-rich shithead. And it wasn't going to be quick and painless. He'd earned something special. What he'd put me through was bad enough, but to cap it with letting Mom die—Nope. Sorry. End of story.

It wasn't all just revenge for Mom, either. Okay, mostly? But there was more to it. I feel stupid just saying it, but yeah, I really do love my country. Maybe I haven't done much to show it—I mean, I don't think too many people go around bragging about how the world's greatest thief is from the USA. But I'm pretty sure I wouldn't *be* the world's greatest thief if I'd been born in China or Romania. And if that's not enough, well, I've been all over the world, and I've never found a place that's better, or even as good. And I love living here, being from here, and coming home to this country.

So I really and truly had been planning to do the patriotic thing and give Prescott to the FBI. I kind of liked the idea of the Ivy League scumbag living out the rest of his days in an orange jumpsuit in Federal lockup.

That wasn't going to happen now. He took my mother, and now she was dead. So Prescott wasn't going to live out his life in lockup. He wasn't going to live out his life anywhere, because he was about to run out of life. It was just a matter of deciding how.

"Listen, dumbfuck, we all know what you're thinking, and it's crazy. You go after him alone, you come back in a body bag," Chaz said.

Tough love is always a beautiful thing, isn't it? But I wasn't in any mood for beauty. "Fuck off," I told him.

"Look around you, Riley," he insisted. "You got friends here that can help."

"No help," I said. "I do this alone."

Winston cleared his throat and leaned forward. "He doesn't go anywhere without a couple of guys, Riley," he told me. "You know, like bodyguards. And I know those guys: They're shooters, and they're good."

I looked at Winston. I was surprised that he spoke up. He was kind of new to the Riley Wolfe show, and it was pretty obvious that I was not in a patient and understanding mood. "This is none of your goddamn business," I said.

"Yeah, but, you know. It kind of is?" he said. "I mean, I bailed on my job to help you, and I did that. I proved myself, Riley, and I need to do this with you."

It was a fair point, but I didn't care. I only cared about one thing: snuffing Prescott. Ever since they'd told me that they found Mom at that castle and she was dead, gone forever, taken away from me for all time until that beautiful day when we meet up yonder. Which, let's face it, was never going to happen, because there ain't no "up yonder." I was going to get him here and now and make him suffer, and I wasn't going to cheer up and play nicely with others until it was done. And I wasn't going to do it as some kind of team-building exercise.

"No," I said. "This is mine."

"Right, I get that," he said. "But I know Prescott, how he thinks, and I know the guys who'll be guarding him."

I looked at Winston. He didn't blink. I was getting to like the guy, and he was right. I had sold him on jumping ship—and it was kind of ironic: I had fed him a made-up story that Prescott was a traitor, and even though it turned out to be true, I kind of had been shoveling BS at him for my own selfish reasons. So maybe I owed him, and he had some good usable talents, too. I didn't want to alienate him. But he was pushing in where he didn't belong. "Stay out of my way, T.C.," I told him.

"No."

I stared at him. I thought I must have heard wrong. "What?"

"No. I won't stay out," he said. "I want in."

"I have to do this, T.C."

"Yeah, I get that," he said. "But goddamn it, I do, too. I mean—look, you know what I'm all about, okay? I've given my life to serving my country, and fucking Prescott—" His breath hissed out between his teeth, and for a second he looked scary as hell. "Goddamn it, Riley, he used me. He betrayed his country, and that's as bad as it gets. Except it's worse, because he took me along and made me betray my country, too." He shook his head. "I can't let that go. So okay, you have to do it. Fine. But I proved I'm on your team at the castle, and I'm coming along to help now."

He looked stubborn as hell, with some of that scary mean face mixed in, and I thought about what he said. I mean, I wasn't scared of him, and I knew I could slip away from him easily. But if I was being fair, I had to admit that Prescott had screwed Winston, too, and for years. Hell, he'd screwed both of us in a thousand ways.

A line popped into my head. Maybe it was because Prescott kept quoting him, but it was Poe again, "The Cask of Amontillado" this time. "The thousand injuries of Fortunato I had borne . . ."

And just like that, I thought of how I was going to do it.

"Okay," I said.

CHAPTER 58

C hase Prescott had always been proud of his emotional control. He'd learned early in the game that anger, yelling, and threatening were tools. Used judiciously, they were effective at keeping the troops in line. But if the anger was uncontrolled and came out at the wrong times, it was guaranteed to be counterproductive. Right now? Pure, red-hot rage was boiling just under the surface, and if something didn't break soon, it was going to erupt and there was no way he could stop it.

It was Riley Wolfe, of course. It had been a week since his team had botched the hit on Wolfe. And if that wasn't bad enough, there had been no sign of him since. He had completely vanished, and nothing Prescott tried had been able to find a trace of him. Even worse, he'd lost his hostages, the only safeguard he'd had. He still believed Wolfe wanted the money he'd been promised—but would he try to get more somewhere else? No way to know—but goddamn it, Prescott needed to know, and needed that flash drive. But it had been seven days with no clue about where the thief was or what he was going to do with the precious flash drive. The key to Prescott's future, and it was off in the wind somewhere.

So when his personal cell phone rang, he was in no mood to answer it. Especially since he didn't recognize the number, meaning it was probably another call about the extended warranty on the vehicle he didn't own. But his anger boiled over, and he answered anyway, determined to let some of it out on whatever sick stupid bastard was on the other end.

"This better be good," he snarled into the phone.

There was a soft chuckle on the other end. "Oh, I think it's pretty good," a slow drawl told him. "I mean, if you're still interested in the flash drive?"

All the anger hissed out of Prescott. "Wolfe? How did you get this number?"

"Let's not waste time with stupid questions, okay?" Wolfe said. "All either one of us cares about is getting that flash drive back to the US authorities, isn't that right?"

"Really? You're still pretending you care about this country?"

"And you're still pretending you didn't try to kill me last week?" Wolfe said.

Prescott felt sweat popping out on his forehead and even on his hands. He was losing his grip, and he had to hold it tight until he had the drive. "That was for national security," he said. "I couldn't take the chance that you had seen what's on it."

"Cut the bullshit, Prescott. You sent a hit team for me, and the only reason I'm talking to you is because yes, goddamn it, I care about my country, and I don't know how to get this thing to the right people. You do. So let's quit playing dumbass games and get this done, okay?"

Prescott felt a surge of sick relief. He could still get the flash drive.

The idiot still wanted to give it to him. "All right, fine. When and where?"

"Syracuse," Wolfe said.

Prescott couldn't believe he'd heard right. "Syracuse, New York? Why?"

"Because I will be there," Wolfe said patiently. "And I will have the flash drive. There's a minor league ballpark there, NBT Stadium. Be on the pitcher's mound at midnight. Be alone. And I better see your face, or it's over. This is your last chance, okay?"

"That's crazy, Wolfe. Why not just meet someplace—" He stopped talking because the line had gone dead.

Prescott put the phone down, surprised to see that his hand was trembling slightly. A drink—he needed a drink, that would steady his nerves. He dropped ice into his glass and poured on some brandy. *Syracuse. A ballpark,* he thought. He sipped the brandy. He would have to show himself this time and he didn't like that. He avoided exposure when possible. But this time it wasn't possible; Wolfe had made that clear.

He sipped some more and thought about it. *Well, why not?* he decided. *Get my team there early, put a good man up on top with a good view. Birchette is the best at this sort of thing. He won't screw it up. I stick my face out and wave, that's all. One shot and it will be all over. Minimal risk.*

He drained the glass and poured another. *It's finally over,* he thought. *Especially for Riley Wolfe.*

Brett Birchette didn't know a hell of a lot about Syracuse, but what he knew wasn't positive. He'd done some training at Fort Drum, an hour north, and they'd hit the bars in Syracuse one weekend. Salt City, they called it. Like, we have salt, big whoopy-shit. That was about all they had. A bunch of crappy bars, and salt.

Well, this wasn't a pleasure trip, and Birchette was pretty sure he wouldn't have time for the bars. Just as well. One shot, and he could head back to home base. And it looked to be a pretty simple setup. Inside a stadium, with minimal crosswinds, and the target would be a hell of a lot closer than anything he'd shot in Afghanistan.

So Birchette was feeling pretty loose as he drove into the lot at NBT Stadium in Syracuse, between the downtown area and the airport. It was a little after eight, and Prescott's meet was at midnight. Plenty of time to get in position, so he took his time and drove around the perimeter twice. No other cars, no sign of anybody lurking. Simple and clean all the way around.

He parked in a deep pool of shadow close to the corner of the stadium. There was a small stand of trees there that would hide his car.

He opened the trunk of his car and took out his weapon, a beautiful M24 that had been with him since Afghanistan. He closed the trunk and approached the doors at the base of the corner tower. It took two seconds to jimmy the doors open and step inside. He closed the doors behind him and started up the ramp.

Birchette figured to go up top, tuck himself in where he'd have a good clear bead on the pitcher's mound. And then, just wait. He was good at that; patience was one of a sniper's essential skills. Four hours, and Prescott would show up. Bang, all done, home for breakfast. Maybe an omelet, and some of those good smoked sausages.

Birchette turned a corner at the first landing, thinking about those sausages. He could almost taste them now.

Aside from surprise and a flash of pain, that was the last thought Brett Birchette ever had.

T.C. Winston didn't have anything in particular against Birchette. He was kind of a douchebag, but most of Prescott's guys were, and he was nothing special. Kept to himself, was always sort of quiet.

Well, he was going to be a lot quieter now. Permanently quiet. Too bad, but that was the only way. And what the hell, he'd been a sniper, so he had plenty of kills to answer for anyway. So Winston stepped out of the shadows, slipped behind Birchette, and got the wire garrote around his neck without too much guilt.

It was over quickly, and Winston got the body back outside easily enough. He took the car keys from Birchette's pocket, popped the trunk, and stuffed the body and the rifle in. He slammed the trunk, locked it, and went back inside the stadium to wait.

Prescott arrived at the ballpark at five minutes before midnight. There was no sign of anyone at all; it was the off-season, so there was no need for any cleaning crew, and if there was a night watchman, or several of them, he was confident that they would have been neutralized, either by Wolfe or by Birchette, his sniper, who had arrived hours earlier.

"Get in place, get sighted on the pitcher's mound, and wait for my signal," Prescott had told him. "I will raise my left hand—*left* hand, clear?"

"Yes, sir," Birchette had said. "No sweat."

"All right. Don't screw the pooch."

It should be simple. A clear and unobstructed line of fire, no witnesses. And Birchette would have a suppressor on his weapon, so no sound of a gunshot and very little muzzle flare. Prescott was as confident as he could be with so much riding on it.

He walked through the parking lot and up to the stadium's gate. It had been unobtrusively jimmied open, and he slid through, closing it behind him. The interior of the stadium was dim, lit by a few security lights, and his footsteps echoed strangely. But there was no hint of any human presence other than himself.

Prescott made his way down to the arch that opened out onto the field and paused, still inside in the darker shadows of the interior. Ahead he could see out onto the field. It was illuminated by a three-quarter moon. There was Wolfe, on the mound, sitting in one of those folding canvas chairs. What a shithead. He took one more step forward—and stopped as something bit his neck, a bug of some kind, or something. Instinctively, he put a hand up to slap at the bite—

And then it all went black.

CHAPTER

59

The argument with his father was not going well for Chase Prescott. They never did, but this one was simply absurd. Chase badly needed a drink, and Old Benson kept grabbing away the decanter. When Chase tried to grab it back, his father levitated out of his chair, up to the ceiling and out of reach. That was something Father had never done before, and he knew damned well that Chase couldn't do that. But his father just laughed. Pure mean on his part; Chase wanted that drink. He was as thirsty as he'd ever been. He tried to point out that his father was long dead and didn't need to drink, but Benson simply blew out at him, a great blast of frigid air that cut through Chase to his very bones and left a dozen pains in its wake. So cold. And his head hurt, and his shoulders and arms and ankles and—

Prescott blinked awake, shivering, teeth chattering. He was still as cold as if his father had really hit him with a blast of arctic breath. Why? He focused one eye on his torso—he was naked?! What the hell!

He moved his arms to rub some warmth into his body—and the arms traveled two inches and jerked to a stop, accompanied by a metallic jingling.

With great effort, Prescott turned his head to one side and then the other. His arms were in manacles. The manacles were chained to a stone wall. He looked down and found that his feet, too, were in fetters. He lifted his head and looked around with a complete lack of comprehension. The weird dream of his father made more sense than what he was seeing now. He blinked harder, several times, and looked again, but he saw the same thing.

Stone walls, dripping with condensation. A small drain in the center of the stone floor. No window, just a doorway that led out to a stone-lined hallway. He was in some kind of cell. No, not a cell—a *dungeon*, for Christ's sake! He was chained to the wall of a dungeon!

It wasn't possible. It had to be some kind of weird practical joke. Somebody thought it would be funny. He couldn't think who that might be, but by God they'd regret it. They'd have to let him out sooner or later. He was a Prescott, and if he couldn't persuade them, he'd buy them. And then—then they would discover that there was a price. Whoever was behind this, he'd show them funny.

First, of course, he had to get them in here. "Hey!" he yelled. "Hello!"

He waited. No response. His nose was itchy, and without thinking he tried to scratch it. Of course he couldn't get his hand within three feet of his nose. The chains yanked his hand back, jingling happily, and now his nose was itchier than ever.

"Goddamn it. Hey! Somebody!"

No response. He shivered, and this time it wasn't all from cold.

What the hell was going on?

I let Prescott stew so he'd have a good long while to wonder what was going to happen to him, who was going to do it—and, of course, how much it would cost him to get out of it, which is just the way your brain works when you're born into wealth and privilege. Everything has a price, and you always have it. Until now. I wanted him to hang there, naked and shivering, long enough to get scared when he realized maybe this time he couldn't buy his way out. So I left him there half an hour after he started yelling. Not out of pure meanness, of course. It was only about 80 percent meanness. The other 20 percent? What the hell, I guess that was meanness, too. Sorry.

Winston and I were sitting in a couple of chairs we'd dragged down to the end of the hall, to what was supposed to be the guard room in this big fake castle. Some of the props were real enough, though. There was a beautiful suit of armor that was genuine fourteenth-century French. And one of the hanging tapestries had me drooling—it was St. Sebastian, pierced with arrows, and I swear it was thirteenth century.

Anyway, we found a couple of overstuffed chairs that were just twentieth-century Salvation Army and dragged them down to the dungeon to wait for Prescott to wake up. When Prescott started to yell, Winston jerked up to his feet, but I motioned him back down. "Let him cook for a few minutes," I said. He sat back down, but he kept glancing at me nervously. Conscience is a terrible thing. Glad I don't have one.

When I waited long enough for Prescott to appreciate how helpless and hopeless he really was, I went down the cold stone hall to his cell. I admit I'd been looking forward to this. All of it, the whole thing. But seeing him awake, naked, hanging from the wall like some medieval heretic or something—that was special. One of those great moments that lives in your memory all your life. So I stood there just outside the cell looking in for a minute, until he finally saw me.

"Wolfe! You sonofabitch!"

"I'm so glad you're awake."

"Let me out of this, goddamn you!"

"Oh, I don't think so," I said. "After all the trouble I've gone to arranging this?"

"You think you've seen trouble? You don't let me go, I'll fucking show you trouble!"

Really, the things people say. I mean, it was probably just reflex. His whole life, he'd just had to say "Boo" and everybody would jump. But now? Naked and hanging from a wall and he's threatening me? "Do you hear yourself?" I asked politely. "If I don't let you out, I'm in trouble? Isn't that kind of a contradiction? What can you do to me chained up in a dungeon?"

"You fucking idiot, when the Agency finds out that you've got me—"

I couldn't help it. I walked in, laughed in Prescott's face. "Let's not pretend anymore that you're still working for the Agency," I said.

I could see all the blood run out of his face and into his feet. "That's crazy," he said. "Of course I am."

"Really?" I said. "So I can call them right now, tell them where you are?" He moved his mouth a few times, like a fish out of water, but didn't manage any words. "I thought not," I said. "You don't want the Agency any more than I do."

I watched him think. I was pretty sure I knew the way his mind worked, like any .1 percent, overentitled piece of crap. And sure enough, I was right.

"All right," he said. "How much do you want to let me go?"

I was right. "Oh, Chase," I said, shaking my head. "How predictable you are. Do you really think I want money?"

"Of course you want money," he said. "I know all about you and where you come from, Wolfe. Always broke and living in a trailer with—"

He stopped dead, and it's a good thing he did. "With my mother," I said. "That's right, my mother—who you kidnapped. And then you let her die. And now we're up-to-date, aren't we? Now you know why you're here."

"For Christ's sake, that was an accident," he said. "Let me go and I swear I'll make it up to you."

"How? You going to buy me a new mother?"

There wasn't a whole lot he could say to that, but what the hell, he had to try anyway. "Be reasonable, Wolfe. She'd been brain dead for years, and there was no real hope she'd ever wake up."

"Well, I guess we'll never know for sure, will we?" I said. And then I slapped him, hard enough to rattle his teeth. "Sorry. That was an accident, too." I took a step back and smiled at him. "What happens next, though—that's not an accident."

I let him see my smile for a good long minute. And then I turned around and walked out of the cell. His yells followed me down the hall, part threat and part begging, and it was as sweet as listening to Yo-Yo Ma playing the Bach Cello Suites. Just pure beautiful music that lifted my soul.

Riley, fuck, I think you're enjoying this too much," Winston told me when I walked into the room where we'd been waiting for Prescott to wake up.

"You're right, I am," I said, still smiling. I sat back down in the easy chair we'd dragged into the room. "You want a turn?"

"Kind of?" he said with a really guilty look. "But I don't know, it seems like—" He shrugged. "I don't know. Like maybe crossing the line?"

"Really? But betraying our country wasn't crossing the line? Killing my mother, that was okay?"

"Yeah, okay, I know," he said. He sighed. "I just thought, like, doing this would be more fun."

"Oh, well, if it's fun you want, fine. Let's move on to the final step." I stood up. "Get the wheelbarrow and we'll get this done."

Prescott couldn't be sure how long he hung there waiting. It was long enough for him to wonder if maybe Wolfe had just gone away and left him there dangling from the chains, so he'd starve to death. But finally he heard something in the hall—footsteps approaching, and a kind of muted squeaking, like a rusty wheel turning on a scooter or something, which didn't make any sense.

The sound paused in the dim hall outside his door and Prescott could make out—a wheelbarrow, not a scooter. A full wheelbarrow, with an overflowing load of bricks? Not that that made any more sense than a scooter.

And it wasn't Wolfe pushing it—it was his dopey foot soldier, Winston! Prescott felt a surge of relief. Winston would obey his orders. He always did; he couldn't help it. "Winston!" he yelled. Winston looked up. "For Christ's sake, don't just gawk—get me out of this!"

Winston eased the full wheelbarrow down. Then he stepped around it and into the cell, and he just stood there, looking at Prescott.

"How are you doing, sir?" he said politely.

"Goddamn it, cut the shit and turn me loose!"

And Winston smiled. "I can't do that. Sir."

"Of course you can! Don't be an idiot!"

Winston shook his head. "No, sorry, I really can't."

"Why the hell not?"

The smile got bigger. "Because I'm enjoying this too much," he said.

Prescott couldn't think of a thing to say. He could only watch as Winston unloaded the bricks in the doorway.

Winston had the bricks unloaded and stacked neatly beside the door when I joined him in the hall outside the cell. He shook his head and greeted me with, "Goddamn it, Riley. I really am having fun with this. And I hate myself for it."

I sketched a cross in the air. "*Ego te absolvo*, my son. Lose the guilt, because it's about to get even better."

He saw what I was holding and frowned. "What's that?"

"A hat," I said.

"Okay. Why?"

"Very important piece of the story," I said. "Watch his face when he sees it."

I stepped past Winston and into the cell. Prescott tried to look authoritative when he saw me—really tough when you're naked and hanging from chains, but he tried. "Wolfe! This has gone far enough."

"You're right," I said. "We need to get you dressed." And for a second he actually looked hopeful. "Actually, you gave me the idea." I held up the hat. It was a jester's cap, with five droopy points, each point a different bright color, each festooned with little bells.

"No," he said hoarsely. "Jesus Christ, no! You can't—"

"You got it right away! I'm so happy," I said.

"You were right," Winston called from the doorway. "That look on his face is epic."

"Wolfe, this is insane, you can't go through with this, Jesus, just let me go—keep the flash drive, it's worth billions, it's all yours!" Prescott said. He was starting to babble, which was kind of a nice flavor.

"That's not how this goes, you know that." He kept babbling as I pulled the hat onto his head. It fit nicely, and I stepped back and admired it for a minute.

He was still gabbling away when we started laying the bricks across the doorway to his cell. Curses, threats, promises, pleas, more threats and curses. They just kept pouring out of him, and the bells on his cap jingled merrily in perfect rhythm to his ranting. But his voice got hoarser and weaker, and by the time the new wall was half done, it was almost a whisper. He finally got quiet for as long as it took to lay in three more rows of bricks.

"Please, Wolfe," Prescott said at last, and his voice was a guttural whisper. "Please . . . ?"

I stopped laying bricks. "You've never said that word before, have you?"

"Let me out, Wolfe, I swear, anything you want."

I put my head to one side and looked like I was thinking about it. "How about this," I said. "If you can think of the right thing to say, I just might let you go."

He looked desperately confused. "The right thing to— What does that even mean? Jesus, Wolfe, please!"

I shrugged. "That's my final offer," I said, and I went back to laying bricks.

And Prescott went back to an increasingly weaker and frantic stream of blather, until I was on the last row of the new wall. Then he stopped. I looked in at him. He was slumped in the chains, like he was already dead.

"Last chance, Prescott," I said.

The bells on his cap jingled happily as he looked up, but he didn't speak.

"Come on, play the game," I said. "Say it."

He stared at me, and there was actually a tiny flicker of hope in his eyes. But it was fighting with his near certainty that it wouldn't do any good, no matter what he said. In the end, though, he had to take the chance that I really might let him go, and he said it: "For the love of God, Montresor."

Word for word, just the way Poe wrote it. It was amazing how good it felt. "Yes," I said. "For the love of God."

And then I finished the wall.

CHAPTER

60

Special Agent in Charge Frank Delgado still wondered what had gone wrong. It had been two weeks since the debacle at Grand Central, time spent in endless postmortems, intensive searching for either Wolfe or the flash drive, and no one had turned up a hint. Everyone else, from the DNI to the other agents at the Bureau, was sure that either Wolfe had sold them out for a ton of cash, or else the whole thing had been a prank from the start. Delgado didn't think so. He had spent his career listening to con men spinning stories, and he'd developed a pretty reliable facility for detecting when they were lying. Additionally, he felt that he *knew* Wolfe, understood him and how he operated. And he had believed that Wolfe truly meant to turn over the flash drive, and the rogue agent who had stolen it, when he'd set up the operation.

That hadn't happened. And there had been no further contact from Wolfe. Something must have happened, something that changed things for Wolfe. But what?

And more important, of course—what had happened to the flash drive? The plans it held were vital to national security. The DNI himself had said so. Delgado had gathered that they were for some kind of endgame weapons system, something utterly terrifying. He still had no real idea what the details were, but the few people who did had gone straight into completely hair-on-fire panic mode and stayed there at the thought of a foreign government getting it.

And Wolfe still had it. Either that, or he was dead, and the flash drive was already in the hands of a hostile power. Either possibility was awful to contemplate, and irrationally, Delgado felt responsible and thought he should—

"Fornicating on the front lawn."

Delgado heard the words quite clearly, and with a start he turned to see where they came from. He was sitting in Dulles International with Miranda Shaleki, waiting for their flight back to Moscow. And clearly, the words had been hers. She was looking at him with an expression of mild amusement. "My mother used to say that," she said. "When she thought someone wasn't listening to her."

"Oh, that's— I'm sorry," Delgado stammered. She still had a knack for getting under his guard. "I guess I wasn't listening."

"True that," Miranda said. "I was saying something like, let it go, it's not your problem anymore. And you were lost in the ozone?"

"Sorry," Delgado said. "I was just wondering what happened. With Riley Wolfe."

"The dude scammed you, bro," she said. "Accept it."

"I just can't believe that," he said.

"What's to believe? He's a total outlaw, and he didn't show. Do the math."

Delgado shook his head. "I did," he said. "It doesn't add up for me."

"Well, shit," Miranda said, clearly exasperated with him.

"I guess so," he said.

"At least we're headed back to sunny Moscow," she said. "Where we know exactly where everybody is coming from."

"I guess that's something," he said. He stood up. "I'm going to the restroom," he said.

"I hope everything comes out all right," Miranda said with mock sweetness.

It was only about a hundred feet to the nearest men's room, but by the time Delgado reached it, he was already back in a mental fog, wondering what had gone wrong. He was still pondering when, standing at the urinal, he heard someone move to the spot on his left. The man was very large and brushed against him accidentally. "Oh, my, I do beg your pardon," the newcomer said with a gentle Southern accent.

The hair on Delgado's neck stood up, and all his senses came online. He whipped his head to the left.

It was him.

Riley Wolfe.

Wearing the same fat, sweaty persona he'd had on when they'd met a few weeks earlier. "It's been two weeks," Delgado said. "I thought we had a deal."

"We did, and I am sorry for the disappearing act?" Wolfe said. "Something . . . unexpected came up at the last minute. It required a certain amount of time to unfold." He smiled. "I believe sufficient time has elapsed now."

Delgado couldn't help noticing that Wolfe wore his character so completely that even his vocabulary was spot on for an aging, overweight Southern gentleman of the old school. But even as he admired that, he didn't let it distract him. "What about the flash drive?" Delgado said.

Wolfe nodded. "I have it for you right here," he said. "And I have to say, I do feel a little more at ease handing it over in a confidential tête-à-tête like this? Without the possibility of overzealous interference from the gentlemen on your side of the field. If you don't mind me saying so." He tipped his head toward the sinks. "Shall we wash up?"

They moved to adjacent sinks, and Wolfe began to wash his hands. "You have probably noticed that I did not bring the other part of the deal? A certain quisling from a brother agency of yours?"

"I noticed," Delgado said.

Wolfe dried his hands with a paper towel and then reached into his coat pocket. He removed a plain white envelope and handed it to Delgado. "Inside, along with the flash drive, you will find a note revealing his location," he said. "Bless his little heart."

"Are you sure he'll still be there?"

Wolfe's smile this time was not quite as pleasant. "Oh, yes, quite sure," he said. He cocked his head to one side and regarded Delgado. "This has been a curious affair, Mr. Delgado. And not at all a pleasant one. But it has been some small recompense to make your acquaintance at last." Nodding, Wolfe said, "I feel quite certain that our paths will cross again." And he turned away and walked out of the restroom.

Delgado watched him go without making any effort to stop him. Wolfe had been as good as his word, even if somewhat tardy. Delgado waited a decent interval and then went back out to rejoin Miranda.

"That must have been an amazing pee," she said. "Judging by the smirk on your face."

Delgado picked up his carry-on case. "I'm afraid our return to Moscow is going to be delayed," he said.

"Oh, crap," she said. "I'm not eating at another McDonald's."

—————

Well, that's Chase Prescott," the man from the Agency said. "A real bastard, and he sold out the country, but even so, a bad way to go." He shook his head. "Jesus, that's hard to look at."

Delgado agreed. It truly was not a pretty sight. Even though he knew the man had been a traitor, it was hard to look at what was left of him. Just the old, emaciated, naked body of a man who had died slowly, in great physical and mental pain, hanging from chains in a completely dark, cold dungeon. There were crusty wounds at his wrists and ankles where he'd yanked at the chains, and the floor below him was coated with dried blood and excrement. Then there was the jester's hat, drooped atop the mess on the floor. Delgado nodded. A truly bad way to go. Had even Prescott deserved it?

It had taken some detective work to find him. The note from Wolfe had led them right to the castle.

It looked oddly familiar as they approached, but it took a minute before Delgado got it. *Of course. The castle Miranda's search program found.* So much had happened, he hadn't thought of it until now— hadn't had time to think of it. But there was no doubt that this was it.

He led his team in, confident that they were in the right place.

But a rapid sweep of the castle hadn't found a trace of Prescott. It was Delgado who had noticed the brick wall in the dungeon. In the first place, nothing else in the castle was made of brick. Additionally, the bricks themselves were still bright, obviously much newer than anything else. Delgado had run a hand over them and remembered Wolfe's smile when asked if Prescott would still be there.

Half an hour later the team had taken the brick wall out—and there was Chase Prescott. And truly, he wasn't going anywhere. Not ever again.

Delgado knew that Wolfe had killed many times and showed no hesitation about it. But this? Sealing a chained man into a small room to die gradually, in complete darkness, of hunger, cold, and thirst? This was a terrible, slow, agonizing murder, cruel and sadistic. It seemed uncharacteristic.

"Special Agent Delgado?"

Delgado turned to the speaker. It was Agent Fraleigh, who'd been leading the Bureau's sweep of the castle. "Fraleigh," he said. "What did you find?"

"Not a lot," Fraleigh said. "There's a room with a bunch of medical equipment in it?"

"What kind?" Delgado asked, more to be thorough than from any interest.

"Looks like life-support stuff," Fraleigh said. "A ventilator, an IV rig, I think it's a dialysis machine? And a rack of monitors, tubes. You know, the kind of setup for maintaining somebody in a coma."

An alarm bell went off deep in Delgado's brain. Fraleigh had all his attention now. "Any medicines?"

Fraleigh nodded. "Yes, sir. A bunch of 'em."

"Show me," Delgado said.

Fraleigh led him to the room. As he'd said, it was clearly intended for someone in a coma. A hospital bed, a rack of electronics, everything you'd find in an ICU at a hospital—or an extended-care facility. Beside the bed was a table that held several IV bags. Delgado picked them up, one at a time. They each had a label detailing their contents. Some of the medicines were rare and expensive, but they were all from a list Delgado knew by heart.

Riley's mother used them. Needed them to stay alive. But they had been left behind. Why?

Delgado dropped the last IV bag and stared at nothing. It began to make sense. Prescott had taken Wolfe's mother, used her as leverage against him. That explained why Wolfe was working with the Agency. And the tactic would probably have been enough to infuriate Wolfe, lead him to killing Prescott.

But kill him like that? In such a vicious way? He shook his head. Not enough, not for that. But . . . The meds had been left behind, and they were expensive and difficult to get. Whoever took her would have to take the meds, too. Unless . . . What if the mother had died while Prescott held her?

Yes. That would do it. Delgado nodded. The whole riddle made sense now.

He turned back to Fraleigh, who had been watching him as he stared at the wall. "Did you find anything else of interest?" he asked. "Anything at all?"

Fraleigh hesitated. "Not really?" he said. "But there was a room upstairs where someone else was being held. Small room, one window high up, a single bed, and a nightstand. The door was kicked in, and there was a body, a woman in a white medical jacket." He shrugged. "There's no real sign to indicate who was locked in there. Just some art stuff. Some drawings."

"Drawings of what?"

"A man's face, mostly. Same face over and over. And a couple of a big dog? Or maybe it's a wolf?"

"Show me," Delgado said. "Show me the drawings."

The upstairs room was just as Fraleigh described. The door had been knocked off its hinges and lay inside, next to the body on the floor, the body of a skeletal woman with three bullet holes in the front of her white coat, surrounded by a black pool of dried blood. She'd clearly been dead for a couple of weeks.

On the nightstand beside the bed Delgado saw the sketchbook. He glanced at Fraleigh. "We've already dusted it, sir," he said. "You can pick it up."

Delgado did. He flipped through the pages one at a time. He paused at the first page with a face drawn on it. Below it was a good likeness of a wolf. Delgado nodded and turned the page.

The drawings of the face evolved slowly, page by page; the chin changed, the nose got bigger and then smaller. And then, the changes stopped. Two drawings in a row, on consecutive pages, showed the same face. The final drawing was a full-page portrait of the face.

Delgado studied it for a long time. He flipped back to the first page and looked again at the drawing of the wolf. Then he turned to the last page again, the fully realized drawing of the face. For several minutes he didn't move, just stared at that face. Then he nodded. He was sure. There was no explanation for who had drawn it or why. He had no real reason to feel certainty, but he felt it anyway.

It was him. He was looking at Riley Wolfe.

At last.

CHAPTER
61

Everything ends. Nothing lives forever. We all know that. We don't think about it if we can help it, and if something rubs our nose in it we mostly think, okay, sure—but not *me*, not now. We push it away. We can know it, but we can't really believe the lights will go out for that *me* someday.

But they do. They have to. Everything dies, and there's no way around it. That doesn't make it any easier to handle, when something does end. When someone dies.

I had known all along that Mom would die someday. But I knew it the way I knew that the capital of Argentina is Buenos Aires. It was a fact that didn't have any real meaning to me.

And now it had happened. Mom was dead, and there was a gigantic black hole inside me that felt like it went on forever and would never end. I had done everything possible to keep Mom safe, and it hadn't been enough. She was dead anyway, and I couldn't shake the feeling that it was my fault.

Once I'd taken care of Prescott and tidied up with Special Agent Delgado, I had time to think about it. She was gone, I couldn't bring her back any more than I'd been able to save her. The dark fog rolled back over me.

So I wasn't a whole lot of fun to hang around with. Chaz and Winston tried anyway. They did all the normal stuff to make me feel better. None of it worked. I just snarled at them and told them to piss off. Finally, they did. I guess they both got tired of my attitude, and I don't blame them. I went back to staring into the deep dark nothing.

At least I wasn't alone. Monique had hung on to me like her life depended on it. I took her back to her apartment and watched as she slowly remembered it. But when I tried to leave her there, she freaked out. She grabbed onto me and wouldn't let go, and that's how it stayed. At first it was kind of nice. Then it began to get annoying. Until suddenly one day, it wasn't annoying at all.

When I realized she wouldn't let me leave, I threw myself into getting her well. It gave me something to do, something that made the deep dark pit fade for a while. I took her to the best specialists, doctors who knew more about recovering from traumatic brain injuries than anybody else in the world. They started her on a course of rehab and mental and physical therapies that would bring back the real Monique, the one I knew before this happened. And they all said it would definitely maybe have a really good chance of possibly working perhaps.

I'd heard all the could-be crap before. It's what doctors always said, just to cover their asses. It didn't mean anything. I knew she would recover. I would damn well make her. And she worked hard at it, and I worked hard with her—partly because I wanted to help any way I could. Mostly because she started to panic if she lost sight of me. If nothing else, it kept me busy, and that filled the black hole for a while.

On top of that, I started to feel like it was what I should be doing, helping Monique get well. With Mom gone, she was all I had in the world. I mean, I didn't have her, not really, not in any sense of us being a couple or anything. And even if that never happened, there still was a bond between us.

So we worked at rehab, and I could see her improve a little every day. She was remembering things, and her speech got better. She still stuttered a little, but not as much. And every now and then she'd pause in the middle of a sentence and get this lost look, like she didn't know where she was. But that happened less frequently as the weeks passed, and I thought I could see the old Monique peeking through the clouds. She was drawing a lot, remembering how that part of her had worked. But I wanted more. I wanted all of her back. I tried to think of something that might do the trick, and finally I did. I talked it over with the doctors, and they thought it might be good for her, or at least it couldn't hurt.

So when they said it was safe for her to travel again, I took her to my island. It's kind of like my Fortress of Solitude, and just as hard to find. That's on purpose. But it was a long trip, and it wasn't easy to take even if you're in great shape. It's a chartered jet for the long first lap, to a remote island where I keep a boat. Okay, I guess a yacht, because it's thirty feet long and the cabin is air-conditioned. It also has a couple of monster engines, and a hull designed to cut the waves, so it can really fly.

Even so, it's eleven or twelve hours to my island, depending on weather. But when you get there, it's worth it. There's a very tight channel, booby-trapped, of course, and that empties into a beautiful tropical lagoon with a white-sand beach. My house is on a bluff looking down at the water. It's fully stocked with food, beverages, music, and books, and it's as close to perfect for me as I could make it.

Monique had been there once before. She had helped me pull off a miraculous job, and I thought she deserved a very cool vacation afterward. Sure, we could've gone to Tahiti or something, but this was a whole lot more private. And yeah, that last time here I had ulterior motives, but who can blame me? A few years back, when we'd pulled off a truly outstanding job together, we'd celebrated the best possible way. An epic night, and I know she felt the same way.

So after that second outstanding job, I brought her here, to my island. I figured the sun, the sea, bonfires on the beach, and a really good wine cellar would all add up to a great time and some healing. Maybe something more than that, too. And it almost did work.

Almost. At the last second, something knocked it off the rails, and we went back to just good friends having a nice vacation. But it was a great memory anyway, and the doctors said that made my island just the place to round out Monique's rehab and get her all the way back, if that was going to happen.

Of course it was. It was definitely going to happen. I knew that like I know the sun will come up tomorrow. Monique would recover. She had to.

For the first couple of days, though, she seemed to go backward. She spent way too much time staring around her, like it wasn't just that she didn't know where she was; more like she couldn't figure out what sand or water was and what she was supposed to do with them. I pretended I didn't see that and kept her as active as I could. We painted my house, and we paddled a kayak all around the island, and we built a new stone wall I didn't need. I made sure she was so tired at the end of each day she didn't have the energy to wonder what a rock was for. And then I'd wake her up early the next day and start all over again.

It worked. She got so mad at me she forgot that she couldn't remember things. She would flop into her bed after dinner and be out all night. And I would go down to the beach with a bottle of something and hope that maybe the waves would explain to me why Mom had to die. But either they didn't know, or they just weren't telling. I asked them if they could maybe suggest some explanation for the whole life-and-death thing, but they had the same answer for that. They just rolled in and then out again. I watched them until the bottle was empty, and I'd finally go back to the house, flop into my own bed, and start all over the next morning.

But at least I could see it working for Monique. She got a spring in her step, an energy and positive attitude that had been missing. Every day she remembered more, and more of the Lost Girl face dropped away. Monique was coming back. I'd still catch her looking at me, but it wasn't with the expression I'd gotten used to, the kind of who-the-hell-are-you look. I wasn't sure what the new look was, but it was conscious, aware. It was Monique.

And then one night, something woke me up.

It wasn't much, just the creak of a floorboard. But in my house, that's a feature, not a bug. The Japanese did it in their castle floors—they called it a "nightingale floor." It was designed to make a noise if somebody steps on it, because back in the day, the samurai lifestyle involved a whole lot of assassination. So the old feudal lords built in a floor that squeaked when someone, like an assassin, walked on it. I built my floors that way, too, because there are plenty of very serious people who would feel a whole lot better if I was dead. And yeah, in theory nobody knew where this island was, and there was lots of security to keep people out. But in theory, my mom had been protected, and look how that ended. So when the floor squeaked, I woke up with a Glock 19 in my hand.

It turned out I didn't need it.

A silhouette appeared in the doorway, and just before I pulled the trigger, I recognized who it was: Monique, in the terry cloth bathrobe she'd been wearing after swimming. She paused for a second, and I figured she probably woke up and wondered where she was, or something like that. I put away the pistol. I could gentle her down for a while and get her back to bed.

I was wrong about that, too.

When she saw me sit up to stash the Glock, she took a step forward. "Riley . . . ?" she said, in a whisper.

"I'm right here," I said.

She took another step. "I—I remembered something," she said. Step. "Something important."

"That's great," I said. "What is it?"

One more step. She was standing right by the bed. "This," she said, and the robe dropped to the floor.

"Uh," I said. I mean, I've always been quick with a clever comeback, but what did I say to that?

Turns out I didn't need to say anything.

Time slowed down after that. The days got longer, because we were waiting for night. And the nights got longer, too, because we weren't sleeping a whole lot. It was everything I'd been hoping for ever since our one-nighter. We were together for real, and that's what really mattered, that feeling of truly being together, growing closer and closer until we were both part of one thing. Or maybe there wasn't any "both" anymore, just the one thing. I don't know if I can describe it any better than that. Just, we'd been two separate people—friends, and sort of partners, but there'd been a lot of lines we drew around each other, just to make sure we didn't get too close. Now those lines were gone, and we were more than close; we were simultaneous. And if that doesn't make any sense to you, I guess maybe you've never felt it, and I kind of feel sorry for you.

So we had this special time, a time out from everything, kind of a temporal loop where nothing was so important that it couldn't wait—nothing except being together. The days went by. I know, they do that most of the time. This was different. Most of the time, days go by like a technical document, step-by-step work. Now they went by like poetry, or maybe a really good song. Time sang. We didn't do anything mystical or magical. It was just being together, swimming or paddling around the island, sometimes just lying in the sun together. Time didn't really mean anything. It was all good, and it was going to last forever.

Except it didn't. Nothing does, especially if it's good. And this was. It was too good, and I should have known what that meant. Riley's Eighth Law says very plainly: Nothing good ever lasts. There's a Paragraph Two to the Eighth Law, which says: If it's really good, you pay for it big-time.

The day came when I found Monique sitting on the beach and staring out to sea. She looked up at me, and all the happy, goofy stuff I was about to say leaked out of me and died on the sand. Something about her expression was different, like she'd thought of something important she had to do. I knew when I saw her like that, and she didn't have to tell me.

She told me anyway. "Riley," she said. "I need to thank you. For—for rebuilding me, I guess. I was pretty far gone, and it was a long way back." She looked away and bit her lip. "I couldn't have done it without you, and I know that, and I will always be grateful . . ."

I sat down on the sand. Have you ever noticed that when somebody says something like, "I will always be grateful," what it really means is, "It's all over now"?

That's sure as hell what it meant this time. "But I think . . . I just— For this to mean anything, I need to get back to normal. To my life, the way it was. Do you understand? I'm not . . . *cured* if I can't be who I was. If I have to lean on you. So I think it's time to go," Monique said. "To get back to, you know. New York, my real life, and . . ." She waved an arm. "Everything?"

I could have said something like, "I thought we had everything here." Or maybe I could have tried pleading, or even saying something bitter and angry, because I was feeling all that and more. I would have said it, too—if I was stupid. Which I'm not, and I could tell she'd already made up her mind and anything I said would just be spitting into the wind. I mean, I was thinking a whole lot. But I didn't say any of it. I just looked out at the water.

I felt her hand on my arm. "Don't be upset," she said. "This was never real or, you know. Permanent?"

That kind of hurt. I mean, I hadn't actually thought that we were going to motor off to find a preacher or anything. I hadn't really thought anything through. I was just enjoying it, lost in a time without time, an endless moment that just went on, no thoughts of the future. If you had asked me, I would've said hell no, this isn't permanent. Marriage? Forget it. Riley Wolfe can't be tied down. I would've meant it, too. But to have *her* say it was over—

Well, shit. Maybe that was it. Maybe it was just that I was supposed to be the one who gets to say it's over, and I wasn't ready yet. Which meant it was all nothing but my ego getting stepped on, and I was pissed off because she had said it first. But I never thought a bruised ego hurt like this.

It doesn't matter. It was over. We packed up, mothballed the house, and left early the next morning. Two days later we were back in New York.

———

That's when the depression really took me. It just rolled me over and wrapped me up like a dark, wet blanket, and it took me back into that deep black pit to where I couldn't see anything at all except what a fuckup I was. Riley Wolfe, the all-time greatest. The smoothest operator there ever was. Except I didn't get my score, I let my mom die, and somehow I even screwed up the thing with Monique.

Remember that old saying the Brits have? The one about how a hard lesson gives you a wrinkle in the ass? This time I didn't just get a wrinkle. I got cut, and cut deep, with a three-edged sword. Just like the one that suit of armor had. Because one swipe of the blade, and I had *three* new cuts. To do that? That takes talent. Practically genius. Yeah, I really was the best ever. The best fuckup.

I'd never lost so much at once. I mean, sure, when I was ten my dad died and we lost our house and everything in it. But that wasn't *me* losing it. I was just a kid. This time, it was all on me.

So I admit it. I wallowed for a while. There's something about feeling so completely worthless and stupid that is totally satisfying to the soul on some weird, masochistic level. It's like, I don't need to do anything, shouldn't even try, because I would just screw it up, so there's no point trying. I can just sit here and try to open another beer without ripping open an artery and bleeding to death.

I couldn't stop thinking about all I'd lost. From the day I climbed on board the DC-3 at the Keresemose Mine, the whole thing had been a total flaming shit show. I ended up with less than I started with, which is a good trick. I had to pay Chaz a big chunk of cash, since there was nothing to split. Winston had to get something, too, and Kondor. And of course I paid for all the doctors and therapy for Monique, all that. I didn't mind. I have plenty of money. It's just that everything added together added up to a whole lot less than nothing.

On top of that, Mom was gone, and that was the biggest, darkest loss of my life. For a while I'd been able to hide that pain away, during the time I was living on Fantasy Island with Monique. And now that was lost, too.

Was it gone for good? Who knows. In New York, she went back to her apartment, I went back to my place in Brooklyn. And then? We got back to normal, just like she wanted. Hurray, normal. They should have a holiday, with a parade. Happy Normal Day. Please put everything you care about on the bonfire.

Anyway, Monique took on a couple of small jobs, trying to get all her old skills back. I finally decided I should do that, too, and I started looking around for something impossible to do. I would call Monique when I was in town and we'd have dinner, a few drinks, a couple of laughs. But that's all. No more holding hands, watching the sunset, none of that. I didn't try to push it. The wall was back up, and I was outside looking in.

Maybe someday we'd happen again. Maybe if I took her back to my island it would re-spark something. Maybe I'll think of something that will help her remember one last thing—how good it was on the island, when we were together. It could happen. There is always a way.

In the meantime? There's work to do. Pretty things to steal, over-privileged assholes to send off into the deep dark forever, impossible heists to pull off. Plus, all this castle stuff had me thinking. For instance, I've heard this rumor about the Irish crown jewels? I mean, there have been all kinds of rumors for over a hundred years. None of them panned out. The jewels were stolen in 1907 and haven't been heard of since—until now. Nothing really definite. There was just one soft whisper on the dark web about a completely insane collector who got the jewels from a guy whose grandfather was in the Irish Republican Brotherhood back in the day, and this collector built a totally impregnable fortress in a cave, out in the wilderness in Ontario, and he keeps the jewels there, along with a bunch of other shiny things. So maybe I'll go get them if it turns out to be true, and impossible enough for me to spend time on it. We'll see. The important thing is for me to find my way back to being me again. So I keep busy.

That way I don't have to think.

ACKNOWLEDGMENTS

I am very lucky to have had help from someone with a truly unique per-spective, Dr. Jillian Armour. She is not only an expert on Traumatic Brain Injury—she is also a survivor. I am grateful for her help.

And as always, endless love to Hilary. Nothing can happen without her.

ABOUT THE AUTHOR

JEFF LINDSAY is the award-winning author of the *New York Times* bestselling Dexter novels, upon which the international hit TV show *Dexter* is based. This is the third book in his Riley Wolfe series. He has also written two dozen plays and, among many other things, he has worked as an actor, comic, voice-over artist, screenwriter, columnist, singer, musician, bouncer, DJ, teacher, waiter, chop-saw operator in a foundry, TV and radio host, gardener, sailing instructor, and girls' soccer coach. Jeff is married to writer-filmmaker Hilary Hemingway. They have three daughters.